A WEDDING IN THE COUNTRY

Lizzie has just arrived in London, determined to make the best of her new life.

Her mother may be keen that she should have a nice wedding in the country to a Suitable Man chosen by her. And Lizzie may be going to cookery school to help her become a Good Wife.

But she definitely wants to have some fun first.

It is 1963 and London is beginning to swing as Lizzie cuts her hair, buys a new dress with a fashionably short hemline, and moves in with two of her best friends, one of whom lives in a grand but rundown house in Belgravia which has plenty of room for a lodger.

Soon Lizzie's life is so exciting that she has forgotten all about her mother's marriage plans for her.

All she can think about is that the young man she is falling in love with appears to be engaged to someone else . . .

KATIE FFORDE

A WEDDING
IN THE
COUNTRY

Complete and Unabridged

CHARNWOOD
Leicester

First published in Great Britain in 2021 by
Century
London

First Charnwood Edition
published 2021
by arrangement with
Century
Penguin Random House UK
London

A catalogue record for this book is available
from the British Library.

ISBN 978–1–4448–4780–2

Published by
Ulverscroft Limited
Anstey, Leicestershire

Printed and bound in Great Britain by
TJ Books Ltd., Padstow, Cornwall

This book is printed on acid-free paper

To all my wonderful writer friends. The writing community is so generous and supportive. This book is for you; a huge thank you. I couldn't have done it without you. Actually, it's been the same with all my books — I've just never got round to thanking you before.

Acknowledgements

For Bill Hamilton and everyone at A M Heath.

Richenda Todd, who is so much more than the best copy-editor ever.

My sister-in-law, Susan Makin, who was so helpful with my research.

Fellow author Sarah Steele for her tremendous knowledge of 60s clothes.

My children and children-in-law, Guy, Frank and Briony, plus Nastya, Heidi and Steve Wilson-Fforde for the huge amount of time they put into sorting my technical problems with my computer. And for sorting me out afterwards.

To Elizabeth Lindsay for her support through this.

Selina Walker and Ajebowale Roberts, my wonderful editorial team, without whom I would be lost.

To Joanna Taylor, who was so good when we had technical meltdowns.

To the unsung heroes who make my books look great, who get them into the shops so people can buy them — thank you! Rachel Campbell, Mat Watterson, Claire Simmonds, Sarah Ridley, Ceara Elliot, Jacqueline Bisset, Linda Hodgson, Helen Wynn-Smith, Sophie Whitehead, Klara Zak, Charlotte Bush.

You are my team, and I love and appreciate you very much!

PART ONE

1

London, Spring 1963

'Garlic should be the same size as an 'azelnut in its shell,' said Mme Wilson in her strong French accent. She was looking at a collection of pale, curved shapes on a plate in front of her that could have been toenail clippings given both their appearance and Mme Wilson's look of utter disgust.

Lizzie regarded the despised items. She had no experience of garlic. It was one of the things her father regarded as 'foreign muck' and so had no place in her family kitchen. And yet just then, Lizzie was grateful for her father's fondness for 'good plain cooking', for without it she wouldn't have been sent to London to do a cookery course.

So here she was, in a rather cramped basement in Pimlico, with nine other girls, being lectured by a Frenchwoman who, if first impressions were anything to go by, was fairly terrifying. Almost everyone was wearing a white buttoned-up overall covered by a white bibbed apron, as specified in the prospectus.

Mme Wilson had moved on to olive oil and the outrageous fact that you had to buy it in chemist's shops. Lizzie gathered this meant that olive oil had another function, apart from use as a cure for earache. Mme Wilson seemed to despise most ingredients available in England, and Lizzie couldn't help wondering how she managed to live here when it was obviously a culinary desert.

She surreptitiously studied her fellow pupils, hoping that at least one of them would turn out to be friendly, otherwise her time in London might be lonely.

Most of them seemed to be very aristocratic, with smooth white skin, their glossy hair in elegant chignons, fat ponytails or discreetly backcombed so it rose smoothly from their foreheads and ended in perfect 'flick-ups', a style she had never managed to achieve herself. Under their all-covering garments glimpses of cashmere and silk could be seen. They wore pearls, round their necks and in their ears. Lizzie had a string of pearls, given to her by her godmother, but they were for best, not for every day. She had to ask her mother whenever she wanted to wear them.

One of the girls was a bit different. She had ignored the white overall and instead wore a blue-striped butcher's apron over what seemed to be a man's dress shirt without the collar. She was wearing black cigarette pants and round-toed shoes which buttoned up across her instep. Her long hair (glossy, like the other girls) was tied up into a pile on her head. She had a thick fringe which gave her a look of Audrey Hepburn. She was wearing pearls too, but hers were much larger, twisted round her neck like a rope. Lizzie suspected they were fake, and she warmed to her. She was just as glossy and well bred as the others and yet she wasn't as haughty. This girl was looking around the kitchen as if she didn't quite know how she'd got there.

Another girl caught Lizzie's attention because she was writing everything down with single-minded attention. She sometimes asked questions and, judging by Mme Wilson's response, they seemed to be the right questions. She was obviously seriously interested

4

in learning to cook, not filling in the time until the next social engagement which, going by the snippets of conversation Lizzie overheard, was what most of the other girls were doing. When she caught Lizzie's eye, she smiled, shy but friendly. Lizzie began to feel more confident.

'Now, girls, you know it is easier to cook good food if you are accustomed to eating it. However, I know that many of you are not experienced in a kitchen. You may be forbidden to enter because your cook doesn't like people interrupting her.'

Lizzie gulped inwardly. Her mother would hire a cook for the evening if she had to entertain her father's business colleagues but she did all of the everyday cooking herself, often helped by Lizzie.

'Now I'm going to take you through the *batterie de cuisine*. Each of you will introduce yourselves, and then I will see if you know what each item is for.'

There was an inward gasp of horror as the haughty debs looked around, obviously aware of how little they knew about kitchen equipment. Lizzie was anxious herself. Her mother had a cooking set consisting of a ladle, potato masher, long fork and palette knife that hung in a set on the wall. They had been a wedding present, Lizzie knew. If she was asked about anything more complicated she might well fail and draw the opprobrium of Mme Wilson down on herself.

Yet here was an opportunity to learn everyone's names as well as a test and Lizzie paid attention. The girl in the striped apron was called Alexandra and the one who seemed to know her way round a kitchen (she identified a garlic squeezer without difficulty) was Meg, presumably short for Margaret. The others were called things like Saskia, Eleanor and Jemima.

At school Lizzie's friends had more ordinary names: Rosemary, Anne and Jane, or Elizabeth.

Lizzie was still wondering what it must be like to have the same name as a duck in a Beatrix Potter book when Mme Wilson called on her. Fortunately, Mme Wilson was holding up a cheese grater, which she could identify without difficulty.

After this trial-by-egg-whisk the girls were told to get out their notebooks (Meg was ahead on this, Lizzie spotted) and write down the recipe for sardine pâté. After that they were to cook steak, and for dessert, oranges with caramel.

'Come on,' said the tall girl who looked like Audrey Hepburn — Alexandra — at the end of the morning session, hurrying Meg and Lizzie out of the kitchen. Meg had found herself doing the washing up and Lizzie had felt obliged to help her. 'Follow me.'

Lizzie didn't have a better idea and she liked the thought of getting to know this girl who didn't seem to care much about the rules. She herself had always done what her parents had expected of her but it now appeared there were options.

Alexandra obviously knew her way around Pimlico very well. A short walk, a left-hand turn and they were walking down a side street and into a small café.

The windows were almost totally obscured by condensation and the noise of the steam from the coffee machine was loud and disconcerting. The machine was about the same size as a car and sounded as if it was about to explode. But as no one seemed remotely bothered, Lizzie followed the others inside.

The moment the girls entered, the man behind the counter, who was buttering bread and baguettes, came out. '*Bella*!' he said to Alexandra, hugging her

6

and kissing her soundly on the cheek. 'Where you been? We've missed you! Maria! Alessandra is here!'

A woman, her black hair in a bun, a slightly grubby apron covering her clothes, appeared from the kitchen and kissed Alexandra for even longer. Then she said, 'Sit! Sit! Are these your friends? Welcome! Now — coffee! Food! You must eat!'

It took a little while for the three of them to be herded into a booth and shortly afterwards three foam-covered cups of coffee arrived. Lizzie wasn't sure about coffee. She made it for her parents when they had dinner parties but she didn't like it much herself.

'Capuccinos,' said Alexandra, 'they're lovely but you'll need sugar. Lots of sugar.' There were large wrapped lumps of sugar on the saucers and she started unwrapping hers.

The other two did likewise and, copying their new friend and gang leader, put in both lumps of sugar and, when the sugar had found its way through the foam, began to stir.

'Oh my goodness, that's delicious!' said Lizzie, having taken a sip. 'I didn't know coffee could taste like that.'

'It's not like any coffee I've ever had before,' said Meg.

'I've known Maria and Franco for years,' said Alexandra. 'They taught me about coffee.' She paused. 'I had an Italian nanny for a short time. She used to bring me in here when I was a child.'

'Sorry to have to point this out,' said Meg, 'but you can't be very old now.'

Alexandra laughed, not offended by this. 'I'm nineteen, so at least twelve years older than I was when I first came.'

7

'Did you always have nannies?' asked Lizzie.

'Always.' Alexandra took another sip and sighed in satisfaction. 'I'm an orphan. But don't feel sorry for me! I never really knew my parents and have managed perfectly well without them.'

'Goodness,' said Meg. 'I can't imagine what that must be like. My mother and I are very close.'

Alexandra shrugged. 'It's what you're used to, I suppose. I had nannies, then I went to boarding school and in the holidays, if I didn't stay with my stuffy relations, I had governesses or companions or whatever they liked to be called. My relations only care about my money.'

Lizzie nearly choked. She had been brought up to respect her relations although her Aunt Gina had proved to be a bit of a surprise when she met her last evening. She wasn't sure her father would approve of Gina!

'I am — or will be — quite rich,' said Alexandra, as if it was a bit of a nuisance, 'but I'm not due to inherit until I'm twenty-five. It was arranged like that to keep the fortune hunters at bay.'

'My goodness,' said Lizzie, weakly.

'My relations — and I have a lot of them — take a very personal interest in my fortune. I think they're intending to find a cousin to marry me when the time comes who's not so closely related that we'd have strange children but who'll keep the money in the family.'

'My mother's very keen on me getting married,' said Lizzie. 'It's why I'm on this course, so I can learn to cook and other housewifely skills and be more marriageable. Although I don't have to have fortune hunters kept away.'

8

'Has your mother got anyone in mind?' asked Meg, who seemed to find this very odd.

'I think so,' said Lizzie. 'Not that they'd make me marry him, but I think I met him when I was about six and his parents are friends of my parents although they've moved away since.'

'And you don't mind?' asked Alexandra and Meg, more or less at the same time.

Lizzie shrugged. 'To be honest, I mostly go along with what my parents want but I'd never marry someone I didn't love.'

'But you do have your hair done at the same hairdresser as your mother?' asked Alexandra.

'Can you tell?' said Lizzie, patting her hair.

Alexandra nodded. 'It's quite an old-fashioned style,' she said. 'And now I can see what you're wearing under your overalls, your clothes were probably chosen by your mother too.'

Lizzie exhaled. 'The thing is, I don't think it's worth fighting about things you don't really care about.' She looked at Alexandra's shirt and slacks with envy. 'My mother has been planning my wedding day since I was tiny. I reckon if I was marrying a man I really loved I wouldn't care about the day all that much. And she does. I am their only child, after all.'

'I'm an only child too,' said Meg. 'But I don't think my mother has given my wedding day a thought.' She paused. 'Mind you, she works so it's different for her.'

'Your mother goes out to work?' said Lizzie, curious and a little intrigued.

'Well, she stays in to work really,' said Meg. 'Until recently anyway. She used to be a cook-housekeeper for an old man. He was lovely. We live in his flat. He always said he'd make sure we could stay in the flat after he died, but somehow his nieces made sure this won't happen. Luckily, he had a really nice solicitor who's arranged it so we can stay for three months — well, it's been two months now. It's why I'm on this course. I want to start earning as soon as possible.'

'Goodness me!' said Alexandra. 'But in my experience relations always do that. Whenever anyone dies there's always an ugly fight for the money, even if they have quite a lot already.'

'And when I've done this course and got my certificate I'm going to cook directors' lunches,' Meg went on. 'And if I can, I'll do catering in the evenings or something similar.'

'Why have two jobs?' asked Lizzie.

'I want to earn enough to get a deposit on a flat for my mother,' Meg said. 'She'll quite likely get another live-in job but we both feel we want something that's ours. If we get a flat, we can rent it out if Mum doesn't live in it.'

'My mother would have a fit if I even thought about having two jobs,' said Lizzie. 'My parents will expect me to do something until I meet Mr Right, but it won't really be for the money.'

Meg shrugged and Lizzie worried that she might have offended her. 'My mother was widowed young. She's always had to work,' she said.

'My mother only does voluntary work,' said Lizzie. 'And I think she only does it for the social life.' She thought about the coffee mornings and cake sales where women got together and talked about each other until the subject of their conversation appeared and they switched to another poor woman. She'd done enough assisting at these events to know what they were like.

'Let's have something to eat,' said Alexandra. 'I

10

know we tasted what we made today but it was only a taste and I'm hungry. It's flower arranging this afternoon, isn't it? I really wanted to do a course that only focused on cooking rather than doing different things in the afternoon, but this was the one people thought I should go on.'

Lizzie nodded. 'I quite like the thought of flower arranging. I've done lots of that. And I like dressmaking. But the thought of French conversation terrifies me!'

'You've done flower arranging for your mother?' Meg said.

Lizzie nodded. Her mother always roped her in if there were church flowers to be done. Lizzie tended to complain a lot but actually she enjoyed it and was considered to be quite good.

'But I hardly know any French,' she said, in case her friends thought she was claiming to be good at everything. 'I've never been abroad.'

'I don't know any French or about flower arranging,' said Meg. She looked at Alexandra. 'Is the food here likely to be expensive?'

Alexandra shook her head. 'It's very reasonable and the toasted cheese sandwiches are really filling. I may be an heiress but I know all about watching the pennies so the pounds can take care of themselves.'

'How come?' asked Meg.

Alexandra shrugged. 'I'll tell you one day. It's quite boring really.'

Lizzie had the impression there was quite a lot about Alexandra she wasn't ready to tell them.

In the end, they weren't allowed to pay for the cheese sandwiches, or the coffee, and Lizzie and Meg felt as much part of the family of the café owner as

11

Alexandra was.

They walked back to the cookery school, which was in the basement of a delicatessen. 'I'm quite looking forward to learning about other things, apart from cooking,' said Lizzie. 'I don't think I'm ever going to be any good at it. I might have a chance with flowers or dressmaking. That's my hobby.' At least she was confident in her needlecraft. She used to embroider tray cloths for her mother, add lace to handkerchiefs, and other fancy but basically fairly useless things. But she'd always made clothes for her dolls and, although her mother discouraged it, she also made things for herself.

'I like dressmaking,' said Alexandra. 'It's easy if you have plenty of space. And you have a sewing machine.'

Lizzie yearned for access to a sewing machine; she'd left hers with her parents. 'Do you make your own clothes?' she asked, keen to know about Alexandra's rather strange garments.

'Kind of. I mostly adapt stuff.' She frowned slightly. 'My life sounds really weird now I'm talking about it to other people. Although of course it's normal for me.'

Lizzie opened her mouth to ask another question and then closed it again. How could this glossy, aristocratic girl, who had told them she was rich, possibly need to save money? She shrugged and walked on. She'd find out soon enough, she was sure.

2

Lizzie was on the bus to her Aunt Gina's house, having asked the conductor to tell her when she should get off. Tired but very happy, she thought about her day.

Firstly, she felt she had found potential friends in Alexandra and Meg, which was very important. Her best friend from school, Sarah, had gone away to train as a nurse, and Lizzie missed her.

Secondly, although Mme Wilson was frightening, compared to some of the other girls who seemed not to have even ventured inside a kitchen, Lizzie felt she knew a bit more about cooking and so hoped she wouldn't be the focus of her sarcasm.

As the bus drove through the streets she spotted landmarks. There was Harrods (which she'd visited with her mother), and the Victoria and Albert Museum (which she hadn't). In spite of her tiredness she was excited and thrilled to be in London.

She got off the bus at the right place and set off, relatively confidently, in what she thought was the right direction for the little cul-du-sac where Aunt Gina lived. She was soon climbing the steps. As Gina hadn't given her a key, she rapped on the door.

'Oh, darling!' said Gina when she saw her standing there. 'You're back quite early!'

As there had been a fair amount of chatting among the girls after the French conversation and flower arranging, it was now half past four. Some of the others had been rushing off to tea parties as part of

13

their Season. It didn't seem early to Lizzie.

'I hope it's not inconvenient.'

'Don't worry about it!' Gina smiled, obviously a bit put out. 'Come in. I have a friend here for tea. I'm sure it won't be long before you can rustle up little French fancies and make yourself useful!'

Her parents had driven her up the night before so she knew her way round Gina's flat, which Gina had recently moved into. Although Gina was her mother's younger sister, they had very little in common so family visits were infrequent.

Now, Lizzie put her outdoor clothes in her bedroom and then went into the little sitting room at the front of the house. Gina and a man were sitting on the sofa. There were teacups on the little table in front of the sofa and Lizzie noticed that one of the teacups had fallen over.

'Let me introduce you,' said Gina as both she and the man got to their feet. 'Barry, this is Lizzie, or Elizabeth as her mother prefers, Lizzie, this is Barry.'

Barry took Lizzie's hand and kissed it. 'And what name do you prefer?'

'Lizzie,' she said, trying to take her hand back and failing.

'Sit down,' said Gina briskly, managing to make Lizzie feel even more that she'd intruded on something private. 'Tell us about your course.' She patted Barry's knee. 'Lizzie is learning to cook — among other things. Such fun! What did you learn today, darling?'

Lizzie got the impression that Gina was asking this in order to make conversation rather than because she cared. 'We learnt a lot about garlic and olive oil and how to make caramel. Never stir the pan, just shake it.' Lizzie smiled, wondering how soon she could leave

14

the room again. 'Would you like me to make more tea, Aunt — ' She remembered too late that her aunt had told her the previous evening that being called Aunt made her feel old. 'Um — Gina, or shall I just take these things out?'

'Oh, take them out, do. Thank you!'

Having escaped, Lizzie didn't return to the sitting room. She washed up the tea things, dried them and put them all away.

Eventually, when the little kitchen was spotless, she heard Barry leave. It seemed to take a long time.

'Oh, darling, you've cleared up. How kind. My char comes in the morning. Mrs Spriggs. Salt of the earth but rather short-sighted. By the way, your mother telephoned earlier. If you could ring her back? She wants to find out about the course.' Gina smiled. 'It can't be easy for her, letting her little girl go to London on her own.'

'I'm not on my own,' Lizzie protested. 'I've got you, Gina!'

★ ★ ★

Lizzie sat in the hall by Gina's telephone table. 'Mummy?' she said, when the phone was answered. 'It's me.'

'Elizabeth!' said her mother. 'Don't move; I'll ring you back. We don't want you running up phone bills.'

A few seconds later her mother was back on the line. 'So, how did it go? Were the other girls nice?'

'Yes. A couple of them were really nice. The others were quite — haughty. They're the ones doing the Season.'

Her mother sighed. If her dreams had come true,

Lizzie would be doing the Season too, going to balls, tea parties, sporting events, all with the object of meeting suitable young men: good husband material who could provide for a wife and family and keep them all in a suitable upper-class manner. Lizzie knew this but as her ambitions did not include forcing herself into a group of girls where she knew no one, she didn't know what to say to please her mother. 'One of the nicer girls seems quite grand though,' she said, hoping this would give her mother a little titbit of joy.

'Really, darling? What's her name?'

'Alexandra.'

'You must bring her down for the weekend as soon as you can. Maybe this weekend?'

Although Lizzie was the most obedient, compliant daughter possible, she could manage her mother to some extent. 'I won't know her nearly well enough to invite her down in a week, Mummy. Besides, I think Gina wants me to do something this weekend.' This was a lie, obviously, and although Lizzie considered herself to be a truthful person, sometimes lying was necessary. Lizzie didn't think she'd be ready to go home after only a week. She felt she'd only been in London for five minutes — she wanted a bit longer to stretch her wings.

Her mother, who had pressed on Lizzie exactly how important it was to keep in Gina's good books — Lizzie was staying for a very reasonable rent — didn't argue. 'I expect she wants you to clean the silver. It certainly needed doing yesterday. I was only in the house for five minutes and I noticed.'

Lizzie didn't point out that her mother wouldn't need a whole five minutes to spot the gaps in Gina's housekeeping skills.

'I think I'd better ring off now, Mummy. Gina might like help with supper.'

'All right, darling. Ring and tell me if you can pop home at the weekend. And find out more about this Alexandra. She sounds like such a nice girl.'

Lizzie knew that Alexandra was a nice girl but how her mother could have come to that conclusion on so little evidence she didn't know. Or rather she did know. It was because Lizzie had described her as 'grand'.

She went downstairs into the little kitchen where she found Gina. 'Can I help?'

'You can scrub the new potatoes. But it's a very simple supper. Unlike you, my darling, I'll never be able to cook anything too complicated.'

Lizzie was grateful. The night before she'd been confronted with an avocado pear — a fruit entirely new to her. It was so waxy and dense it took her a few moments to decide if she liked it or not.

'Maybe when I've learnt a little bit more, I'll be able to cook some meals for you,' she suggested.

Gina smiled and nodded but didn't seem exactly enthusiastic at the prospect of being cooked for by Lizzie.

Bearing in mind her mother's advice about being useful she went on, 'I'm also very good at mending. If you've got anything that needs a stitch, give it to me and I'll have it mended in a jiffy.'

'Really? Did you learn at school?'

Lizzie nodded. 'A bit, but my mother taught me to sew lace round bits of fine lawn to make handkerchiefs. They go down very well at the Bring and Buy sales she organises. My hems are invisible too, although I did learn that at school.'

'Oh. Well, after supper, I'll give you my mending basket — see what you can do with it.'

Gina was thoughtful throughout the meal and topped up Lizzie's wine glass, seemingly without thinking. Lizzie's parents didn't have wine with meals as a regular thing but, as her father had said, Gina was very 'modern'. Lizzie's father obviously did not approve of modernness.

After the washing up was done — although Gina said she was quite happy to leave the dishes until the following morning when her charwoman would come and do them, Lizzie turned her attention to Gina's mending.

It was in a bag and there was quite a lot of it. Lizzie discovered that Gina just shoved things in there and never looked at them again. She just bought a replacement. So there were quite a few dresses that needed the hemming, some buttons to be replaced and a torn sheet.

'Don't worry about the sheet, darling,' said Gina, seemingly a bit embarrassed. 'I'll get the laundry to do it.'

'Is that how it got torn?' asked Lizzie.

'No,' said Gina. 'Now, have you got everything you need?'

3

On Friday, Gina drew Lizzie into the sitting room the minute Lizzie had taken off her coat.

'Lizzie, I know we're not quite there yet, but what are you planning to do for the weekend?'

This was more than a casual query, Lizzie could tell. 'Well, my mother wants me to go home but I said I'd prefer to explore London a little. But of course, if it's inconvenient — '

'No, no. You should definitely get to know London a little. I'll give you an A to Z and you can spend Saturday exploring and, in the evening, Barry will take us to the theatre.'

This sounded very jolly and after supper, having washed up and left the kitchen so even her mother would have been satisfied, Lizzie went to bed, excited at the prospect of being free to explore her new surroundings.

Thus, on Saturday, having had a slightly hurt conversation with her mother who had wanted her at least to visit for the day on Sunday (her mother had always been excellent at making Lizzie feel guilty), armed with the A–Z Gina had given her, Lizzie set forth. She wasn't used to doing things on her own but it wasn't very long before she began to revel in her solitude.

She could stop and look in shop windows, or not, as the mood took her. She could look at the people who inhabited the King's Road — very different from the people in her own market town. There were Beatniks, with beards — Lizzie couldn't think of a single person who had a beard that she knew except the man who ran the wholefood shop, who wore sandals all year round. But here people had beards and longer hair. She saw a woman in a sack dress — a style she'd only seen in magazines.

Her plan was to explore the King's Road in the direction of Sloane Square and from there make her way to Knightsbridge and Harrods. She and her mother used to visit Harrods when they came up to Daniel Neal to buy her school uniform. Once they'd bought the school blouses for another year, they'd get into a taxi. If Lizzie's mother was feeling generous they'd buy something from Harrods, a pair of gloves or a hair clip, so they'd have a little green bag with gold writing on it.

While still in the King's Road, Lizzie spotted a dress shop with only one dress in the window. It was scarlet, plain and short. It had no sleeves and a deep round neck. In the shop it was put over a black polo-neck jumper, as unlike the full-skirted shirtwaister dresses her mother liked her to wear as was possible.

Lizzie gazed at it thoughtfully. She did have a little money but if she bought the dress she wouldn't have any money until her next month's allowance was due. And did she need to buy it? Could she just buy a pattern and make it for herself? She thought longingly of the sewing machine left behind at home and then moved on to the hairdresser next door.

This was also very different. At home the hairdresser was full of women sitting under dryers like giant eggs, reading magazines. This one was small, didn't seem to have any overhead hairdryers and had pictures outside of models with very different hairstyles from the ordered curls favoured by her mother's generation.

20

She was just trying to imagine herself with short hair when a young man came out.

'Excuse me! Miss!'

It took him a couple of goes before Lizzie realised he was talking to her. 'Oh! Hello?'

'I was just wondering if you fancied having your hair cut? I'm looking for a model, you see. I have a new stylist. She's good but inexperienced in the kind of cut people want now.'

'Er . . .'

'It would be free.' He hesitated. 'Would you mind stepping into the shop for a minute? Your hair is in great condition. I'd love to — '

Without finishing his sentence he somehow steered Lizzie into his shop and seated her in front of a mirror.

A gown was flung round her shoulders.

'Come over here!' said the man to someone hovering in the background. 'Come and see this hair. Unpermed, unbleached, in really lovely condition.'

A nervous young woman appeared in the mirror and watched as the man ran his fingers through Lizzie's hair. 'And look!' he said. 'A perfect widow's peak. So, er, Miss — what is your name? I can't go on calling you Miss.'

'Lizzie,' said Lizzie, charmed and unnerved at the same time.

'And I'm Terry. This is Susan; she's my student. She's good but she hasn't done a proper geometric cut before. If you let her cut your hair I'd pay you.'

'I'm not sure . . .'

'Ten pounds! Can't say fairer than that!'

Ten pounds was more than her monthly allowance. It seemed a huge amount of money to Lizzie.

'Really? You'd pay me ten pounds to have my hair cut?' It seemed too good to be true and her father always said that if it seemed too good to be true it probably was. 'But it might look awful!'

'It won't,' said Terry, still playing with her hair as if it were the finest fabric. 'I'll supervise every step of the way. You can even choose which style. We're not like some places who make the models have whatever we want. I'm just training one stylist who's good already, not dozens of them. Come over to the basin. We'll cut it wet.'

Lizzie was there for a long time but she was not put in front of a mirror. She was given cups of coffee and biscuits and then a sandwich. Every snip of the scissors was checked and supervised. But although Terry and Susan examined her closely, she couldn't see what they were doing to her.

'Does it look all right?' she asked once, after what seemed to be a big lock of hair fell down into her lap.

'It's great!' said Terry. 'You really look something! You have great bones and of course perfect skin. So lucky! I was a mass of acne when I was your age.'

'You look really lovely,' said Susan shyly. 'Almost like a model.'

'Not quite like a model?' Lizzie wasn't satisfied by the 'almost'.

Susan shook her head. 'Your clothes are all wrong and you need some make-up.'

Lizzie's mother sometimes wore a little 'eye blue', as she described it, as well as lipstick and powder. And of course she always pencilled in her eyebrows. But it had to be very discreet: Lizzie's father disapproved of women who painted their faces. He would have had a fit if Lizzie had worn make-up. She thought of the ten pounds she was going to be given. Some of it would definitely go on make-up.

Lizzie hardly recognised herself when at last she was allowed to look. Her eyes were enormous, her face pixie-like and appealing and the slanted fringe and the geometric shapes of hair on her cheeks made her look, she felt, very modern.

'Gosh!' said Lizzie. 'I can never go home again! My father will go mad.'

'I'll just take some pictures,' said Terry.

When he'd finished, he produced two ten-pound notes. 'I know I said ten, but it's worked out so well . . . ' He handed over twenty pounds. 'Take a tip from me. Go straight next door and buy that dress in the window. You won't regret it.'

Lizzie took his advice. She bought the black polo-neck sweater, too. She had her own dress put in a bag so she could wear her new outfit straight away. Then she walked to Peter Jones and found a remnant of gaberdine in a plain dark green. She wouldn't need a pattern, she decided; she could just copy the dress she already had.

* * *

Lizzie practically skipped back down the King's Road towards Gina's house. She hummed a pop song and swung her bag and generally felt as if she was in a film. She was like a real London dolly bird, not the boring Home Counties girl she had been when she'd first arrived. She ran up the steps to Gina's front door and rang the bell, hoping her aunt would soon give her a key. She lived in London, she had made some great new friends and she looked the part.

23

Gina opened the door and looked blankly at her for a few seconds.

'Good Lord! I hardly recognised you!' she said. 'You've had your hair cut.' Then she frowned. 'Sorry, stupid thing to say. You know that. Come in.'

'What do you think?' Lizzie asked. 'Is it an awful mistake? I was looking in a window and this man came out and begged me to be a model.'

'Your father will hate it,' said Gina, 'but that probably means you've done exactly the right thing. Come and have some tea. Barry will be here soon to take us to the theatre. I wonder what he'll think about you, with your skirt showing your knees and your hair so modern.'

Barry was impressed. He made a big fuss of Gina's 'little niece' to the extent that Lizzie felt quite uncomfortable. He gave her a large glass of sherry — not like the thimblefuls Lizzie's father thought were appropriate for the fairer sex. Then he wondered aloud if she and Gina would like to go to a club after the theatre. The Ad Lib, he said; he had a contact who could get them in.

Gina wasn't at all keen and although Lizzie did want to go to a club sometime, she didn't want to go with Barry and Gina in a bad mood.

The theatre trip was somewhat marred by Barry's attentiveness and the fact that other people, strangers, also noticed her. Lizzie didn't really like being the focus of attention. While she was in the Ladies, having queued seemingly for hours, someone admired her hair and asked her where she'd had it done. She happily told them. She only noticed a couple of other people with hair cut short like hers in the theatre and they all looked very stylish.

★ ★ ★

On Sunday afternoon Gina seemed on edge. Lizzie walked to the park and then came home and made toast for tea. She took a tray through to the sitting room where Gina was sitting by the gas fire. She smiled and made a space for the tray, pushing the Sunday papers off the table and on to the floor.

'I'll miss these little attentions,' she said. 'You're a good girl, I must admit.'

Lizzie was alarmed. Her aunt wasn't given to sentimentality.

She poured a cup of tea and handed it to Gina. Then she offered her the plate of buttered toast.

'What would your parents say if you told them you didn't want to live with me any more?' Gina wiped her buttery fingers on her handkerchief.

Lizzie went hot and then cold. 'I — I don't know — I can't imagine.' Then she thought a bit harder. 'They'd say I had to go home. They wouldn't let me stay in London.'

'OK, well, we won't say that then. But, darling, I can't have you here. I made a mistake. You'll have to share a flat with other girls. Lots of people do it. It's fine. I'll help you. Help you with the rent, too.'

'But why can't I stay here?'

'You're far too pretty! I was relying on you looking like your mother, but you're far prettier than she ever was.'

Lizzie blushed but didn't speak.

'The thing is, Barry means well, but if he made a pass at you, I'd have to ditch him and he helps out quite a lot with bills and things.'

Lizzie was a bit shocked but she could see the

25

sense in this. It was a shame that Gina obviously felt it was easier to get rid of her than to keep Barry under control.

'When do you want me to leave?' Her voice was hardly more than a whisper. The thought of leaving Gina's cosy little house in the best part of London was devastating. And how would she cope living with girls she didn't know?

And then she took a breath and thought back on all the new experiences she'd had in the past week — was it really only a week? — and here she was, looking different, being different from how she had been all her life. She would be fine, she told herself. Of *course* she would be.

Fortunately Gina was unaware of the mixture of excitement and terror that was filling Lizzie's head.

'Well, I'm not going to throw you on to the street! I'll give you at least a couple of weeks.' Gina smiled, obviously pleased to have got the difficult part of the conversation over. 'I've got the evening paper from last week here. We'll find you somewhere lovely. It'll be far more fun than living with your old aunt.'

'You're not at all old!' said Lizzie.

'I'm older than you, sweetheart, which is why I can't have you living here.'

4

Lizzie's new hairstyle and short dress attracted a lot of attention when she arrived at the basement kitchen on Monday morning. Not all of it was positive.

'How will you put your hair up? If you want to wear a tiara?' said one girl, Saskia, whose long chestnut locks were currently confined into a chignon. She was one of the haughtiest girls there and Lizzie felt flattered she even spoke to her, even though it was to say something negative. Saskia didn't mention Lizzie's short dress.

'I don't think I'll ever need to wear a tiara, ' said Lizzie, but sensed her mother would probably say something very similar to Saskia.

Saskia went on, 'I mean, I'm going to have my photographs done and the photographer definitely said I shouldn't cut my hair beforehand. I'm hoping to get into *Country Life*. The 'girls in pearls' photograph? Although I've got diamonds.'

'Diamonds aren't suitable for a very young girl,' said Mme Wilson, breaking into the conversation.

'And can we all settle down? It's time for class to begin.'

'You look wonderful!' whispered Meg to Lizzie as everyone found places. 'Very 'with it'.'

'You don't think it's a bit — modern?' asked Lizzie.

'Of course not,' Alexandra declared. 'You're very trendy!'

Mme Wilson was less impressed. She merely looked at Lizzie and suggested she put on her overall quickly to cover her knees.

'I won't be able to hang around,' said Lizzie, the moment they were on the pavement at the end of the day. 'I need to go and look at a flat. I have to move out of my Aunt Gina's house.'

'Really?' said Meg. 'Why?'

Lizzie hesitated before speaking. She didn't want to imply Gina was unkind, or that she herself was a flirt out to 'get' Gina's man. 'Because Gina has a boyfriend — a manfriend — and Gina thinks he might turn his attentions to me.' Lizzie bit her lip. It seemed terribly unlikely to her that Barry would prefer her, so young and unsophisticated, to her dashing Aunt Gina. But he had made very flirtatious remarks when he'd taken them to the theatre so it was a possibility.

'How awkward,' said Meg. 'So, you're going to look at a flat now?'

Lizzie nodded. 'Gina seems quite keen to get me out of the way, even though I was really helpful and was doing her mending!'

Alexandra laughed. 'How ungrateful of her.'

Lizzie laughed back. 'I know! Outrageous!'

'Where's the flat?' asked Alexandra.

'Tufnell Park? Have you ever been there?'

Alexandra shook her head. 'I'm afraid not. It's quite far out.'

'I'll walk to the Tube with you,' said Meg. 'It's not far.'

But at the other end of her Tube trip, the flat seemed an awfully long way from the station, Lizzie thought as she checked her A–Z once again to make sure she was in the right place. She was already deeply depressed by her surroundings. The huge Victorian houses seemed unkempt and run down. This part of London was very different from Chelsea. And how long would it take her to get to the cookery school from here? She realised it would be quicker when she knew the way, but it would still take over an hour, she reckoned. An hour away from Gina and her cosy little house, from her new friends. And it seemed a world away from her home in Surrey.

Although Lizzie was naïve she was not stupid and she realised that Gina was justified in not wanting her pretty young niece to live with her. She also accepted Gina couldn't give Barry the brush-off — he was too wealthy and generous for her to be able to afford to. But Lizzie did wish that Gina could have put up with her for just a bit longer. The cookery course was only for a few weeks, and she would go home when it was over.

However, although her going home after the course was always the plan, Lizzie was beginning to think she might prefer to get a job and stay in London. Meg was going to work after the course. Why couldn't she? She wasn't as talented a cook as Meg was, of course, but she was OK, better than the debs, who never seemed to pay attention and just wanted to talk about the next party, weekend in the country, or event on the social calendar, while yearning for their picture in the *Tatler*.

At last the numbers of the very long road she was walking down were a bit nearer to the number of the address she had written on a bit of paper in her hand. Two more houses and she was there.

The front door wasn't promising. It was very dirty and had a piece of cardboard pinned over a broken pane. Lizzie rang the bell and hoped no one would answer. Then she could go home and tell Gina she'd tried. Before she attempted to find somewhere else again, she would check very carefully the area the flat-share was in, although she realised the reasonable rent had probably been a sign it would not only be miles from anywhere she wanted to be but also very scruffy.

A young woman opened the door. She had long hair tucked behind her ears like curtains. She had greasy skin and didn't smile.

'You here for the room? You'd better come in, but I warn you, there's plenty after it.'

Lizzie felt it would be rude to leave before she'd even crossed the threshold so she went through the door.

An unidentifiable but powerful smell hit her nostrils: a combination of old cooking fat, cabbage and drains were all she could identify. Maybe there was a hint of body odour but that could have been coming from the girl.

'It's upstairs, follow me,' said the girl. 'I'm Monica, by the way.'

Monica opened a door off the first landing. 'In here.'

Monica had been right about there being others after a share in this flat. Lizzie found herself in a tiny hallway with doors opening off it and nearly bumped into a fellow viewer.

'I'm so sorry!' said a very tall, smartly dressed young man. 'Did I step on your foot?'

'No, it's all right, you didn't.' Lizzie would have smiled at him except his good looks and well-cut suit increased her natural shyness. His voice was very upper class.

'Living room through there,' said Monica, who was now pushing past Lizzie.

The man went into the room first and Lizzie followed.

It had a bay window draped in yellowing net curtains, a large black plastic-covered sofa with a tear in it, two other armchairs, and a small scratched coffee table. There was an electric fire in the fireplace. Her mother, who had an inbuilt sense for such things, would surely say it was damp — yes, the wallpaper was detaching itself from the wall and there was mould on the wall behind the door.

'There's a meter for the electric,' said Monica. 'Bedroom's here.'

Lizzie's room at Gina's wasn't large but it made this little boxroom seem spacious. There was no window and no other furniture apart from the bed.

'It's a single,' said Monica, stating the obvious, 'which is why it's a bit dearer. Hook for your clothes on the door.'

'Kitchen?' asked the man.

A grubby gas stove, a sink and a Formica table with two chairs completed the furnishings but at least it had a window.

Monica flapped a hand at the window. 'Keep your milk on the sill. Label your bottle.'

'What about the bathroom?' asked Lizzie. She knew she wasn't going to take the room, she'd rather go home and travel up each day from there than live here, but she would have felt rude if she hadn't seen the entire offering.

'Shared with the flat above. There's a rota.' The doorbell rang and Monica withdrew.

'Do you want to take it?' asked the man.

Lizzie shook her head. 'It's all yours.'

'It's pretty dreadful, isn't it? But cheap.'

Lizzie thought he looked like someone who could afford to live somewhere far nicer than her. He had a prosperous, glossy air about him — in fact he was the sort of young man her parents would approve of. She quite approved of him herself. He was attractive.

★ ★ ★

'So what was the flat like?' asked Alexandra the following morning while they hung up their outdoor clothes.

'Ghastly,' said Lizzie. 'It would be easier to live at home and commute from there.'

'Do you want to do that?' asked Alexandra.

'No,' said Lizzie. 'Definitely not. I mean my parents are perfectly nice people but I want to live in London! At least for as long as the course lasts.'

'I have an idea,' said Alexandra. 'Talk to you about it at lunch.'

Although Lizzie was fairly preoccupied with her own problems she couldn't help noticing in the morning session that Meg was a bit distracted — not as focused as she usually was. Mme Wilson had to ask her twice to recite her recipe for shortcrust pastry. Meg managed it the second time.

'My advice, girls,' said Mme Wilson, 'is to use this recipe for everything that requires a short crust. The egg yolk makes it easy to handle.'

★ ★ ★

'Let's go to the café,' said Alexandra after all three girls had made quiche cases and baked them blind — a process new to Lizzie.

32

'I was thinking,' Alexandra continued, when they had cappuccinos in front of them and were lowering in the sugar lumps. 'Why don't you come and live in my house? It's silly me living there almost all by myself when you have to go home to live with your parents, or find some ghastly flat-share somewhere.'

'Oh my goodness! That would be amazing!' exclaimed Lizzie. 'But what would your — your guardians think about it?'

'They won't know and why would they object? Me sharing with a nice girl from the Home Counties would be just what they'd want for me if they ever gave the matter any thought.'

'That would be perfect!' Lizzie said, thinking how her mother would react to the thought of her sharing with a posh girl who lived in the very best part of town. She'd be so thrilled she'd possibly forgive her daughter for her geometric haircut.

'Excellent!' Alexandra clapped her hands. Meg cleared her throat. 'Might there be room for two people in your house?'

'Of course,' said Alexandra. 'It's huge. Why?'

'It's just I need somewhere to live now too. Urgently.'

'But why?'

'My mother's got a job, which is brilliant, and it's live in, also brilliant, but it leaves me homeless,' said Meg.

'Come and live with me then! We can all be together, which will be lovely. It's quite lonely living in that huge house more or less on my own.'

'There's just one problem,' said Meg, who, Lizzie felt, wasn't quite delighted enough at the prospect of having her housing problem solved so happily.

'What?' said Alexandra.

33

'There's Clover.'

'Who's Clover?' said Alexandra and Lizzie together.

'She's my dog. Well, not my dog really; she used to belong to the old man my mother looked after — where we've been living for the past five years.' 'And he left her to you in his will?' suggested Lizzie.

Meg became a bit emotional. 'The thing is, the old man's family — distant family; they never came to visit — wanted to have her put down. Clover isn't young, she's seven, but that's not old either!'

'Oh, that's awful,' said Alexandra. 'Of course she can come and live with us.' She paused. 'There is one thing though.'

Lizzie and Meg regarded Alexandra with trepidation. Was the answer to their problems to be snatched away so soon?

'I told you I live more or less on my own . . . well that's a lie. I've got into the habit of lying to people — self-preservation — but it's an awful habit.' She took a breath. 'I live with David. He's the kindest, nicest person you will ever meet and he's always looked after me — well, for about three years anyway. He's an antiques dealer and an actor.'

'Why might that be a problem?' asked Meg.

Alexandra didn't answer for a second. 'He's a homosexual.' Lizzie and Meg both swallowed.

Alexandra went on: 'As you know, being gay is illegal. If you think you might have a problem sharing a house with someone like that, or might tell the authorities or anything, I can't have you in my home.' She paused again. 'And I'm not sure I can have you as my friends.'

'It's not a problem for me,' said Meg. 'Although nothing was ever said, I'm sure William, the old man

34

my mother looked after, and who we lived with, was homosexual. He was the nicest, kindest person too.' She smiled shyly.

'I'm sorry to be stupid,' said Lizzie. 'But I'm not absolutely sure what a homosexual is.' She found herself blushing at her ignorance. 'I've led a very sheltered life,' she added apologetically.

'It's when men don't fancy women, they like other men,' said Meg. 'I don't know why it's illegal.'

'OK,' said Lizzie. 'I don't think I've ever met a gay person.'

'You probably have,' said Alexandra. 'Only you didn't know. Let's go and see the house,' she went on. 'It's walking distance, if you don't mind walking,' she said confusingly. 'You may hate it!'

'It would mean missing upholstery,' said Lizzie, slightly shocked.

'I don't think it would matter,' said Meg. 'The debs quite often miss the afternoon sessions. They're only there as a filler, to make the course seem worth the money.'

'She's right,' said Alexandra. 'But we could make it after upholstery if you'd rather, Lizzie.'

'Let's do that,' said Meg, looking at Lizzie and obviously guessing that Lizzie would be more comfortable doing this.

But the moment the workroom was tidy at the end of the day and the girls could go, they didn't dawdle. Alexandra led the way and London suddenly seemed at its best. There were cherry trees along the way bursting with blossom. Window boxes full of bulbs, daffodils, tulips and hyacinths decorated the smarter houses. Small shops, larger ones as they reached Victoria and then residential streets again. Lizzie couldn't

35

stop smiling, she was so excited. London seemed so full of possibility and promise. Living in this area would be wonderful, and completely different from the ghastly flat in Tufnell Park and even better than Chelsea had seemed?

Alexandra led them to a crescent full of tall, stately houses of at least four storeys. In front was a garden, surrounded by a wire fence. Lizzie thought it had probably once had iron railings, taken down during the war. It was full of mature trees and through the wire could be seen flowers, paths, seats and a little hut.

'Is this the only garden?' asked Meg anxiously.

'No, no, there's a small one at the back. Let's go in. I have to warn you, the house hasn't been properly redecorated for years.'

The hallway was dark and somehow got darker when Alexandra pressed a switch. A single bulb shone from a chandelier, throwing shadows everywhere. The light was dim but it was enough to reveal faded grandeur, a house that once had been aristocratic and elegant but now was in desperate need of a good clean. There was a staircase leading up but Alexandra said, 'Come downstairs to the kitchen. It's a bit cosier.'

It was cosier but it was still big. Lizzie got the impression that several small rooms had been knocked through to make a large room that ran from the front of the house to the back, so there were windows at each end. But because the room was below ground level it still wasn't very light. Lizzie could see it was roughly divided into three areas. As you came through the door there was a large table. It was clearly for working on rather than sitting at, as there were no chairs and it had quite a few boxes of china and a broken candelabra on top. Further along there were a couple of sofas and some chairs ranged around a gas fire in the middle, like a sort of sitting room. There was an upright piano against the wall between this seating area and the kitchen area up the far end.

Here there were a couple of dressers against the wall and on them were some large stoneware storage jars full of cooking implements and wooden spoons. A blue enamelled gas stove stood next to the large wooden draining board and attached to the wall above there was a large, two-tier plate rack.

A wooden table stood opposite the sink and in the corner was a tall saucepan rack, with saucepans, all different sizes, on the separate shelves. There was a knife rack attached to the wall and Lizzie was impressed to see knives like those Mme Wilson had at the cookery school. They were not the small, serrated, wooden-handled knives Lizzie's mother struggled with. Nothing matched but everything seemed to be in a logical order.

'Someone who lives here cooks,' said Meg, walking further into the room.

'That's David. He could have taught me to cook and, to be fair, he has tried. But I'm on the course because my guardians thought I'd meet nice girls there,' said Alexandra. 'And of course I have!' She made a gesture towards Lizzie and Meg.

'Does he also play the piano, or is that you?' asked Lizzie.

'I can play a little bit, but you're right, that's David too,' said Alexandra. 'We love community singing! He's a great sight-reader and so I've got quite good too, although as the singer, I only have to sight-read one line.'

'I can't read music at all,' said Meg, possibly feeling inadequate.

'Oh, you don't have to! You'll know most of the songs. Anyway, wait until David's here. He says everyone can sing. Now come and sit down. I'll get the fire going and then make us some tea.'

After a lot of popping and minor explosions the gas fire was alight and Alexandra went over to fill the kettle.

'So how often do you see your guardians?' asked Lizzie, amazed by the apparent freedom Alexandra had.

'Hardly ever. I write them a lot of letters, full of news, never telling them everything, and giving each of them something a little different. I know what worries them individually, you see. It keeps them happy.' She looked around her. 'Of course one day they'll come over from Switzerland and see I've knocked together all the small rooms — you know: the laundry, the pantry, the room where the china was kept — and there'll be hell to pay, but I'll deal with that when it happens.'

She looked a little wistful, Lizzie thought.

'Someone once told me it's easier to ask for forgiveness than for permission.' Alexandra brightened up again. 'In the meantime, it makes down here really cosy, don't you think?'

'Weren't you worried that the ceiling might come down while you were bashing away at the walls?' asked Meg.

Alexandra, who had finally got the gas to light under the kettle, flapped a hand. 'Oh, it was all right. Some builder friends of David's did it. They made sure it was safe.'

Alexandra was now opening and shutting cupboard doors looking for something. Finally she brought out a beautiful china teapot with a chipped spout. 'I thought we should use the best china instead of the old tin teapot. Just this once.'

'I really want to live here,' said Lizzie. She'd spotted a sewing machine amid the clutter on the table up the other end of the room.

'You haven't seen the bedrooms yet,' said Alexandra, apparently on the hunt for the rest of the tea service.

'I'm sure the bedrooms are lovely,' said Lizzie, thinking at least they'd be large.

'And I don't care about the bedrooms,' said Meg. 'I want to cook in this amazing kitchen. It's so spacious! The one we've had — me and my mother — is fairly tiny. But can I take a quick peep at the garden? Make sure it'll be OK for Clover?'

'Go through that door at the end,' said Alexandra, at last finding cups and saucers. 'There's a key on the shelf by the back door. Unlock it and you'll see the garden. It's just a bit of lawn with a tree in the middle really. The tea should be ready by the time you come back.'

Meg came back several minutes later, apparently satisfied that the garden would be suitable for Clover. 'You could grow herbs, parsley, things like that there,' she said. 'My mother was brought up in the country and her mother grew all sorts of things. We've always had whatever we could fit into pots, wherever we've lived. Although with William, we planted things in his garden.'

'Does Clover need much exercise?' asked Alexandra, making tea now the kettle had finally boiled. 'We do have a key for the square garden — communal, obviously, but they don't let dogs in. Or unattended children. And they're not allowed to play ball games. Not much fun at all, although I suppose the flowers are pretty.'

'Do you go in it much?' asked Lizzie, still fascinated by what seemed such a different sort of life.

'In the summer, yes. I suspect one of the neighbours is a spy for my relations so I let her see me at least once a year, looking healthy. I make sure I have a friend to take with me. Not that I've got many friends, but David produces a nice young actress for me to wander round the paths with. Ah! Here he is!'

Lizzie found herself stiffening with nerves at the prospect of meeting the first man she knew to be homosexual. But when she saw him and realised he looked just like any other man, she relaxed again. He was older than they all were, possibly in his mid-thirties, and very handsome; he looked kind.

'David!' Alexandra went across to him and took his arm, leading him to the fireside. 'This is Lizzie, who I said I was thinking of asking to come and live with us, and Meg wants to come too. There's plenty of room.'

Meg smiled. 'Only I've got a dog, so you may not want me as a flatmate.' She paused. 'Although this is hardly a flat.'

'A dog? Where?' David looked around expectantly.

'I haven't got her here now,' said Meg, laughing. 'Will you mind?'

'Darling, I adore dogs! There's nothing I'd like more than having one in the house. Can I take it for walks? What kind of dog is it?'

'It's a little spaniel,' said Meg, obviously relaxing. 'And of course you can take her for walks. I'm not

40

sure where you'd take her though. We take her out on Wimbledon Common at the moment.'

'There are a couple of small parks nearby and if you wouldn't mind, I could pop her in the car and take her to one of the larger ones,' said David.

'She'd love that,' said Meg.

After they'd all finished second cups of tea, Alexandra said, 'Come and see upstairs.'

Through the faded hall and up the stairs they went. 'Those rooms are closed off,' said Alexandra when they were on ground level. 'Follow me.' On the first floor, Alexandra opened a door and ushered them into the drawing room. 'It's got double doors, so if there's a really big party you can use the whole room.'

'It seems quite big enough as it is,' said Lizzie, awestruck by the high ceiling, the two floor-length windows that opened on to balconies and the magnificent marble fireplace.

'I prefer this room,' said Alexandra, opening the doors to the smaller room.

This room contained a dusty grand piano as well as a sofa and chairs. 'David plays the piano sometimes, but he prefers the old upright one in the kitchen. It's too cold to come up here in winter.'

It was fairly chilly now, in April, thought Lizzie.

'You can see why we live in the basement,' said Alexandra.

'Would you mind if Clover slept with me?' asked Meg. 'She's used to living in a flat and I'm not sure I'd like to think of her all the way down in the basement if I was up here.'

Alexandra nodded. 'And you'll be up a level, on the second floor. Come and see the bedrooms. I don't mind where Clover sleeps.'

41

'David's in the nursery, at the top, which has its own bathroom, complete with a frieze of little ducklings,' said Alexandra, opening the door to a vast bedroom. 'I'm in this one at the front. There's another next door, and a small bedroom at the back. The bathroom's in here.' They went into a bathroom revealing a large bath with ball and claw feet and a lot of complicated-looking brass pipes indicating some sort of shower arrangement.

'Let's have a look at where we'd sleep,' said Meg.

'I'd like to say I was leaving the best until last,' said Alexandra, 'but I'm not, really. Here: it's next to mine.'

The bedroom Alexandra showed them was very large but the once pretty floral wallpaper was falling off and there was a damp patch on the ceiling. There were two single beds, a dressing table and cupboards, one of which revealed a washbasin.

'We could share this,' said Lizzie. 'It's massive!'

'But what about Clover?' asked Meg diffidently. 'How would you feel about sharing a room with a dog?'

'Does she howl in the night or anything?' Lizzie asked.

'No, she just sleeps on my bed and snores,' said Meg. 'Although that can get quite loud.'

'I'm sure I won't mind,' said Lizzie. When she used to go and spend the night with her friend, she always liked hearing someone else breathing in the dark nearby. She was slightly prone to having nightmares and liked the thought of having company, at least until she'd got used to living in this slightly spooky house.

'How much is the rent?' she asked, hoping she could afford it.

'Yes,' said Meg. 'We need to know. I probably can't

42

afford what it's worth.'

Alexandra's face screwed up in a way that indicated she'd thought about this but hadn't reached a conclusion. 'Well, to be honest, as I never anticipated renting rooms, I expect it would be fine if we all chipped in for housekeeping. I don't see myself as a landlady, all enormous bosom and wrap-over pinny.'

'We've got to pay you!' said Lizzie. 'Otherwise we'd just be scroungers.' Her father had very strong opinions about scroungers and while Lizzie rejected a lot of what her father thought, the bit about people who expected to get something for nothing had rubbed off on her.

'OK,' said Alexandra, and named a ridiculously small amount. 'And we'll all pitch in for food and household bills, how about that?'

'And would you mind if we decorated this room a little bit?' asked Meg. 'Stuck the wallpaper back on?'

'Not at all! Help yourselves. Actually, I think there's wallpaper in the attic we could use,' said Alexandra, seemingly enthusiastic about this plan.

'What about bedding?' asked Lizzie. 'Sheets, blankets, eiderdowns, pillows?'

'There's a huge airing cupboard full of it. Don't worry. It's all going to be enormous fun! Let's go downstairs and make toast.'

When they'd gone back down and had more tea — in mugs this time — and eaten toast, Lizzie got up. 'I ought to go and tell Gina I've got a lovely place to live.' She paused. 'My mother will be delighted too. I mean, she'll be worried about me leaving Gina, but when I tell her I'm living in Belgravia . . .' She looked at Alexandra. 'Will I be? Living in Belgravia? Pimlico seems a bit racy, somehow.'

43

Alexandra shrugged non-committally. 'I'm not absolutely sure. I think so.'

'I'll tell her I am,' said Lizzie. 'She won't know one way or the other.' She frowned. 'I'd better go and see my parents, I suppose. They'll have a fit when they see my hair.' She ruffled it thoughtfully.

'And I'm worried about how I'm going to get Clover up here,' said Meg. 'She's never been on the Tube or a bus or anything.'

David, who'd been chopping something in the kitchen end of the room, looked up. 'Why don't I go down in the car and pick you both up? You live in Wimbledon at the moment, don't you?'

Meg turned to him. 'Yes! And that would be wonderful! Could you really do that?'

David smiled and nodded. 'It's not that far, you know. And I could bring your things as well.' He frowned. 'Would your mother be all right about that? You being picked up by a strange man?'

Meg laughed. 'If it means Clover has a good home, my mother wouldn't mind who I ran off with!'

'It'll have to be on Friday though,' David went on. 'I'm doing Portobello — that's the market — on Saturday.'

'That would be perfect. I'll make you a cake to say thank you,' said Meg. 'I'll go and ring my mother now, if that's all right. I'll leave some money for the call, of course.'

Lizzie had a flash of inspiration. She thought about her mother's tea parties, cake, little sandwiches and scones and more importantly, guests. 'I don't suppose you'd fancy coming home with me, Alexandra? For tea, this weekend? My mother wouldn't make a fuss about my hair if you were there, and she'd be so

44

thrilled to meet you, given that we're going to be flat-mates.' She didn't add that Alexandra had the sort of confidence that revealed her rather grand roots.

Alexandra made a gesture. 'I'd love to, especially if it helps your escape plan. I promise to wear something conventional. I know all about pulling the wool over the eyes of people who may love you but have no chance of understanding you.'

Lizzie put her hand on Alexandra's. 'That sums it up perfectly. Thank you!'

5

'Thank you so much for coming with me,' Lizzie said again, a few days later. 'They absolutely loved you!' She and Alexandra were on their way back from visiting her parents.

In fact, she had been a bit embarrassed at her mother being so obviously impressed by Alexandra's casual aristocracy, coupled with perfect manners and genuine friendliness.

'They were sweet! They're just very concerned for you,' said Alexandra. 'And I do agree that Gina should have hung on to you for a bit longer before telling you you had to leave.'

'But my father did believe her when she said the whole house had to be rewired,' said Lizzie. 'Gina didn't say, 'I'm worried that my boyfriend will make a pass at Lizzie because basically he's a sex maniac.''

Alexandra laughed, taking off her coat and slinging it over the bottom of the elegant staircase. 'That would not have gone down well! Now I must go and change. This skirt is a little tight.'

'I'd be happy to let it out for you if you'd like,' said Lizzie, not sure if the skirt was a favourite. Being mid-calf-length and full, it was a bit New Look for current fashion.

'Thank you, but don't bother. I do have lots of other clothes I'd love your help with, though.'

Lizzie now had the courage to ask what she'd been longing to know since the first day at the cookery course. 'Don't your guardians give you a clothing allowance or anything?'

'They do, but of course everything cost sixpence in their day and all their frocks were 'run up' by seamstresses who worked by candlelight for nothing. Besides, I'd rather spend the money on other things.'

Alexandra was poised to run upstairs so Lizzie put her hand on her wrist. 'What other things?'

'Junk really, although I prefer to call them antiques.'

★ ★ ★

By Sunday evening, all three girls were installed in the big house in Belgravia.

David, having brought Meg's things and her dog over on Friday, collected Lizzie and her things from Gina's house. David and Gina discovered they had friends in common and so the three of them had enjoyed a glass of sherry together before David drove her back to the house. Gina, possibly feeling guilty for throwing her niece out of the house quite so soon, handed Lizzie a smart carrier bag full of clothes.

'These are things that aren't right for me but I never took back. You're such a genius with a needle and thread you might be able to make something of them.'

Lizzie looked in the bag. She saw some lovely fabrics and a tangle of interesting belts and scarves. 'Oh gosh. It looks like there are some really nice things in here.'

Gina shrugged. 'Some are only from La Boutique Saint-Michel but there are one or two better things. I know you'll be able to alter them to make them a bit more up to date.'

'La Boutique Saint-Michel?' asked Lizzie, aware

Gina expected her to know about this apparently famous shop.

David laughed. 'Oh! Jolly old Marks and Sparks? I shall never call it anything else from now on.'

Now the penny dropped. 'I do like that, Gina,' said Lizzie. 'Although I didn't get what you meant at first. Being a girl, my vests all had St Margaret in them, not St Michael.'

'And we mustn't forget Charles et Antoine,' said Gina.

David frowned for a moment. 'C and A! That's delightful!'

When David was putting Lizzie's cases in the car, Gina said to Lizzie, 'He's a very nice man. He'll look out for you.'

'You know he's . . . ' Lizzie paused.

'Homosexual? Yes,' said Gina firmly. 'It doesn't make any difference. I feel much happier casting you out now I know someone like him is sharing the house.'

Lizzie was very pleased. If her father ever got to learn of David and was concerned, she would set Gina on to him. Gina would tell her father what was what.

★ ★ ★

A little later, when Lizzie had moved properly into the room she was sharing with Meg, she and the rest of the household gathered in the cosy basement.

Up the kitchen end, Meg and David were cooking something for supper. David had produced a lot of ingredients which would have impressed Mme Wilson but baffled Lizzie's mother. Apparently, Meg told her, he shopped a lot in Soho. The market in Berwick

48

Street provided all sorts of exotic produce as well as more usual things. Meg, seeing what he'd brought home, had become very excited. She and David loved food in a way that Lizzie and Alexandra admired but didn't quite share.

In the middle, in front of the popping gas fire, Alexandra lay with her feet up on one of the sofas. Clover, the spaniel, was lying on top of her. Alexandra had propped her book against the dog and was happily engrossed in *Angélique and the Sultan*. Clover had fitted into the household as if she'd always been there. Although all three girls made a big fuss of her, it was David who'd taken her for a walk that morning. Clover adored him.

At the far end, Lizzie was trying to make a paper pattern from her new dress without taking it apart. She had the ironing board, a big table, an Anglepoise lamp and a sewing machine. She felt she was in heaven. Gina's clothes, all lovely, all in need of adaptation, were back in their bag for now.

'I know it's very early days, but I love sharing a house with you lot,' said Lizzie.

Alexandra looked up from her book. 'Me too! I hope you agree, David?'

'It's bliss having someone who appreciates food as much as I do,' said David. 'Meg has actually heard of Elizabeth David.'

Meg laughed. 'I feel so lucky to have found somewhere so lovely and a home for Clover.'

'Clover is a very easy guest,' said Alexandra, scratching the little dog behind her ears. 'Although I don't know if I'd describe the house as lovely. It's very tatty.'

'But it's in Belgravia, darling,' said Lizzie, imitating her mother, 'and that's all that matters.'

49

A few days after the large house in Belgravia had become a cosy home, it was the dressmaking class at the cookery school. Vanessa, one of the other students, was struggling to lay the pieces of the paper pattern on her chosen fabric. She wasn't the only one who was finding this hard but Lizzie liked her best. Unlike most of the debs, she was fairly friendly and possibly lacking in confidence.

'It just takes practice,' said Lizzie, rescuing the pattern piece which had drifted to the floor.

'I don't suppose you could do it for me? I was never any good at sewing at boarding school, either.' Vanessa gave a shy, entreating smile.

Lizzie saw that the teacher, a friend of Mme Wilson — like all the people who taught the afternoon activities — was occupied elsewhere. 'OK.'

Later, when the class was over, Vanessa came over to where Alexandra, Meg and Lizzie were sharing out shopping bags to carry home. 'Would you three like to come to a dinner party?'

All three girls were a bit taken aback. Thus far, there'd been no social interaction between them and the other girls on the course.

'It's for my brother,' she went on. 'He's been away for a while and has come home to live. My parents won't be there. It'll be fun.'

'That sounds great!' said Lizzie, eager to see what Vanessa's house was like.

'Yes,' agreed Meg.

Alexandra was less enthusiastic. 'OK.'

'When is it?' Lizzie asked.

Vanessa didn't answer immediately and Lizzie was

surprised. She'd have thought Vanessa would know this.

'Well,' Vanessa said slowly, 'when can you all make it?'

Alexandra shrugged. 'When would you like us?'

'OK,' said Vanessa. 'During the week. Next Tuesday. Is that OK?'

When it had been agreed that it was, Meg said, 'What are you going to cook?'

Vanessa looked at Meg as if she was completely mad. 'Lord, I'm not going to cook! We'll get caterers. Our cook is in the country with the parents.'

'Golly,' said Lizzie, and then wished she'd said 'Lord' like Vanessa.

'Dress code?' asked Alexandra.

'Long, I think,' said Vanessa. 'More fun.'

The girls set off for home, carrying their shopping bags and talking about the dinner party. Lizzie was excited but trying not to show just how excited. She'd never been to a dinner party given by her contemporaries before. She'd attended her parents' parties, of course, but never one especially for people her own age.

'Long dresses means Vanessa has got one she wants to wear,' said Alexandra. 'But have we all got long dresses?'

'No,' said Lizzie, 'but we've got time to make them. Or adapt something.' She glanced at Alexandra. She was longing to get a look at her stash of old clothes.

'Oh yes,' said Alexandra. 'I've got lots of old things that I'm sure Lizzie could alter.'

★ ★ ★

Meg was slightly less enthusiastic than Alexandra and Lizzie about spending time in the attic searching for clothes. It was dark and very spidery. 'Let's bring the trunk down,' she suggested.

'Will we get it down the stairs? They're terribly steep and narrow.' Lizzie had been a bit wary of going up them, although Alexandra had run up with practised ease.

'It should be possible,' said Alexandra. 'Although we can wait until David's home if you like.'

Lizzie, eager as she was to get her hands on this treasure trove of fabric, clothing, lace, ribbon and accessories, agreed this might be the sensible course. Luckily, they heard David arrive back shortly afterwards and he and Alexandra soon had the trunk (one of several) down in the basement.

'OK,' said Lizzie. 'We don't want to look as if we think it's a fancy dress party. We can look different, but not peculiar.'

'I think I always look a bit peculiar,' said Alexandra.

'Eccentric maybe, but not peculiar.' Actually, Lizzie thought her friend *did* verge towards peculiar sometimes but somehow she always managed to carry it off.

Once in the basement, in better light and without the smell of damp and mothballs that permeated the attic, they found a skirt for Alexandra almost immediately. It was in a wonderful dark green velvet, and she said she could wear it with a lacy blouse that was already in her wardrobe. When forced by the others to try on the entire outfit she definitely looked a bit 'period', but also stunning with her hair piled up.

David, who came over from the kitchen end of the basement, had an old biscuit tin shaped like a country cottage in his hand. From it he produced a big

52

cameo brooch. He pinned it on to the high neck of the blouse, at Alexandra's throat. It was the perfect touch.

'You can borrow it, but not keep it,' said David. 'It's quite valuable. Now, Meg, what are you going to wear?'

'Nothing fancy,' said Meg. 'If it must be long, it'll have to be fairly plain. Lots of this stuff is very frilly.' She picked up a dress that was not only heavy but seemed to be made of enough material to make a small pair of curtains.

'OK, we'll find something that's not bustley,' said Lizzie. 'Sorry!' She turned to Alexandra. 'I seem to have taken over your clothes.'

'Fine by me,' said Alexandra. 'Just don't try and take over my junk!'

'Oh, it's junk now, is it?' said David. 'I thought it was all antique.'

'Well, as you know, a lot of it is antique, it's just very damaged,' Alexandra said. 'Which means I don't have to sell it.'

'Did you know we're going to have a lesson in how to mend china?' said Lizzie. 'It seems a bit odd but Mme Wilson has a friend who does it, so naturally, we're going to learn it. I suppose it's in case the debs on the course break the priceless antique Ming vase when they go to meet their future mothers-in-law.'

'That'll be really useful,' said Alexandra. 'I have a couple of items I was given because they were in pieces.'

'You seem far keener on bits of broken plate than clothes,' said Lizzie, amused.

'I am keen on clothes,' said Alexandra, 'but I can't be bothered to keep changing or having different

53

ones. But I do love china and I don't care if it's glued together.'

'So, what about you, Lizzie?' said David. 'You seem keen to sort everyone else out with dresses but you haven't said what you're going to wear.' He pulled out something that was possibly worn for riding side-sad-dle in. 'Actually, darling,' he said to Alexandra, 'you really should keep these somewhere better than in this trunk.'

'I'll help you,' said Lizzie. 'Is there an empty ward-robe anywhere?'

'Oh yes,' said Alexandra with a casual flick of her hand. 'So what are you going to wear, Lizzie?'

'If you don't mind, and it's not a historic heirloom or anything,' said Lizzie, looking at the dress David was holding up, 'I'll take this apart and make a new dress with it. It's a really fine cord, if you look at it, and I love the little flowers.'

'I think that's dimity,' said David.

'Cool,' said Lizzie. She'd seen a dress in a shop, long, with sleeves slightly puffed at the top, she thought she might copy. It had a yoke and a high neck but she was considering doing without the high neck. She planned to wear a velvet ribbon round her neck. She didn't have much jewellery; her pearls were safely sitting in a satin-lined box in her mother's dressing table. Her mother was probably waiting for the day when Lizzie had met a nice boy (picked out by her), when she'd put them round her daughter's neck for a studio photograph that they could display on the piano with pride. Well, she didn't need them yet.

6

'We don't still smell of mothballs do we?' asked Meg.

A week had passed since they rummaged in the trunk for clothes during which there had been a lot of washing, sewing and ironing going on. Now they were standing in the hall waiting to go to Vanessa's dinner party.

'No,' said David. 'Now you mostly smell of Lizzie's scent.'

'Je Reviens,' she said. 'But it's fine. Vanessa smokes like a chimney so soon we'll all be smelling of Balkan Sobranie.' Lizzie was keen to get going. This was her first dinner party and she didn't want to be late. David was taking them in the car and was going to drop them off on the corner of the London square where Vanessa lived.

Once on Vanessa's doorstep, Lizzie started to giggle. 'I'm sorry! It's nerves! It reminds me of a time when I went with my best friend to visit a boy she liked.'

'I'm a bit nervous too,' said Meg. 'I'm only used to mixing with old people really, not people my own age. And certainly not boys my own age.'

'Oh come on, they're only people,' said Alexandra and pressed the doorbell.

Lizzie was half relieved and half disappointed that the door was opened by a girl who was obviously a guest and not by a butler. They were led to an upstairs drawing room and given glasses of wine. Vanessa wasn't there, which seemed a bit odd to Lizzie, but it was her first dinner party: maybe it was normal.

She looked around to see what everyone else was wearing. She was relieved to see that they all fitted in with regard to their clothes, although she was aware that everyone else probably bought theirs from Harrods or Harvey Nichols or else had them made by their mother's dressmaker.

A boy came over to her. 'I like your dress.'

Lizzie took a breath to tell him that she'd made it herself but then realised he wasn't looking at her dress but at her cleavage. It hadn't seemed too much on show when she'd made the dress. She'd consulted the other two girls and they had agreed. This man made her feel it was far too low cut. 'Thank you,' she said glumly.

'How do you know Vanessa?' he asked. Now Lizzie took time to inspect him she realised he wasn't what she'd expected to find at a society dinner party. Instead of a dinner jacket, he was wearing a corduroy jacket over a polo-necked shirt.

'We're at the same cookery school. How about you?'

'Friend of a friend,' he said. 'Cigarette?'

Lizzie shook her head. She'd never got the hang of smoking. She'd tried it once in a friend's garage and it had made her feel dreadfully sick and dizzy. Her father had been furious when she'd got home, smelling of cigarette smoke, so she'd never persevered.

She took a breath to say something else although she had no idea what, when she noticed the man who had just come into the room. It was the man she'd met when she was looking at the flat in Tufnell Park. She felt shocked and for a moment didn't want him to see her and then she realised that was ridiculous, they were at a dinner party. But he might not recognise

56

her. She didn't want him to: he might somehow guess that she'd spent a lot of time thinking about him.

Vanessa came into the room wearing a gown with spaghetti straps, one of which was halfway down her arm. 'Sorry, sorry!' she said. 'Me and Ted got caught up with something.' Ted was wearing a leather jacket over a shirt with half the buttons undone, the done ones all wrong. She giggled and looked up at Ted. Then she made a gesture to the man Lizzie had seen. 'This is my brother, Hugo. Can't be bothered to introduce everyone. Just introduce yourselves.'

The man she was standing by took hold of Lizzie's hand and looked down into her eyes. 'I'm Rich — that's my name not my financial status.'

'I'm Lizzie.' She smiled, glad to have someone to talk to. She drank some more wine and began to relax. 'So, what do you do?' she asked, hoping she didn't sound like one of her mother's friends.

'I'm a music journalist,' said Rich. 'Do you like music?'

'Yes,' said Lizzie. No one would ever say they didn't like music but did she like the same sort of music that Rich did? Probably not. He would mock her musical taste: she could tell just by looking at him.

To her enormous relief, a woman in an apron, obviously one of the caterers, appeared. 'Dinner is ready,' she said.

It seemed that they weren't eating in the formal dining room, but in the basement, probably because of its proximity to the kitchen. As everyone wound their way down the stairs, Lizzie, who'd realised her dress was just a bit too long and hiked it up a bit, heard a voice.

'Hello! I know you! You were at that ghastly flat!' It

was Vanessa's brother, Hugo.

Lizzie smiled. He had recognised her, which was embarrassing, but at least she was prepared. 'Oh yes!' she said. 'Did you take it?'

'No. Better to go on living with my parents than suffer running water down the walls.' He paused to let another couple go ahead. 'I'm Hugo Lennox-Stanley.'

'Lizzie Spencer.'

'Hello, Lizzie.' He looked at her with a slightly quizzical look that Lizzie didn't understand.

Then Lizzie received a shove in the back that nearly made her stumble.

'Hugo, darling, would you mind getting a move on? You're holding everyone up.'

Lizzie looked round to see a very soignée young woman, her hair in a chignon, wearing a long, straight dress that made Lizzie's feel childish and fussy. Although the woman hadn't addressed her, Lizzie said, 'Oh, so sorry. Do you want to get by?'

The woman pursed her lips. 'We all do!' She pushed past both Hugo and Lizzie and everyone moved on.

Once everyone was seated, Lizzie found it easier to sort people out. There was the woman who'd been so rude on the stairs, who was now lighting a cigarette. Vanessa, who was sitting practically on the lap of the man she'd introduced as Ted; a jolly-looking man with short curly hair who had been talking to Meg and still was; and Hugo, who was sitting next to the rude woman. Alexandra was talking to a man who seemed to be a bit older. She looked interested in her conversation, which Lizzie was pleased about. Alexandra didn't suffer fools and hadn't really wanted to come tonight. Then there was a tall girl with a red face and fuzzy hair who didn't seem to care what impression she gave, who was with a man in a dinner jacket who obviously found her hilarious.

Rich made sure he sat next to Lizzie, which was flattering but then he lit a cigarette which was annoying. He and Ted exchanged bits of conversation which indicated Rich was the friend he was a friend of; he and Ted were mates.

The first course arrived, landing in front of people more or less at the same time. It was half a melon with the melon shaped into balls and surrounded by a dark red liquid.

'Lovely to have something that isn't fattening,' said the girl who was smoking and sitting next to Hugo. She was apparently attached to him and Lizzie had heard that her name was Electra. Electra speared a bit of melon, ate it and then threw down her fork.

'I don't like girls who think about diets all the time,' said the man on Lizzie's left, the one who laughed easily.

'I've never been on a diet,' said Lizzie.

'Jolly good show! No need, after all.' He glanced at her décolletage, but only briefly. 'I'm Anthony. I'm a friend of the family. I've known Hugo and Nessa all my life.'

'Lizzie. Vanessa and I go to the same cookery college. I've got two friends here. There's Meg, talking to the man with curly hair . . .'

' Charles,' said Anthony. 'Nice chap.'

'And Alexandra. She's the one looking a bit like an Edwardian lady.'

'Right. She's got stuck with Duncan. Nice enough but obsessed with ancient ruins.'

Lizzie smiled. 'That might suit Alexandra. She's very keen on antiques.'

'So, what do you do, Lizzie?' Anthony asked.

'I'm on the same course — '

'Oh yes. Sorry, wasn't paying attention there for a minute. Too busy looking into your eyes.' He laughed to indicate he was joking, but also not joking.

Lizzie began to enjoy herself. The food was lovely — the melon had been drenched in port — and the men on either side of her vied for her attention. She felt attractive, interesting, someone worth talking to. It was very exhilarating.

When the last cigarette had been stubbed out in the last traces of profiterole (Lizzie noticed she was not the only one present who winced at this), the party was led upstairs by Vanessa.

'Come on, more drinks,' said Vanessa. 'I know where the parents keep the good stuff.' As Lizzie went upstairs, followed closely by Rich, who seemed to have claimed her for the evening, she thought that perhaps Vanessa was behaving differently because she was with Ted, whom she probably wanted to impress. She wasn't like this when she was struggling to fillet a fish with the rest of them. Alexandra had thought there was a reason that the three of them had been invited tonight and although Lizzie hadn't worked out what this was, she now definitely agreed with her.

Someone had put on some music and a couple of people were dancing. Rich took hold of her wrist and pulled her into the group. He stood very close but he didn't put his arms round her. Then he put his hand on her shoulder. He had just leaned in to kiss her when Vanessa's friend, Ted, called out.

'Hey, Rich! Are you going to the Earl of Sandwich on Friday night?'

Rich took Lizzie's hand and led her over to where Vanessa and Ted were standing. 'I do want to hear a new group who are playing.' He paused. 'Come with me, Lizzie?'

'It's a very cool place,' said Vanessa. 'Not like a usual pub. Me and Ted are going. It'll be more fun if you come too.' She made a face. 'I don't like being the only girl.'

'It sounds fun,' said Lizzie, slightly wary. She liked Vanessa but they weren't quite on the terms where they could exchange girly confidences in the ladies' loo.

Rich tipped up her chin with his finger. 'Do come. I really want to see you again.'

'You could see her again without taking her to the Earl of Sandwich,' said Hugo, who had joined the group without Lizzie noticing.

'It's a great music venue,' said Rich.

'Nothing wrong with the Sandwich,' Ted agreed.

'Come on, Hugo! Don't be a spoilsport!' said Vanessa, wheedling.

Hugo raised a hand in submission. 'I only implied there were other places in London for first dates.' Then he turned away and went over to his girlfriend, Electra, who was gesturing at him.

When he was out of the way, Rich said, 'Well?'

Lizzie nodded. 'I'll come.' She felt very daring to be accepting his invitation.

He took a cigarette packet out of his pocket and found a pen. 'Give me your number then?'

* * *

'The best bit of a dinner party is tearing it apart afterwards,' said David. 'I want every detail.' He was making toast and the kettle was on.

It had been a long time since they'd eaten the beef Wellington and profiteroles and they'd all accepted his offer when he suggested more food. Alexandra lay down on the sofa and Clover instantly climbed up and sat on her.

'I had a lovely time!' said Lizzie, a little dreamy.

'You were the belle of the ball,' said Meg. She was standing over the grill, butter at the ready. 'The men were flocking round you.'

'No, they weren't!' said Lizzie, pushing her friend on her way to an armchair. 'It was just Rich.'

"Rich' is a good place to start,' said David.

'His name was Rich.' Lizzie explained, not enjoying being the centre of attention.

'And he asked her out,' Meg explained to David, buttering now, another two pieces under the grill. 'It obviously doesn't happen often.'

'It doesn't!' said Lizzie. 'Honestly, when I lived at home I only went out with the sons of my parents' friends. They used to have to come to the house to pick me up. I never felt they really liked me for me. They were just going out with me because their parents made them.'

'What was this Rich like?' said David. He had warmed the pot and was waiting for the kettle to reboil.

Lizzie looked at him. David was really, really nice, hugely kind but he did seem like a parent sometimes. Which probably wasn't a bad thing. 'He's a music journalist.'

'Hmm,' said David. 'Be careful.'

'I'm very careful, David,' said Lizzie. 'Boringly so.'

'Rich was very good-looking,' said Alexandra, 'in a bad-boy way. Although I'm sure he isn't a bad boy!' she hurried on, before David could comment again.

'I met the caterers,' said Meg. 'We had a long chat. They quite often want waitresses and are happy to give me a trial straight away. It's a way into the business. They said if it goes well they'll take me on, and as I learn more they'll let me help with the cooking.'

'That's good,' said David. 'I know you planned on getting a job as a barmaid, but really, that is a bit risky, especially in London.'

'You are such a mum!' said Alexandra. 'If you want your daughter to stay safe and a virgin forever, get her to live with a gay man!'

'Nothing to do with being gay, sweetheart,' said David. 'It's all about being caring. So, tell me more about the other guests, then I can be waspish.'

'Well,' said Alexandra, pulling Clover's ears. 'I met a very sweet man who knew everything about old buildings.' She paused. 'I still haven't worked out why Vanessa invited us. I'm sure she must know lots of other girls. Why invite three of them you don't really need?'

'Perhaps it was something to do with the man — her brother? — who was with that very skinny woman who smoked all the way through?' said Meg. 'He didn't seem quite like the other guests. It's so rude to smoke during meals, I always think.'

'She wasn't the only one,' said Alexandra.

'And she stubbed her cigarette out in the chocolate sauce,' added Lizzie, shuddering.

'I think you're right, Meg,' said Alexandra. 'I think she invited us because we're not connected with her parents in any way. The fact that she has some dodgy friends won't get back to them.'

'But wouldn't Hugo tell them?' asked Lizzie. 'He's her brother!' Then she realised Meg and Alexandra were looking at her; she was the only one of them who'd remembered his name.

7

Lizzie couldn't decide if she was really excited about her proposed date or plain terrified. So much was so romantic — the way Rich had torn up his cigarette packet for her to write her telephone number on and put it in his top pocket looking intensely into her eyes. But other parts made her scared stiff. Supposing he wanted to meet her in the pub? She had never gone into a pub on her own, not even the cosy pubs in her home village, pubs where she'd gone first with her parents on a Sunday morning when they met their friends. If she wanted to meet her friends at a pub, they met up outside.

Supposing Rich didn't ring her? He might either lose the cigarette packet or lose interest. She examined how she'd feel if this was the case. There was a large amount of disappointment but a good measure of relief too.

But he did ring, the next evening when they were all settled in their multi-purpose basement. Alexandra answered the phone and then said, 'Lizzie? It's for you.'

'Hey,' said Rich, sounding sexier than ever on the telephone. 'Do you still want to come and hear that new group we were talking about at Nessa's?'

It took Lizzie a second to work out that he meant Vanessa. 'Oh yes. Please,' she added, the manners of her childhood deeply embedded.

'Cool. But you will never find the Earl of Sandwich on your own. We'll meet at the Odeon, Leicester

Square. Can you find that?'

'Of course!' said Lizzie blithely. She'd heard of it, which was halfway to knowing where it was. Besides, she knew Alexandra would help.

'Good. I'll see you there at seven o'clock on Friday.'

'Lovely,' said Lizzie and then could have bitten her tongue out. She should have said 'cool' or 'great' or any bloody thing apart from 'lovely'.

Everyone was looking at her when she put down the phone. 'Was that your date being organised?' asked David.

'Yes,' said Lizzie, as casually as was possible given that she couldn't breathe properly from excitement. 'We're meeting outside the Odeon in Leicester Square.'

'When?' asked David.

'Friday.'

'Damn,' said David, 'I can't give you a lift. I'll have to have the car packed. I'm doing Portobello on Saturday morning.'

'And I'm going with you,' said Alexandra. 'I haven't done a market for ages and I have things to sell.'

'It's OK!' said Lizzie. 'I'm perfectly capable of going on the bus.'

'What you must do', said David, in fatherly mode towards his young housemates again, 'is put money in your bra, in case you get separated from your handbag. Then you can always get home.'

'That sounds just the sort of thing Gina would say,' said Lizzie. 'And I'll definitely do that.'

'It always gives you a bit of a shock when you wake in the morning and see a pound note in your bra,' said Alexandra, obviously a money-in-your-bra veteran. 'You feel as if you've become a call girl without noticing.'

'I'm sure even I would notice if that happened!' said Lizzie. 'Now I must think of what to wear.'

'Why don't you make something with that length of velvet we found?' suggested Alexandra. 'We can sprinkle it with Eau de Cologne to disguise the musty smell.'

Lizzie considered. 'It would have to be a short dress,' she said. 'There isn't a lot of it. Or much time.'

★ ★ ★

'You look gorgeous,' said David on Friday evening when Lizzie appeared in the basement for inspection. 'That little dress has worked out really well. You know how to work a sewing machine, young Lizzie.'

'Not too short?'

David pursed his lips. 'Well . . .'

'It's fine!' said Alexandra. 'And I like your hair. It's softer now it's grown a bit. '

'I couldn't get my fringe to lie flat even though I put Sellotape on it when it was damp.' Lizzie peered in the mirror that hung near the door but as it was antique and the light was bad just there, she didn't get much of an impression of what she looked like.

'Just don't get into trouble,' said David. 'And if things get difficult, or you want to escape, ring me.'

'But, David, I've got the money in my bra if that happens! I can take a taxi home.' She smiled at him and shook her head. 'You do look after us well — you are so kind.'

He shrugged. 'Someone has to look after you skittish young things.'

Meg laughed. 'No one has ever called me skittish

67

before! Now come on, Lizzie, I'll walk with you to the bus stop. I'm going that way,' she added hurriedly as Lizzie opened her mouth to say that she was perfectly capable of walking to a bus stop on her own. 'I've got my first waitressing shift in the area. But I don't want to be late.'

Because Meg had to be at her destination a bit earlier than Lizzie, Lizzie found herself outside the cinema a good twenty minutes before she was due to meet Rich.

She was grateful that there were lots of film posters to be examined outside the Odeon. While she studied them intently, her earnest expression didn't prevent several young men trying to pick her up. She was tempted to walk round the block but she was worried in case she missed Rich, or possibly Vanessa and her boyfriend. Lizzie pulled up the collar on her coat (one of Gina's — she had moved the belt loops) and made herself as unapproachable as possible.

At last Rich appeared. 'Am I late, sweetie?' He kissed her casually on the cheek and Lizzie found herself flinching. She kissed her relations on the cheek, no one else.

'Where are Vanessa and Ted? Or are we meeting them there?' she asked to hide her awkwardness.

'Oh, they're not coming. Does it matter?' He put his arm round her and turned her so he could study her.

She looked back at him. 'No,' she said. Part of her was lying.

They walked along together, with his arm round her, clamping her to his side. It made her feel safe and protected after feeling so exposed while she waited for him.

He took her down a side street and through a narrow door that would have been easy to miss, and up a steep flight of stairs on to a dark landing. Then Rich pushed open a door and noise, light and cigarette smoke flooded out.

'It's like a Speakeasy!' Lizzie shouted to Rich.

He smiled and nodded. 'Drink?'

'Half a lager,' she said. 'Please.' She knew where she was with lager. She would have to find her way to the Ladies eventually, but she knew two halves wouldn't make her drunk.

Rich guided her to a table that had a couple of spare seats. He said, 'You'll be OK here.' Then he headed for the bar.

Lizzie looked around. The pub was very full and there seemed to be a great range of people present. There was a group on a small stage who were currently playing jazz. Round them stood young men in corduroy trousers, shirts and cravats, who wouldn't have looked out of place in her local pub at home. There were people in denim jackets covered in badges, tight jeans and winkle-picker shoes. She even spotted a few men in suits.

The girls were wearing an even greater range of clothes, from long, elaborate dresses to tiny short skirts worn with fishnet tights and spangle-covered tops. There was even a group of women who could have been teachers from Lizzie's old school wearing mid-calf skirts with thick stockings and clumpy shoes. But what pleased Lizzie, as she completed her survey, was that the prettiest girls were wearing short dresses quite like her own.

'On your own?' said a voice, two seconds after Lizzie had removed her coat and stuffed it behind her on the chair. A young man who looked as if he'd had a few pints already swayed slightly as he looked down at her.

'No,' said Lizzie firmly. 'I'm with my boyfriend. He's over there.' She gestured towards an enormous man in a leather flying jacket that was making him sweat quite a lot. He looked dangerous.

The drunk lurched away and Lizzie felt quite pleased with herself because she had seen him off, but realised that she was going to have to toughen up quite a bit if she was going to live in London for the foreseeable future.

A couple more men tried to pick her up before Rich came back with the drinks. She was very relieved to see him.

'It's great here, isn't it?' said Rich.

'Mm,' said Lizzie, trying to look enthusiastic. But as she sipped her drink and relaxed she realised she liked the music and the variety of people. It was unlike anywhere she'd been before.

'The group I'm interested in is on later,' said Rich. 'Let's sit on this sofa, now it's free.'

It was hardly a sofa but it made it possible for Rich to put his arm round Lizzie properly and kiss her cheek again. Then he turned her chin and kissed her on her mouth. She couldn't decide if she liked it or not and realised, to her dismay, that she didn't feel strongly either way. It wasn't distasteful, having his tongue in her mouth, but it wasn't sexy either. She broke the kiss and sat back in her seat.

She realised that Rich was looking at her in a speculative and possessive way and began to worry that he might want more from her than she was happy to give. But then he smiled and she realised he was really attractive and she did fancy him a bit. She could always say no later, if he tried anything on.

'Another drink?' Rich asked.

Lizzie was only halfway down her glass of lager. She didn't really like it. 'No, I'm OK, thank you.'

'I'm going to have to go backstage and see my boys in a minute. I don't want anyone else taking advantage of your empty glass.' He smiled sexily.

'I'll drink slowly,' she said. While she gave him what she hoped was a confident smile, inwardly she didn't like the thought of being left in this crowd. It seemed to be full of predatory men on the lookout for a girl on her own.

He put his hand on her knee and stroked it for a bit in a way that made her think of rubbing embrocation rather than anything sexy. She was grateful when, just as his hand was moving from her kneecap to her thigh, he sighed and said he had to go.

At that moment the music stopped and the lights went off and on again.

'Oh shit!' said Rich. 'It's the fuzz.'

Before Lizzie realised what was happening, Rich had stepped over her and started heading for the stage area. She looked around and saw that the door they had come in by was now flanked by two police-women. Other policemen were arranging themselves along the walls.

Lizzie was confused. What should she do? Should she wait for Rich? Or make her way home when she was allowed to leave?

'What's going to happen now?' she asked the man next to her.

He slid into the seat just by her. 'They'll search us. No bother if you haven't any grass on you. Your boyfriend obviously had.'

Lizzie gulped. There had been a girl at her school who'd been to a party where there were drugs. The school had somehow found out and she had been expelled. This had given her a fear of anything to do with drugs. She knew it was irrational but this girl's life seemed to have been ruined by this small connection with them.

The man patted her knee. 'Don't worry, Kitten, I'll look after you.' He put his arm round her and squeezed. 'Stick by me. I'll sort you out.'

Lizzie tried to get up. There had definitely been a double meaning in the way he'd said he'd sort her out. He pulled her back down again.

'They won't let you move. Just stay quietly until you've been searched and then we can head off somewhere. My flat's not far. I've got some tequila. Have you ever tried tequila?'

She'd never even heard of it. 'No,' she said.

'You haven't lived, little girl,' said the man. He ran his hand up and down her arm, finding the flesh under her short sleeve.

'Please don't touch me!' she said quickly. 'I don't like it!'

'That's only because you're a frigid little virgin. When I've finished with you, you'll yearn for my touch.'

Lizzie burrowed behind her and found her coat and put it on. 'I'm cold,' she said crossly and tried to get up again, only to find herself pulled back down.

'Don't run away. We have to wait to be searched.'

Lizzie had never been so glad to see the police. A pair of young female officers reached their table. 'Can you turn out your bag for us, love,' said one.

Lizzie obligingly tipped the contents of her bag on to the table, glad that it was one of Gina's and so wouldn't be full of old sweet wrappers and bus tickets. Then, as she watched one of the WPCs take the bag and search the lining she suddenly wondered if Gina might smoke dope.

She realised she was panicking unnecessarily. If Gina did smoke anything illegal she wouldn't keep it in an old handbag. She tried to calm her breathing, hoping her over-reaction wouldn't make her look guilty.

She was just wondering how to escape when the policewoman indicated that she should stand up. This was her chance, she realised. The moment the search was complete she could make a dash for the door. Then she saw that there were several policeman blocking the door. She wouldn't be allowed to leave.

When she had been searched (in a fairly cursory way, she recognised with relief) she sat back down again. The man who had been trying to pick her up had now been searched too and snuggled up to her as if they were soon to be lovers. Not if I have anything to do with it, thought Lizzie.

'Oh, there you are, darling,' said a male voice. 'I've been looking for you everywhere. Let's go or we'll be late.'

Lizzie saw Hugo Lennox-Stanley looking down at her with his hand held out, smiling encouragingly. She put her hand in his and got to her feet. He put his arm round her in a way that was just as possessive as the man she was so keen to get away from, but somehow she didn't mind.

She let Hugo lead her to the door. 'Sorry to be a nuisance,' said Hugo to one of the policemen. 'We're both clean and we need to be somewhere else. Would you mind awfully letting us out?'

'Oh no, that's all right, sir,' said the policeman. 'No need to detain you.'

The next moment Lizzie and Hugo were outside on the dark landing. 'Where did you spring from?' said Lizzie, breathless with relief.

'You need a drink. Come on, there's a really nice pub near here. I'll explain everything.'

He took her arm and held her close once they were in the street, guiding her until they came to a small pub where there was no music but a fair amount of people, talking hard. He took them to a small room at the back that was quieter. It was cosy and familiar and Lizzie felt herself relax.

'Brandy?' he asked.

She nodded. 'Yes, please.'

She took off her coat while Hugo went to the bar. No one tried to pick her up. No one looked at her. She felt safe.

Hugo came back with the drinks. Lizzie didn't speak. She smiled but waited for him to settle himself. He raised his glass to her and took a sip. Still no explanation.

Lizzie took the initiative. 'Hugo? You were going to explain how you came to be in the Earl of Sandwich? I was really grateful to be rescued but it seems like an amazing coincidence.'

Hugo seemed a bit embarrassed. 'Well, it wasn't really a coincidence, more a happy combination of circumstances.'

Lizzie nodded and sipped her brandy. She'd never had it before and she found it warming and soothing.

'I discovered that Vanessa and Ted had changed

their plans and she mentioned your name. Then I remembered you were going with Rich. I've never had much time for Rich. As I was planning to call on someone over this side of town I thought I'd call into the pub and see if you were all right.'

Did this sound a bit rehearsed? But why would he lie? He'd have no reason to. Lizzie decided to take him at his word. 'Oh well, if you were going to visit someone, you mustn't let me make you late.'

'No need to worry about that,' he said with a smile. 'I cancelled. Shall we find a bite to eat somewhere?'

He took her to a little Italian restaurant in Soho, somewhere she would never have dared to investigate on her own, even in daylight. But with Hugo at her side, a solid presence, she felt she could go anywhere she wanted.

The restaurant was in a basement. The tables were small and covered with gingham cloths. There were straw-covered Chianti bottles hanging on the walls along with plastic lemons and fake strings of garlic.

'Don't be put off by the decor,' said Hugo. 'The food is really good.'

Lizzie looked around. There were pictures of Mount Etna and Vesuvius, lovely Italian girls gathering olives and riding pillion on motorbikes driven by gorgeous dark-eyed Italian boys. 'I like the decor and if the food is good as well, it's all fab.'

Hugo nodded. 'Now, what are you going to have? Say if you need me to help. The menu is in Italian.'

Having agreed they didn't want starters, Lizzie chose lasagne, unfamiliar with this apparently Italian staple. 'And a green salad,' she added.

'I'll have the same. We can share some garlic bread.'

If anyone had suggested that Lizzie might go out to

dinner with Hugo Lennox-Stanley she'd have shaken her head saying it would never happen. The very thought was daunting. And yet here she was, sharing garlic bread (she had never had that before either, although she didn't tell him this), laughing with him, and, even more surprising, making him laugh.

He was very amused with her stories about the cookery course and she even confessed to doing his sister's dressmaking for her. (He wasn't at all surprised to learn that Vanessa had neither the patience nor the willingness to learn.) Then she told him about adapting clothes from the trunk in Alexandra's attic and Gina's cast-offs and making clothes for them all.

'I think working with one's hands is underrated,' he said. 'I loved carpentry at school but if you were academic, you weren't allowed to do it for long.'

'You were academic?'

He nodded. 'Very, although I still make the odd pipe rack if I have a moment. I come from a long line of barristers and so that was where I was steered.' He smiled ruefully and for the first time Lizzie sensed sadness in him. Up until now he seemed successful, in control of his life and everything in it, but apparently that wasn't leading to contentment.

'So did your parents make you go into law?'

'I wouldn't say they made me. They encouraged me, certainly. But as I didn't object, I don't know what they'd have done if I'd wanted to do something different.'

'Do you enjoy it?'

'Yes, but there's still a part of me that would have liked to take another path.'

Lizzie nodded in understanding. 'The reason I'm doing a cookery course is because my mother thinks I

76

won't find a decent husband if I can't cook. And finding a decent husband, with a proper job, preferably with parents they already know, is really important.'

'Is that how you feel?'

'No! At least I don't think so. But it's only really since I've been in London that I've given the matter much thought. I mean Alexandra would never think getting married is all a woman would want from life. And Meg, she's learning to cook so she can earn money so she can save up for a house. Her mother always has live-in jobs and so nowhere is ever theirs.' She paused. 'It's why Clover, their dog, came to live with us.'

Hugo smiled. 'I like dogs. People always say you shouldn't have them in London, but I think you can. If they're small dogs and don't need miles and miles of exercise every day.'

'We manage. There is a park nearby and Clover certainly doesn't need loads of exercise. David puts her in the car and takes her to places where they can walk.'

'Who's David?'

This question gave Lizzie a jolt. She hadn't meant to mention David. Supposing Hugo asked questions about him? Did different sexes share flats in London? What would happen if she accidentally mentioned he was a homosexual?

'He's a friend of Alexandra's,' she said, her voice a little higher pitched. 'They met because they're both antiques dealers. Alexandra does it in a very small way but David does much more of it. He has a stall at the Portobello Road Market.'

'Oh, that sounds fun!' said Hugo. 'Have you ever been?'

Relieved that Hugo didn't start to grill her about David, Lizzie smiled. 'No, but I've said I'll go with them and help them on their stall sometime.'

'I often go there. I enjoy spending Saturday mornings looking for beautiful old things.'

'And what do you buy?' Lizzie imagined silver candelabra, Chippendale chairs, jewellery for Electra possibly.

'Tools,' said Hugo. 'I buy old woodworking tools.' He smiled. 'Now, can I tempt you to some zabaglione? If you've never tried it, it's delicious but not too heavy. In Italy they give it to you if you're ill and need building up.'

'That sounds delicious!' And it was.

When they'd finished, Hugo paid the bill and they took a taxi home; Hugo made the driver wait while he saw her into the house and then sped away. Lizzie stood in the hall getting her emotional breath back. She knew the others would be downstairs, waiting to hear about her date with Rich. David would be pleased that she had been rescued from the Bad Boy by a gentleman who knew exactly how to treat a lady.

8

'Are you sure you want to come to the market with us tomorrow?' asked Alexandra later that night. 'We start extremely early in the morning.'

'I know,' said Lizzie. 'But I thought I'd like to experience it properly, and you don't do the market every week, Alexandra.'

Alexandra nodded. 'That's true. I'll wake you then.'

Lizzie breathed a secret sigh of relief. She didn't want anyone to guess there was a slightly ulterior motive to her eagerness to get up before dawn and stand around in the chilly spring morning. But it appeared that no one had picked up that she was developing feelings for Hugo.

They couldn't know that he enjoyed visiting Portobello Market and that was why she was so keen to be there. She wasn't really willing to acknowledge these feelings herself. There was no point in having them after all; he was spoken for. With Electra as his girlfriend, why would he look at her? She was just Elizabeth from the Home Counties in her home-made dresses. Her edgy haircut was beginning to grow out and, in her own gloomy opinion, her moment of being fashionable had passed.

It felt like being raised from the dead the following morning. 'I've brought you some tea,' said Alexandra. 'But hurry, because David is ready to go now, more or less. I'm going in on the bus. There isn't room for both of us in the Citroën. It's a big car but it's full of stock.'

79

Lizzie took a sip of tea. 'OK.' Her voice sounded as if she were still asleep.

'Morning, Sleepyhead,' said David when she appeared downstairs without having done more than pull on some clothes and brush her teeth. 'Bless you for not dawdling. Now into the car. Bacon sarnies when we get there.'

The big French car, which had been parked somewhere else overnight, seemed to be nearer to the ground than usual, so heavily loaded was it. David had brought it round to the front of the house. Lizzie got in. She had her cloth bag containing a few essential items and put it on her knee.

'Actually, it's rather lovely being up before the rest of the world, isn't it?' she said as they drove through Hyde Park, which looked extra beautiful with dew on the grass and the spring flowers nodding in the breeze.

David nodded. 'It's the getting up that's the hard part and that gets easier when you're used to it.'

'I feel fine now.' She frowned. 'Will Alexandra be OK on the bus?'

'Of course. I've got her stock. It'll take her longer to get there but she won't mind.'

They sat in companionable silence for a while.

'Well,' he said after a few minutes. 'Why are you so keen to experience the Portobello Road Market this early?'

Lizzie looked out of the window. She should have known David would sense she had a motive. 'I just think it sounds fun, working on a market stall. Not a scary fruit and veg market or anything, but nice antiques.' He didn't answer so she blundered on. 'It's living with you and Alexandra. You've made me interested in old things.'

80

David laughed. 'I won't be offended by your reference to old things. And I promise you, even if we don't have to call out our wares to passing trade, things can get heated if two people see the same thing at the same time and both want it. The dealers come first, and then later, the general public drifts in.'

'What sort of people are the dealers?'

'You'll see. But it's all sorts. You get the gentry, with their posh voices and no money. East End types who sound terribly 'cor blimey' but really know their stuff and who've done well. Housewives whose 'little hobby' and fondness for going to auctions has got out of hand and turned them into experts in something or other. And a few who think it's easy to make money out of antiques.'

'And it's not,' said Lizzie. She knew this much already.

David sighed. 'No. But if you get the bug, you love it and don't care if it never makes you rich. Although of course, we're all looking for the one thing that will make our fortune.'

'The thing that no one else spotted and will sell for thousands?'

David nodded. 'That's the thing.'

'Have you ever found anything? Is it rude to ask that?'

He laughed. 'You're all right, Little Lizzie. You can ask me what you like. And yes, I did once find something that turned out to be quite valuable.'

'And? You can't leave me not knowing,' Lizzie went on when he didn't immediately tell her.

'It was a little Delftware mug. A bit nibbled round the edges but no real damage. It was cream with a blue pattern. It was early. It was in a box of other crockery.

I spotted it but didn't say anything. I knew if I drew attention to it the seller would realise it wasn't like the other bits and pieces in the box. I offered him a quid for the whole box and he was glad to have it.'

'Did you keep it? Or sell it?' This was exciting. She longed to hear about David making his fortune. Although she realised that if he had made a fortune it was unlikely he'd be living with Alexandra.

'I put it into auction. I made enough to buy this car.' He patted the steering wheel of his big old estate car, which was now completely packed with boxes. There was a trestle table on the roof, lashed down with rope. 'I paid off my debts, bought some new stock. And that was it. But it was exciting. And you never know that something similar won't happen again. It's the thought that it might which keeps us going.'

Lizzie didn't speak for a while. She was admiring London before dawn, when although there were people about, there weren't many of them. Milk floats, some drawn by horses, could be glimpsed as they drove along the Bayswater Road towards Notting Hill. Dustcarts, the men emptying the dustbins wearing leather caps with flaps, even an ice cart, delivering ice in huge blocks. Lizzie realised how much went on while most people were asleep.

'Right,' said David as they approached the Portobello Road. 'I'll drive up to my spot and we'll unload. You'll guard the stuff while I go and park the car. Then we'll set up. OK?'

The stallholders either side of David were already there and noticed Lizzie getting out of the car when they were obviously expecting Alexandra.

'So, you turned in Lexi for a new model, did you, Dave? She's a pretty one,' one of them said as Lizzie helped David get the trestle table off the roof. He was definitely a cockney geezer type, she decided.

'Nah.' David grinned, obviously well used to his teasing. 'Lexi's coming on the bus. I've got two dolly birds helping out today.' David nodded towards the man. 'This is Terry, Lizzie. Watch him.' He gave a knowing look. 'I'll be off to park the motor.'

Lizzie felt a bit self-conscious about being referred to as a dolly bird. In her mind they were fashionable and pretty. She hadn't had time to put on any make-up that morning and felt a bit frumpy. She put her hand up to her hair, and ran her fingers through it.

'He does all right for women, considering he's an iron,' said Terry, eyeing up Lizzie when she tried to make sense of the trestle table.

She smiled at him. 'Give us a hand with this?' she asked. She'd never heard the expression 'iron' before, but she could work out Terry meant homosexual.

In spite of his rather aggressive manner, Terry was very helpful and between them they got the table up. Lizzie had found the cloth and spread it out and was beginning to unpack the crates when David got back.

'You've done well, Lizzie,' he said. He handed over a paper bag. 'Here's your breakfast.' He handed another bag to Terry.

In the bag was a floury white roll full of crispy bacon. Lizzie took one bite and felt she'd gone to heaven. Soft bread and butter yielded to her bite until she reached the crispness of the bacon. 'Oh, that is so good!' she said. 'Nothing I've learnt with Madame Wilson tastes half as good as that.'

'You can't beat a bacon sarnie and a cup of strong Rosie,' said Terry with his mouth full. 'Rosie Lee, tea,' he added helpfully when he'd stopped chewing.

'Don't let Terry fool you with his rhyming slang,' said David. 'I happen to know he went to Eton.'

Lizzie put on an expression she hoped was quizzical. She didn't know if David was telling the truth or not. Maybe Terry *had* been to Eton. 'What would you like in the front of the stall?'

'Well, as you can see I mostly deal in silver and china,' said David, 'with a bit of jewellery thrown in. I put a bit of silver at the front: the plate — hairbrushes, mirrors, trinket boxes. But I keep the really good stuff at the back, where I can keep an eye on it. Why don't you put it out in a way that looks nice to you and then I'll tell you you've done it wrong.'

At this moment Alexandra appeared; she was carrying paper bags too. 'I see you've got your breakfast already,' she said. 'But bacon rolls never get left uneaten. Who's for seconds?'

'Me, please,' said Lizzie, suddenly realising how hungry she was.

'The stall's beginning to look nice,' said Alexandra. 'Has David told you it's all wrong yet?'

'Not yet,' said Lizzie. 'I think he's planning to let me finish it before he dismantles it.'

'Sounds about right,' said Alexandra. 'So, Tel? How are you doing?'

'Mustn't grumble, Lex,' said Terry. 'So David's got two of you to help out today? He planning to get some new stock? I've seen some of that for months now.'

'Always on the lookout for something good, Terry,' said David. 'So I'll give your stall a miss. If you two girls don't mind setting up, I'll have a wander. See if anyone's else has got anything worth buying.'

Lizzie, who was setting up a row of little figures she assumed were Chinese, looked at her friend in horror.

'But, Alexandra! Supposing someone wants to buy something? We won't know what anything costs!'

'David's got a book,' Alexandra explained. 'We find out what he paid and then add on as much as we think we can get away with.'

'What I wouldn't do to get a look at David's book,' said Terry, eyeing up Alexandra, judging his chances on getting one.

'Don't you mean a 'butcher's hook', Tel?' said Alexandra, one eyebrow raised, looking her most aristocratic.

Terry laughed loudly.

'When David's back, we can put prices on,' said Alexandra. 'You've got neat writing. He'd love it if people can read the tickets. He likes to be descriptive but no one can ever read my writing.'

Lizzie laughed. Mme Wilson had said her friend's writing looked like 'loose knitting'.

Lizzie enjoyed writing on the little tags that David attached with cotton thread to the items. *Victorian silver tea caddy, hallmarked Chester, 1900.* And the price.

People came and went on the stall. At first it was all dealers, who used expressions like 'What's the absolute death on that?' when they wanted to buy something.

David really reduced prices for 'the trade', he explained, when someone walked off with something for less than half the price on the tag. 'The real punters, the ones who pay proper retail prices, come later. You carry on getting those tags written. You have such nice writing!'

★ ★ ★

85

The hours passed quickly. They sat on their chairs, Lizzie carefully writing labels, David and Alexandra talking to passers-by, sometimes selling something.

Later, after lunch had been bought from the same stall as the one that had provided breakfast, Lizzie tried her hand at selling and Alexandra was pleased with her for getting rid of a little tea caddy that was quite damaged. 'I've been trying to get rid of that for ages. It's pretty, but its condition is poor.'

'Condition is all important, sweetie,' said David. 'I've told you that enough times.'

'I know!' said Alexandra. 'But you need never see that battered tea caddy again!'

Lizzie was just inscribing 'Danish art nouveau silver Liberty-style flower buttons' — items she would have loved to buy for herself had they not been so pricey, when she heard a voice she thought she recognised.

'Now this is more like!' said Electra, picking up the buttons although Lizzie hadn't quite finished writing the tag. 'Much more appealing than those boring old tools. Maybe you could buy them for me?'

Electra turned her head to talk to Hugo, who was looking attentive. He had a brown-paper-wrapped bundle under one arm and was holding several carrier bags in the other hand.

Lizzie wanted to die. She'd gone to all this trouble to try and see Hugo again but somehow it hadn't occurred to her that Electra would be there too. Now, she didn't know if she should try and keep her head down, or look up and say hello. She had decided not to draw attention to her presence and hope they'd go away when Alexandra spoke.

'Oh, hi! Electra! We met at Vanessa's. Alexandra.' Alexandra put her hand out so Electra was forced to drop the buttons in order to shake it. 'Do you like those? They're so stylish, aren't they? Contemporary somehow, although of course they are old.'

Lizzie knew she couldn't pretend she wasn't there any longer. 'Hello!' she said. 'I'm just writing the price tag for those buttons.'

'And what does the price tag say?' Hugo asked, his gaze making Lizzie blush, even though he could have just been looking at the stall.

'Oh, don't take any notice of the price tag. David will give you a good deal, won't you, David?' Alexandra seemed determined to sell those buttons. Lizzie wondered if she was on commission, she was being so helpful.

David laughed, every inch the charming actor/ antiques dealer. 'I'm sure we can do something. What price were we putting on them, Lizzie?'

Lizzie told him.

'My goodness!' said Electra. 'That's ridiculously expensive, even if I'm not paying!'

Lizzie felt offended on David's behalf. 'They are unique. Buttons like this are rare and would make any garment extremely special.' Then she decided to relax a little and smiled. 'I've got my eye on them myself, so I don't want you to buy them. I have a dress they would look lovely on. Sometimes changing the buttons can make the world of difference.'

This was all true. She had a short, pale pink velvet fitted dress she had adapted from one of Gina's discarded garments. It had sleeves to the elbow and she had added a satin frill. It had a deep round neck and Lizzie was really pleased with it. But the buttons would make the dress something really special.

Knowing there was competition for the buttons

made Electra became far more enthusiastic. 'So, what would you sell them to me for?' she asked.

Lizzie told her again.

Electra laughed. 'No one ever pays the price on the ticket.'

'Mostly they do,' said Lizzie, finding some steel she didn't know she had. She tried as hard as she could to look pleasant.

'Well, as you're a friend,' David said, 'I could let you have them for . . . ' He took an amount off the price which wouldn't count as a discount if Electra had been a dealer.

Electra put her hand on Hugo's arm in what seemed to Lizzie to be a gesture of ownership. 'What do you think, Hughie?' Electra asked. 'Would you get them for me?'

He seemed undecided.

'I think I deserve something after dragging round after you while you bought ancient coping saws or whatever it was.' Electra's voice was beginning to sound less persuasive and more insistent.

'I can maybe do a little bit better than that on the price,' said David, his foot pressing against Lizzie's in some silent message. He gave a new figure.

'Oh, please, Hughie!' said Electra. 'I've got this darling little frock that I bought at another stall. It's brand new — couldn't wear anything anyone else had sweated in — but it just needs a little something to make it extra special. Here . . . ' She took the bags Hugo was holding and began to delve into them.

While Electra was hunting through her purchases, Lizzie wondered why, if she wanted the buttons so much, she didn't just buy them.

Eventually Electra took out a dress that had stylised

daisies on it. It looked modern and attractive, but the buttons down the front did indeed let it down a bit. She showed the dress to Lizzie. 'It's this!'

'You don't think the buttons you're considering buying would look better on something a bit plainer?' said Lizzie. 'The buttons are like daisies. You might have too many daisies if you add more.'

Electra snatched back the dress, not at all happy that her taste had been questioned. 'We'll have the buttons, and the price you first offered, but I want you' — she stabbed at Lizzie with a manicured finger — 'to sew the buttons on for me now.'

'Hang on, Electra,' said Hugo, embarrassed by his girlfriend's demanding attitude. 'We're buying buttons, not a sewing service. Lizzie may not have a needle and thread.'

'It's OK,' said Lizzie. 'I never go anywhere without my sewing kit.' Just for a second, her eyes met Hugo's. She felt an electric charge going through her. She knew it was a one-way effect, that he was just looking at a young woman he'd inadvertently put in a tricky position, but it still made her joints turn to water.

She rummaged at her feet and brought out her bag. 'Here we are.' The home-made cloth bag that contained her sewing things made her feel like a particularly unsophisticated Girl Guide.

'Great!' said Electra. 'Pay the man, Hughie, and then let's get on.' She glanced at David. 'We're meeting some friends for drinks soon and I want to change first.' Then, looking down her nose, she turned her attention back to Lizzie, who had already started removing the buttons on the daisy-covered dress. 'Ten minutes long enough?'

'I'll need a bit longer than that,' said Lizzie.

'We'll come back and see how you're doing in half an hour,' said Hugo. 'There's no huge hurry.'

'And I want them sewn on properly! I'll be furious if one of them comes off after we've paid so much for them.'

Hugo took her arm and hurried her away.

'That was a nifty bit of salesmanship,' said Terry. 'And a handy service to be able to offer button-buyers. Not that you sell a lot of buttons, I don't suppose.'

'She's quite a difficult person,' said Lizzie tactfully, threading her needle.

'She's a bitch,' said Alexandra simply.

'She is,' David agreed. 'And when you've done that, Lizzie, I'll give you some really pretty buttons. Much nicer than those. The ones I have in mind are antique, for a start.'

He rummaged about at the back of the stall and then produced a battered leather box. 'Here.'

Lizzie gasped as he opened the box. Six large buttons glittered against the velvet lining. 'Are those diamonds?'

'I've never seen those!' said Alexandra indignantly, looking over Lizzie's shoulder. 'Have you been keeping secrets from me?'

'Certainly not. I've only just bought them,' said David, getting out his magnifying glass and peering at them even more closely.

'They are so pretty!' said Lizzie. 'What can you see down that glass?'

'You mean his jeweller's loupe?' said Alexandra.

'I suppose so,' said Lizzie impatiently. She just wanted to know about the buttons.

'Well, they're not diamonds,' said David. 'They're

90

paste, but very good quality. Georgian.'

'How much did you pay?' asked Alexandra. When David had told her, she whistled. 'Isn't that rather a lot for paste?'

He shook his head. 'They are extremely rare. Here you are, Lizzie. They're yours.'

Lizzie looked at the buttons. They were huge, nearly an inch across, the stones set in spirals. 'They look like fireworks,' she said. 'They're stunning. But I don't think they'd look right on my dress. It's quite a soft pink. Pearly buttons would be better.'

'You could put them on another dress? Black velvet?' David suggested. He obviously really wanted to give them to her.

Lizzie shook her head. 'It's too much. I'm only sewing on a few buttons. Besides, I think Electra's dress would look better without them.'

'But you got me the sale. I charged that woman a lot and I just found those Art Nouveau buttons in a button box I bought. They were practically free.' David was being very insistent.

'It was a pleasure! Really, it was.' She felt a bit sad that it had been Hugo who'd paid the extra, but supposed the buttons had still been good value.

'I'd like to do something for you,' said David.

'I know what you could do, David,' said Alexandra.

'What?' David asked.

'You could cook for a dinner party,' said Alexandra. 'You're a brilliant cook.'

'What dinner party?' Lizzie made a start on her sewing task.

'I think we should have one,' said Alexandra. 'Definitely.'

Lizzie felt a bit strange at the thought of giving a

dinner party — she had so little experience of them — and was trying not to think of the people Alexandra might want to ask. 'Do you really think that's a good idea?'

'Definitely! Firstly, we should invite Vanessa back, and secondly, it would be fun to get out all the silver and candelabra and make the dining room look lovely.' Alexandra seemed very happy at the prospect.

'A dinner party?' said Terry. 'Can I come?'

'Of course,' said Alexandra. 'We'll make a guest list. Put you on it. Do you have a wife you'd like to bring with you?'

Terry had not been expecting to be taken seriously. 'Well, yes . . .'

'We'll send you an invitation,' said Alexandra, taking pity on him. 'Then you can decide at your leisure.'

'I've never given a dinner party,' said Lizzie, not sure how she felt about the idea.

'Meg would love it.' Alexandra was excited now. 'She and David would be in charge of the food, and we'd help them.'

'Why do you want to do that, all of a sudden?' said Lizzie, tackling the next button.

'Well, we owe Vanessa one, don't we? She invited us. We should return her hospitality,' said Alexandra.

'You're up to something,' said David.

'Not really.' Alexandra rearranged a chain evening bag and a chatelaine hung with items considered useful for a nineteenth-century housewife. 'I just think that Lizzie should have a proper crack at Hugo.'

Lizzie gasped and blushed as she cut off her thread.

'Don't you want to see him again properly, Lizzie?' asked Alexandra.

Still blushing, Lizzie shrugged and picked up the

last button. 'Well, yes, but we'd have to invite Electra too. They're a couple!'

'We can invite her,' said Alexandra. 'But she might not want to come. She might have a prior engagement.'

'I think I have a prior engagement, if it's all the same to you, Madame Hostess,' said David. 'Although I'd be happy to cook.'

'Well, if Dave's not going, I won't come,' said Terry obviously glad of an excuse to refuse the invitation.

'We'll manage without you both if we have to,' said Alexandra.

'Who else do we know to ask, Alexandra?' said Lizzie, sewing hard.

'Vanessa, obviously, and Ted.'

'We'll make up a list. If necessary, we'll invite some of David's actor friends, to add a certain louche glamour to the occasion.'

Terry laughed. 'You're a one, Lexi, you really are.'

'Does anyone else ever call you Lexi, apart from Terry?' asked Lizzie.

'Lexi is what my antique friends call me,' Alexandra explained.

'Friends who are a hundred years old?' said Lizzie, feeling a bit better about life. 'That's amazing! They look so fit and healthy!'

'Honestly!' Alexandra rolled her eyes.

Lizzie looked up and saw Electra and Hugo in the crowd and felt she really didn't want to see them. Electra had somehow made her feel belittled, as if she was beneath her in some way. She wasn't going to be made to feel like that again. 'OK, I've done the buttons. Would anyone mind if I had a quick look at the other stalls?'

Alexandra looked at her quizzically. 'No, go on. You should have had a look before. But don't be too long. We'll be packing up in about an hour.'

'And don't pay the asking price for anything,' said David. 'Say 'What's the death on that?' for everything.'

Lizzie put her head on one side. 'What? Even for a bunch of bananas?'

And then she walked quickly into the crowd.

9

'I can't believe you invited Electra and Hugo to our dinner party while I was buying bananas!'

They were back in Belgravia and Lizzie was putting the fruit on the table in the kitchen.

Alexandra shrugged. 'No time like the present!'

'What's all this about a dinner party?' said Meg, inspecting the bananas, possibly deciding if they were ready to eat. 'When and where, and am I involved?'

'Yes, when is it?' Lizzie was still indignant. She had very mixed feelings about seeing Electra and Hugo again. Much as she liked Hugo — and she knew her feelings were more than 'like' really — she didn't want to see Electra again, ever.

'Sorry, Meg,' said Alexandra. 'I thought it would be fun to have a dinner party here. We'd invite Vanessa and some of the other people at her dinner party. The ones we liked and have telephone numbers for.' She smiled endearingly. 'David is going to cook, with you, if you fancy it? But not if you don't. You could just be a hostess, like me and Lizzie?'

Meg made a face. 'A hostess? That sounds very odd, if you don't mind me saying so.'

'You know what I mean! We all live here and we're having a dinner party, so we're joint hostesses.'

'I'll cook but I'm not being a guest, or even a hostess,' said David.

Alexandra made a sad face. 'Not even if we acquire a trolley?'

'Not even if you give me a frilly apron.' David was

95

very clear about this. 'I don't want to be involved in all the social chat: 'What do you do?' 'Where do you live?' I'm too old for your friends, anyway,' he finished.

'So what did you do about dates?' said Lizzie, wishing she'd said no to this idea right at the beginning.

'Electra had her diary with her — from Smythson, naturally, I couldn't help noticing — and we chose a couple of dates. Midweek. They go to the country at the weekend.' Alexandra did seem very slightly sheepish about this.

'I can't believe Electra was keen enough to give provisional dates,' said Lizzie.

'Well, no, actually it was Hugo,' said Alexandra.

'I think he was a bit embarrassed by Electra's high-handedness about those buttons,' said David.

'So which date shall we choose?' said Lizzie, feeling further protest would be futile. 'Meg? When would suit you? How did it go last night — have you got a job now? If so you'll be working in the evenings.'

'I can do that date,' said Meg, looking at the list Alexandra had scribbled down. 'The Thursday. But book me now. Don't want to boast but the caterers loved me! It seems my waitressing skills will be in demand — the caterers are extremely busy during the season. The other girls I met were very like the girls at Mme Wilson's. Apparently it's a socially acceptable thing to do.' She reflected for a second. 'I think maybe they appreciate someone who really needs to work.'

'They're very lucky to have you,' said David.

'OK,' said Alexandra, after a suitable pause. 'Lizzie, I've got Electra's number and she's in charge of Hugo's diary. Ring her and tell her that's the date.'

'Absolutely not!' said Lizzie. 'She already thinks

I'm a seamstress for hire. If I telephone her, she'll think I'm a secretary. Besides, I hate ringing people I don't know.' She really meant that she hated ringing people she knew despised her.

Alexandra studied her. Lizzie felt she was being read like a book.

She was relieved when Alexandra nodded. 'I'll do it. Now, who else shall we ask?'

'More importantly, what are going to cook?' said Meg. 'David? What do you think?'

'What's the budget?' asked David.

'Budget?' said Lizzie and Alexandra together.

'You know, cost per head?' Meg looked at her friends with a slight frown.

'Well,' said Alexandra, looking crossly at David, who was laughing, 'why don't we think what we'd like to serve and then work out if we can afford it?'

'How many people do you want to invite?' said David. 'My favourite for a dinner party is six.'

'No!' said Lizzie passionately. Then she went on, 'I mean, there are three of us: we can't just invite three more people. One more, actually, if Hugo and Electra are already coming.' Had she sounded as if she cared too much?

'Well,' said Alexandra, 'there are twelve chairs that fit round the table in the dining room. But I suggest we have ten people.'

David sucked his teeth. 'That's quite a lot to cope with, if you haven't got staff.'

'Oh, come on,' said Lizzie, who was delighted by the prospect of Electra and Hugo being lost among a large group. 'We don't need staff! There are three of us girls who are nearly trained chefs — '

'Not quite chefs, Lizzie,' said Meg. 'And staff would

97

be helpful. I could ask the people I work for if — '

'No,' said Alexandra. 'We'd have to pay staff. Lizzie is right, we may not be trained chefs and we won't even be trained to entertain for our husbands' — she glanced at Lizzie — 'for another couple of weeks, but we can certainly cook and serve a jolly good meal for ten people. Between us.' She looked at David.

'OK,' said David. 'But we need to choose the menu carefully. More Elizabeth David than Fanny Cradock.'

The three students of the Mme Wilson School of Cookery looked at him, disdain etched clearly on their faces. 'Don't even say Fanny Cradock to us!' said Meg. 'Mme Wilson told us very firmly that piping is vulgar.'

Lizzie laughed. 'It's not often that I appreciate being told something is vulgar because it's usually something I want to do, like eat in the street, or go out without gloves or something. But I'm very happy not to pipe anything.' She frowned. 'Although I'm not sure how you'd write on a birthday cake without piping . . . Sorry! Thinking aloud!'

'Can I suggest pâté to start?' said David. 'With melba toast. You can put it all on the table before they sit down.'

'Won't the melba toast be tricky?' said Alexandra.

'No! I have a handy hint for that I learnt the other day,' said Meg. 'Not at Mme Wilson's sadly. You toast sliced white bread, cut off the crusts and tease the two halves apart. Then you dry it off in the oven.'

'OK,' said Alexandra. 'What sort of pâté?'

'Kipper,' said Meg. 'My favourite.'

'Kippers are so bony!' objected Lizzie.

'We'll buy fillets and there are lots of us to take the bones out,' said Meg. 'They're cheap.'

'Or chicken liver?' suggested David.

'Fiddly to do,' Meg objected. 'Though delicious . . . '

Eventually Lizzie yawned. They couldn't agree on what to serve for pudding. She said, 'Well I'm off to bed. I'm going to have Sunday lunch with my parents tomorrow. Anyone want to join me?'

There were polite murmurs but no one accepted. Lizzie nodded. She understood why. 'OK!'

'Would you like me to drive you there, Lizzie?' asked David. 'You were such a trooper today at the market.'

Lizzie shook her head. 'Easier if I go on the train, really. It's what they're expecting.'

She would never be able to explain David to her parents, even if he wasn't gay. Her mother would have them down the aisle before you could say 'hire a marquee'.

★　★　★

Her father picked her up from the station, as arranged, the next morning. Lizzie hugged him, which he found rather surprising although he managed to pat her back awkwardly. Lizzie had suddenly realised how much she was growing up — away from the confines of her family. They were suffocating and yet very precious to her.

Her mother had the roast lamb all ready, the oval table laid in the dining room for the three of them. Sunday lunch had been like this ever since Lizzie could remember. Her father carved, her mother served the vegetables and passed the gravy. Lizzie would clear the table afterwards, then make coffee for her parents and bring it through to the sitting room for them to drink.

99

'It's lovely to have you home for a little while, darling,' said her mother when everyone was served and her father had started eating. 'When will you come back for good after your course is finished? I'm so looking forward to having my Elizabeth with me again.'

Lizzie chewed to avoid having to answer.

'Daddy could pick you up from where you're staying, couldn't you? Bring you home with all your things.'

Lizzie's mother hadn't actually called her husband Daddy since Lizzie was about thirteen, but she always tensed in case her mother went back to doing it. It embarrassed her, even though it was just the three of them.

'Of course,' said her father. 'Anything to help get my little girl home!'

Lizzie smiled warmly. She could put off replying no longer. 'Actually, I was thinking of staying in London. I'd like to get a job. After all, you've spent a lot of money having me taught how to cook; I feel I should earn something to justify the expense.'

Her parents looked at her, their mouths slightly open. Lizzie wasn't exactly arguing but she wasn't just nodding and smiling as she usually did.

'But you must let me tell you what I was up to yesterday.' Lizzie ploughed on, smile still bright. 'I was behind an antiques stall at the Portobello Road Market! It's famous,' she added, wishing her parents would stop looking like startled goldfish.

Her father was the first to find his voice. 'An antiques stall? How come?'

'Darling,' said her mother. 'Are antiques people quite respectable?'

'Oh yes! Alexandra — you remember? She came here? — has a stall with a friend. I helped them with it. I sewed on some very pretty buttons for a customer and she was delighted.'

'You always were handy with your needle,' said her mother.

'And my sewing machine.' Lizzie always had the impression that her mother would be happier if she just embroidered tray cloths and made peg bags for the sales of work her mother was so involved with.

'Yes, you did run yourself up some pretty dresses,' her mother acknowledged.

'And I managed to make that coat and skirt you had look so much smarter by altering it, didn't I? We changed the buttons on that if I remember correctly.'

'Elizabeth, would you mind passing me the water jug?' said her father, although she was far too far away to make this possible.

She passed the jug to her mother who passed it on. 'Have you managed to do much in the garden yet, Daddy? Or has it been too chilly?'

'Darling, we have Mr Edwards to do the garden now. Have you forgotten?' Lizzie's mother seemed disappointed by her daughter's memory lapse.

'Oh yes. I used to love pottering about with you in the old days, Daddy. I had my own bit of garden. Do you remember?'

Why was conversation being so difficult, Lizzie wondered. These were her parents: there should be lots of things they wanted to say to each other.

'Oh!' Inspiration hit her. 'We're giving a dinner party in the house where I'm staying. We're just working out a menu.'

For the first time since the meal began her mother

seemed to relax. 'Well, if you want my advice . . . '

'Yes please, Mummy!'

'You'll start with something simple, like grapefruit, with a cherry in the middle. It's attractive and easy to do.'

Lizzie nodded, picturing the faces of her house-mates if she suggested this.

'And then coronation chicken. It's served cold which is easier if you haven't got a hostess trolley.'

'And for pudding?' asked Lizzie.

'Chocolate mousse is always a nice sweet,' said her mother. 'All easily prepared in advance.'

Lizzie nodded. Chocolate mousse was indeed always nice so this might be a very good choice. 'Thank you for those ideas, Mummy. That's really useful.'

'I'd have thought your course would have taught you all these things,' said Lizzie's mother. 'Who are you going to invite?'

'Girls from our course,' said Lizzie. 'And their boy-friends, if they've got them. We will have to have even numbers of course.'

'Well, keep it small,' said Lizzie's mother. 'Other-wise it's just too difficult, even if you have got a simple menu.'

'Don't offer too much to drink,' said her father. 'One glass of sherry beforehand, sweet for the girls, drier for the men. And then a glass and a half of wine per person.'

Lizzie nodded, thinking of the amount of alcohol served at Vanessa's dinner party. 'What about cana-pés? Or just crisps?'

'I'm very partial to a cheese straw, myself,' put in her father.

'But they are tricky to make, darling,' said her

mother.

'Elizabeth's been on a fancy course so making them should be easy for her,' he said.

'I think I could manage cheese straws. Mme Wilson made us practise making pastry a lot and mine is very good now, if I say so myself.'

Lizzie regarded her parents who were still looking at her strangely. She was puzzled for a moment but then realised that she was talking very much more than usual, which had surprised them. It surprised her, too, but they were barely contributing to the conversation. She realised her announcement that she wasn't coming home immediately after the course was over had been a shock. Although they hadn't forbidden it — which was what she'd been expecting.

'We did like Alexandra,' said her mother when her father had been pressed into eating the last roast potato. 'And I like to think of you having friends like her. But what sort of work would you do?'

'I would like to practise all I've learnt with Mme Wilson,' said Lizzie. 'One of my other new friends, a very nice girl called Meg, has just got a little job with a catering company. She'll be working for them in the evenings as a waitress, but soon she hopes to be helping with the canapés too — they're very fiddly to do.'

'She's on the same course as you are?' asked her father.

'Yes! Her mother is widowed. She brought her sweet little dog with her to the house. We all love her.'

'I don't like the idea of you being a waitress,' said her mother slowly.

'It's not quite like being a waitress in a café,' said Lizzie, knowing her mother pictured her only child in a black dress with a white pinny and a little cap

103

falling over her eyes. 'It's quite smart. The other girls are from really good families. They do it because they want to earn a little bit of extra money, for clothes and things.' She saw that her parents still didn't understand. 'You'd like Meg, if you ever met her.'

Her mother smiled. 'I'll get the sweet. It's your favourite, darling. Pineapple upside-down cake.'

Lizzie had never liked pineapple upside-down cake but having said she did for good manners, when her mother had first produced it, she couldn't now tell her. However, for tea, two hours later, her mother produced her real favourite, Victoria jam sponge.

'Oh, Mum! This is lovely! So light!'

'Call me Mummy, darling. Just as you always have. But I'm so glad you liked it. You're the expert now!' Her mother waved her finger archly.

'You'll always be the expert at making Victoria jam sponges, Mummy,' said Lizzie. She gave her mother a little smile and hoped she wouldn't think she was being insincere. Why was she was finding the day so awkward? She was shocked to realise she was longing to go back to London, to leave the place she'd always thought of as home. She deeply loved her parents but she didn't think she could live with them any more.

★　★　★

Lizzie had gone up to her room to see if there was anything she wanted to take back up to London when her mother came and sat on her bed. 'Sit down. It's been a little while since we had a motherand-daughter chat.'

Lizzie put down the dress she had been holding. She didn't like it but it had a very full skirt and she had been wondering if she could make something else from it.

Her mother patted the bed. Lizzie's mind went back to the time when her mother had told her 'the facts of life' — about periods and how babies were made. It was lucky she had known all about this already; the little lecture had been so full of embarrassment and euphemisms Lizzie felt she would never have worked out what really happened.

Now her mother seemed more confident. 'I just want you to reassure me. If you stay in London when your course finishes, and get a job as a waitress, will you be in a position to meet suitable men?'

'How do you mean, suitable?' Lizzie knew the answer really, but she was still a teenager, and surely, even by her mother's standards, far too young to think about marriage.

'Darling, don't be naïve! I mean young men with good career prospects, who'll be able to look after you, give you the finer things in life. A doctor, possibly, who has a good private practice and will become a consultant. Not a GP — you'd end up being his receptionist, which wouldn't do at all. Or someone in the City. Or a barrister.' Her mother smiled, obviously enjoying choosing fictional husbands for her daughter.

'Oh, come on, Mummy! I'm far too young to think about getting married!'

Her mother shook her head. 'And I know exactly what sort of wedding you'll have. Obviously the service will be in our church here. It's old, about the right size and has a very pretty churchyard. And then I'd like to have the reception here, in a marquee in the garden, a proper country wedding in the bride's house. We could easily fit in three hundred guests, I think. It would have to be a buffet, of course.'

'Really?'

'Oh yes. Daddy's already buying the champagne. A contact from the golf club is a wine merchant so he's getting it on very favourable terms. And I know who we'll have to cater.'

Lizzie couldn't decide if she should be outraged or amused. 'How many bridesmaids should I have?'

'There are four on our side and of course your groom might have suitable young relations.' Lizzie's mother smiled. 'I suggest you only have small bridesmaids.'

'Are you worried big ones would outshine me?'

'Certainly not. Bridesmaids are there to set off the bride. Enhance her, not compete with her.'

Lizzie nodded. 'I see.'

Her mother was looking into the middle distance. 'I have your wedding dress very clear in my head.'

Lizzie realised she wasn't supposed to have an opinion on this. 'And what's it like?'

She'd known her mother's greatest ambition was for her to marry well but she hadn't realised she'd thought about it in quite so much detail.

'Full length, I think. A tight waist — you have a lovely small waist although no one would ever know it with those straight-up-and-down bits of cloth you seem to like nowadays. And my mother's veil of course. She wore it, I wore it and I want my darling daughter to wear it.' Her mother's voice broke a little.

She got up and headed for the door, dabbing her eyes. Then she stopped and turned. 'My daughter's wedding. It'll be the best day of my life!'

Her mother had wrapped up the remaining cake in greaseproof paper and put it in a tin for Lizzie to take back to London. She had it ready when Lizzie came down with a few clothes.

'Well, if I'm to get my train, I'd better go.' Lizzie was aiming for the earliest train back to London that she decently could catch.

'Don't worry, darling,' said her mother. 'We've decided to drive you back.'

'How sweet of you! But no need. I've got my ticket. I only need a lift to the station.' The thought of it made Lizzie sweat slightly.

'No,' said her mother firmly. 'We've decided. But we do want to go immediately. Your father has to work in the morning and the traffic might be bad.' She patted her daughter's arm. 'Daddy is getting the car out now.'

As Lizzie went to the car she frantically tried to think of an excuse to telephone her housemates but couldn't think of one. David might easily be there on a Sunday night. How would she explain him? Her parents would never accept her living in a mixed household.

Because Lizzie didn't want to get there, the traffic was surprisingly light considering everyone was going back to London after their weekend in the country. With the help of Lizzie's mother's skilful use of the A–Z they were soon parking in front of the big house in Belgravia that Lizzie now called home.

'That was so sweet of you, Daddy, driving me home. Now I know you want to get off so I won't keep you.' Lizzie was out of the back seat and on the pavement in seconds.

'We're not in that much of a hurry, darling,' said her mother, opening the passenger door and getting out. 'We'd love to see where you live, wouldn't we, Edward?'

'Indeed. It's why we wanted to drive you back. We need to know you're living somewhere half decent. All this talk of you wanting to stay in London to be a waitress is worrying. You'll be wanting to be a barmaid next!'

Lizzie had suspected this was the reason for her lift back to London. She decided to take her parents in through the front door. She had a key to the basement, via the area steps, but if she rang on the door someone would have to come up and open the door and maybe alert the household to what amounted to intruders.

Alexandra opened the front door. She was wearing hut slippers: embroidered red woollen stockings attached to leather feet, going up to her knees, as well as a pinafore dress that might have been from a little boutique or from a long-dead ancestor, Lizzie couldn't tell.

'Oh, hello, Mr and Mrs Spencer?' she said. 'You've brought Lizzie home. How nice.'

'Her name is Elizabeth, and we've brought her to her temporary home,' said Mr Spencer crossly. 'We'd like to reassure ourselves about where she's living.' Then he smiled, possibly aware he had sounded rather grumpy.

'Of course!' said Alexandra, holding the door open wider. 'Do come in!'

'We'd better go down to the kitchen,' said Lizzie, knowing the dust-sheeted drawing room would be anything but reassuring to her parents.

'Yes! It's a bit of a mess,' said Alexandra. 'You know how it is on a Sunday night, everyone getting ready for Monday.'

Her parents followed Alexandra down the stairs and Lizzie came behind them. She was hoping that the obvious grandness of the property would make a greater impression on them than the equally obvious fact that the house hadn't seen a paintbrush for fifty years or so.

'We live in the kitchen,' Alexandra explained. 'It's so expensive to heat the whole house.'

'The kitchen?' Lizzie's mother seemed bewildered by this thought.

'You'll see, Mum — Mummy!' said Lizzie.

In the basement Meg was experimenting with aspic, it seemed, as there was a tray of shapes on a sheet of greaseproof paper. Alexandra had a collection of tiny copper moulds and so there was a row of green pods with peas in them, made out of some sort of mousse. It must have taken ages, thought Lizzie, waiting for the mousse to set so Meg could turn out the shape and re-use the mould.

Where was David and how on earth could she explain him to her parents if he appeared?

He appeared from behind the kitchen table, obviously having been doing something to the sink. He was wearing a brown apron and a put-upon expression. 'I've done my best with it, but I can't guarantee anything,' he said, in an accent more Cockney than Terry's from the antiques market.

'Have you a problem?' asked Lizzie's father, going further into the room.

'It's the trap under the sink, sir. Dripping something chronic,' said David.

109

'It's making the sink smell dreadfully,' said Meg.

'Mummy, Daddy, this is Meg,' said Lizzie. 'She's the best of us at cooking. And this is Clover, who used to be Meg's dog but we all sort of own her now.' Clover wagged her tail politely.

'How do you do?' said Meg. 'I may be the best cook, but Lizzie is by far the best at sewing. There's nothing she can't make!'

'Her name is Elizabeth,' said Lizzie's mother. 'But yes, she's always been adept with her needle.'

'Can I offer you a cup of tea or something?' said Meg. 'I've made some rock cakes that could go with it.'

'We had tea some time ago,' said Lizzie's father, 'before we left for London.'

'Come and sit down by the fire, anyway,' said Lizzie.

David, possibly dissatisfied with his walk-on part as plumber, cleared his throat. 'If I may be so bold as to make a suggestion, Miss Alexandra, you have a very nice amontillado sherry that the lady and gentleman might find acceptable.' David bowed, slipping seamlessly into a new role as butler, but not a very grand one.

'Have we?' said Alexandra. 'Right! I'll find some glasses.'

'If you'll allow me, Miss Alexandra,' said David, 'I will do that for you.'

Mr and Mrs Spencer were now seated on the scruffy sofa in front of the popping gas fire looking confused. Lizzie was fighting laughter and a scream of panic; something like a sneeze came out. Meg joined Lizzie's parents on the sofa. 'It's so nice to meet you. Li— Elizabeth always talks so fondly about you.'

'That's nice!' said Lizzie's mother.

'So why doesn't she want to come home after the cooking course is over?' asked Mr Spencer.

Meg smiled warmly. 'Swinging London, probably! But I'm sure she'll keep in touch. I chat with my mother on the phone almost every day.'

Lizzie wished Meg hadn't mentioned Swinging London. Her parents probably hadn't heard of it before but were bound to worry about it now that they had.

'Are you Elizabeth's friend who works as a waitress?' asked Mrs Spencer.

'I was explaining how really quite nice girls work in your catering company,' Lizzie put in quickly, trusting that Meg would pick up her mother's anxieties and put them to rest.

'Oh yes,' said Meg. 'It can get quite annoying. The waitresses meet their friends among the guests and just gossip instead of getting the trays round. And lot of them have titles.'

That seemed to go down well.

'I will phone you as often as possible, too. There's no need to worry about me working.' Lizzie regarded her parents tenderly. She knew they loved her and she knew they worried about her, but she couldn't let this stop her living her own life.

David served sherry and both Lizzie's parents accepted a glass, along with some Twiglets he'd put in a cut-glass dish. However, they drank it quite quickly and got to their feet.

'We should be going, darling,' said her mother. 'I had wanted to see your bedroom, just to make sure it's — er — you know . . .'

Lizzie did know. She wanted to make sure it didn't

harbour bedbugs or cockroaches but with luck her mother felt reassured now.

'I'll show you out,' Lizzie said. She really didn't want her parents seeing the flapping wallpaper and hearing the creaking floorboards.

Once the front door was open and Lizzie felt the joy of the soon-to-be-released, her father stopped, one foot still in the house.

'Seems a bit strange, being able to get a plumber on a Sunday night. Especially one who seemed to know where everything was, including the sherry.'

Lizzie had been dreading this, but in dreading it, she had thought up something to say. 'He's a family retainer, Daddy. But he also does plumbing. As a sideline. He's really awfully handy. If any little thing goes wrong, if a light bulb needs changing, he comes round and does it for us.'

Mrs Spencer nodded. 'I thought it must be something like that. Alexandra does come from a very aristocratic family, doesn't she?'

Lizzie nodded, very happy to be able to speak nothing but the truth for once. 'Yes, she does.'

She kissed her parents goodbye several times and then, at last, watched them drive away.

She went back downstairs to the kitchen. 'You're a family retainer, David, who does plumbing on the side. Now please can I have a glass of sherry? I'm practically shaking! I didn't know whether to laugh or cry!'

'Me too!' said Meg. 'I kept asking myself, what sort of plumber could serve sherry so elegantly?'

'One 'oo's an hactor,' said David, ''oo 'appens to 'ave plumbin' skills!'

10

It was four days before the dinner party. Lizzie was at the kitchen table with a list. It had many crossings out and she was considering starting again and writing it all out neatly so she could read it.

Meg was making Béarnaise sauce, flicking bits of butter into the top of a double boiler and mixing it in with a bunch of birch twigs, as preferred by Mme Wilson, who was convinced a metal whisk would spoil the delicate emulsion.

Alexandra was scraping glue off the edge of the arm of a cherub she had bought, broken, for very little money, at Portobello the previous weekend.

Clover was snoring loudly in front of the gas fire, happy to be surrounded by well-occupied humans.

'I don't know why you're making that sauce again, Meggie,' said Alexandra. 'You're brilliant at it already.'

'Not brilliant,' said Meg. 'And Mme Wilson has been very tough on me lately. Besides, I want to add it to my repertoire. People like it.'

'I do wish Madame would just tell us what she's going to ask us to make,' said Lizzie. 'Why can't she have a more conventional method of testing us? The way she picks on someone at random and orders them to make meringues, or a béchamel or whatever, is just terrifying.' She had experienced this the previous week and was still shaken.

'Your meringues were fine, Lizzie!' said Meg, laughing at the memory.

'Only just!' said Lizzie, remembering the scene in

113

detail. 'And Madame was definitely disappointed that the egg white didn't flop on to my hair when she made me hold the bowl upside down over my head.'

'It was quite funny though,' said Alexandra, 'watching you holding the bowl as if it might explode at any moment.'

'Now it's funny,' Lizzie conceded. 'It wasn't at the time — for me that is. It was obviously hilarious for you lot!'

Meg put down the birch twigs, took a teaspoon and tasted the sauce. 'Oh, that's really delicious, though I say it myself.'

Lizzie reached over and picked up the spoon. Using the other end she took a sample. 'That is delicious! You'll be fine if Madame asks you to make it now. We'll have to have poached eggs or something so we can try it.'

Meg frowned. 'To be honest, making the sauce is far easier than tidy poached eggs. You're good at them, Alexandra.'

'Practice,' said Alexandra. 'All that cooking in the nursery. I watched my nannies do it and learnt how not to.'

'Can I just ask,' said Lizzie. 'Why are you taking off all the glue you've just put on to that bit of cherub? Was it the wrong kind?'

Alexandra shook her head. 'No. But if you scrape off as much as you can you don't get the glue oozing out.'

'Lexi's ability to scrape off all the glue is the key to her success as an antique dealer,' said David. 'Proud of her.'

'How are you getting on with your list, Lizzie?' asked Meg, spooning her sauce into a bowl.

'It's a bit of a nightmare to be honest. I'm not sure of the numbers.' Lizzie chewed her pen. It didn't help.

'Why not? I thought it was all fairly straightforward,' said Alexandra. 'It's us three, plus men for us. Then Hugo and Electra, Vanessa and Ted!'

'It may be straightforward in theory, but I don't know any boys who I could have as a partner and Vanessa has split up with Ted. I'm not sure if she's bringing someone else, or if we have to find her someone.'

'How annoying!' Alexandra applied a cherub arm to a cherub and held it firmly. 'Can't you ask her?'

'I have, a couple of times, but I never get the same answer twice,' said Lizzie. 'And it still leaves me partnerless. David, I don't suppose . . . ?'

'No, Lizzie!' said David. 'Apart from the fact that I bat for the other team, the age gap would look ridiculous.'

'I didn't actually mean — ' Lizzie began.

'I know a nice boy,' Meg said. 'He's a music student and gets jobs as a waiter because he's got a dinner jacket and patent-leather shoes.'

'He sounds perfect. Do you think he'd like to come?'

'I should think so. Free food. Always attractive,' said Meg.

'Have you got someone nice for yourself?' said Lizzie. 'I don't want you giving away a lovely boy and leaving you short.'

David shook his head, laughing. 'You're talking about real-life people here, people, not packets of tea!'

'We're just getting the numbers right, David,' said Alexandra. 'Everyone will just mix in once they're here.'

'I've got a boy I work with sometimes for me,' said

Meg. 'He's fun and he likes free food too.'

'But it will show if Vanessa hasn't got a partner,' said Lizzie. 'Won't it? She's quite upset about Ted and I don't want her unhappy.'

'Ask her again tomorrow,' suggested Meg. 'And if she's vague, I'll find her someone.'

'If not, we'll just put an ad in the paper for spares,' said Alexandra. '*Wanted: several presentable young men for a party. Must be hungry.*' She picked up her cherub and looked at him, satisfied. 'You'll do!'

'What? For Vanessa?' said Lizzie. 'A cherub? Talk about age gaps!' She shot David a look, pretending to be resentful.

'No, for the market,' said Alexandra calmly. 'For the party, I'm inviting a boy I knew from when I was really little. He wore shorts, white socks and shoes with buttons. I have kept up with him, and he looks normal now.'

'I expect you looked normal then, for the times,' said Lizzie. 'I bet you had a coat with a velvet collar and a velvet beret to match.' She threw down her pen. 'OK. I'll ask Vanessa one more time if she's bringing someone, and if she's at all doubtful, I'll tell her we'll ask someone for her.'

'And if she turns up with a man, the one we invited can be a waiter,' said Meg.

'No!!' said Lizzie. 'That's an outrageous idea! The man thinks he's been invited to a nice meal and is sent down to the kitchen to get on with the washing up?'

'I was joking,' said Meg.

'I bet it's just the sort of thing Electra would do,' said Alexandra. 'I can almost hear her saying it. 'As your services as a guest are no longer required, can you put on an apron and clear the table?'

Now she'd finished her Béarnaise sauce, Meg went to get her own list. 'Can I just confirm we all agree? We're having kipper pâté with melba toast. Boeuf bourguignon. Chocolate mousse for pudding — '

'I'll look out some teacups for the mousse for you,' said Alexandra. 'There's a cupboard full of miscellaneous china at the end of the corridor. It'll look elegant and I like the thought of that china being used.'

'And I thought I'd really like to make some sort of big cake,' Meg went on. 'A gâteau Saint-Honoré perhaps. I'd use frozen puff pastry for the base.' Meg looked at her co-hosts. 'You know, crème pâtissière? Circles of choux pastry?'

Lizzie shook her head. 'Sorry, never heard of it. You have to remember I grew up in a household where no one liked foreign food.'

'I haven't heard of it either,' said Alexandra, 'but if you want to make it, Meggy, carry on! Now, wine?'

David looked stern. 'I can't approve of you using all that lovely wine that's in the cellar, Alexandra. I'll get it for you. I have a contact in Soho.'

'I suppose you're right,' said Alexandra. 'It's just it's been there for years and no one has ever drunk it. If it was so wonderful, wouldn't my esteemed relations have come over from Switzerland and taken it back there with them?'

'Wine doesn't always travel,' said David. 'And to be honest, they've probably forgotten about it. Or just assumed it will be safe. Either way, you can't drink it.'

'Well, if you can get us something that's drinkable and cheap, that would be really useful,' said Alexandra.

'We have got a fairly economical menu,' said Meg.

'We planned it to be cheapish.'

'You planned it,' said Lizzie. 'And you're cooking it too. You've been brilliant, Meggy.'

Clover woke from her nap and, hearing her mistress's name, looked up and wagged her tail in agreement.

'I enjoy it!' said Meg, not comfortable with praise. 'You know I do.'

'We'll be your kitchen maids,' said Lizzie.

'When we're not being char ladies and parlour-maids,' said Alexandra. 'David? Will you get the wine tomorrow? We need to know how much it's all going to cost.'

'I will. You can get good wine cheaply if you know the right people,' said David.

'And you do!' said Lizzie.

'Yes,' said Meg. 'You have Soho sewn up! All the dealers, fruit and veg suppliers — '

'I used to have a flat there,' David explained. 'I shopped in the market every day. I got to know all the stallholders and shopkeepers.'

David got up from where he'd been waxing a small wooden tea caddy, went over to the piano and started to play. He had a habit of doing this if he felt the mood or subject needed to be changed, as he obviously did now. It never failed: he didn't seem to like having his past delved into.

Lizzie, delighted to abandon her list-making, soon joined him. She began to leaf through the music on top of the piano. While David could play by ear, he would also play any bit of music put in front of him. She put a song in front of David.

Alexandra, hearing the words 'Can't help loving that man of mine', got up and stood next to Lizzie at the piano. 'You're a sentimental sausage, aren't you?'

Lizzie nodded. 'I am.'

'But we love you for it,' said David and broke into something more upbeat.

* * *

'I don't think this dining room has been used for at least fifteen years,' said Alexandra, coughing and sneezing from the dust she had dislodged from the mantelpiece with a feather duster.

It was the day before the dinner party, as they felt they'd need all their time and energy the following day on getting the food right to have time for cleaning. They started out just wanting the dining room clean and respectable-looking. But when they went downstairs for more cleaning supplies they discovered that David had brought back several buckets of flowers from a friend who worked near Covent Garden flower market.

'They were practically giving them away,' he said. 'A big society wedding was cancelled.'

'Flowers! Lovely! I'll do them,' said Lizzie. 'Or some of them,' she went on, seeing quite how many there were.

'There's a whole cupboard full of vases,' said Alexandra. 'It's upstairs.'

'Your house is like a huge antiques emporium,' said Lizzie, panting slightly as she followed Alexandra.

'It is,' Alexandra agreed. 'But it's much more fun living in one since you and Meg came.'

When they reached the first-floor landing, Alexandra opened what appeared to be a wooden pillar, revealing a mass of things that, clearly, no one had used for years.

119

'Oh my goodness!' said Lizzie, peering in. 'Not only vases but candelabra! They're massive!'

Alexandra put in her hand and extracted one. 'And filthy,' she said, looking at it with horror.

'Never mind!' said Lizzie. 'We can leave them tarnished, pretend it's on purpose.'

'David's got a trick with tin foil and soda crystals,' said Alexandra, extracting candelabra one at a time until there were six of them on the floor beside Lizzie. 'If you wanted them clean. We ought to clean the knives and forks anyway.'

'Have you got any low vases that we could put on the table?'

Alexandra was leaning so far into the cupboard she was practically inside it. 'What about this for the table! I think it's called an epergne.'

Lizzie couldn't speak for a few moments. Her friend was holding a huge, highly decorated silver object which, at first glance, seemed to be a candelabra only with dishes instead of places to hold candles. 'What's it for?'

'Apart from hiding the person sitting across the table? I think it would have fruit or flowers or little sweets in the dishes. What do you think? Do you want to use it?' Alexandra looked very dubious at the prospect and Lizzie agreed with her.

'I don't think so. I mean it's gorgeous but there wouldn't be room for any food on the table if it had that on it,' she said.

'You weren't supposed to talk across the table in Victorian times anyway,' said Alexandra, replacing the epergne and dislodging a couple of the little dishes from their holders as she did so. The dishes bounced on the floor. 'Oh, don't worry,' said Alexandra, picking them up. 'It's not very special.'

'And they seem OK anyway,' said Lizzie, having inspected both dishes.

'So, what vases do you want? Don't forget we'll need flowers for the drawing room.'

Lizzie chose three of them. 'I'll start with these. They should be enough.'

'Well, you know where they are if you need more. Let's get back to cleaning the dining room. The drawing room only needs the flowers and a quick dust.'

'Shall we have a quick look, to check?' suggested Lizzie. 'We don't want to be caught out.' She had a vision of Electra running her finger over the mantelpiece and then dusting off her fingers afterwards.

The three young women inspected the room. 'It does look a bit Miss Havisham-ish,' said Alexandra.

'A lick and a promise should do it,' said Meg.

'Maybe I'll vacuum the rug,' said Lizzie. 'And run the oil mop round the edges. That's the trouble with cleaning, once you start you don't seem able to stop.' She put her hands on her hips, trying to see what her mother would see if she was inspecting a room before guests were expected. 'Flowers will make all the difference,' she said.

'OK. Now let's check the dining room,' said Alexandra. 'That hasn't been used for years. There'll be cobwebs and spiders everywhere.'

'We could bring Clover up,' said Meg. 'She catches spiders. It's the only useful thing she does, really.'

'Darling Clover!' said Alexandra. 'She's so decorative, she doesn't need to be useful as well.'

'Well,' said Meg. 'We're being neither just now. Let's get going.'

★ ★ ★

Meg had decided to polish the table, which came up beautifully and, she declared, would add a wonderful background fragrance to the scent of flowers. But it was time-consuming and when she was about half-way through, she decided she needed to get into the kitchen to start on the canapés. The beef was already marinating. She handed her cloths and polish to Lizzie. 'I suppose if you get fed up we could put sheets on the table as tablecloths.'

'No! I'll carry on,' Lizzie insisted. 'It looks so beautiful and smells divine. But I will start on the flowers when I've finished.'

Alexandra disappeared to find table napkins although Lizzie tried to persuade her that paper ones would do. 'No,' said Alexandra. 'If we're doing this, we're doing it properly.'

'But we'll have to iron them!' said Lizzie. 'They'll be very hard work.'

'Not if we don't have to wash and iron them before using them, in which case, paper ones will definitely do. We can send them to the laundry afterwards.' Alexandra had been firm.

'You go and look while I finish the table,' said Lizzie, dipping her duster in the tin of polish yet again.

David helped Lizzie do the flowers in the end. He also helped carry the vases; they'd needed far more than three for both the dining room and the drawing room. The dining room was huge and a table for twelve with chairs didn't take up all the space. There were tables at each end, and in the corners of the room. David and Lizzie agreed that all the tables needed a floral display.

They did huge ones for the end tables, and con-
gratulated themselves on the wonderful sprays of
delphiniums, freesias, irises and lilies. The fragrance
mingled with the wax of the polish.

'I really like your arrangement so let's put mine
this end,' said Lizzie, 'so they'll see yours when they
come in.' She bit her lip. 'I didn't think I'd say this,
but we haven't left ourselves enough flowers for the
side tables.'

'Let's not bother. We can keep one side table free
to serve from and the other has a timepiece on it. It's
handsome, even though it's broken. But I'll go into
the garden and see what I can hack off the bushes.
Extra greenery will make it look lavish.' He looked at
her and smiled. 'I have to say, you do have a gift for
arranging flowers, little Lizzie.'

She liked it when David used his nickname for her.
'It'll help make me a perfect wife one day,' she said, a
little bitterly, thinking of her recent conversation with
her mother. 'I'll be able to go on the church-flower
rota, and decorate my lovely home when my husband
wants to entertain business colleagues.'

'Is that the plan?' asked David.

'It's my mother's plan,' said Lizzie. 'She does usually get her own way.'

'But you wouldn't marry to please her?'

'No, I wouldn't go that far. And I did hold out
when she suggested grapefruit with a cherry as an
easy starter for our dinner party.'

David was highly amused. 'You're not as much of a
walkover as your mother thinks, obviously!'

★ ★ ★

123

Lizzie awoke on the day of the dinner party wishing they didn't have to spend the morning in the basement kitchen in Pimlico learning how to prepare partridges and other small game birds. Although she liked to spring surprises, Mme Wilson had given them that snippet of information before they'd left the day before.

Meg was already in the kitchen, frying bits of braising steak, when Lizzie came downstairs.

'I'm going to get this in the oven, really low, before we have to leave,' said Meg. 'Then I can just heat it up tonight. It's going to be quite tricky doing all this on only four burners, although David's promised to provide some sort of double burner thing you just plug in.'

'You're enjoying yourself,' said Lizzie, accusingly. 'And you've obviously been up since before dawn!'

'I have — and I know! But I do just love the challenge,' said Meg. 'I feel if this dinner party goes OK I could actually go into people's houses and cook. If I did directors' lunches and cooked in the evening, I'd earn a proper salary.'

Lizzie nodded, opening the bread bin so she could make toast. 'You just need a job in a café making breakfast and every minute of your day would be filled!'

'Don't tease. I love cooking and I love working and I especially love earning money,' said Meg. 'And if you could make me some toast while you're grilling, I'd be grateful.'

Lizzie put two slices of bread on the grill pan and lit the gas. She would have to wait until the toast was done before she could leave her post. There were only moments between well done and burnt and she didn't want to have to scrape it. It made such a mess. And giving Meg a properly made piece of toast seemed the least she could do.

11

Alexandra was looking very like Audrey Hepburn when she opened the front door to the first guests that evening. She was wearing a long black sleeveless dress and long white kid gloves she had found in one of the chests of clothes in the attic. Her hair was in a pile on top of her head, and strings of pearls were looped snugly round her neck before falling down her front. Her eyeliner was a perfect curve with an Audrey flick at the corners. Demure but extremely sexy had been the verdict.

Lizzie was standing a little way behind Alexandra as part of the welcoming committee, wearing a very pretty long dress with elbow-length sleeves and round neck that showed just a hint of cleavage. She had a velvet ribbon round her neck and antique earrings that looked like daisies. Alexandra had done her make-up too, so she was wearing a bit more than usual. Her hair was growing out but she'd fashioned kiss curls of the ends and it had a certain look, she felt.

Meg was in the kitchen and would have to be prised away from it later. The fact that Meg was wearing make-up at all was down to Alexandra's strength of character. Meg had protested that it would all be sweated off and there was no point in putting it on.

Lizzie wasn't at all surprised to see that their first guests were Electra and Hugo.

'I hope we're not early,' said Electra, not giving anyone time to greet them. 'But we may not be able to stay late.'

126

'Do come in,' said Alexandra at her most stately.

'Good evening, Alexandra, Lizzie,' said Hugo, kissing them both in turn. He was wearing a suit that Lizzie thought looked smart and elegant. He was a perfect foil for Electra.

'Can I take your coats?' said Alexandra. 'Oh, you're not wearing any.'

Electra smiled. 'Easier to make a quick get away without.' Although she'd smiled to indicate she was joking, no one was fooled. She was wearing a two-piece with a stand-up collar in oyster satin. It was knee-length and, with her elegant upswept hair, large pearl earrings and matching choker-length double strand of pearls, the clasp at the front, she could have come from the cover of Vogue.

Lizzie forced her smile a bit wider. 'And you don't want the ladies' cloakroom?' Then, realising she'd asked Electra if she wanted to use the lavatory, she hurried on. 'Then do come upstairs.'

Blushing at her gaucheness, and feeling her long dress and daisy earrings made her look like a child who'd got into the dressing-up box, she led the way up to the drawing room. There she could pass her guests on to the young men who were waiting, bottles open, ready to serve. They were guests, but they had duties.

Why had Electra been so keen to come? Lizzie asked herself, listening to Electra swishing up the stairs behind her. She wasn't going to enjoy herself. Hugo probably wouldn't either. Probably no one would; the dinner party was a horrible idea, she concluded.

Still, she had been trained as a hostess by her mother from an early age, and didn't follow her heart and run from the room.

127

'Electra,' she said, 'this is Ben, who's studying at the Royal Academy of Music; Philip, a childhood friend of Alexandra's — sorry, Philip, I should have found out what you're doing now! And Luigi and Piers, who are friends of Meg's. Guys? If you could kindly serve drinks, I'm going to pop down and get some canapés. Meg hasn't let them leave the kitchen until people were here to eat them hot.'

'How delicious,' said Electra smoothly. 'I can't wait to try them. Is the champagne vintage?

This gave Lizzie a little reason to smile as she left the room. What Electra was about to be served with certainly wasn't vintage; in fact it wasn't even champagne. It was *crémant*, a sparkling French white wine made outside the area that was allowed to use the name; David had been put on to it by a wine merchant friend of his. Lizzie had thought it was delicious when they'd all had a glass as a pre-party stiffener, as David had put it.

In spite of what David had said about going out for the evening, when Lizzie got down into the kitchen, she found him helping Meg add cod's roe to little tartlets filled with cream cheese.

He looked up when Lizzie arrived. 'I know! But I couldn't abandon Meggy, could I?'

'I'm so grateful, David,' said Meg, spooning the jewel-like fish eggs on with a mustard spoon. 'I should have kept it simple, like everyone said.'

'It's OK,' said David. 'I love food too. I understand your need to experiment and stretch yourself.'

'We'd never have been able to manage without you being chums with most of the food sellers of Soho,' Lizzie said, wishing she could stay down here in the cosy kitchen instead of going back to where Electra, so beautiful and cold, was, in her imagination, turning the drawing room into a snow palace.

'It's not what you know, it's who you know,' said David. 'Now, are you going to take this up?' he asked.

They heard the doorbell ring and at just the same moment, Luigi, Meg's friend, appeared in the kitchen.

'Oh, Luigi!' said Meg. 'Can you be an angel and take these up? I think Lizzie should answer the door.'

'My pleasure, cara,' said Luigi, taking three plates of canapés in a way that revealed him as a professional as he swept from the room with total confidence.

Luigi, Meg had told them, had been very keen to attend an English dinner party. They had met when Luigi's restaurant had provided the food at an event when Meg was serving and Luigi had been sent to make sure it all went well. His usual job was a head waiter but the restaurant was being redecorated and so he was doing catering jobs until it reopened.

The girls agreed he added some much needed Latin glamour to the event, although Meg confided to Lizzie he might not remember he was a guest. 'Not that I really mind,' she added. 'As long as everyone is happy.'

Lizzie went up to open the door. It was Vanessa, looking flustered. 'Am I late? I was supposed to come with Hugo and Electra but they were so early and I'd only just got out of the bath.'

'Perfect timing. Come with me.' Lizzie took Vanessa's wrap and hung it up. 'Drinks are upstairs.'

'Did it matter I couldn't bring Ted?' Vanessa asked, although Lizzie had known Ted wasn't coming for several days.

'Not at all. There are several nice men for you to choose from. Only Hugo is spoken for and you're hardly going to want to be partnered by your brother. There's an absolutely gorgeous Italian for a start but the one I picked out for you is called Piers and seems really nice.' Lizzie couldn't remember what he did apart from part-time waiting, like Luigi and Ben.

'Sounds promising!' said Vanessa. 'It's not that I loved Ted or anything, but it is extremely galling when a man leaves you, and not the other way around.'

Vanessa's words were nonchalant but Lizzie had the impression she was actually a lot more hurt than she was willing to admit.

Meg finally appeared at the party. She came up the stairs with a plate of canapés in each hand. She was wearing cigarette pants and a white silk blouse and ballet shoes. She had a red apron on top of her clothes which Lizzie had made for her that afternoon out of an old skirt.

Lizzie knew Meg would need to wear what she called a pinny, and she wanted it to be faintly presentable. Meg didn't really care and had argued that, actually, she should just stay in the kitchen and produce the meal. She had been metaphorically jumped on by the entire household except Clover the spaniel.

Ben, Lizzie's partner, whom she had got to know a bit, stepped forward. 'Would you like me to pass them round for you?'

'Oh yes, please!' said Meg. 'I have more to bring upstairs.'

'I could help you?' suggested Luigi, who was standing next to Electra.

'Oh no you don't,' said Electra. 'You were just telling me about your grandfather's olive farm and it is so interesting!'

Lizzie had time to notice that Hugo was looking

amused at his girlfriend being so fascinated by Luigi's dark brown eyes and romantic Italian accent.

'I'll come down with you,' Lizzie said. 'Can someone make sure everyone's got drinks?'

As she left the room she saw that Hugo had taken a bottle and was topping up glasses.

'So far so good.' Lizzie said when they reached the kitchen. 'These little pastry things are delicious!'

'With the Camembert? I used the rest of the puff pastry to make those. I found a copy of Constance Spry and she's full of good ideas for canapés.'

'Don't forget you are here to enjoy yourself!' said Lizzie, taking hold of the plate Meg was handing her.

'I am enjoying myself! I like cooking food people like eating! And there's a lot of money to be made in canapés, you know.'

'Meg!' said David, who had just put down the potato masher. 'Go upstairs and join the party. You've worked quite hard enough already.' He looked thoughtful. 'That mash is really delicious. I have been quite generous with the butter.'

Then Ben arrived in the kitchen. 'Oh! You've got a piano down here too! I didn't notice that before.'

'No time to play now,' said Lizzie, not wanting him to get distracted. 'Take up some cheese straws, there's a dear.'

There was a lot to be said for having a head waiter among your dinner guests, Lizzie realised, watching Luigi get everyone from the drawing room to the dining room like a discreet Collie working a flock of sheep.

Alexandra had a placement (which she pronounced in the French way) and soon everyone was sitting down. Lizzie had suggested writing out place names

131

(her mother always did) but Alexandra said she'd just write it on a bit of paper and issue instructions.

Admiring her friend's confidence, Lizzie sat down between Ben and Piers. Vanessa was paired with Piers but, Lizzie noticed, seemed more interested in Luigi who was proving to be the star guest.

Bowls of kipper pâté, butter (put into dainty curls by Meg, much to the disapproval of Alexandra who'd have preferred plain squares of it) and piles of melba toast were ranged down the middle of the table.

'Do start everyone,' said Alexandra. 'Oh, Electra, let me get you an ashtray so you can put your cigarette out.'

'I'll do it,' said Lizzie. 'No, Meg! You sit down and eat.' Lizzie hoped she hadn't sounded too bossy. She wasn't usually that stern even when she was addressing Clover.

As Lizzie put an ashtray at Electra's elbow and returned to her seat she wondered how to stop Meg getting up and down like a yo-yo and not taking part in the social aspect of the event at all. It wouldn't be easy.

Lizzie did her own share of getting up and down during the evening but so did Ben, Luigi and Piers. Others, Hugo in particular, helped by pouring wine. There was white wine for the kipper pâté and red for the beef. Lizzie didn't allow herself to drink much of either. Although Alexandra was definitely Head Girl of the party, Lizzie had her obligations and wasn't going to fall down on them. Her main focus was ensuring Vanessa had a good time. Although when she had first come across her at the cookery school Lizzie had dismissed her as a 'haughty deb' type, she realised that underneath the veneer of sophistication Vanessa was a nice girl.

Vanessa seemed to like Ben and so Lizzie had a quick word with Alexandra, who rearranged the seating plan after the first course. Hugo was also looking out for his little sister and making sure her glass had something in it — and this included her water glass.

When she had a moment or two to breathe, Lizzie calculated that at the end of the evening with four glasses per person, which included the antique champagne saucers from before dinner, there were forty glasses to be washed, carefully, one at a time, rinsed and dried.

The meal flew by. Everyone loved the pâté, the boeuf bourguignon was full of flavour and the mashed potato was superb. In no time everyone was eating rich chocolate mousse with whipped cream on top out of dainty teacups, charmed by the idea of using such decorative items as dishes. The gâteau Saint-Honoré was much admired too.

'So, you actually made this?' Electra was looking at Meg as if she might be lying. 'Yourself?'

'Yes,' said Meg. 'I didn't make the puff pastry, I didn't have time for that, but I made everything else.'

'Hmm,' said Electra thoughtfully, 'you're rather good as a cook, aren't you?'

'I'm learning to be,' said Meg.

Meg had confidence Lizzie realised, when she was talking about food and cooking.

'So brave to do stew,' said Electra and turned away.

A little later, clearing the table a bit to make room for coffee cups, Lizzie was putting glasses on a tray when Hugo joined her. 'What a lovely evening. I do hope you've enjoyed yourself.'

'I should be saying that to you. You're the guest,

you're the one who should be enjoying yourself.' She smiled and carried the full tray to one of the side tables. She was going to ask one of the professional waiters to carry it downstairs. She couldn't bear the thought of dropping dozens of antique crystal glasses, showering the stairs with lethal shards.

'No,' said Hugo. 'It's very important that the hostesses enjoy themselves too, otherwise it's just a lot of hard work for nothing.'

Lizzie looked at him briefly before gathering more glasses. 'I have enjoyed myself actually. Everyone's been very co-operative — on the whole.' Electra had lit a cigarette while people were still eating pudding, but lots of people did in London, she realised.

'And now they're waiting for you to go through to the drawing room,' said Hugo.

'Oh no! I must go and make coffee!'

Hugo shook his head. 'That's in hand. I promise you. Come and join your guests.'

As she allowed herself to be ushered into the drawing room, Lizzie realised that Hugo could probably tell she was a bit shy and was happiest when doing something practical.

'So who's making coffee?' Lizzie asked, as Hugo was still by her side, although there was a free chair next to Electra, across the room.

'Meg, of course, but also the Italian chap who has so charmed the ladies. How do you know him?'

As Electra seemed to have been more than a bit charmed, Lizzie wondered if Hugo minded, although he didn't seem to now. 'He's a friend of Meg's. She does waitressing work. Luigi is a head waiter but the restaurant he works for is being redecorated so he's been working for the same catering firm as Meg does,

134

while he has nothing else to do.'

'Vanessa seems to be having a nice time which is great. She's been quite miserable since that dreadful man left her, I gather from my mother.'

'I'm really glad too.' Lizzie focused on a buttonhole in Hugo's jacket for a few moments and then looked up. 'I was a bit scared of Vanessa when I first met her but she's really nice when you get to know her.'

Hugo nodded. 'She's not as sophisticated as she likes to appear. Which, from an older brother's perspective, is a good thing. Ted was very bad news for her.'

Philip, Alexandra's childhood friend, came over with a plate of chocolate mints. When Hugo and Lizzie had both taken one, Lizzie said, 'Did you manage to find a flat? Or are you still living with your parents?'

'No, I managed to find one in Queen's Gate. I gave up trying to find somewhere a bit cheaper. It's nice. It has a little balcony. Electra likes it.'

Lizzie didn't think she could ask if he and Electra would live in it after they were married but she wanted to know.

'Does Electra live nearby?' she said instead.

'Not too far. Knightsbridge. She has a part-time job in a very swish office in Sloane Street.'

Lizzie smiled weakly. 'How nice.'

'Yes. She organises wedding lists for people. She makes sure they don't get too many fondue sets or ramekin dishes. Apparently that can be a problem.'

Lizzie didn't know how to respond to this.

'I know!' Hugo went on. 'Who'd have thought that having a wedding could be so fraught with potential problems?'

Lizzie wanted to smile but felt she shouldn't really. 'I wouldn't have thought Electra needed to have a job.'

135

'She doesn't need to have one,' Hugo explained. 'But she likes to have something to do in between shopping trips and social engagements. She does a bit of modelling, part-time, too, and raises a lot of money for charity. She's very committed to her charity work.'

'She is very beautiful,' said Lizzie. 'I can perfectly understand why she models.' She didn't think she could comment on Electra's charitable feelings. They weren't evident in the way her beauty was.

Hugo was looking down at Lizzie in a thoughtful way and she got the impression he was about to ask her what her career plans were. As she didn't have any she cleared her throat to stop him.

'I know you said someone was organising coffee,' she said quickly, 'but I should go and see what's happened to it.'

'It's here,' said Hugo, indicating Ben and Luigi, both holding trays.

Electra came up to collect a cup of coffee. Although she really wanted to move away from her, Lizzie felt it would look rude.

'Have you worn the dress I sewed the buttons on for you?' she asked, making conversation.

Electra made a sorry face. 'No. I didn't think the buttons worked in the end. I cut them all off. They're in the button box now.' She smiled as if Lizzie's interest in the buttons was rather quaint. 'It took me ages! You'd sewn them on so well!'

'Weren't they antique?' Lizzie was appalled. She turned to Hugo.

'Yup.' He didn't reproach his girlfriend for wanting something so badly and then, the moment she had it, losing interest.

'Maybe I should sell them back to your antique-dealer friend,' Electra suggested. 'Is he here?'

A whole chasm of potential disasters opened up in front of Lizzie's feet. She didn't want people to know there was a man in the house and she didn't want anyone to suspect he was in any way different. And she certainly didn't want to have to explain his presence. It had been bad enough when her parents dropped her off at the house and found him there. She decided to step aside.

'Excuse me,' she said, with a sociable smile her mother would have been proud of. 'I must go and make sure everyone's got enough coffee.'

'If you could just top me up first,' said Electra, 'and then, Hugo,' she put her hand on his shirtfront and looked up at him, 'I'd really like to go soon? I'm quite tired.'

Lizzie stepped back. Who'd have thought that worrying about ramekin dishes and fondue sets could be so exhausting? Or maybe Electra had been meandering down a catwalk, pouting and trailing her coat on the floor behind her.

'I don't want to leave just yet,' Lizzie heard Hugo say. 'Nessa is enjoying herself and she's had a rotten time lately.'

'Darling! We've all had unsuitable boyfriends. She needs to forget him.'

At least Hugo could never be described as unsuitable, Lizzie thought as she moved away.

'Has everyone got coffee here?' Lizzie asked the first group of people she came to, who included Vanessa.

'Yes, thank you,' said Vanessa. 'Tell me, does Electra want to go already? I'm having such a nice time, I really don't want to leave yet.'

137

'I think maybe she does,' said Lizzie.

'Oh dear!' said Vanessa.

'Could you take a taxi home, perhaps?' suggested Lizzie.

'I'd be happy to escort you,' said Ben, who had been invited to be Lizzie's partner, but who, it seemed, really fancied Vanessa.

'There we are then,' said Lizzie. 'You don't have to go home just because Electra wants to. Now, is there anyone without coffee?'

As she wandered among the guests checking on coffee cups, she wished she could have chatted to Hugo properly. They'd got on so easily when he'd taken her out for dinner after her disastrous evening in the Earl of Sandwich. Now, surrounded by others, and Electra there to pounce, like a silk-wearing snake, she found she didn't know how to talk to him.

'I think you forgot to bring my top-up,' said Electra from behind her, making Lizzie jump.

'It looks as if we've run out of coffee,' said Lizzie firmly. 'I'm so sorry. If you're desperate, I'll go down and make some more.'

'That would be nice,' said Electra and walked off.

Her parting smile was charming, full of good manners but underlying it was something steely that made Lizzie want to rush to the kitchen and do her wishes. She resisted for a few moments but Electra didn't seem to notice she didn't rush off immediately to do her bidding.

Electra came back a few minutes later while Hugo and Vanessa were talking. She put her arm on Hugo's and looked up at him. 'I promised to call in on Daddy for a nightcap. Is that OK with you?'

Lizzie turned away. What did Hugo see in Electra?

She was lovely to look at, would probably be a perfect hostess and was exactly the sort of wife that could help a man in his career. But was that enough? She sighed. Apparently it was.

Lizzie had stopped worrying about coffee and had been persuaded to sit down for a bit with a group on or around a sofa. Lizzie squashed herself in next to Meg and Luigi.

'That was a fab meal you produced, Meggie,' said Lizzie.

'The chocolate mousse was so scrummy,' said Vanessa, who was sitting on the arm of the sofa, swinging her leg and drinking a glass of wine.

'I'll give you the recipe if you like,' said Meg. 'It's very simple.'

'It is simple,' said Lizzie, 'but what's easy for Meg is often awfully difficult for the rest of us.'

'Glass of wine, Lizzie?' asked Ben, who had pulled up a chair to be near Vanessa.

'It has been a super party,' said Vanessa. 'And it's not over yet.'

'We have got some records,' said Lizzie, wondering if they were the right records. 'We could put them on and dance.'

'I haven't the energy to dance,' said Meg. 'But don't let me stop the rest of you.'

'I really prefer live music to records,' said Ben.

'Do you know that pub?' said Vanessa. 'The Earl of Sandwich? They always have live music there.' Then she appeared to remember something. 'Oh, sorry, Lizzie. I let you down that night, didn't I? Ted changed his mind at the last minute.'

'I don't want to hear any more about this Ted, Vanessa,' said Ben firmly. 'He was obviously NSIT — '

'Not Safe in Taxis?' Vanessa hooted with laughter. 'He certainly wasn't. Not safe anywhere, frankly.'

Hugo came up. 'I'm going to take Electra back now, Ness, but I'll come back and pick you up.'

'No need, Hughie!' said Vanessa. 'Ben said he'd take me home.'

'In a taxi,' said Ben. He got up. 'I don't know if we were properly introduced. Ben Saunders. I'm at the Royal Academy of Music.' He held out his hand.

Hugo took the hand. 'All right, if that's OK with you, Ness?'

'Fine with me. More than fine,' said Vanessa.

Lizzie realised that she and Meg should get up and say goodbye to their guests.

'Don't get up!' said Hugo firmly as Meg and Lizzie began to struggle upright. 'Thank you so much for having us. We've had a wonderful time. The food was superb,' he said to Meg. 'You could go into business.'

'I fully intend to,' said Meg, smiling. 'But not just at this minute.'

As she watched Hugo stride away Lizzie noticed that his hair was a little bit longer than it had been when she first met him.

'Good that Hugo trusts you to get me home safely, Ben,' said Vanessa. 'Electra is quite demanding.'

'Have they known each other long?' Lizzie was delighted to have a chance to find out more about this relationship. She hoped she didn't sound as bitchy as she felt.

'Ages. He's mad about her,' said Vanessa.

Lizzie's mood plummeted. Why wouldn't he be mad about Electra? 'Do you get on well with her?' she asked, trying to give the impression she wanted Vanessa to say how lovely Electra was when you got to know her.

Vanessa shrugged. 'I don't know her well, but if she asks me to be a bridesmaid at least I know she has good dress sense.'

Lizzie now felt as if someone had punched her in the stomach, although she knew it was ridiculous. She'd always known that Hugo and Electra were a couple, if not yet a married one.

'Are they engaged?' asked Meg.

Vanessa shook her head. 'Not yet. I think Hugo is having a ring made. The family are expecting it to be announced any minute.' She laughed. 'Electra will have the best organised wedding list on record! That's one of the many things she and my big bro have in common: organisation. And ambition. Hugo wants to be a high court judge like our father and grandfather and, incidentally, Electra's father. So she knows the ropes and will be the perfect wife for him.'

'Does anyone want to dance?' said Lizzie, not wanting to hear any more about how well suited Hugo and Electra were. She thought about the collection they had hastily acquired for the evening, which included an LP contributed by Luigi that proved to have a lot of sweeping strings and passionate, incomprehensible lyrics. Lizzie had left all her records at her parental home, as had Meg. Alexandra's taste seemed influenced by a French nanny she had once, and so all she could come up with was Françoise Hardy and Johnny Hallyday. Still, thought Lizzie, just because people didn't understand the words, it didn't mean you couldn't dance to it.

'I prefer a band to dance to,' said Vanessa.

'Oh, so do I,' said Ben. 'But then I would. I'm a musician.'

'What do you play, Ben?' asked Vanessa. 'I'd love to hear you.'

Ben got up and took her hand. 'Violin and piano.'

Vanessa gestured to the grand piano pushed as far as possible into the corner of the drawing room, beyond the opened-up double doors. 'Go on then!'

Ben laughed. 'I couldn't get near the keyboard unless I climbed over the top; besides, I don't suppose it's been played or tuned for years. But I do know where there's another one!' he said, and, before Lizzie or Meg could react, took Vanessa's hand and led her from the room.

'Is that all right?' Lizzie asked Alexandra when she joined them a few seconds later. 'Will David mind?'

'He's not precious about the piano. He'll be glad to have a sing song. Not so happy if Ben wants to dive into something deep and meaningful from the classical canon,' said Alexandra. She laughed gently. 'The piano would die of shock if Ben tried to play a Tchaikovsky concerto on it.'

'Let's see what's going on down there,' said someone and people began to drift downstairs until it was just Alexandra, Lizzie and Meg left.

'We cleaned and tidied every inch of this house,' said Alexandra. 'And everyone ends up in the kitchen.'

'It happens at all the best parties,' said Meg. 'Not easy for staff, but we haven't got staff so we don't care!'

'Let's go and join them,' said Lizzie, who'd been dying to. She was in the mood to sing something sad and sentimental and found herself humming 'Can't help loving that man of mine' as she went down the stairs.

★ ★ ★

An hour later, Vanessa was at the piano, singing while Ben played. People were draped over the furniture sipping wine or drinking tea while others sang along to Ben's music. Even Clover was happy, being stroked by whoever was available for adoration duty. Lizzie was helping Luigi polish the glasses. He had lost his voice singing 'O Sole Mio' at full volume. As Lizzie's throat was also a bit sore she decided to help him rather than feel guilty about a guest working so hard.

She heard a tap on the area door. Wondering who on earth it could be, seeing as everyone who used that door was at home, she opened the door.

It was Hugo. 'Oh, hello!' she said. 'Have you come to pick up Vanessa?'

Ben stopped playing and everyone looked at Hugo.

'Hughie!' said Vanessa. 'I said Ben is going to take me home.'

'I haven't come to take you home, Ness,' he said. 'I just came back to make sure you weren't all having too much fun.'

Only Lizzie laughed. Being near to him she could see the twinkle disturbing his usually serious expression.

'We're having absolutely no fun at all,' said Lizzie. 'Come in and see for yourself.'

He made his way to the piano and put his hand on his sister's shoulder. 'This takes me back to that holiday when we were kids. The parents were lent a house in Scotland. It had no electricity so Uncle James played the piano and we sang. We just had oil lamps. We used to get through the entire Scottish Students Song Book every night.'

'That was a great holiday, wasn't it?' said Vanessa.

Looking at them Lizzie could see that Hugo and

Vanessa were really very fond of each other. She sighed. Having Hugo for a brother would be the next best thing to having him as a boyfriend.

12

'I can't believe it's our last day,' said Lizzie, as she, Meg and Alexandra walked to the cookery school in Pimlico. 'So much has happened.'

'I'm so glad you two aren't going back to the comfortable lives you had before we met,' said Alexandra. 'Now you're living in a house which crumbles a bit more each day.'

'I think we all do that,' said Meg. 'And I promise you, my life wasn't that comfortable after William died and we had to kidnap Clover!'

'Did I know you'd kidnapped her?' asked Lizzie. 'Did you demand a ransom?'

Meg gave Lizzie a shove. 'We just told William's relations that Clover was ours, or they'd have had her put down.'

'I remember now,' said Lizzie. 'Will we have a test, do you think? At Mme Wilson's?'

'No,' said Meg. 'We can all make meringues, a good béchamel, pastry and crème patissière. As well as all sorts of other things. I think that's all Mme Wilson could hope to teach us on such a short course.'

'Not to mention dressmaking and flower arranging and French conversation,' said Lizzie.

'It has been fun!' said Alexandra. 'I only went on this course because my guardians insisted but I'm really glad I did. I've learnt it's really good to have girlfriends. David is wonderful, of course, but you do need women friends too, I think.'

'Definitely,' agreed Lizzie. 'I was just thinking I'd

have liked a brother — or a sister. Having you two is probably better!'

'What made you think about that, Lizzie?' asked Alexandra.

Lizzie hesitated, not sure if she felt private about her feelings. 'It was seeing Vanessa and Hugo at our dinner party last night. I envied the way he looked after her, making sure she was safe and happy.'

'I don't think all brothers are like that,' said Alexandra. 'Some are horrors!'

'Although being an only child is a lot of responsibility,' said Meg. 'Especially if your mother is a widow. Being with you two means I can forget about that most of the time. Although my mother is fine at the moment, in her new job, doing well.'

'Sorry, I've forgotten,' said Alexandra. 'Where is her job?'

'She's an assistant matron at a boys' school,' said Meg. 'She says she loves it, although she misses Clover, of course.'

'We're here now,' said Lizzie as they arrived on the street where Mme Wilson had her premises. 'Oh, look, there's Vanessa. She's waving. She looks excited.'

'I can't believe I felt shy of her when I saw her on the first day,' said Meg, still being thoughtful. 'She's really normal and nice when you get to know her better.'

'Most people are OK when you get to know them,' said Alexandra. 'With a few exceptions we don't need to talk about now.'

'Hi, girls!' said Vanessa when they were within earshot. 'Our last day and we've survived! I never thought I'd make meringues that Madame didn't curl her lip at.'

'Nor me!' said Lizzie.

'I'm glad I've got you three alone. I want to invite you to a party at our house in the country. It would be for the whole weekend, obviously. I can't invite everyone on the course to stay as there'll be aunts coming so bedrooms will run out quickly, which is why I'm asking you first.'

'How lovely!' said Lizzie. Then doubt hit her. Hugo was bound to be there and seeing him wouldn't help her get over her crush on him. And Electra's presence — she was bound to be there too — would make it very painful. 'But I'm not sure I can come,' she added.

'You don't know when it is yet!' said Vanessa. 'Don't be a spoilsport. Hugo would be really disappointed if you couldn't come.'

'Would he?' asked Lizzie. 'Why?'

'Because he thinks you're a nice friend for me,' Vanessa went on. 'In fact he thinks you're all nice friends.'

'I think it sounds a lot of fun,' said Alexandra. 'Thank you so much for asking us. I'm sure we can come.'

'Yes, thank you,' said Meg.

'It looks as if we're all accepting your kind invitation,' said Lizzie; then she smiled, pleased to be almost forced into doing something that would bring her close to Hugo. She had tried to be sensible but had been overruled by her friends and social requirements. Her mother would be utterly delighted to think she'd been invited to stay somewhere grand.

'We'd better go in,' said Meg. 'It's nine o'clock.'

★ ★ ★

Mme Wilson got everyone making canapés and when they were done, she produced champagne and everyone toasted each other. Lizzie realised you could tell those who drank champagne fairly often and those for whom it was a rare treat. She was definitely in the 'rare treat' camp.

Meg was given a set of Elizabeth David cookery books as a prize for being the best student. Mme Wilson thanked everyone for being good pupils and told them to tell their friends about her course.

'I only want people who have been personally recommended,' she said. 'My course is very exclusive, for the daughters of the aristocracy and gentry only.'

Meg and Lizzie exchanged glances. 'She slipped up when she let us in!' Meg whispered.

'Not at all! Star pupil!'

After they had been dismissed by Mme Wilson, most of the students went to the pub. When they came out an hour later, everyone was a little tipsy.

'We should have had lunch before we went to the pub,' said Alexandra. 'I know, let's go to Maria and Franco's!'

There was a little gaggle of them in the end, all welcomed and served with good filling Italian food and coffee. Lizzie, Alexandra and Meg were the last to leave and when they finally headed for home and Clover, they had bags full of Italian pastries for David and ham scraps for the dog. A cab home seemed essential!

* * *

The official invitation to Vanessa's party in the country arrived a few days later and Lizzie instantly felt she must get her hair trimmed.

'I'll have to pay for it this time,' she said to Meg and Alexandra as they ate breakfast together in the kitchen. 'But thanks to you, Meg, getting me in as a waitress at that big do at the last minute, I've got a bit of extra money so I can afford it.'

'We'll have to think about clothes,' said Alexandra.

'Right!' Meg agreed. 'We're not turning up at Vanessa's looking like poor relations.'

'Or poor fellow students Vanessa met on her cooking course,' Alexandra agreed.

'Let's look at the invitation again,' said Lizzie. 'We're asked to arrive at teatime on the Friday.'

'So we'll need something to wear for dinner that night,' said Alexandra.

'And clothes for the following day. Then it's the party on Saturday night,' said Lizzie.

'Fancy dress would be easier in some ways,' said Alexandra. 'Think of those trunks of clothes I've got in the attic.'

'Tea gowns, morning gowns, things like that?' asked Lizzie. 'I see your point. In those days you knew what was expected. But I'm sure it's just evening clothes we need to worry about. We can just wear slacks and jumpers during the day, surely.'

'As long as we have shoes we can go for walks in, we'll be fine,' said Alexandra. 'In my experience, weekends in the country always involve walks.'

'I must check David's going to be around for Clover,' said Meg.

'You could probably bring her,' said Alexandra, 'but she might have to stay in kennels or in the kitchen at

149

night. Would she be all right doing that?'

'I doubt it,' said Meg. 'She's got so used to sleeping on people's beds.'

'I'm sure we could smuggle her upstairs if we had to,' said Lizzie.

'I'd rather leave her here with David if possible,' said Meg.

'He'll be up soon,' said Alexandra. 'I think he went to see a friend in a play last night, which explains why he was so late home.'

'Did you hear him come in, then?' Meg asked.

Alexandra nodded.

'Is it all right for me to use the phone?' Lizzie asked. 'I might give Gina a ring and see if she'd like to see me. I feel a bit guilty that I haven't seen more of her since I've been in London.'

'She did throw you out on your ear,' said Alexandra. 'Not that I mind about that at all! Her loss was our gain.'

★   ★   ★

A few days later Lizzie was sitting in Gina's sitting room, her hair newly trimmed. In a bag at her feet was a good haul of remnants from the fabric department of Peter Jones.

'No need to ask how life is treating you, Lizzie,' said Gina, handing her a glass of sherry. 'You look wonderful! Are you in love?'

Lizzie nearly choked. 'Ah — no! What makes you say that?'

'The stars in your eyes, darling. Are you sure there's no one?'

Lizzie took a large sip of sherry and felt she might

150

as well confide in Gina. While her housemates knew some of how she felt it wasn't a good idea for them to know quite how badly she was smitten. She had her pride and they were already far too keen to try and matchmake between her and Hugo.

'Well, there is someone I really like but he's spoken for. And there's no earthly chance anything is going to change. He's practically engaged to this perfectly beautiful girl who does modelling.' Her rueful smile was intended to make it clear there was nothing to be done about it.

'Oh, a model!' said Gina, refusing to pick up the signal. 'That means she's all skin and bone and flat as a pancake in front.'

Lizzie considered this. 'Well, she is pretty thin, but she wears lovely clothes.'

'I bet you're prettier, and you have a bosom.'

Gina obviously didn't understand. 'Clothes look better if you don't have a bosom and Electra has long hair which she wears up or down. Either way it's always perfect.' A sigh escaped her. 'And she makes me feel childish and immature with my short hair and miniskirts.' But it wasn't only that. It was as if Electra knew how Lizzie felt about Hugo and thought it was ridiculous and pathetic.

'Skin and bone and behind the times,' said Gina.

Lizzie laughed, determined to change the subject this time. 'Have you got any news, Gina?'

'Not really. Life goes on pretty much the same. Enjoyable enough. I want to hear about you! How did you convince your parents to let you stay in London now your course is finished? I'd have thought they'd have been parading you round the social whirl of all of what Surrey has to offer in the way of clubs, dinner

151

dances, garden parties and the like.'

'Well, I was helped in that they drove me back one Sunday after I'd been home for the weekend. They saw the house where I'm living and were impressed.' Her parents had never commented on David changing from plumber to butler. It was possible they were convinced by his 'family retainer' performance.

'Also I was able to convince them that if I got jobs waitressing for this catering company my friend works for, I'd meet eligible men.' She shrugged. 'All my mother wants for me is to have a nice wedding in the country. A lovely marquee, pretty bridesmaids, the dress of her choosing and of course a bridegroom who'll keep me in the manner to which I'm accustomed. Dead boring!'

'So you're not so keen on the wedding idea?'

'Absolutely not! I mean, I'm sure if I had a lovely man I wanted to get married to, I'd love it. But as that's out of the question for the time being, I certainly don't want to think about it.'

'Good for you! Being single and independent is very underrated in my opinion.'

Lizzie acknowledged this accolade. 'But on the other hand, my mother is absolutely delighted that we've all been invited to a party at a country house. It's for the whole weekend. That's partly why I was so keen to have my hair trimmed and get some material. We may need new dresses.'

Gina leaned forward. 'Tell me all about it!'

Gina made all the right comments and was reassuring when it came to the right clothes. 'The upper classes very often have no dress sense at all. As long as you wear different clothes, they probably won't notice what you're actually wearing. As long as you don't frighten the horses.'

Lizzie giggled. 'My mother seems more worried about me impressing the servants, and says I must leave a little something in my room for the maid.'

Gina nodded. 'You probably should do that. It reminds me of when I went to stay in Ireland once when I was in my teens. All my evening dresses were rather low-cut. When I went up to change for dinner I found someone — the maid presumably — had sewn net backs and fronts into my frocks.'

Lizzie was amazed. 'Golly, Gina, did you put up with that?'

Gina nodded. 'I didn't really have a choice although I'd have been happier if the inserts had been made of winceyette, frankly. The house was absolutely freezing. All grand houses are the same temperature, winter or summer, and it's always a lot colder than you'd want. Make sure you take warm clothes with you.'

'Twin set and pearls?'

Gina nodded. 'Horribly outdated, I know, but maybe best for the first tea. You've been invited for tea?'

Lizzie nodded. 'Will it be OK to wear slacks in the morning?'

'I should imagine so. But take a sensible skirt in case. By the time you've had tea, dinner and breakfast you'll know. Do take sturdy shoes. There'll be walks.'

'That's what Alexandra said.'

'It sounds like you're in good hands with her to advise you. More sherry?'

Gina held the decanter encouragingly over Lizzie's glass but she shook her head. 'No thank you. I should be getting back. But it has been really lovely to see you.'

153

'And you! And don't forget, I'm here if you need advice or help or anything you can't talk to your mother about.'

Lizzie bit her lip. 'Which is almost anything!'

'She's overprotective but you're her only chick, and she doesn't have much else in her life.'

Lizzie knew that Gina and her mother had never really got on and appreciated her understanding. 'I know. And I do appreciate all they do for me — have done for me — but I need to grow up a bit!'

At the door when they'd said their goodbyes, Gina put a banknote into Lizzie's hand. 'Be a proper Chelsea girl. Take a taxi home. You'll get one as soon as you get into the King's Road.'

Lizzie kissed her aunt. 'How very kind. I'd love that!'

13

David had very kindly offered to drive the girls down to Vanessa's house in the country in time for tea on Friday. Although they set off in good time, they got lost several times when trying to find the house.

But at last they saw it. It was on a small rise and the river circled the park that surrounded it.

'Good Lord!' said David. 'That is gorgeous! Queen Anne, I reckon. Probably the wings are a bit later. But a really lovely country house.' He sighed. 'I hope you girls appreciate where you'll be staying.'

'I'm sure we can smuggle you in, David,' said Alexandra. 'They'd never notice you, I'm sure.'

'Ha ha,' said David without humour.

Lizzie's mouth went dry. Hugo's parents lived in a stately home. How could she even have a crush on someone who came from a house like this?

She was now worried about what would happen should a butler or footman appear to open the car doors for them. David's old Citroën wasn't exactly smart. But in fact no one seemed to notice their appearance at all and they had to bang the lion's head knocker on the front door.

'Are we horribly late or early?' Lizzie said. 'And do we look all right?' She had worked hard to look appropriately dressed. She wore a pinafore dress over a white polo-necked jumper (remembering the house was likely to be cold). Using the fabric she'd cut out to make the deep scoop neckline, she'd made a little triangular headscarf and little handbag. What had seemed so clever when she'd been making it now seemed far too 'matching' and she felt as though she was modelling a paper pattern or a fashion tip from a magazine.

'We all look lovely,' said Alexandra, who, as always, was understatedly stylish. Her handbag dated from before the war but was so elegant she might have bought it in Bond Street that week.

'I wish there'd been a time on the invitation,' said Meg. 'But I expect we're late. It's half past four, after all.'

'We've arrived now,' said Alexandra, 'and they're very lucky to have three such beautiful young women to grace their establishment. Ah, someone's coming.'

Lizzie had been beginning to hope no one would come and they could just tiptoe down the drive, carrying their cases, and tell Vanessa they'd had an accident on the way there. What had started out as a jolly invitation to a party had become something full of social anxiety.

'Miss Alexandra Haig and party,' said Alexandra.

'You are expected,' said the butler with a bow.

Much to Lizzie's relief, Vanessa appeared. 'You're here. Thank goodness. Would you mind just washing your hands or whatever you want to do before coming into tea? We've started and Mummy's quite hot on punctuality.' She seemed flustered.

'We got a bit lost,' said Lizzie. 'We're so sorry.'

'Oh. Didn't you take a taxi from the station?' asked Vanessa, leading the way to a downstairs cloakroom.

'David drove us down,' said Meg.

'Just leave your bags here. Someone will take them up to your rooms.' Vanessa paused. 'Actually, you're sharing. Will that be all right?'

'Of course,' said Lizzie.

'I'll wait while you get ready,' said Vanessa.

When they emerged, as smartened up as was possible given the basic nature of the downstairs cloakroom, Vanessa looked at Lizzie with a worried expression.

'Gosh, your dress is a bit short. Stay out of sight of my father. He'll make a sarky comment. He doesn't approve of any modern fashions. Aren't you worried your stocking tops will show?'

'No!' said Lizzie. 'I'm wearing tights!' They'd seemed awfully expensive and she really hoped she didn't ladder them. A run in one leg meant that both legs were ruined.

'Oh well, at least it means you won't give Uncle Bertie an unexpected thrill by showing the tops of your thighs.' Vanessa gave Lizzie's hair a frown and then said, 'Come on. The house is heaving with relations, I'm afraid.'

Her heart in her kitten-heeled slingbacks, Lizzie followed the others. Her dress was shorter than she'd have liked it but the remnant she'd bought had been rather narrow. She'd thought about putting a border on it but had got distracted.

The huge drawing room seemed to be full of sofas and armchairs surrounded by little tables. On the little tables were cake stands, teapots, side plates and cups and saucers. Uniformed maids were hovering round passing things. It was like something out of a film, thought Lizzie. Only it felt horribly real. Why had they come? No party could be worth going through all this first.

'I'll just introduce you to Mummy and Daddy,' said Vanessa. 'Don't worry if they seem a bit — formal. It's just their way.'

157

Lizzie tucked herself behind the others and held her bag in front of her knees, hoping it would make her skirt look longer. If she'd known she would have carried her scarf, too, instead of leaving it with her case.

'Mummy? Daddy? Can I introduce my friends from Mme Wilson's to you?'

Vanessa's parents seemed to be an off-putting combination of bewildered and cross. 'Oh yes,' said Vanessa's mother. 'The last-minute guests.'

'This is Alexandra . . . ' Vanessa introduced each one of them and they all nodded in turn. Vanessa's parents' smiles were icy and their interest in their daughter's friends only fleeting.

Alexandra had warned Meg and Lizzie that Hugo and Vanessa's father was a baronet and so should be addressed as Sir Jasper. His wife, therefore, was Lady Lennox-Stanley, but they didn't get a chance to speak. Vanessa whisked them away as quickly as she could and took them to where there was an old leather pouffe and a couple of spindly dining chairs with arms.

As they walked away (Lizzie was slightly surprised they weren't expected to walk backwards), Lizzie heard Sir Jasper say, 'That girl seems to have forgotten to put on a skirt. I do hope she'll be decently dressed for dinner.'

'Let's get you a cup of tea and something to eat,' said Vanessa. 'Dinner will be at eight and unless you had an enormous lunch you'll be starving by then.' She stopped a passing maid who was carrying a plate with some curling sandwiches and a couple of slices of cake.

Lizzie sat on one of the upright chairs. Even wearing tights, she didn't want to risk her dress riding up another fraction.

'Most of these people aren't staying,' said Vanessa, gesturing to the room. 'But quite a lot of people are, I'm afraid.'

'Does that matter?' asked Meg.

'Yes! Although Electra said she'd help Mrs P. — she's our housekeeper — sort out bedrooms, she forgot to tell Mrs P. that you were coming.'

'Do you need us to go home?' asked Lizzie. She was hoping against hope that Vanessa might say yes.

'No!' Vanessa laughed. 'Don't be silly. We've got plenty of room it's just . . . ' She paused. 'Why don't you take the sandwiches and I'll show you your rooms? Don't let Mummy see you.'

When they were in the hall, Alexandra said, 'Has something gone wrong, Vanessa?'

'Yes and no! Come up and I'll tell you.'

Vanessa couldn't actually wait to tell them and so shot bits of information over her shoulder as they climbed the stairs. 'I asked Mummy if I could have a little party here. I thought they were going to be at the races and we'd have the place to ourselves.'

They were on the first floor now. A galleried landing ran in several directions but, rather to Lizzie's surprise, Vanessa headed for another set of stairs.

'Then Electra decided she wanted to have a party — I think Hugo is planning to propose — and Mummy instantly invited every aunt and uncle. It was no longer going to be something small and fun, and Mummy had completely forgotten I'd invited you first.'

There was no doubt about it, they were heading for the servants' quarters now. At least they weren't lugging their cases. There'd been no question of packing light. They all needed dance dresses, morning clothes, afternoon clothes and probably (Meg had muttered) elevenses clothes. Lizzie had dithered more than the other two and felt she'd packed for a month.

Vanessa stopped at a door and opened it. 'I've given up my bedroom to Electra — Mummy asked if I would. So I'm in my old nursery.'

They followed Vanessa into a large room with a long row of windows. You'd know it was a nursery without being told, Lizzie thought.

There was a rocking horse in front of the window, a doll's house on a table in the corner and a child-sized table and chairs next to it.

There were some small mismatched armchairs drawn up in front of a fireplace with a gas fire in it. Round it was a metal fireguard, just like the one Lizzie had had as a child. Shelves, still holding some toys and children's books, filled a wall. The single bed with a small bedside cabinet next to it looked a bit lost in the space.

'This is lovely!' said Alexandra. 'You could make this really nice.'

Vanessa nodded. 'There're bedrooms through there.' She pointed to the doors in the corner. 'My nanny used to sleep in one, and there's a bathroom next to it. This would make a fab sitting room. I did suggest to Mummy that I had a little flat up here but she looked at me as if I'd suggested a family outing to the moon.' She smiled and shrugged. 'I pick my battles. I'm usually on the first floor and I have a lovely room, which is why Electra's got it now.'

'So where are we sleeping? We could all have fitted in here,' said Meg.

'I did suggest that,' said Vanessa, 'and got a lecture

160

about giving the staff extra work moving beds when they've got so much to do anyway. You're in here.'

Vanessa opened the doors to two small bedrooms. One had two beds in it, the other, one. 'The single room was for the nursery maid. I'm so sorry and embarrassed that you have to sleep here. I think Mummy thought I'd uninvite you once I knew you'd been put here. But you're my friends! And why should Electra take over my party? Which she jolly nearly has!'

Lizzie stepped into the narrow room with two beds in it, tucked under the eaves. A thin rug, thin curtains: it felt like a servant's bedroom. There was a tiny fireplace which probably hadn't seen a fire in years. It had a simple charm but was a bit Spartan. But: 'Oh, look! Flowers!' said Lizzie as her eye suddenly caught a little posy on the small chest of drawers between the beds.

'Well, yes. I thought they made the room look a bit more welcoming. I had to do flowers for all the other bedrooms — took hours — but as you're the people I actually invited to stay, I thought you should have flowers too.'

'I think we're going to be quite happy in here,' said Meg. 'Don't worry.'

Alexandra nodded in agreement. 'We'll be fine here.'

'I do hope so!' said Vanessa. 'I had such a nice time at your dinner party. It really cheered me up after Ted — well, you know — after Ted. Anyway, Ben's coming tonight. He's staying with friends locally.'

'Ben?' said Meg. 'That's nice.'

'Tonight?' said Lizzie. 'I thought the dance was tomorrow?'

'I'll explain,' said Vanessa. 'Let's go through to the

161

nursery. Come to think of it, I brought bread and butter up for breakfast. We could make toast now.'

'Ooh, can we have cocoa?' said Alexandra. 'Like they did in all those school stories I used to love but not at my actual boarding school!'

'We can. We could have breakfast here. Proper breakfast isn't until nine and ladies are supposed to have trays in their rooms.' Vanessa giggled. 'But Mummy said I couldn't possibly ask for trays to be brought up here. So I asked Mrs Crannock — she's the cook — if we can have breakfast in the kitchen. She doesn't mind.'

Lizzie felt very confused. There seemed to be so many rules which didn't make sense. 'So, if we're in the servants' quarters,' she asked, 'where do all those maids who were serving tea downstairs live?'

'In the village,' said Vanessa. 'Far more comfort-able!'

14

Vanessa ushered them back into the nursery after Lizzie had extracted a cardigan from her case.

'It's lovely up here,' said Alexandra, looking out of the window. 'You can see everything.'

'You can. It's quite private, which is why I like sleeping here.' Vanessa opened a cupboard and brought out a bottle of wine. 'Shall we drink this?'

'Shouldn't we be changing for dinner or something?' asked Lizzie, who was keen to get out of her too-short dress and her paper-pattern matching bag. Apart from anything else, she was cold in spite of the cardigan.

'Don't worry,' said Vanessa, producing tooth mugs for the wine, 'there'll be a bell. We'll hear it.'

'A bell?' said Meg.

Vanessa poured out the wine. 'To tell us when it's time to dress.'

'Good Lord,' said Lizzie. 'Who'd have thought. A dressing bell!'

When everyone had taken a sip of warm white wine, Alexandra said, 'So, what's the plan?'

'Let me start from the beginning,' said Vanessa, who obviously felt her story needed everyone's proper attention. 'And thank you so much for coming. Electra is driving me round the bend.'

'How?' asked Lizzie, delighted to have the chance to share catty remarks about her least favourite person.

'She's just taken over! Honestly! Instead of just

having friends — people our age for a dance — it's become a huge formal ball thing.'

'A ball?' asked Meg, worried. 'I have got a long dress but it's hardly a ball gown.'

'It's a lovely dress,' said Lizzie, who'd had a lot to do with adding a flounce to one of Gina's castoffs so that it reached the ground.

'I'm sure your dresses are fine,' said Vanessa. 'At least for tonight.'

'Two parties?' asked Alexandra.

Vanessa nodded. 'Honestly, it was the only way to do it. Otherwise it would have been dire.'

'Why?' asked Meg. 'It's not that I don't believe you, I just want details.'

'Apart from the fact that tomorrow's bash is going to be the most formal event that doesn't actually have royalty at it, you mean?' Vanessa went on. 'That's not really the problem. It's the music.'

'Oh?' said Alexandra. 'They've hired a band, have they? I think I know the kind. They're fine with fox-trots and waltzes but anything more up to date they play sounds really strange.'

Vanessa nodded. 'The same one they always have. They wear white DJs, will take requests and there's only five of them so that's not too many to feed.' Now Vanessa was getting indignant. 'Can you believe it? Electra wondered if they had to be fed and yet they're expected to play from about eight o'clock till four in the morning.'

'Golly.' Lizzie wondered if she'd have the stamina for dancing all night.

'People will waltz to old dance numbers from the war, and then, worst of all, someone will ask for a Beatles number and they'll play it — and they are not the Beatles — and the old people will try and do the twist and give themselves slipped discs.' Vanessa stopped for breath.

'It sounds hilarious!' said Meg.

'I think it sounds quite . . . romantic,' said Lizzie. 'I can just imagine people waltzing round the room in their lovely dresses, jewels sparkling.'

'Yeah, it is sort of sweet,' Vanessa agreed. 'But it is so far from what I had in mind when I asked Mummy if I could have a party for my friends.'

'And this is Electra's fault?' asked Lizzie.

Vanessa nodded. 'But good old Hugo has saved the day!'

'How?' asked Lizzie.

'He's arranged for us, and the rest of the younger crowd, to have a party tonight! After dinner, obviously, but it'll be brilliant fun. He's bought lots of records. The Beatles, the Beach Boys, all sorts — '

'Won't the noise annoy the grown-ups?' asked Meg.

'And won't it make an awful lot of work for the servants? Having parties on consecutive nights?' Lizzie was now obsessed with the well-being of people about whom she'd only previously read in books.

'Hugo had a brilliant idea — we're going to have it in the barn!'

'A barn dance?' asked Alexandra. 'Like in *Seven Brides for Seven Brothers*? I love that film!'

'Oh, so do I!' said Lizzie.

Vanessa frowned a little at their enthusiasm. 'It'll be a normal party but in the barn, which is empty. There are bales of hay to sit on. And no band, just records. Hugo has bought so many! I think he felt guilty about Electra taking over. And of course he's got his old rock and roll records out from his room.'

165

'I love rock and roll,' said Lizzie.

'Come on,' said Vanessa. 'Let's finish the bottle. The bell will go at any moment. Daddy will expect everyone to wear long for dinner but you can change into whatever you like afterwards. The party in the barn doesn't start until nine.'

As Lizzie got ready for dinner, in her discreet, long velvet dress, which no one could possibly object to, she thought of the dress she'd wear afterwards. It was one of the few dresses she'd brought from home: the last dress her mother had bought for her from the local department store that she had actually liked. It was primrose yellow with tiny little white dots on it. It had a full skirt and a boat neck and ended on her knee — perfect for jiving in!

Dinner was as about as tortuous as it could be, Lizzie thought, given that the food was quite nice and she was seated fairly near Hugo.

It started off badly when she heard herself referred to by Sir Jasper as the girl who was wearing the non-existent skirt. Electra, to whom the remark was addressed, giggled and said, 'She does lack in sartorial taste although she is rather a clever little needle-woman.'

'Do we invite our seamstresses to stay for the week-end these days?' Sir Jasper went on. 'It seems we do.'

The meal was made worse by the man on one side of Lizzie talking about nothing except hunting, a subject which was of no interest to Lizzie at all. But although she thought it was cruel, she didn't have the nerve to say so.

The man on the other side said, 'Aren't you cold having such short hair?'

Lizzie said, 'Aren't you? Mine is probably a bit

166

longer than yours is.'

'But I'm a man, I'm used to it,' he said.

Lizzie was annoyed with herself for swallowing all the hunting talk and had drunk quite a lot of wine by now, given what they'd had in the attic and the sherry they'd been given before dinner. 'Well,' she said, 'I'm a woman, and I'm used to it too!'

The man stared at her. 'What a very rum thing to say! Never heard such nonsense!' He turned away from her to talk to his neighbour although Lizzie knew (Vanessa had told her) that he was supposed to talk to her until they'd finished eating their chicken chasseur. All this made it doubly annoying when he put his hand on her knee. She jerked it away with all the vigour she could manage, given the lack of space under the table.

* * *

'Just a minute!' said Lizzie, seemingly hours later but in fact a mere thirty minutes. She was scrubbing her little brush over the block of mascara she had just moistened. 'I want to put on a little bit more.'

Dinner had been awful but the one good thing had been the men all being keen to get the women to leave the table so they could get on with the port and the smutty stories. While the older women had gone to the drawing room, Vanessa had asked her mother if it was all right for her and her friends not to join them. Given the snatches of conversation overheard by Lizzie, Vanessa's mother had been delighted.

'Actually,' Lizzie said, 'you go down. I'll find you.'

'We're in the barn — you'll find that all right?' said Vanessa. 'I'd wait but people will be turning up. I

167

should be there to greet them.'

'We could wait with you,' said Meg.

'No, you go down. I want to dither about changing my dress,' said Lizzie. 'I'll do that better if I haven't got you all looking at me!'

'OK,' said Vanessa, obviously keen to get away. 'We'll go down and if you're not with us in fifteen minutes, we'll send out a search party.'

Lizzie hadn't wanted comments from her friends when she got out her dress. It felt old fashioned now of course — her mother had chosen it! — but she was definitely going to wear it. It was sleeveless, which would be cool if she got hot dancing, its full skirts had underskirts which swished delightfully, and she knew she looked nice in yellow.

As Lizzie made her way down the stairs she realised that had she arrived for tea wearing that, instead of the short, sharp, fashionable dress she had worn, Vanessa's parents wouldn't now have her down as a bit tarty.

She let herself out of the house by a side door, walked down a short passage that Vanessa had told her about and found herself in a gravelled area, the main house behind her and a collection of outbuildings ahead and to the right.

To the left she could see glimpses of a beautiful garden, with lawns and large trees. There was obviously a ha-ha in the lawn because there were fields and then there was the river. It caught the sun and glinted like a strip of silver. In the distance beyond the river Lizzie could just see a church tower.

She walked across the gravel towards the barn thinking that Vanessa's parents weren't nice enough to own such a beautiful house in such a glorious setting.

But on the other hand, Hugo was, and presumably he would inherit it all one day. She could easily imagine Electra arranging flowers for the large drawing room and having career-enhancing dinner parties in the dining room. Electra could probably imagine all that too, Lizzie thought ruefully.

She could hear music coming from the barn and saw that plenty of people had arrived already. No wonder Vanessa had been keen to get there after dinner.

As she got closer, she realised the music was rock and roll and Lizzie hurried over. But when she got to the barn, although it was full of people all standing round the dance floor with glasses in their hands, no one was really dancing. There were a few people jigging from foot to foot on the edges but so far the middle of the big barn was empty.

Someone had gone to a lot of trouble to make the barn attractive. There were coloured light bulbs strung across one wall. There was a bar made out of barrels and planks of wood and bales of hay surrounded the dance floor for people to sit on. People were clapping to the rhythm, obviously enjoying the music. Why was there no one on the floor? It was such a waste, Lizzie thought.

She went inside and stood at the back of the crowd, looking for her friends. She'd just spotted them over the other side, when someone said her name.

'Hey! Lizzie!' It was Hugo. The last time she'd seen him he'd been wearing a dinner jacket. Now he was in jeans and a dark shirt, open at the neck. 'Come and dance with me!'

'OK,' Lizzie said casually. Inside she was fizzing like a firework.

He led her into the middle of the barn and they waited a couple of beats and then they started.

Lizzie loved to jive and was good at it. Hugo was good at it too. He spun her round, sent her under his arm and out again, their feet going in perfect time to the music. And as they danced others joined them.

The other dancers made Lizzie even braver and she and Hugo did some more extreme moves when he lifted her in his arms and swung her around. She landed neatly and it encouraged him to try more.

At last the song ended and they were both panting hard. 'You're good! When did you learn to dance like that?' Hugo exclaimed.

'I could ask you the same question! But I'll go first. My mother sent me to ballroom-dancing classes and afterwards the teacher added rock-and-roll or jive classes for those who were interested. I always stayed for them. I loved it.'

'That explains it. But you know some pretty nifty moves.'

'So do you!'

'What would you like to drink? Beer, cider or squash?'

'Cider please,' said Lizzie. She was still short of breath and knew it was because she was so close to Hugo and not just because they'd been dancing.

Hugo seemed a lot calmer. He got them both drinks and they headed for a vacant hay bale.

'I learnt at boarding school,' he said. 'Sometimes we were allowed to go to dances with the local girls' school and one of the teachers thought we should be encouraged not to slow-dance with the girls. They got in someone to teach us to jive, or rock and roll, whatever you call it.'

'My parents weren't keen on my learning how to do that,' said Lizzie.

'My parents don't even know.'

'Can Electra jive?' asked Lizzie.

Hugo looked apologetic. 'Not really her sort of thing. She waltzes beautifully though.'

Before Lizzie could comment, Electra herself appeared. 'There you are, Hugo!' she said irritably. 'I've been looking for you everywhere. What on earth are you doing here when you should be in the house?'

'I was just making sure Vanessa's party got off to a good start,' he said calmly.

'Which didn't need to include making a fool of yourself on the dance floor!' said Electra. 'Anyone would think you were a Teddy Boy, dancing like that. Now come on!'

'Say hello to Lizzie first, Electra,' he said, in the same calm way.

'Hello, Lizzie,' said Electra, 'although as we've already spoken this evening, it hardly seems necessary. Now, your mother is looking for you, Hugo, so come on.'

Lizzie had no shortage of dance partners but only Hugo had wanted to jive. But she was a good dancer generally and enjoyed herself. She quite often managed not to think about what was going on in the house.

The party was winding up and Lizzie was thinking of asking her friends if they were going to bed soon when she heard the cousin who was in charge of the records put on 'Rock Around the Clock'. The next minute, Hugo was in front of her, in his dinner jacket again, but with his bow tie hanging undone.

'Come on. This is for us!' he said, and pulled her

on to the floor.

This time they were completely confident with each other, knew each other's moves and when they were planning something a bit complicated. Everyone gathered to watch them. Vanessa whooped and people clapped.

She had just been set back on her feet after being swung around in his firm and confident grasp when she spotted Electra. She looked as if she'd swallowed a scorpion.

Electra stalked across to the record player and lifted the needle, ignoring the complaints from the audience who had been enjoying themselves.

'Hugo, this is ridiculous. Come on! Your father is expecting you in the library. And as for you!' Her attention felt like a lash across Lizzie's face. 'You need to learn that it's not the done thing to go around making sheep's eyes at other people's men!'

She pulled Hugo away and they left.

Meg and Alexandra were at her side in a moment. 'What a cow!' said Alexandra, furious. 'How dare she? You were only dancing!'

'Are you OK?' said Meg. 'You and Hugo were amazing!'

'Thank you,' said Lizzie.

A boy came over. 'Hey! You're a terrific dancer. Can I have a go?'

Lizzie smiled and shook her head. 'I'm worn out now. I think I'll go back to the house.'

'I'll come with you,' said Meg.

Lizzie wanted to be alone. She had a lot to think about. 'No need for that! You stay until the end.' Seeing Meg hesitate she put her hand on hers. 'Honestly, I'd like a few minutes on my own. To clear my head.'

172

The evening air was cooling and, to give herself longer in it, Lizzie walked round to the front door rather than slipping in at the side. The door was ajar when she arrived and she had just pushed it further open when she heard angry voices. She realised that Hugo and Electra were having words at the foot of the stairs she needed to go up. And a second more told her the subject of their heated conversation. It was she.

'I don't know what's got into you, Hughie!' said Electra, sounding like an angry nanny. 'Making a fool of yourself with that girl!'

'You know perfectly well she's called Lizzie. You've been to a dinner party at her house, in case you've forgotten.' While Hugo was obviously annoyed, he was calm.

'Don't be ridiculous. It wasn't her house. She's just a lodger. God knows why Vanessa insisted on inviting her here tonight! If I'd known she was coming I'd have stopped it!'

'Electra, when I last looked, you didn't have the right to say who could or could not be invited to this house.'

'Oh, for goodness' sake! I get on brilliantly with your mother!'

'That's hardly the point.'

'No, the point is, I am not at all happy with you being so ridiculous with that girl, in public! It reflects on me, you know.'

'I danced with Lizzie twice. You don't like jiving. She's very good at it.'

'That's your excuse for picking her up and flinging her all over the place, is it? She's *good at it*?'

'Look, I'm sorry if me dancing with another girl

173

has offended you. It isn't usually a problem. We've been to lots of balls together and we've always danced with other people.'

'Other people on the same table. That's quite different!' snapped Electra.

'It's not really different. Lizzie is a guest in my parents' house. It's my duty to see that she enjoys herself.'

'Well, she very obviously did that! And so did you! Jiving, for God's sake!'

'Not many people can jive so well these days. I was having fun. It's hardly a crime.'

'It's not very polite when you know I can't do it.'

'It's not hard. I could have taught you if you'd let me.'

'I wouldn't waste my time!'

'That's your choice. Occasionally having a jive at a party is mine.'

'At least I don't spend it dancing with other men.'

'Are you accusing me of being unfaithful? Because I danced twice with another woman?' Hugo asked quietly.

Electra laughed. 'I'm certainly not doing that! Not with that little nobody.'

Lizzie didn't wait to hear more. She went out of the door and back to the dance as quickly as she could. She met Alexandra and Meg coming out of the door.

'Oh, I thought you'd gone in,' said Meg.

'I got a bit — er lost,' said Lizzie, relieved to see them. 'Let's go upstairs together.'

15

Lizzie was extremely relieved she wasn't obliged to have breakfast in the dining room the next morning, with Lady Lennox-Stanley and Electra. The kitchen option, with the cook, Mrs Cannock, was much more fun.

The four girls all sat up one end of the kitchen table. Vanessa was obviously a great favourite with the cook.

'If you girls don't mind serving yourselves,' said Mrs Cannock, whom Vanessa called 'Canny'. She was busy with scrambling eggs for the dining room. 'I've done you some sausages, as requested, Miss Nessa, and I've got some fried bread going if you fancy that.'

'Canny's breakfasts are guaranteed to cure a hangover, if you've got one,' said Vanessa, holding a spitting frying pan and sliding sausages on to plates. 'I don't know why greasy food helps, but it does.'

Lizzie didn't have a hangover in the alcoholic sense. But she still felt dreadful after the previous evening and what she'd overheard. She ate a sausage slowly and refused fried bread.

It was all she could do not to leap to her feet when Lady Lennox-Stanley and Electra came in. Fortunately, they were both very preoccupied.

'There you are, Vanessa! I hope you're not getting in Mrs Cannock's way,' said her mother, obviously for form's sake, not because she greatly cared if her cook was inconvenienced. 'We have an emergency.'

'Yes,' Electra went on. 'The florist I booked for tonight has let me down and we'll need you to do the

175

flowers. No one else has time. The party has to be perfect for our announcement.'

'We can help Vanessa with the flowers, Lady Lennox-Stanley,' said Alexandra. 'Lizzie is really good at them.'

Lady Lennox-Stanley frowned at Lizzie and then smiled at Alexandra. She could obviously smell aristocratic blood, thought Lizzie, and didn't like to waste smiles on common people.

'I'll help if I possibly can,' said Electra. 'They need to be first rate. A lot of important people are coming, and these details are important. Now I'd better check about *The Times* . . .'

Lady Lennox-Stanley and Electra swept out of the kitchen again, like a pair of dogs, working as a team.

'I'm not awfully good at flowers,' said Vanessa. 'And I promised I'd tidy the barn.'

'I'll do them,' said Lizzie. 'If you give me the things, and maybe the flowers. Will your mother have bought flowers?'

Vanessa shook her head. 'Not if she was expecting a florist to just bring arrangements.'

'You want to take Lizzie to see Mr Dudley,' said Mrs Cannock. 'He's the head gardener. Here . . . ' She handed a tureen of scrambled egg to a waiting maid. 'Take the towel; the dish is red hot. It's the only chance of getting it to the dining room in an edible condition.'

Relieved of her egg-scrambling duties, and apparently also other breakfast making, Mrs Cannock pulled out a chair at the head of the table. 'Vince — Mr Dudley — his father was head gardener here too. He used to arrange all the flowers. He kept on doing it long after the lady of the house had taken over that duty in most big houses.'

'I just stick flowers in vases when I do flowers,' said

Vanessa, 'but I know Electra will want something better for tonight.'

'The flowers you did for our room were lovely,' said Alexandra.

'What's Electra's big announcement?' Lizzie had to steal herself to ask this.

'Oh, the engagement! Electra and Hugo,' Vanessa said.

'Hmm,' said Mrs Cannock. 'I can't say I'm sorry I'll be retired before that one takes over as lady of the manor here. Lady Lennox-Stanley has her ways . . . but that one?' Mrs Cannock shook her head as if words were inadequate to express how she felt.

★　★　★

Lizzie was really glad to have a task to keep her occupied. During the night, while trying to get to sleep, she had wondered how she could somehow leave. But although she spent what felt like hours trying, she couldn't think of anything that didn't involve a very elaborate set of lies. Leaving early would cause problems and embarrassment for the others, too. It was supposed to be Vanessa's party, even though Electra had taken it over. Lizzie would just keep out of the way of Vanessa's parents and Hugo and Electra as much as she could.

★　★　★

'Mr Dudley, this is Lizzie,' said Vanessa, a little while later. 'She's doing the flowers for the ballroom and anywhere else that needs flowers. My sister-in-law-to-be had booked a florist but they've let her down. So we have to do them.'

177

Mr Dudley nodded. 'It would have always been done in house in my father's day. He used to do them.'

'I know. Mrs Crannock told us.' Vanessa smiled. 'Would you mind helping Lizzie find things? Lend her secateurs and tell her what she can pick? Would it be a lot of trouble for you? I'm clearing out the barn and it would be better if you did it.'

'I would hate to pick the wrong things,' Lizzie said. 'The garden is so beautiful. It would be awful if I spoilt it.'

'Bless you, my dear! You wouldn't spoil it! But come with me and I'll show you where you'll find the best blooms. You'll need buckets of water, and tarpaulins when you go into the house. There used to be a flower room but it's used for storage now. I've got the bits and pieces in a shed. There's chicken wire, and those heavy plates with pins sticking up. They're good for the smaller arrangements.'

'Do you like arranging flowers?' asked Lizzie. 'I don't want to do it if you'd rather do it instead.'

'No, no. I never had my father's eye for flowers, not once they've stopped growing. Now, let's find you something to put the flowers in.'

Mr Dudley found tarpaulins and spread them under the two huge vases that were to be filled with flowers for the ballroom. Then he found buckets, gave her secateurs and some stronger loppers for thicker stems and took her on a rapid tour of the garden. Then he set her loose.

★ ★ ★

Lizzie had become entirely absorbed in her task. Never had she had such wonderful material to work

178

with. When she did church flowers with her mother and usually a couple of other women of the parish, she was always restricted by what people had in their gardens, plus some carnations or chrysanthemums, depending on the season. While in theory her restrictions here were the same, she had vast borders, a rose garden, shrubby areas and a small arboretum to pick from. She was in a flower-arranger's heaven. And if she didn't have enough of a flower or type of foliage, she could have more. Even more useful, she didn't have anyone pursing their lips and tutting if she did anything a bit different.

Mr Dudley kept a close eye on her. He carried the picked flowers to the ballroom for her and found extra buckets from deep in the potting shed for more. The most helpful task was when he explained to Sir Jasper what she was doing when he came rushing out into the garden having spotted Lizzie hacking at some variegated pittosporum (such a good backdrop to the flowers) from an upstairs window. She had kept her head turned well away, grateful for the capacious apron she was wearing which added to her disguise.

Vanessa brought her sandwiches at lunchtime in the ballroom. Lizzie had been aware of getting hungry but didn't know what she was expected to do for lunch and was terrified of intruding somewhere she wouldn't be welcome.

'Oh my goodness, those flowers are so beautiful! You could definitely be a professional florist if you wanted to be!' said Vanessa, putting down a plate and a mug of tea.

'Not if I'd be paid by the hour,' said Lizzie, taking a sip of tea. 'It's taken me so long.'

'But you didn't know where anything was. Those

179

flowers are so unusual but lovely. You've used so many different kinds of foliage. We never learnt how to do that at Mme Wilson's!' Vanessa was walking round, looking at the large arrangement from every angle.

'To be fair to Mme Wilson, she didn't have an acre of wonderful garden to acquire her foliage from. And I learnt how to be resourceful from doing church flowers with my mother,' said Lizzie. 'We just had to use what people had brought with them and I often used to have to rush out into the churchyard and get more material from there.'

Lizzie had been thinking fondly of her mother as she'd selected different flowers or sprigs of leaves. She had so wanted to get away from home but now she was in exactly the sort of house her mother wanted her to visit, she realised she much preferred her own smaller and simpler home. For although (being fair-minded) she was sure that not all people who lived in grand houses were raging snobs, Sir Jasper and Lady Lennox-Stanley definitely were.

Electra came in to check on proceedings, possibly hearing Lizzie and Vanessa chatting. She looked like the perfect society fiancée, as seen in *Country Life* or *Tatler*. Her hair, nearly shoulder-length, was back-combed so it had height and was held back from her face by a black velvet headband. It curled evenly all the way round the bottom in a Jackie Kennedy flip. She had on a knee-length gaberdine dress in pale yellow, a matching cardigan and an Hermès scarf tied round her neck, somehow not interfering with the string of pearls that matched those in her ears. Her shoes were patent leather and had low, square heels.

Lizzie immediately felt scruffy in her apron and slacks. At least her hair was too short to get in a mess.

'Oh, haven't you finished the flowers yet?' said Electra. 'You've been at it for hours! We still need flowers for the drawing room. I thought you were good at this?'

'Electra!' Vanessa couldn't contain her indignation. 'Lizzie is doing this to get you out of a spot! You could at least be polite!'

'Oh, sorry. Yes, you are only an amateur so I suppose you're not doing a bad job.'

Electra's grudging praise made Lizzie feel even worse. She started gathering some of the detritus and putting it in an empty bucket.

Lady Lennox-Stanley came in. 'Oh, Electra, dear! Those are lovely!'

'Not quite finished yet.' Electra laughed prettily. 'I'd love to ask your advice about flowers in the drawing room . . . ' Electra drew the older woman out of the room with the skill of a magician.

'Did you see that?' Vanessa was puffing with indignation. 'She let Mummy think she'd done the flowers!'

'Well, thank goodness I've already done them in the drawing room.' Lizzie was pleased that Vanessa had noticed Electra's duplicity.

'If the flowers are anything like this, they'll be wonderful!' Vanessa was firm. 'Now have a break. Eat your sandwiches and drink your tea. I wasn't quite sure what drink to bring you but Meg and Alexandra thought you'd like tea. They've been brilliant at helping me clear up the barn. We've made it so we can escape there tonight if Electra's ball gets too dire.'

Lizzie didn't want to think about Electra's ball and changed the subject. 'I love tea and the sandwiches are amazing. Cheese and tomato. You can't beat it, can you?'

'They're a bit door-steppy I'm afraid. Canny would have had a fit if she'd seen me do them. She was supervising the caterers.'

Lizzie looked at Vanessa, seeing a kind girl who liked to enjoy herself and wanted everyone to be happy. She knew that if Vanessa hadn't thought of it, no one in the house would have cared if she had starved. 'Nessa, can you tell me what the plans are for the afternoon?'

'Well, it's nearly teatime now,' said Vanessa.

'I won't be finished — '

'Dinner will be before the ball, obviously. I think that's at eight — or may be seven — I'll have to check with Mummy.'

Lizzie felt she could not bear to suffer another dinner like the one the previous night. 'I think I'll need to make sure all the flower arrangements are fresh and that nothing's gone flop and that the chicken wire isn't showing. Would it be awful if I didn't come to dinner?'

'No, no, that would be fine.' Vanessa said this without needing to think. Lizzie wondered if there'd been a conversation with her mother on this very subject. Lizzie suspected that Lady Lennox-Stanley would be delighted not to have Lizzie at her dinner table.

'I'd like to have a bath, get the soil out of my fingernails,' Lizzie went on. 'If I skip dinner I'll be ready for the ball.'

'Well, you'll have to come to that to hear Electra's big announcement.'

Something about the way Vanessa said this made Lizzie ask, 'Are you happy about Electra and Hugo getting engaged — married?'

'Oh yes. They're terribly well suited and have been

together forever.' The words came out very pat but without a lot of conviction.

'But . . . ' Lizzie really wanted to hear Vanessa's misgivings. She knew it was childish and probably a bit catty but couldn't help herself.

Vanessa sighed. 'She's not a lot of fun, Electra, is she? I mean, you've seen her. She looks like a dream, does everything perfectly — '

'Except organise florists.'

'But you wouldn't find yourself drinking warm white wine with her in the attic, would you? I bet she went all through school without going to a single midnight feast.' Vanessa obviously felt this said it all.

'Hugo is quite grown up like that too, though, isn't he?' Except when he jived and forgot he was training to be a barrister.

Vanessa sighed. 'He used to be great fun but Electra's made him much more serious. But everyone says they are perfect for each other — so I suppose they must be!'

'Let's hope they're very happy then,' said Lizzie, her jaw rigid with the effort of getting the words out.

'Oh, I don't suppose they'll be happy in the jumping-up-and-down, skipping-round-the-room way,' said Vanessa, 'but they will be very successful and both sets of parents will feel they'd done a brilliant job.'

This flash of cynicism was unlike Vanessa and Lizzie was about to ask her about it when Vanessa looked at her watch. 'Is that the time? I must drag Alexandra and Meg out of the barn and make them change for dinner.'

'And I'd better get on and finish. Electra is right. I've been doing these for hours!'

The clearing up seemed to take as long as the

arranging, but at last Lizzie had tipped the final dust-pan-load of leaves and petals, stalks and bits of stick into the bucket. The ballroom looked perfect.

She allowed herself a last look before leaving. Sisters, but not twins, the two arrangements, in identical vases, stood on tables at opposite ends of the room. A yard wide at the base, every sprig of green enhanced every bloom. Tall bearded irises were ranged at the back, interspersed with white foxgloves and pale camassias that looked like huge bluebells. Sprays of lilac in white, purple and palest pink added fragrance and white peonies gave the arrangement added abundance. One of the church-flower ladies had told Lizzie that a butterfly should be able to flutter through an arrangement. She had said she was quoting someone else and Lizzie thought it was good advice.

Just as she was leaving Hugo came into the room. 'Good Lord, those really are stunning,' he said.

'Electra told your mother that she'd done them,' said Lizzie, hating herself for being so petty.

'Well, I know she couldn't have. She has allergies. Thank you so much, Lizzie. It was so kind of you to do them.'

'My pleasure,' she said, her throat suddenly clogged with tears.

She didn't move until he'd left to go to the drawing room for tea. She didn't dare, certain that movement would cause the gathering tears to fall. She picked up the two buckets that were left and had to wipe her face and her nose on her arm as she walked.

She got to the bottom of the long staircase and went to the side door to let herself out. It was locked. Now her tears were threatening to turn into sobs and she went quickly to the front door, desperate to escape.

Just as she arrived, Sir Jasper shot out of a room — perhaps the library? — nearly bumping into her. He looked at her with horror, and then took in the buckets, the apron and the fact he'd already shouted at her for cutting his shrubs.

'Oh, you're the florist! For a moment I got you confused with one of those ghastly young women Vanessa inflicted on us. I'll open the door for you.'

The next moment she was free, walking down the shallow steps to the gravel drive.

She found her way back to the potting shed. Mr Dudley had gone but left the key in the door so Lizzie went in. She put down the buckets and hung the apron on the back of the door. Then she found the hook for the secateurs.

For a while she inhaled the musty, particular smell of the shed. It was very different from the heady fragrance of the flowers in the ballroom but it was comforting. Now she was supposed to go back to the house, walk up many flights of stairs to the nursery for a bath. Would there be hot water? She doubted it. The more she thought about it the less appealing the thought of getting ready for a ball was. But she couldn't stay in this shed and hide all night.

The garden was lovely and although now she was crying freely, she still appreciated its beauty. In fact, the beauty made her cry more: for herself, certainly, but also for Hugo. He was going to marry a woman who could help him in his career, would bring up his children properly, stand by his side, beautiful, useful but possibly demanding. But would Electra love him as she did?

While she thought she walked until she found herself at the ha-ha, looking over it to the water meadows, and beyond them, the river.

Mr Dudley had told her that the river often flooded and thinking of this made Lizzie want to go and look at it. Running water would be soothing, she thought. She wasn't going to the ball. She wasn't going to hear the announcement of Electra and Hugo's engagement. Knowing there was going to be one was quite painful enough. And while the entire party would think that Electra had arranged the flowers, she and Hugo (as well as her friends) would know that, in fact, Lizzie had done them. That was good enough.

Without quite knowing how she did it, she found her way to the fields and was soon on the riverbank. She did find the water soothing, and laughed a little, picturing herself as Ophelia, lying in the water with daisies in her hands. She walked along until she found a bench, obviously put there because it had a perfect view across the river and more meadows to where the little town sat on the horizon, visible mostly because of the church tower. Everything had a sort of golden hue, like a painting by Constable.

This weekend — and it was still only Saturday — had seemingly gone on forever. Lizzie thought back to their arrival. If only she'd worn something different! If only she hadn't been so set on being a dolly bird with her short skirt and headscarf.

Then something Vanessa said came into her mind. It was while they were apologising for being late. 'Didn't you take a taxi from the station?' Now she thought more about it she realised that meant there must be a station at the little town that looked so pretty in the distance.

A station meant a train — to London. It felt so near — within sight — but so far. How on earth would

186

she get there?

She sat there for a while, working it out. Now she'd had the idea she so wanted to carry it through. If she left now she wouldn't be a pathetic little Cinderella figure, stuck in an attic instead of a kitchen; she'd have taken charge of her own destiny and got away from a place where she was clearly not wanted.

She got up and started walking again, thinking hard as she went. At last she reached a slight bend in the river and there, tied up to the bank, was a small boat.

She hurried forward to inspect it. It had oars. It looked fine. She made her decision and turned back to the house at a run.

She knew the side door was locked and so went in through the kitchen door, which was open for the caterers. As quickly as she could, without actually knocking anyone over, she made her way through the people, out of the kitchen, through the green baize door and into the main part of the house. People were in the drawing room, gathering before dinner, and she had to wait while a couple came downstairs, cowering at the end of the passage. It seemed early for dinner to Lizzie but remembered Vanessa thought it might be at seven — earlier than usual because of the ball afterwards.

She was panting when she reached the attic but didn't stop. She went into the bedroom she was sharing and found her case. She found a jumper and tied it round her waist with its sleeves, to save carrying it. Then she put on her raincoat, got her handbag and slung it round her neck. She was ready!

Just as she was leaving she thought to write a note. She had to tear a sheet out of her diary and write with the tiny pencil.

Dear Alexandra and Meg, I'm going back to London. I'll be fine. Please don't worry about me. See you on Sunday night. Love, Lizzie. Although she was still running, she tiptoed past several open doors and back down to the kitchen. She thought she heard someone call after her but didn't stay to investigate. She was going to get out of that house and away; nothing would stop her.

16

It took Lizzie a little time to find the boat again. Also, she had no idea of train timetables so she knew she might be stuck on the station all night. It wasn't a tempting prospect but she'd got this far, she wasn't changing her mind. Also, there might easily be a train back to London. It was still relatively early, after all.

Lizzie knew she wasn't an experienced rower — the little boating lake in the park in her home town was the only place she'd ever done it — but how experienced did she have to be? The river wasn't all that wide. She just had to get in and row to the other side. Getting out might prove a bit tricky, but she'd manage. Then, using the church spire as a guide, she would walk across the fields to the town.

She had to jump into the boat from a bit of a distance as it wasn't as near the bank as it looked. Nor was there a proper jetty. But she managed to scramble on and, after trying for a while to unhitch the rope tying the boat to the post, she gave up, and untied the rope from the boat end, which was far easier.

It took her a little while to get the oars into the rowlocks — she knew she couldn't row unless she did so. It was a bit disconcerting to realise the boat had travelled downstream quite a lot while she was doing that. She hadn't noticed the river had much of a current. But at last she had the oars where they needed to be and soon she was rowing.

Because she wanted to cross the river she manoeuvred the boat so it was pointing at the opposite bank, although this only lasted a short time as the current swept her along sideways and the bow turned so she was parallel to the bank and not going towards it.

She'd been struggling to take control of the little boat for a few minutes before she began to feel frightened. This was not working out as she had imagined it. She had no idea where the boat would end up if she allowed the current to take it. She was aware that it had started raining and, worse, the boat seemed to be leaking. The wind had also got up so she was fighting that as well.

A sudden squall spun the boat round and Lizzie realised she was in real trouble. She had to get to the bank: either side of the river would do. She took hold of the oars so she could start rowing but one of the blades missed the water's surface as she pulled back and the oar bounced out of the rowlock. She leant forward to try and get it back in and then the other bounced out too. She shipped both oars and held on to the sides of the boat, wondering what to do. Surely the river would end somewhere, or there'd be a fallen tree or something to stop the boat even if she couldn't?

For about ten seconds she felt doing nothing was her best course until she became aware of how much water had gathered in the bottom of the boat. A small leak had lowered the boat in the water and it was leaking from the sides as well now.

The boat was sinking.

Lizzie couldn't decide if she should stay in her little cockleshell or if she'd do better swimming. She wasn't a strong swimmer and decided to hang on as long as she could. Surely there'd be a branch she could cling to — or something?

Seconds before the boat sank she heard her name

being called. She looked around wildly, registering the voice just as, to her great shock, she found herself completely submerged.

She kicked underwater, hard. Her shoes had come off but her handbag was still round her neck; her raincoat was dragging her down. Somehow, she got to the surface of the water long enough to take a breath before sinking again. She floundered back up, paddling with one hand and trying to unbutton her coat with the other, but her freezing fingers couldn't do anything useful.

And then, miraculously, there was a lifebuoy. She put her hand on it, and although she went under again, she managed to hang on to it. When she resurfaced, she got both hands on it.

'Well done!' said a voice she knew was Hugo's. 'Now try and put it over your head and then get one arm through it. Then I can pull you to the bank.'

It seemed to take a lifetime but at last she managed this. For a second or two she felt herself being pulled then suddenly the tension went out of the rope. She looked around and could see no one and then she realised that Hugo was in the water with her. They were both going to drown together.

The next second, Hugo was holding on to the lifebelt and shaking the water out of his eyes. 'Hang on tight. I'll tow you in.'

Lizzie realised that the bank must have given way, which was why he was swimming instead of pulling. But the current was sending them both downstream at quite a rate. She concentrated on keeping her head above water and keeping sight of Hugo.

At last they stopped for a second and she realised he had his feet on the bottom but was struggling to keep them there. He suddenly went under but Lizzie could see he was still clutching the lifebuoy and he reappeared again quite quickly.

Then Lizzie spotted a fallen tree. She opened her mouth to tell Hugo and got a mouthful of river but as they travelled towards it she waved to Hugo and he turned round. They both caught hold of branches as they sailed past, Lizzie getting a nasty scrape across her face at the same time.

Hugo was holding on to a strong branch and he had time to catch his breath a bit. 'OK,' he said. 'I'm safe here. You hang on while I pull you. Now we have to get up the bank.'

It looked so near and yet it felt as if they'd never reach it. They both had their feet on the ground but the ground was mud and was full of roots which caught their feet. But eventually, slipping and sliding, they managed to get up on to the riverbank.

They lay there, coughing and spluttering, trying to get their breath back.

'I never thought we'd make it to land,' Lizzie gasped eventually, her teeth chattering so hard she could barely speak.

'It did seem a bit of a struggle, but we made it.' Hugo shifted so his body was lying as close to hers as he could make it. 'You're so cold. We must get you somewhere dry and warm.' His teeth were chattering too but not as badly as Lizzie's.

She could feel warmth coming from him but she didn't know if this feeling was real or just an illusion. She felt she'd been in a nightmare and the only good part was that Hugo was there. Lizzie realised she had no idea where they'd ended up and she wondered if she'd lost her mind and that soon she'd wake up and be in bed. She closed her eyes and tried to imagine heat and comfort but she couldn't.

'Come on,' said Hugo. He pulled at her and suddenly she was off the ground and in his arms.

She put her arm round his neck. 'You're wearing a dinner jacket.'

'Yes.'

He staggered with her a little further, up the slope until the ground grew more level. Then he set her on her feet but kept her close.

'Where are we?' she asked.

'We're quite a way from the house but there's a boathouse not far. Can you walk?'

'Of course,' said Lizzie.

He kept her clamped to his side but she felt she could hardly move along. Her limbs felt like lead and her feet slipped.

'Come on, you've got no shoes on and we need to get you out of the rain.' He picked her up again.

Lizzie kept her eyes closed but opened them when he said, 'OK, change of position.' He set her down and then picked her up once more so she was over his shoulder. She shut her eyes again quickly as she realised he was carrying her up a flight of wooden steps.

'Please God, let the key be in its place . . . It is. Thank the Lord for that,' she heard him muttering.

He set Lizzie back on her feet and opened the door. 'It's not a palace but at least it's not raining in here,' he said.

A strong smell of mustiness hit them as they went in and it felt warm. It was dark but Lizzie could see they were in a triangular space, like the top section of a tent.

'Welcome to the boathouse,' said Hugo. 'My father

isn't boat-minded so this place has always been a sort of den to Vanessa and me. I think he's forgotten it exists. Now, let's find you somewhere to sit.'

It was like an attic, full of strange things hanging from hooks in the ceiling. There were oars, fishing rods, oil lamps, a saw, and many things Lizzie couldn't identify. The only light came in through dusty windows and she felt in a state of shock.

He guided her to a wicker chair that creaked loudly as she sat in it.

A thought occurred to her. 'You should be at the ball.'

'No, I shouldn't,' he said firmly. 'I should be here, looking after you.'

No longer worried about drowning, she began to wonder how Hugo had found her in the river. But she didn't want to ask just yet.

As her eyes became accustomed to the lack of light Lizzie saw random bits of furniture and a bundle of something that could be sails in the corner. There was a solid old table with a toolbox on top of it. There was something draped with a cloth next to the box. This old boathouse might have been forgotten by Hugo's parents, but someone still came here.

'I'm hoping there are some blankets in here,' said Hugo, opening a large wicker laundry basket. 'Vanessa's Girl Guide troop camped here once, years ago, and left bits and pieces behind. It all got dumped in here.'

He pulled out a couple of blankets. 'Now all we need is a box of matches.'

'I think that would be pushing our good luck too far,' said Lizzie as he wrapped a very smelly blanket round her shoulders and put another on her knees.

'I don't think so.' He went over to the table in the corner and reached up to a shelf made under the eaves. 'Here we are. They've been here a while but it's dry here. They should be all right.'

'What do you want matches for?' However much she craved warmth, surely there wouldn't be a stove or anything here?

'This.' He went to another corner of the boathouse and found a hook with an oil lamp hanging from it. 'I think it's still got oil in it.' He shook it.

He found a tea chest which had obviously been used as a table before and set the lamp on it and lit it. The light instantly made the space feel warm and cosy.

'You're still shivering,' he said. 'Maybe you'd better get your wet things off.'

'You're wearing a dinner jacket,' she reminded him. 'And you're shivering too.'

He turned back to the wicker basket and produced a sleeping bag. 'If you took off your wet things you could get into this. Lie on one of the blankets and put the other on top.'

'What's in that pile over there?' She pointed, reluctant to undress in front of him. 'Isn't there a sail or something we could lie on?'

'That's a good idea. I'll have to chase the spiders out first.'

Soon he had made a bed out of old sails, Guide blankets and a sleeping bag. 'Get in,' he said encouragingly.

'You get in first. I need you to check there aren't any spiders.'

'OK. But we won't both fit in the sleeping bag. We can have it as a mattress.'

When he was lying down she lay down next to him, suddenly wishing she had taken off her clothes. 'I'm making you wet,' she said.

'We're as wet as each other,' he said. 'Lie next to me. We'll warm each other up.

He pulled her close so she was lying with her head on his chest. She could hear his heart thumping under her ear. She wrapped her arms round him and closed her eyes. So many things were wrong and uncomfortable but at that moment she wouldn't have been anywhere else in the world.

'How did you know I was in the water?' she whispered.

'I didn't, but I'd seen you run out of the house earlier. I came to find you. I wanted see you were all right.' His voice was deep and low; she could feel it rumble as well as hear it.

'Why?' It was hardly a spoken word, more a breath.

He sighed very deeply. 'Because I care about you.'

'Oh.' She sighed deeply too and tried to get even closer to him.

'I thought I'd lost you,' he said.

'Lost me?'

'I thought you were going to drown.'

He moved so he could lean over her and kissed her.

She kissed him back, matching his passion, putting her hand on his cheek and then pulling him down. She wanted to climb inside his body, become part of him, she wanted him so much.

Soon they were struggling out of their wet clothes until at last they were skin on skin.

At one time he tried to pull away but she wouldn't let him. She felt as if this was her last moment of happiness on earth and she couldn't relinquish it.

196

17

Afterwards they lay panting on the canvas in a musty heap of blankets. Lizzie had an overwhelming desire to cry, and tears did start to leak out of the corner of her eyes as she lay there. She couldn't let Hugo see her. She didn't want him to know it was her first time. He'd be worried and upset — angry, possibly.

'Are you all right?' he asked, still short of breath.

'Mm. A bit cold. I think I'm still in a state of shock.' She didn't know if it was from nearly drowning or from making love. She had never dreamed she would do that before she was married, or at least engaged. She wasn't completely naïve, she knew it did happen, but not to girls with her background and upbringing. Thank goodness her parents would never find out.

'We need to get you back to the house, so you can have a hot bath and get warm. When did you last eat?'

'I don't want to go back to the house yet, Hugo. I can't face all the fuss people would make. But if you went back you could send Alexandra or Meg with some clothes for me? And shoes? Would they be able to find this place?'

'I think so.' He paused, looking at her. She kept very still so the light wouldn't catch her tears. 'Why don't you want to go to the house?'

'I'm too tired to walk, especially barefoot. I'd rather just rest here for a bit.'

'Presumably you left the house in the first place because you didn't want to be there, but circumstances alter cases, as they say.' She saw him smile.

'I just want some dry clothes and a bit of a rest. How are you going to explain being so wet?'

'That's my problem.' He stayed looking at her for an agonisingly long time. 'We will have to talk about this, Lizzie.'

'But not now.'

'Fair enough. Not now.'

He got to his feet and she watched him in the lamp-light, fighting his way into his wet trousers. 'I'll get some clothes to you, Lizzie. And then we will talk.'

When she was alone she allowed herself to shed the tears she'd been keeping in so firmly. Then she sniffed hard and wiped her nose on her hand.

She realised she was getting stiff and cold so she got up, to see if moving around would help.

Two things had happened to her in the past few hours and she felt they were both life-changing. She had nearly drowned — *very* nearly drowned — and she had made love, for the first time, with a man she really loved but could never have. She didn't want to regret either of them. It was something she could think about in future years when she was married to someone else — someone she felt she couldn't possibly love as much. And if it hadn't been for the first thing the second wouldn't have happened — and surely that made nearly drowning worth it.

With the blankets wrapped round her, she went over to the large table with the box. She pulled off the cloth covering the item next to the box and found another box. This one was quite different. Much smaller, for trinkets rather than tools, the lid was inlaid with wood of different colours making an intricate pattern. She picked it up and shook it gently. It seemed to be empty and so she opened it. The inside was made

198

just as carefully and the smell of some aromatic wood caught her nostrils. There was fine sawdust in the box. She closed it and put it down. Then she opened the tool chest. Inside were tools similar to the ones Hugo had bought at the Portobello Road Market, seemingly a lifetime ago. This boathouse must be where Hugo used those tools he loved, maybe not recently, but sometime.

A wave of fatigue swept over her and she went back to the nest on the floor. When she'd straightened it up and made it more comfortable, she put on her underwear. It was damp and difficult to get on but she couldn't be discovered without it. Then she sank back down and let herself sleep.

★ ★ ★

She was woken by the sound of voices. It was
Alexandra and Meg.

'We thought we'd never find you!' said Meg.

'Vanessa wanted to come with us to show us the way, but she would have been missed,' said Alexandra. 'She was very concerned about you though, and sends lots of love.'

'It's so lovely to see you both!' said Lizzie. 'Have you brought my clothes?'

'Clothes, food and wine,' said Meg, handing Lizzie a paper carrier bag. 'Here are the clothes we thought you might like for now. Vanessa has lent you some shoes. I think they were her school shoes. I hope they fit. I think her feet are a bit bigger than yours.'

Lizzie looked at the round-toed lace-ups. They would fit but they were very unattractive.

'Vanessa doesn't want them back,' said Alexandra.

'And I reckon we can see why.'

'It's very kind of her to find them for me,' said Lizzie.

'Vanessa got the picnic together, too,' said Meg.

Lizzie's underwear was more or less dry now but she was very glad to get into the jumper and pair of slacks Meg had brought. And fortunately Vanessa's old school shoes fitted well enough.

Meg unpacked the picnic and spread it out on one of the Guide blankets. Vanessa had obviously put a couple of plates of canapés into the boxes from a picnic set. Then there was a wedge of cheese and some rolls. There was butter in another box and a paper bag with tomatoes in it.

'It was really kind of Vanessa to do this when she must have been so busy,' said Lizzie, having put cheese and butter into a roll and taken a delicious bite. 'I didn't realise I'd be so hungry.'

'Well, according Hugo, you nearly drowned!' said Alexandra.

Lizzie looked at her friends, who obviously needed to know how she'd got herself into this position.

'We got your note,' said Alexandra. 'What happened? Why did you feel obliged to leave?'

'Pour the wine and I'll tell you everything,' said Lizzie, knowing there was at least one thing she'd leave out. 'But you have to tell me if it caused an uproar when Hugo came back? Presumably it was while you were all finishing dinner?'

'You go first, Lizzie,' said Alexandra. 'We've been so worried about you.'

It didn't take her long to get through what had happened while she was arranging the flowers, the overheard remarks, the snobbish behaviour, her plan to get to the nearest town. She ate while she talked and when she'd finished her story and her wine, she said, 'Your turn. Tell me everything.'

While she sounded as if she just wanted some really good gossip, in fact she wanted to know if Hugo's sudden reappearance would affect his life forever.

'But you could have drowned! Why did you get in that boat?' asked Meg, distressed.

'I didn't drown. It was awful, but it's over. Tell me about Hugo. He rescued me and it was just before his engagement party. His and Electra's.'

'Well, it was a bit awkward,' said Alexandra. 'But he handled it brilliantly, I must say.'

Meg carried on. 'He missed dinner, but came into the drawing room while everyone was having coffee later, wet through and said, 'So sorry, everyone, there's been a minor emergency,' and he laughed, in the way people do when something awful's happened and they're trying to pretend it hasn't. 'I got a bit wet. I'll just go and change and I'll be with you.'

'And then he caught my eye and gave me a look and I got out of the room as soon as I could, when everyone had stopped looking at him,' said Alexandra.

'Electra turned into the Snow Queen,' said Meg. 'Utterly beautiful but sort of frozen, as if she couldn't speak because if she did her face would fall off.'

'Golly,' said Lizzie. She took a breath and steeled herself to ask the next question. 'And did they make the announcement?'

'Not while we were there,' said Alexandra. 'Hugo told me what had happened to you, though. Vanessa had seen the look too and joined us. Then I went to get your things, Nessa did the picnic and Hugo went to change.'

'I didn't hear anything either,' said Meg as Lizzie turned to her for information. 'I followed Alexandra.'

'They might be doing it right now,' said Lizzie blankly. 'Announcing their engagement.'

No one spoke. Meg rubbed Lizzie's arm, obviously not knowing what else to do.

'Well, whatever happens,' Lizzie went on, 'I have to leave, as soon as possible.'

'David is coming to pick us up after lunch tomorrow,' said Alexandra.

'I can't wait that long. I suppose I could get a cab to the station really early tomorrow morning,' said Lizzie. 'Or maybe walk? I don't want to disturb the household.'

'But why do you feel you have to leave?' asked Meg. 'I know Sir Jasper has been vile and Electra is a statue that moves and breathes but has no heart, but Vanessa invited you. You have a right to be here.'

'I know. But I think I may have completely messed up Hugo's life — or at least his engagement plans. I don't want to witness that, and also, I know they'd all blame me for it.'

'No one need know he rescued you — ' Alexandra began.

'It would get out. Things like this are bound to,' said Lizzie.

'I agree with Lizzie,' said Meg. 'Electra will hunt out the truth like a truffle hound.'

'You're very imaginative with your analogies today, Meggie,' said Alexandra.

'She's already been horrible to Lizzie. If she sees her, she'll be on her — ' Meg began.

'Like a dog on a rabbit? Something like that?' suggested Alexandra.

'Yes!' said Lizzie. 'I can't stay!'

'OK,' said Alexandra after a few seconds' thought. 'I'll drive us back to London.'

There was a moment's shocked silence. 'Couldn't we just take a train?' said Lizzie.

'It's Sunday and it's after midnight,' Alexandra explained. 'There's a timetable pinned up in the kitchen: I looked at it and there isn't a train until late in the afternoon. And we can't ring David to come and get us because I know he's out tonight. There's no other solution.' She paused. 'I've been thinking about this. I guessed Lizzie would want to get away from here as soon as possible.'

'But how on earth are you going to drive us?' Lizzie asked. Alexandra seemed to have all the answers at the moment, she thought.

'We'll borrow a car. I'll take you home, and then drive it back. I'll get David to follow me in the Citroën. If we leave early, we'll have the car back by breakfast. No one will know.' Alexandra regarded her friends with satisfaction at having solved the problem.

'Can you drive?' asked Meg.

'Yes. I haven't actually taken a driving test but my driving's OK. And if we go really early, there won't be much traffic. Hardly any, in fact. It'll be easy.'

'Who can we borrow a car from?' asked Meg. 'I mean, we want to be discreet about this. Going round asking people we don't really know if we can borrow their car is going to draw a lot of attention to our mission.'

'And they're not going to say yes, anyway,' put in Lizzie. 'People are funny about their cars — they won't lend them. I remember suggesting to Daddy that I had driving lessons and practised on his car. He had a nasty turn and had to be given a large G and T to calm him down.'

Alexandra didn't reply immediately. She brushed the crumbs off her skirt. 'I wasn't going to ask.'

'What do you mean?' said Meg.

'I was going to borrow the car and put it back so no one would know. Like when you borrow a bit of face cream or something. Or a hairbrush — you just use it and put it back.'

'A car is a bit different,' said Lizzie. 'No one would notice a bit of face cream but they would notice if their car was missing.'

'The thing is, they won't notice,' Alexandra said. 'Why would they be looking at their cars? They're here for the weekend. They won't think about their cars until it's time to go home.'

'Unless they want to go out and get a paper or something,' Meg said.

'But they won't! All the papers — far more papers than anyone wants — will be delivered here. This plan is foolproof, I'm telling you.'

'But cars have keys! How will you get them?' Meg wasn't at all happy with Alexandra's mad idea.

'A lot of people will leave the keys in the ignition,' Alexandra explained. 'Why not? Who is going to steal their car, here?'

'Well, you, obviously,' said Lizzie, poking Alexandra.

'But they don't know that, do they?' Alexandra wasn't going to be talked out of her plan. 'And if by any chance we can't find a car with the keys in it, I'll hot-wire it.'

Meg and Lizzie looked at their friend, half impressed, half horrified. 'How did you learn to do that?' said Meg.

'A friend of David's taught me. It's a long story. It was the same friend who taught me to drive. He used to take me to Richmond Park to practise.'

'This is all so wrong.' Lizzie wailed. 'I'm a nicely brought-up girl from the Home Counties! I don't consort with people who hot-wire cars!'

'Do you want to leave this house or not?' Alexandra asked tersely. 'I'm sure you could stay in the attic, like a kidnap victim, until David collects us. It's up to you.'

'People would ask where you were,' said Meg. 'Vanessa, for instance.'

'Did I hear my name?' Vanessa came into the boathouse. She had a bottle of champagne in each hand.

'How did you get out of the house with these?' asked Alexandra, relieving her of the bottles. 'And aren't you supposed to be at the ball?'

'Practice. I've been smuggling bottles of wine up here for years. And no one will notice if I'm not at the ball. Now what's the plan?' Vanessa looked at the girls excitedly. 'Shall we get one of those bottles open and you can tell me everything?'

'I'm not sure we should,' said Lizzie. 'Alexandra has a plan and it's so awful! I mean, I think the plan would work but it involves grand larceny.' She frowned. Her brain felt too addled to be certain of what this was, exactly.

'Blimey!' said Vanessa.

'Lizzie's exaggerating,' said Alexandra. 'She wants to go back to London as soon as possible. She feels she can't stay here after all that's happened. She feels terribly unwelcome — '

'Although you've been absolutely lovely,' said Lizzie quickly, 'and Hugo — well — he saved my life.'

205

'I knew it was something like that!' said Vanessa, thrilled. 'He and Electra had a massive row — or rather she did. He just stood there, dripping on to the carpet, looking noble, while she said vile things.'

'Not in public, surely?' asked Alexandra.

'No. I just happened to be passing my — her — bedroom and the door was ajar. It took me rather a long time to pass, for some reason.' Vanessa looked mischievous.

'Are they still getting engaged, do you know? asked Meg.

Lizzie knew her friend had asked on her behalf.

'Well, no. At least there's been no announcement yet,' said Vanessa. 'Alexandra, are you opening that bottle?'

'Got it,' said Alexandra as the cork came out with a gentle phut.

Lizzie swallowed, wondering how much longer she would have to wait to hear the finer details of Hugo's engagement. It seemed to take an age before the champagne was poured.

'Does that mean there won't be one?' went on Meg, like the true friend she was.

'No. Electra won't want him to get away. She may have ripped him to shreds — not that he appeared to notice — but she won't let him slip through her fingers. He's a catch. Heir to all this . . . ' She made a gesture indicating the boathouse, which would have been funny, Lizzie thought, in different circumstances.

Vanessa took a gulp of champagne and belched delicately. 'I imagine they'll be announcing it any time now.'

'Oh,' said Lizzie.

'So, tell me about the plan!' said Vanessa, unaware

that Lizzie's heart was shrivelling like a splash of water on a hot frying pan.

'Well, as Lizzie said,' Alexandra began, 'it is probably a bit illegal, but not immoral, which I think is more important, don't you?'

Vanessa nodded. 'Go on.'

'Well —'

'It's my fault,' Lizzie interrupted. 'I nearly drowned and now all I want to do is go home.' Nearly drowning had nothing whatever to do with why she wanted to leave but while she didn't want to lie to Vanessa, she wanted to distract her from the thought that her departure might have anything to do with her brother. Or her father. Or her soon-to-be sister-in-law.

'Oh my God, this is such fun!' said Vanessa a little later, when she'd heard all the details of Alexandra's plan. 'I wish I could come back to London with you! But the sky would fall in so I can't. But I can tell you which would be a good car to steal . . .'

18

With Vanessa leading them back to the house, carrying picnic things, there was a distinctly boarding-school-jape atmosphere in the group. Lizzie did her best to smile and giggle with the others when it was the last thing she felt like doing.

The ballroom was already full of people but Vanessa took them through the servants' quarters and up the back stairs so Lizzie got to the nursery without anyone seeing she looked like a half-drowned cat dressed in old Girl Guide blankets.

Alexandra, Meg and Vanessa sat round her.

'There's no earthly reason you shouldn't come to the party,' said Vanessa, sitting on the bed where Lizzie was now huddled. 'Have a bath, get into your frock and join us! You're my guest. Daddy won't notice you.'

'I just want to get into a hot bath and sleep,' said Lizzie. 'I'm dropping with tiredness. But thank you.'

'You don't need us to stay with you?' asked Meg, her hand on Lizzie's.

'Certainly not! You go to the ball and tell me all about it later.' Lizzie paused. 'When are we leaving?'

'Five,' said Alexandra, who had obviously thought about this. 'Then we can definitely get the car back here by nine.'

'My cousin Anthony definitely won't be up before eleven at the earliest,' said Vanessa. 'He never takes his keys with him and always parks in the spot easiest to get out of. He'll be leaving on Monday morning, early, to go to the City.'

'You go and have a bath, Lizzie,' said Alexandra. 'I'll wake you tomorrow, bright and early.'

As much as Lizzie loved and appreciated her friends, she was relieved when she was finally alone. She went into the bathroom and turned on the hot tap in the bath. Suspecting it would take ages for the hot water to get to the top of the house she held her hand in the stream until the water got hot. It seemed to take forever but at last she felt confident that her bath would be hot and put in the plug.

While the bath was filling, extremely slowly, she went back into the main part of the nursery to look for some paper. She needed to write Hugo a letter.

While she and her friends had stumbled and giggled their way across the fields to the house, Lizzie had been thinking she would only be able to get over Hugo if she stopped seeing him. But Hugo, being a gentleman, and very kind, would want to get in touch with her after what had happened between them. She had to stop this.

She opened all the visible drawers in the nursery until she found what she was looking for: an old exercise book. She didn't think she could write a proper letter on tiny bits of paper from her diary. She needed space.

She had to keep stopping to check on her bath but eventually she managed to write something that sort of expressed what she wanted to say.

Dear Hugo,

I don't suppose I'll ever be able to thank you enough for saving my life. It's one of those things that is beyond thanks. But of course I am extremely grateful!!

209

It's because I am so grateful that I don't want to mess up your life for ever. I completely understand that what happened after you rescued me was just a reaction to the whole near-death experience and it shouldn't affect your future life. It would be awful if anyone found out because there would be dreadful consequences.

Because of this, I don't want you to contact me. There's no need and it could be bad for you. I want you to be happy! I promise that I'll be all right!

She really didn't know how to end it so she put: *Yours sincerely, Lizzie.*

She had to copy it out neatly but in the end she was happy with it.

She got in the bath, which wasn't quite hot enough, and washed herself until she was sure she no longer smelt of the river. Now all she had to do was work out how to get the letter to him.

As she lay in bed she had cause to be grateful that she was so tired and would fall asleep quickly. Because she knew in her heart she would have plenty of time to think about — and possibly regret — the passion that nearly dying and then being saved had brought out in her.

19

Vanessa insisted on tiptoeing out into the chilly dawn to direct the girls to her cousin's car. What she hadn't mentioned was that it was a sports car and would be a squash for the girls and have very little space for luggage. It also had its top down and so was open to the elements.

They looked at the little MG in silence. 'It's not the sort of car I'm used to,' said Alexandra. 'Could we steal something a bit more — conventional? Like that one?' She pointed to a stately Daimler.

'Uncle Robert's car? Good God no!' Vanessa went pale at the thought.

Alexandra hesitated for a bit and then exhaled. 'OK. Cars are much the same really. Aren't they?'

This was obviously a rhetorical question so no one answered.

'Where are we going to put our luggage?' asked Meg. 'It's only big enough for the three of us.'

'I'll put your bags in one of the stables,' said Vanessa. 'You can pick them up when you bring the car back. I'll try and be here. I want to find out how you managed.' Vanessa looked worried suddenly. 'You won't crash the car, will you? It's my cousin's pride and joy!'

'Of course not,' said Alexandra with dignity. 'I'm a very careful driver and there won't be much traffic.'

'Supposing we get stopped by the police?' said Meg.

'Alexandra will talk her way out of it,' said Lizzie, who was anxious to get going. 'It'll be all right, I'm sure.'

'OK,' said Meg. 'Do you mind if I go in the front, Lizzie? I get a bit car sick.'

'No, no, that's fine. I'd rather hide in the back. I'm not a natural rule-breaker.' Lizzie smiled and then turned to Vanessa. 'Can I ask you the most terrific favour?'

'Of course. What is it?'

Lizzie produced her letter, now rather crumpled. 'Can you give this to Hugo for me? It's only a letter thanking him for rescuing me. But I don't want Electra knowing about it. She'll be vile to him about it, I know. And he risked his life to save me, and it wouldn't be fair.'

Just then there was the sound of a window being opened, making Lizzie jump. 'Do you think we could go?'

'Yes, of course,' said Alexandra. 'Jump in.'

Once her passengers were installed, Alexandra made the car inch forward. 'It would be lovely to shoot off in a shower of gravel,' she said, 'but we are sneaking away. We don't want to make a noise.'

'No, we really don't,' said Lizzie. 'I don't think I've ever wanted to get away from anywhere as much in my entire life!'

Alexandra continued to go extremely slowly. Lizzie, huddled in the back, convinced they would be spotted from the house and instantly arrested, kept her eyes shut. She would open them again when they were safely out on the road.

'I know you're being careful, Alexandra,' she said when they seemed to have covered about a yard. 'And I appreciate that, but could you go a little bit faster?'

'I will in a minute,' said Alexandra. 'I've just realised how different this car is from David's Citroën.

I'm just trying to get a hang of the gears. Agh!'

There was a huge sound of metal on metal which made everyone wince. 'Sorry,' said Alexandra. 'Second gear wasn't where I was looking for it.'

As neither Lizzie nor Meg understood what she was talking about, they didn't comment. Lizzie, in the back, tried to hunch down into an even smaller shape, convinced discovery was imminent.

Lizzie kept her eyes shut, wondering if her system could cope with two near-death experiences within twenty-four hours when the car bounded forward.

'Sorry again! Kangaroo petrol!' said Alexandra, not sounding all that apologetic. 'That's what David calls it. But don't worry, I'm getting the hang of things. We'll soon be home.'

'Just off the premises would be a good start,' muttered Lizzie, careful that Alexandra didn't hear her. She knew she was being neurotic.

But at last, the crashing and bouncing ceased, they reached the end of the drive and were out on the open road. Lizzie uncurled and began to look around her. It was cold without the roof on the car, but the feeling of the wind on her face was exhilarating. It was spring, the leaves were coming out and bluebells could be seen like lakes in the woodland. Although in some ways she felt her world had ended, she still felt herself uplifted by the beauty of the morning.

Her feelings were so mixed about what had happened with Hugo, she didn't know if she felt truly awful about having made love to him or deliriously happy. It was a dreadful thing to have done. But it had made her so happy at the time. It had felt right, being in his arms, feeling his skin against her skin; it had been thrilling and comforting at the same time.

No, she refused to regret it. It would never happen again but she was happy that it had happened once. Even though the fallout might be disastrous.

'Does anyone remember if we came in from the left or the right here?' Alexandra asked, bringing the little car to a graceful halt at a junction. She'd got the hang of the mechanics now and was obviously enjoying driving a sports car.

'No, I'm afraid not,' said Meg.

'Nor me,' said Lizzie from the back.

Fortunately, Vanessa's cousin had an AA map in his car. 'Meg, can you map-read for me?' Alexandra said, having studied the map for a while.

Meg shook her head. 'Sorry. I'm OK if I look out of the window and sit in front, but if I even try and look down . . .'

'It's all right,' said Lizzie. 'I'll do it. Hand me the map.'

After that, navigating took up all Lizzie's concentration. She knew she had packed all sorts of emotions away to be examined later, but now she had to focus on tiny road numbers and signposts.

'I do hope David is in,' said Alexandra when at last they'd reached London and she was on home ground (apart from the one-way streets, which sometimes interfered). 'He was out with a friend last night and I've just realised he might have stayed the night.'

'I hope he's there too,' said Lizzie. She hesitated. 'The sooner we can get that car back the better.'

'You don't have to come with me! I'll manage,' said Alexandra. 'I realise you must feel a bit worried that someone might see you. And I do rather like this sporty little thing now.'

Lizzie didn't answer. She really didn't want to go all

the way back to that house which she had left under such a cloud. But she couldn't let Alexandra down.

'Thank goodness we didn't get stopped by the police!' interposed Meg.

'The traffic was light, it being so early,' said Lizzie, 'which would have helped.'

'It won't be so light on the way back,' said Alexandra. 'But I know the car now, so that will be fine.'

'I *will* come with you,' said Lizzie, suddenly stricken with guilt. If this caper went wrong, it would be all her fault: she was the one who'd wanted to leave. The other two would have been perfectly happy to stay until David collected them. 'You need me to map-read, and no one — except Vanessa — will be out of bed if we go straight back now.'

'Thank you, Lizzie,' said Alexandra. 'I'm not always as brave as I pretend to be.'

David was at home, and, after a lot of explanation, he brought the car round to the front, ready to set off to the country.

'You girls,' he said. 'I never know what pickle you're going to put me in next.'

'We keep you young!' said Alexandra, unrepentant.

'I'm quite young enough without needing you lot to help,' said David, patting his pockets to make sure he had everything he needed. 'Look, I've got things to do, apart from rescuing you. Have you got money if you need petrol?'

Lizzie prised apart the layers of her handbag which were still wet. The little wallet where she put her bank-notes was still fairly soggy. 'I'm not sure. I did have.'

David sighed. 'I'll lend you money. You can dry out yours and pay me back later.'

'Right!' said Alexandra. 'Here I go again! I must

say, this is awfully good driving practice.'

'And on someone else's car, too!' said David. 'That's the part I like.'

'Come on,' said Lizzie. 'I'm on navigating duty.' She wanted to be useful. So far she'd just caused everyone problems.

When they were in the car and sitting at a set of traffic lights, Alexandra patted Lizzie's knee. 'I am really enjoying myself. Don't feel guilty.'

'You're very kind. And if ever I get the chance to help you out of a spot, I will.'

'I know you will. I love having friends,' said Alexandra. 'Ones who are my own age, I mean.'

Lizzie was glad that she had to concentrate on where they were going, turning the map book round in her hands to help her navigate. It stopped her thinking too much about what had happened. Her spirits swung violently between deepest despair — she was deeply in love with a man who could never be hers — and utter joy.

Rightly or wrongly, she and he had shared a wonderful experience. She could hold on to that for ever.

PART TWO

20

Lizzie was in the kitchen. It was late morning and the other two girls were out. She was sitting at the table fiddling with things while David was cooking something behind her.

'What's worrying you, chicken?' David asked. 'You're not your cheery little self and haven't been for a while. Are your parents nagging you to go and live with them? Get a proper job? Or are they happy with you being a waitress to the aristocracy with Meg?'

All those things were true and were, indeed, worrying Lizzie. Any of them would be perfectly acceptable reasons for her anxiety. She wondered which one she should give. Instead, she found herself saying, 'I'm late for my period.'

'How late?'

'I've missed one completely. I didn't notice at first. I've been busy and I lost my diary for a bit.' She felt obliged to explain how she could have been so careless. 'I'd stuffed it into a coat pocket after it dried out — you know after I nearly drowned and then I lent the coat to Meg and she left it somewhere and it was a while before I got it back.' She paused. 'The next one was due a few days ago,' she finished bleakly.

'Ah,' said David. 'And it hasn't come, so you could be pregnant?'

'Suppose so.' Lizzie knew in theory it was possible to get pregnant the first time you had sex but it had always seemed so unlikely. She appeared to be a rare example of when it had happened.

'Do the others know?'

'That I could be pregnant? No. I don't want anyone to know. I feel so ashamed.' She suddenly felt like crying but not in front of anyone, not even David.

'Oh, lovey! Why ashamed?' David asked.

Lizzie shrugged. 'You know, sex before marriage, getting caught out — it's shameful! I'm so pleased you're not shocked. Although I suppose being an actor . . . ' She didn't finish her sentence, not being sure where it was leading.

David's expression was a picture of kindness and understanding. 'Do you really believe, in your heart, that what you did was wrong?'

'No.' Even knowing she was probably pregnant didn't change that.

'Not shameful then.' He sounded very certain. 'I'm going to make you a hot drink. What do you fancy?'

Lizzie chose Bovril. She wanted something salty. 'I may not even be pregnant, but I no longer want to drink coffee.'

A minute or two later he put the mug in front of her and came and sat opposite her. 'Do you want to tell your Uncle David all about it?'

Lizzie managed a smile. 'Probably not, if I had an Uncle David. But I would quite like to tell you.'

'I'll find you some crackers. You need to keep your strength up.'

'You seem to know a lot about being pregnant, considering you've never experienced it,' Lizzie said, eating a cracker a few moments later and feeling a bit better.

David laughed. 'In the theatre you get close to people, women in particular, and they tell you their problems. Cheating boyfriends, periods, pregnancy, morning sickness. I've heard it all.' He seemed to assume there was no doubt about her condition.

This sent Lizzie into despair. 'Oh God, David! I can't be pregnant! I just can't! My parents will die!'

'No one actually dies because someone else gets pregnant, even if it's their beloved daughter.'

'Are you sure?'

'Yup. Never ever happened, not unless they top themselves and I don't suppose your parents would do that.'

Lizzie considered this. 'No. They're more likely to move somewhere far away where they don't know anyone.'

'But what about you?' said David. 'The man didn't force himself on you, did he?' This obviously bothered David a lot more than how her parents would react.

It was Lizzie's turn to be shocked. 'No! Absolutely not. It was me. I wanted to so much. I hardly dared speak in case he guessed I was a virgin. I was so grateful that he obviously couldn't tell.'

'It was Hugo, wasn't it? After he rescued you?'

She nodded.

'Well, he's an honourable man. He'll do the right thing. But you will have to tell him.'

'No!' It was almost a shriek. 'I can't tell him! I can't do that to him.' Lizzie felt unable to adequately express how unthinkable this was. 'He's all set for a brilliant career at the Bar, with exactly the right sort of wife! My being pregnant could ruin his life.'

'It's very much more likely to ruin yours, love,' David said gently.

'I know!' She took a couple of breaths. 'It's not that his life is more important than mine, but my life is more fluid. I haven't had it all mapped out for me

221

since I was a baby.' She paused. 'Actually I have, by my mother. But as I've never agreed with her plans I don't feel obliged to follow them. It's not the same.' She paused and looked David firmly in the eye. 'I can't tell Hugo. He mustn't find out.'

David pursed his lips and sighed deeply. He was obviously not at all happy with how she saw things. 'Well, the first thing you need to do is find out for certain if you are pregnant. You had a huge shock when you nearly drowned. That could have knocked your cycle off balance.'

Lizzie took another cream cracker. 'You are very easy to talk to. You don't judge. And you offer snacks.'

David laughed. 'I expect you feel better for having told someone.'

'I do. I'm always so regular I know I must be pregnant. But how am I going to find out for sure?'

David shrugged. 'Sadly, I've run out of specialist knowledge. I think you should go home and go to your own doctor and see what he says.'

'But what shall I tell my parents?' demanded Lizzie. 'I don't want them worrying that I'm ill.'

'Tell them you've got something you wouldn't want to go to a strange doctor about?' said David. 'Anyway, lots of people go back home to see their doctor, or their dentist. God, some travel miles to have the same hairdresser they've always had.'

'I'll think of something,' said Lizzie. 'And thank you. You're such a good listener.'

'And my reward for being a good listener is you telling Alexandra and Meg? I think you'll feel better about it if you're not trying to keep it secret from your housemates. And I don't want to have to keep this a secret on my own.'

'OK. Now I've accepted it myself, sort of, I don't mind them knowing. And you're right, it would be hell trying to keep it secret.'

Two minutes later the back door opened and Meg and Alexandra came in. Their arms were full of flowers.

'These were going cheap at the market,' said Alexandra. 'We couldn't resist buying them.'

'Oh, are they for me?' asked David.

'Naturally,' said Alexandra. 'And you too, of course, Lizzie.'

'Good,' said David. 'Because our Lizzie has something to tell you.'

'What?' said Alexandra and Meg at the same time.

If it hadn't been for David looking at her sternly, Lizzie might well have backed out, but she knew she had to say it. 'I think I might be pregnant.'

People's jaws really did drop, Lizzie noticed, feeling detached from reality.

'What?' said Meg.

'Hugo?' said Alexandra.

'Probably,' Lizzie said.

'You mean it's probably Hugo?' said Alexandra, rubbing Lizzie's arm to show she was joking. Who else might be responsible?

'So when he rescued you from drowning . . . ' said Meg.

'Well, afterwards, obviously,' said Lizzie, laughing with embarrassment.

'He didn't take advantage of you?' said Meg, looking worried. 'While you were grateful for him saving your life?'

'No! Really not! Although I was grateful, obviously.' It was awful that people suspected Hugo of seducing

223

her when Lizzie felt it was far more her fault than his.

'I think we need tea,' said Alexandra, the voice of reason. 'And we bought cakes.'

'Japoise cakes,' said Meg. 'I hadn't heard of them. I had to try them.'

Lizzie began to feel calmer. Her friends, sitting at the table, sharing out cake, hunting for vases for armfuls of carnations, was normality.

The jap cakes, little macaroon-like confections with a crisp meringue coating on top of coffee icing, were delicious. Lizzie spent quite a long time praising them and discussing with Meg how difficult they'd be to make.

'So,' said Alexandra, wiping her sticky fingers on the tablecloth, 'have you told Hugo yet?'

'I've hardly had a chance. But anyway, I'm not going to tell him.' Lizzie didn't meet her eye. She knew Alexandra would disapprove of her decision. Meg too.

'Why not?' said Alexandra at the same time as Meg said, 'That's ridiculous.'

'It would ruin his life,' said Lizzie.

'But what about your life?' said Lizzie and Meg in unison.

'That's what I said,' David muttered.

'Seriously, Lizzie!' said Alexandra. 'Have you thought about this properly? It's not a minor problem that will go away if you don't think about it.'

'Well . . . '

'Honestly,' Alexandra went on. 'My nanny had a friend who was another nanny. This nanny came over to tea and told my nanny about her sister who was pregnant. She was Norwegian, I think. Anyway, her parents made her marry some man she didn't know just to give the baby a father.'

'My parents won't do that,' said Lizzie, but as she said it, she wondered if she was right. Supposing they did? They couldn't make her marry anyone, but they could try.

'But what are they going to do?' Meg asked. 'Are they going to say: 'Come home, darling, we'll help you bring up the baby. We don't mind in the slightest if you have a baby out of wedlock — it's the sixties now after all'?'

Lizzie felt sick. There was no way they would say anything like that. Her mother's loss of face would be terrible. She'd never be able to hold her head up in her community again — attitudes there hadn't changed. Her father would be livid. He might not throw her out into the street, but he'd want to.

'I won't go home. I won't tell them,' she said. It seemed the only answer.

'Don't be ridiculous,' said Alexandra, firmly but not unkindly. 'They love you. You can't not see them for nine months and then somehow conceal the fact you've got a baby.'

Lizzie put her elbows on the table and her head in her hands. 'I haven't thought about it properly yet. I may not be pregnant.'

'Lizzie is going to get an appointment with their family doctor,' said David. 'She'll think of something — some female thing — to tell her mother, to explain why she doesn't want to see a doctor in London.'

'That's a good idea,' said Meg.

'Cystitis,' said Alexandra. 'Never had it myself but I'm told it's agony.'

'By one of your nannies?' asked Lizzie, glad to have

the attention drawn from her for a moment or two.

Alexandra nodded. 'One of the few advantages of having been more or less brought up by people very much younger than my parents is that I know all sorts of things most people my age don't.'

'It's not necessarily a good thing, Lexi,' said David. 'There is such a thing as being too sophisticated for your age.'

Alexandra shrugged. 'Anyway, this isn't about me. We have to get Lizzie sorted out.'

'Are you sure you're pregnant?' asked Meg. 'This may be a false alarm.'

'I'm not sure at all!' said Lizzie. 'But I think I am because I'm so regular usually and I feel a bit strange.'

Alexandra cleared her throat. 'OK, I'm going to ask the question but I think I know the answer: you wouldn't want the problem taken away by a very expensive clinic where you book in under an assumed name?'

Lizzie's reply was instinctive. She shook her head in horror. 'No.'

'You seem very certain,' said Meg. 'Have you thought about it a lot?'

'No. I haven't thought about it at all because it's just not an option for me,' said Lizzie. 'I don't know why I'm so certain. I just am.'

'Are your parents likely to want you to have an abortion?' asked Alexandra gently.

'How would I know? It's not a conversation I've ever had with them.' Lizzie felt suddenly tearful. Perhaps she wasn't pregnant, just very premenstrual and emotional. 'I think they — well, it's my mother really; I would never talk about any of this with my father — I think she just assumed I wouldn't have sex

226

before marriage.'

'Which brings us back to the beginning,' said David. 'Don't you think Hugo would marry you? If he knew you were pregnant?'

'He's engaged to someone else, David!' said Lizzie. 'I thought you knew that.'

'We don't know that he's engaged to Electra,' said Meg. 'I know he was supposed to be making the announcement but I didn't hear it.'

'It probably happened while we were trooping over the fields with Lizzie's dry clothes,' said Alexandra. 'Or when we were all coming back.'

'Wouldn't Vanessa have said something?' asked Meg.

'Why should she?' said Lizzie. 'Announcing the engagement was the whole purpose of the ball, after all.' She sighed. 'I think it happened. If he's engaged, he's engaged. That's it.'

'Being engaged isn't the same as being married,' David pointed out.

'I'm not going to ruin his life because of this,' said Lizzie. 'How many more times must I say it?'

'OK,' said Meg. 'Changing the subject, who's hungry?'

'I'm full of jap cake,' said Lizzie. Now everyone had stopped nagging her she said, 'Imagine poor Hugo having to take me to his parents, tummy out here, telling them he wants to make an honest woman of me. Sir Jasper would die. Or kill Hugo. Or both. It's funny, really.'

No one laughed.

★ ★ ★

Later that evening, Lizzie telephoned her mother.

'Mummy,' she said, after the usual greetings, exclamations and questions had been gone through. 'I wonder if you could make me a doctor's appointment?'

There were more questions and exclamations.

'And could it be with the lady doctor? What I've got — it's a bit — embarrassing.'

'But, darling, we don't know anything about the lady doctor. Why don't you want to see Dr Sharp? We always go to him.'

'I said, it's a bit embarrassing.' Lizzie lowered her voice. 'It hurts when I spend a penny. And I keep needing to go.' She and Alexandra had looked up the symptoms of cystitis, so she knew what to say.

'Oh, Elizabeth! You don't need to be embarrassed. Doctors know all about these things.'

'Really! I'd rather see a woman!' Lizzie didn't actually care that much if her doctor was male or female but she did want to see one who didn't know her.

Her mother sighed. 'I'll do my best.'

'Thank you, Mummy. I'm really grateful.'

21

'Darling!' said her mother, enveloping her in a Chanel-perfumed hug a few days later. 'You're here at last! We were beginning to think you'd forgotten your address you come home so little! And it's so lovely that you're staying the night. Your father's got to go out so we can have a lovely woman-to-woman chat. I've got a bottle of wine we can have with our meal.'

Her mother was so delighted to see her that Lizzie felt swamped with guilt that she hadn't been to visit her parents more recently. She'd had time since the fateful weekend when she'd nearly drowned, but she hadn't been. She suspected it was because she thought her mother might be able to tell that she was no longer a virgin. How much worse were things now? She hugged her mother back.

'I've managed to get you an appointment with our dear Dr Sharp. He's looked after you since you were a baby,' her mother went on.

This was not good news. 'But, Mummy, I asked if you could get me one with the woman doctor? I can't remember her name. Wasn't that possible?'

'I expect I could have managed it but I thought it was better to see a doctor who really knows you. He was so good when you had measles.'

'When I was nine!' Lizzie muttered. 'I wanted to see a woman.'

'Don't be silly. It's far better to see our family doctor. Now, do you want Daddy to take your case up?' The subject was closed.

'No need for that. I'll take it up now.' When would her mother treat her as an adult and do what she asked? Lizzie thought. Probably never!

'When you come down, I'll open the wine.'

Lizzie went up the stairs wishing two things. The first was that her mother hadn't made her an appointment with the doctor who was like a grandfather to her, and the second that the thought of wine didn't make her feel sick. Still, she'd manage. She'd have to.

★   ★   ★

'What I'm really looking forward to', said her mother, when Lizzie's father had been seen off to his meeting and supper cleared away, 'is hearing about the weekend you spent in your friend Vanessa's house. I want every detail! I could hardly believe my ears when you told me you were going.' She topped up both wine glasses although Lizzie had drunk very little of hers. 'I met Mrs Brinklow — you remember they own that electrical shop in the High Street? I had to tell her. She's always telling me how well Christine's doing.'

Lizzie knew this. All her life she had been compared unfavourably to Christine Brinklow. They weren't even in the same year at school, which was a blessing, yet Christine was always held up as the model daughter. Now she wondered what would happen if Christine Brinklow got pregnant out of wedlock. The sky would fall in. Except it couldn't now happen because Christine Brinklow had got married the previous year. Lizzie had been a bridesmaid and worn a very unattractive dress in peach satin. All the bridesmaids had looked hideous.

Lizzie took a deep breath and prepared to tell her

230

mother what she wanted to hear. 'Well! The house was enormous! A stately home. It was a bit intimidating going to stay there, to be honest.'

'I'm sure you were fine. You have lovely manners and, as I always told you, good manners will take you anywhere.'

Except to that house, Lizzie thought, although to be fair to her mother, it was her short dress and not how she held a knife and fork that had made her unwelcome.

'There were lots of people staying. Relations mainly. That meant all the big bedrooms were taken. Vanessa put us all up in the nursery which was lovely. Super views! We had a peep into Vanessa's room which she'd had to give up for someone.' No need to go into detail. 'It was gorgeous. All the furniture was antique.'

'I suppose it would be. Old houses are always full of antiques. And what was the food like? Did you have tea in the drawing room?'

The questions went on and on and Lizzie made every one of her replies positive. When her mother heard her daughter had done the flowers for the ballroom she was beside herself with pride and joy. 'You always were brilliant at flower arranging! As well as needlework. Such a clever daughter! Wait until Mrs Brinklow hears that my little girl did the flowers for an important ball in an English country house!'

Put like that, it sounded like quite an achievement. 'They did turn out quite well, I must say. But I had a huge cutting garden to pick the flowers from. That was so lovely. Not like scrubbing round our gardens to find enough things in flower to make a decent display for the church. It took ages though.'

'Flower arranging does take ages!' Lizzie's mother

sighed. 'We do miss you from the flower guild. It would be lovely if one day you came back down here and could be part of the community again.'

'I was never a proper member of the flower guild, I just helped out.' Lizzie needed to stop her mother from working out ways that this might be possible — the ideas would involve a local boy who lived locally and wouldn't move.

'It was obviously good training for you,' Lizzie's mother said with pride. 'Now tell me about this barn dance that went on before the ball?'

That part was easy to describe — she'd been there. But when Lizzie was expected to describe the ball, dance by dance, her imagination was stretched a bit. She focused a lot on the dresses — some of them were actually real. Then she made up a few dance partners, their abilities taken directly from the various boys who'd attended the dance classes Lizzie had been to while she'd still been at school. By the time she'd finished, Lizzie was almost convinced she'd actually been at the ball, and not frantically tramping across muddy fields before getting into a leaky boat and very nearly drowning.

Exhausted after all that storytelling, Lizzie gave an enormous yawn. 'Would you mind if I went to bed, Mum?' she said. 'I think whatever it is I've got is making me tired.'

'Of course not! I'd forgotten you were ill for a minute. I'll bring you up some hot chocolate. You get up to bed immediately. Have a bath if you want. Very soothing for problems 'down there'. You can use my bath salts.'

An hour later, Lizzie was snuggled up in her old bed, drinking hot chocolate and reading a *Chalet*

School book. She knew she had reverted to childhood, but it made it easier to cope with the smother-love her mother heaped on her.

As she snuggled down under the blankets she realised that her being pregnant was almost bound to shatter all that. It would shatter her parents' lives as much as it would hers.

★ ★ ★

Visiting a doctor who'd given you first prize in a bonny baby competition when you were six months old was about as embarrassing as embarrassing gets. But Lizzie needed to be brave and not beat about the bush.

'And what can I do for you, my dear?' said Dr Sharp. His avuncular expression made her shudder a bit.

Lizzie tried to smile back. 'I think I might be pregnant.'

His expression went from fatherly concern to deep disapproval in an instant. But he didn't comment. 'How late for your period are you?'

'I've missed two periods.'

His frown deepened. 'Could there be any other reason for a missed period?' Disapproval was etched in every line and wrinkle in his elderly face.

'I don't know what else causes it.' She felt less guilty about it all now. If he could be so cold about it, so could she.

'Are your periods normally regular?'

'As clockwork. And I feel perfectly well, apart from not wanting to drink coffee or wine.'

'I suppose we'd better take a test.' He hardly looked at her. He reached into a cupboard behind him and produced a paper cup. 'It may be too soon to tell. It's very early days. Give the sample to the nurse please.'

He got up. The consultation was over.

As she walked out of his room to reception she swore never to see him again if she could possibly help it. She was not having that grumpy old man looking after her through her pregnancy.

★   ★   ★

'How did you get on?' asked her mother the moment Lizzie arrived back on the doorstep.

'Oh, very reassuring, thank you.' Lizzie smiled. 'I've got to go back in about two weeks.' She had been told by the receptionist this was when she could expect her results. 'I've made the appointment.' Guilt which was a constant presence made her say, 'But I could stay with you for a couple of days, rather than go back to London now. If that's OK.'

'Of course it's OK, darling!' said her mother. 'I love having you at home.'

The following morning, her mother insisted that Lizzie did a little shopping with her. This was in spite of insisting that she could have done the shopping without her mother and so save her a trip to town.

'What is it we need to buy, Mummy?' asked Lizzie.

'Er — light bulbs,' said her mother firmly.

So this was it: Lizzie was to be shown to Mrs Brinklow, the owner of the electrical shop and mother of the perfect Christine, so her mother could tell her about her flower-arranging abilities.

Her mother inspected her before they opened the door of the shop. Her mother was within an inch of spitting on her hanky, Lizzie knew. It was only the fact that her face was clean that stopped her doing it.

234

'Morning, Barbara,' she said as they went in. 'You haven't seen my daughter for a while, have you? Isn't she 'with it' with her short hair?' Her mother paused to give her old friend time to observe Lizzie's hair, which was now curling at the ends and giving her kiss curls which had never been part of the original style. 'She's been so busy, haven't you, darling?'

22

Oh, how easily the lies had slipped out, Lizzie thought as she sat on the train, watching the familiar landscape go past. She had lied to her mother, to Mrs Brinklow about a ball she hadn't been to, and, to some extent, the doctor. But if her mother knew the truth, about any of it, she'd die, no matter what David had said about this never happening. She'd certainly never be able to buy light bulbs from Mrs Brinklow again.

Lizzie's friends were all there at the table when Lizzie let herself into the kitchen. She was so happy to see them.

'Well, that was very frustrating!' she said. 'First of all, my mother had booked an appointment with the family doctor who's been banging my back and asking me to say 'Ah' since I was a baby, instead of the only woman doctor there is in the practice — '

Lizzie noticed everyone was looking a bit stunned but she carried on with her story.

'He was really po-faced and horrible about it. I still have to wait two weeks for the results of the test, though. You think it would be a bit quicker than that, wouldn't you? Isn't anyone making tea?'

Meg got up from the table and went to put the kettle on. Alexandra cleared her throat.

'You've missed Hugo by about ten minutes.'

Lizzie just pulled out a chair in time and sat on it before she fainted. She let her head sink towards her knees but was glad when she heard Clover being chivvied off and felt herself being helped on to the sofa.

'I'll make you tea,' said Meg, concerned. 'Perhaps I should put sugar in it? For shock? And maybe you should eat something. Toast and Marmite?'

'He's not going to come back, is he?' Lizzie asked, looking up at everyone looking down at her.

'No. Alexandra was brilliant!' said Meg.

'I said you had a job in Scotland,' said Alexandra, eager to show off her brilliance. 'Somewhere really remote. With no phone and a postal service once a week. I hope I didn't get too carried away with the remoteness. I didn't say how long the job was going to last, in case you run into him somewhere.'

'That certainly was brilliant, Alexandra,' said Lizzie, thinking it unlikely she'd run into Hugo. 'Thank you so much!'

'Here's the tea,' said Meg. 'I hope I let it stand long enough but I thought you needed it now, not in ten minutes.'

Lizzie sipped the tea. 'It's perfect. And yes please to the toast.'

'On its way,' said Meg.

'He was really keen to see you,' said Meg. 'Wanted to know if you were all right. He's quite reserved, isn't he? But I think he wanted to know if you'd had any ill effects from your dip in the river.'

'Oh,' said Lizzie, perversely pleased he'd taken the trouble to visit her, although she'd said he wasn't to.

'So?' demanded Alexandra. She seemed to feel reassured that Lizzie was all right, which meant she could ask the question everyone wanted the answer to. 'You really won't know if you're pregnant or not for two whole weeks?'

Lizzie, who'd been starting to sit up, sank back on to the sofa cushions. 'No, but I think I must be. I've

237

never felt faint like that before.' She cleared her throat. 'Apart from saying I'd left the country you didn't tell Hugo anything?'

'We didn't say you were pregnant, if that's what you mean,' said Alexandra. 'Even though we really should have. He's a good man. He wouldn't abandon you.

But he wouldn't abandon Electra either, thought Lizzie. 'So I'm safe for now? Honestly, I left him a note with Vanessa saying I didn't want to see him. He shouldn't have come here.'

'Yes he should,' said David firmly. 'He's honourable, like I said.'

'It's Lizzie who wants to cut herself off from him. She wants to disappear into the night and never see him again,' said Meg.

'And I won't. Hugo thinks I'm in Scotland so he won't come here again.' Lizzie's churning stomach began to settle, and she swung her legs round so she was sitting, not lying. 'Everything is all right.'

'No, it's not all right!' said Meg, indignantly. 'You can't stay in the house until you have the baby. He will see you somewhere, you can guarantee it.'

'Meggie's right,' said David. 'London is a big city but if there's someone you want to avoid you will meet them, sure as eggs is eggs.'

Lizzie felt sick all over again. She pushed her fingers through her hair so it stuck up in spikes. 'What should I do?'

She hadn't really expected an answer but Meg said, 'Well, my mother works in a school as a matron. They always need assistants.'

'It would be live-in?'

'Yes. But once you really start to show, you'd have to leave,' said Meg. 'Unless you quickly have an affair

238

with one of the schoolmasters and then he can marry you and make everything all right.'

Everyone looked at Meg in horror. 'That wasn't a serious suggestion, but it's what people do, isn't it? I'm not saying you should do it, Lizzie.' Meg paused. 'Unless you fell in love, of course. And then you'd have to tell him.'

'I rather think that ship has sailed, Meggie,' said David. 'And I doubt Lizzie is the type to be able to fall in love again so quickly. You'll have to tell Hugo, my love. None of the other options are going to be at all pleasant.'

Lizzie found herself wanting to cry and realised that being pregnant felt just the same as being due for a period when she could start to cry for no reason and at very little notice. Although this time she had a reason.

'More toast?' said Meg.

Lizzie shook her head. Meg liked to feed people; it made her feel better. 'No, thank you, sweetie, although that was delicious.' Lizzie steeled herself to ask a question. 'Meg, what did your mother do when she had you as a baby, and was a widow?'

'Well,' said Meg. 'It was very hard, I know. A bit easier for her as a widow. Even then, because my father was killed after the war people assumed she'd never had a husband. She suffered a lot of unkindness. But she managed to get live-in jobs. Of course we'd do everything we could to support you — ' Meg looked at David and Alexandra, who nodded fervently. 'Although you might end up finding it would be best to have the baby adopted.'

Lizzie wanted to cry again. I don't think I could bear to do that, she thought. 'This being pregnant lark is no picnic, is it?' she said out loud, trying to sound as if she didn't care.

Possibly hearing the tears in her voice, David said, 'I know you think they will be desperately upset, but shouldn't you tell your parents? They may look after you, and love having a little grandchild without the bother of a wedding and a son-in-law?'

'David,' said Lizzie, 'I don't know if I've told you this already — probably only about a hundred times — but my mother has been planning my wedding ever since she was told she had a baby girl. They care terribly what the neighbours think and their daughter having an illegitimate baby — '

'— would kill them,' David finished for her. 'I know. You said. But women love babies! I've never seen a woman who doesn't go all soppy when they see one.'

'You haven't seen a woman who hasn't *pretended* to go all soppy when they see one,' Alexandra corrected him. 'Babies aren't for everyone. They make a lot of noise and are always damp. And, personally, I never know what to do with them on the few occasions I've been given one to hold.' She sent Lizzie an apologetic smile. 'But I will make a huge effort with your baby, Lizzie. That will be different: it will be our baby, like Clover is our dog.'

'Thank you,' said Lizzie weakly, not sure a baby and a dog were quite the same thing.

★   ★   ★

For the next two weeks Lizzie tried to keep herself busy as she waited for the day when she could ring up the doctor and find out the results of her pregnancy test.

240

She mended some ancient linen sheets for David, turning them 'sides to middle' so he could sell them on his stall. She helped Meg make dainty canapés, cutting grapes in half, piping cream cheese on to biscuits (something she became quite good at), and whatever fiddly, time-consuming thing Meg needed doing for her boss's catering business. Apparently they could charge a huge amount for these salty little morsels. But nothing worked. No matter what her hands were doing, her mind kept turning over her problems.

The day before her results were due, she was alone in the house when the doorbell rang and kept on ringing, even though she tried to ignored it. Eventually she had to give in and respond. She went up from the kitchen to open the front door, terrified in case it was Hugo.

It was her parents. 'Get your things, Elizabeth,' said her father. 'You're coming with us.'

★ ★ ★

Lizzie was allowed to write her housemates a note, to stop them thinking she'd been kidnapped, but she hadn't been given long to put her things into a bag before she was hustled out of the house and into the car. Lizzie sat in back seat, biting her lips, clenching her hands and twisting her fingers, desperate not to cry. Her parents hardly said a word to each other and nothing to her. Although they hadn't said as much there was no doubt that they had found out the results of her test, which also meant she was definitely pregnant.

When they got into the house they restrained themselves no longer.

241

'Elizabeth!' said her father, almost shouting. 'How could you do this to us?'

'After all we've done for you?' said her mother. 'You've been our beloved only child and this is how you reward us?'

Lizzie went and sat on the sofa and looked from one parent to the other. She had to think what to say. She'd have time — it would be a while before she would be allowed to respond. But what could she say? And the only thing she wanted to ask was how they'd found out.

But it appeared getting pregnant was different from missing the last bus and being terribly late home. They both fell silent, staring at her, expecting her to speak.

'I'm terribly sorry,' she said. 'Obviously, I didn't intend for it to happen.'

'And did you also not intend for us to find out?' said her father.

'I had intended to tell you myself,' said Lizzie with dignity. 'I assume Dr Sharp told you?'

'Yes, Dr Sharp told us!' said her mother. 'Imagine the humiliation, the utter shame, of being told by such a respected member of society that our daughter is little better than — than — one of those women who's no better than she should be!'

'I don't think he should have told you! Isn't it against the Hippocratic oath or something?' said Lizzie, a thread of a history lesson coming into her mind.

'Oh, don't be ridiculous!' said her father. 'You're still a minor! He's the family doctor. It's his duty to tell us!'

Lizzie swallowed. Was her father right? Or was he just saying this for his own purposes?

'We'll never be able to hold our heads up in this

town again!' said her mother. 'We have always been so proud of you, but now look what you've done. Brought shame on us, that's what. Have you no sense of duty towards your parents?'

'It was an accident, Mummy!' said Lizzie, fighting tears.

'You should have been more careful!' said her mother, as if Lizzie had broken a vase when she was dusting. Then she heard what she'd just said. 'I mean, you shouldn't have done it — whatever you did — in the first place!'

'I'm sorry, Mummy,' said Lizzie. But while she was truly sorry that she'd caused her parents so much distress, she wasn't sorry for what had happened in the boathouse. She wasn't sorry at all. 'I think I'll go upstairs now,' she said, and left the room.

23

What Lizzie had done was worse, apparently, than robbing a bank and leaving a cashier for dead. No one in the history of the world, it seemed, had been as ungrateful as she was. She wasn't just 'sharper than a serpent's tooth' ungrateful, she was as ungrateful as a whole nest of serpents with entire sets of teeth instead of just the one mentioned in *King Lear*.

Lizzie followed her mother into the kitchen while she made supper. Her father had disappeared into his study and Lizzie felt that if her mother had a chance to get her feelings off her chest, she might calm down afterwards.

'And I suppose you expect us to keep you while you're expecting?' said her mother.

'Mummy,' said Lizzie calmly. 'I'm nineteen years old. I'm not a child. You didn't have to bring me home. I had work I could do; you could have left me where I was perfectly safe and had a good job. I accept I couldn't do waitressing when my pregnancy showed, but until then I could earn my own living. I could save up.'

'And what would you do after the baby was born? How would you work then? Take in washing?'

Lizzie remembered the bags of antique linen David needed help with and thought this was actually quite a good idea. But she didn't tell her mother. It wouldn't help.

She put her hand on her mother's arm. 'I'll help you get supper ready, Mummy.'

As Lizzie had been doing this since she was nine years old, she and her mother didn't need to talk as they worked. Lizzie peeled potatoes, searched the cabbage for what her father called 'livestock' and washed it carefully. Her mother put both cabbage and potatoes on to boil at the same time. Lizzie wondered if she should propose one of the different ways of cooking cabbage she'd learnt at Madame Wilson's but decided this wasn't the time to suggest her mother tried new things. 'Shall I do some carrots?'

'If you want to. I'm not sure there's time to cook them. Your father is hungry and making him wait for his supper will make him grumpy.'

Lizzie rolled her eyes. It would be difficult for him to get grumpier, surely. Although possibly being on his own with a few measures of whisky might help his mood.

'This is quite like it was in the old days,' she said brightly. 'Us in the kitchen, cooking together.'

Her mother gave her a look that told her it was not remotely like the old days. In the old days her beloved daughter had not disgraced the family. 'Go and set the table, please, Elizabeth.'

When they were all seated in the chilly dining room, halfway through their pork chops, her father said, 'I don't like to talk about unpleasant things at mealtimes but we might as well get this over with.'

'We discussed your situation while you were upstairs,' said Lizzie's mother. 'And we've made a plan.'

'I'm not sure you can have made a plan without me being present to share in the discussion,' said Lizzie. She never used to argue with her parents, she always just went along with what they thought best. But since

245

her move to London — and possibly getting pregnant — she was no longer so biddable.

'The plan is', her father went on as if Lizzie hadn't spoken, 'to send you to my cousin Margaret, in Yorkshire.'

'I didn't know you had a cousin in Yorkshire, Daddy,' said Lizzie.

'Please don't interrupt, Elizabeth,' said her father. 'She lives near a Mother and Baby Home. When you are approximately seven months pregnant, you will move into the home. You will stay there for six weeks after you've had the baby, at which time your baby will be adopted.'

Lizzie noticed that her mother was now dabbing her eyes with a handkerchief.

'But I don't want to have my baby adopted,' said Lizzie.

'The only alternative to this plan', said her father sternly, glowering at his daughter and his weeping wife, 'is for you to be booked into a special clinic. I hope you don't want me to elaborate on what would happen in that clinic.'

'What would I do while I'm staying with this cousin I've never heard of before?' asked Lizzie.

'Well, I hope you would be helpful around the house!' Her father suddenly became angry, as if Lizzie had already said she wouldn't help. 'She lives in Halifax in a small house. I don't suppose she has much in the way of modern conveniences.'

'Have you asked her if she'll have me?' There would hardly have been time, Lizzie felt. It was unlikely Cousin Margaret had a telephone.

'She'd be glad to have you, I'm sure,' said Lizzie's mother, rallying. 'We'll pay for your keep. We'll have to pay for your keep at the Mother and Baby Home, too.'

'I think it would be better if I didn't go to the Mother and Baby Home,' said Lizzie.

'But surely, Elizabeth, it would be better to have the baby adopted than to — you know — have an operation. Sometimes you can't have children after — you know — and then I'll never have grandchildren!' She started to sniff as well as dab now. Lizzie got up. 'I'll clear away. Would anyone like a cup of tea?'

Lizzie washed up the supper things and made the tea. Her father had taken her mother to the sitting room and was, if Lizzie knew anything about her parents, now patting her hand while they sat together on the sofa.

She would have to make her own plan. She had time, although not a lot of it — she needed to leave her parents' house as quickly as possible.

She took a tray with tea things through to her parents. 'The thing is, Mummy and Daddy, while obviously I am desperately sorry this has happened — '

Her father moved to interrupt but Lizzie managed to put him off with a smile.

'While I'm desperately sorry — and I know how much I've disappointed you — '

'We sent you to London to better yourself, not to sleep around and get yourself in the family way!' said her mother.

'I didn't — don't — sleep around, Mummy,' said Lizzie, determined to be firm but kind. 'And I have bettered myself, in many ways. However . . .' She was proud of this word, it sounded as if she knew what she was going to say next. 'Things we none of us wanted to happen have happened. One thing, anyway.'

'Are you saying the man forced himself on you? That does put rather a different light on it.' Her mother looked at her father to check this was true.

'No! He didn't force himself on me. It was — mutual.' Although Lizzie was fed up with people asking her if Hugo had more or less raped her, at least her parents were at last showing some interest in her well-being by asking the question. Up to this point it had only been about how her actions affected them.

'What did he say when you told him you were pregnant?' asked her father.

Lizzie picked up the teapot and began to pour. 'He doesn't know. I didn't know! I could hardly tell him before I knew for sure. And I would like to ask why Dr Sharp told you, Mummy, instead of me?'

Her mother looked self-righteous. 'He told me because I'm your mother. He thought — and I totally agree with him — that as your mother I should know anything that affected your well-being.'

Lizzie didn't reply.

'So you're going to tell the man who did this to you now,' her father stated.

'No,' said Lizzie. She did feel a bit ashamed. She knew it would have been the sensible thing to do in any other circumstances.

Her mother gasped. 'Oh, Elizabeth!' she said, horrified. 'He's not married already?'

'No, he's not!' Lizzie was just as appalled at the thought of sleeping with a married man as her mother was but realised a second later that an engaged man was hardly better. After all, the fact he was engaged already was the reason she wasn't going to tell him she was pregnant.

'Then you must tell him,' said her father. 'He must

make an honest woman of you.'

'No!' said Lizzie. 'It's my problem to sort out, not his.'

Her father gave a long-suffering sigh. 'Don't tell me. You've got in with a lot of women's libbers while you were in London!'

'It does take two to make a baby, Elizabeth,' said her mother. 'You can't take responsibility for it all on your own.'

Lizzie felt a pang of guilt. This was true and in any other circumstances — particularly if the circumstances involved someone other than her — she'd wholeheartedly agree. 'I'm sorry but I'm not telling him.'

'If you don't it's Cousin Margaret and the Mother and Baby Home,' said her father.

'Maybe you should write to Cousin Margaret and see what she thinks before you send me off there,' said Lizzie. 'Although I'm not going into any home.'

'You'll do as you're told, my girl!' said her father. 'You've been spoilt all your life, been given everything, and now you'll obey us! And as for this 'not telling the father' nonsense, you'll stay in your room until you do tell him!'

Lizzie could feel everyone, including herself, getting angry and outraged in a way that was far from helpful. 'Daddy! We're not living in a Victorian melodrama! You can't lock me in my room. I'm not a child.' She didn't think this was the moment to point out that she and her friend had once tried climbing out of her window and back in again and had done it quite easily. It would create more unhappiness and upset.

'I'll do what I like in my house, young lady! And

you'll obey the rules while you're under my roof!'

'Daddy, I know I've got pregnant, but I haven't broken any rules,' she said gently. 'Supposing I'd been a widow? How would you treat me then?'

Lizzie's mother became a bit misty-eyed. 'I wouldn't wish that on you, darling, but it would be quite different. You'd live here with us and we'd help you bring up the baby.' Her mother seemed quite taken with this idea.

'Well, couldn't we just pretend? I could live with you here for a bit — get a job — work until I can't any more . . .'

In fact she intended to go back to London as soon as she could — tomorrow morning probably — but she felt she ought to make sure her parents wouldn't look after her before she put her friends in a position where they had to. After all, although no one ever spoke about it, they all knew that staying in Alexandra's house couldn't go on for ever. Her relations could turn up at any moment and turn all Alexandra's lodgers out.

'You are not going into town!' Her misty-eyed mother had turned back into a strict headmistress. 'I'm not having you flaunting your condition in front of all my friends!'

'Mummy! Can you tell I'm pregnant just by looking at me? Really?'

'Of course not, it's far too soon,' said her mother crossly.

'So, while it doesn't show, I could get a little job — '

'No,' said the Voice of Doom that was her father. 'Certainly not. You can live here until it's convenient for you to go north to Cousin Margaret, or you decide to come to your senses and tell the father. But you're

250

not going out!'

Lizzie sighed. 'Daddy, be sensible now. I am an adult. I know I won't be getting the 'key to the door' for a couple more years yet, but are you really expecting me to stay inside the house for the next six months? It would mean I could never do the shopping for Mummy, or pop to the shop if we run out of something.' Lizzie would have liked to be able to specify the something but her mother was a very efficient shopper who bought the same things every week. She never ran out of anything. 'I might need to buy Mummy a box of Maltesers. You know she loves them.'

Lizzie's parents looked at each other, trying to have a silent conversation about how to deal with their disappointing child. It was going to be hard to put up a united front when they couldn't discuss it.

'I think it would be all right if she went to the local shop, don't you? Before she starts showing?' said her mother.

'She'll be up north long before there's any sign of a baby!' said her father. He wasn't ready to make any concessions yet.

'Shall I make some more tea?' suggested Lizzie, hoping that if she gave them some privacy her mother might be able to get her father to soften a bit.

'No thank you!' said her father, unusually outraged at such a harmless suggestion. 'You know perfectly well that too much tea stops your mother sleeping! Not that she'll be doing much of that anyway, now she's found out about your condition.'

'OK. I'll do the washing-up then. Excuse me, you two,' said Lizzie and left the room.

She made sure the kitchen was as her mother liked

it, and that everything was put away in the places that hadn't altered in her lifetime (although some of them were not very convenient). Lizzie realised it would take her parents years to get over the shock of her being unmarried and pregnant. She had to leave as quickly as possible. And although she desperately wanted to be on the early train tomorrow, she felt this would be a bit unkind. And the news was still very fresh; maybe a couple of days seeing that Lizzie was still the same daughter they had always loved would soften them a little.

But if Lizzie had imagined her parents would relent a bit she was wrong; they remained resolutely furious. And after two days of being shunned and shouted at in turns she made a decision. She packed a few extra things into her case, found her Post Office book in her mother's bureau, wrote a message for her mother in a Waverley notelet (a touching picture of a foal sitting in a field of poppies), apologising yet again for her condition and explaining that she'd taken the train back to London, and left the house very early the next day.

★   ★   ★

'They want me to go and stay with a cousin I've never met and then go into a Mother and Baby Home. They'll take away my baby,' said Lizzie when she'd arrived back in Belgravia, while David made her breakfast.

'Don't worry,' said Alexandra. She sat down next to Lizzie, wearing a man's dressing gown made out of silk. 'We'll think of something. You keep calm. We won't let you go into a Mother and Baby Home.'

252

'It's earning my keep I'm worrying about,' said Lizzie. 'I'll need to save up for when I can't work. And I know I can't depend on staying here for ever.'

David and Alexandra were thoughtful for a few moments. 'I can give you work restoring antique linen,' said David.

'And you can do waitressing. And then you can help Meg with the canapés, when you're too big to carry trays,' said Alexandra. Her eyes widened. 'Talking of which, I was working at a cocktail party last night and I saw Vanessa.'

'Oh?' Lizzie almost asked Alexandra if she'd told Vanessa she was pregnant, but knew the answer: of course she hadn't.

'Yes! I was there in my black dress and white apron, of course, so we had one of those conversations without moving our lips. I didn't want to embarrass Vanessa by treating her as my friend. Anyway, I gather she's a bit fed up at the moment so I asked her to come round this evening.'

'It's funny about Vanessa, isn't it?' said Lizzie. 'I was terrified of her when I first saw her and now she's just a jolly friend.'

'She likes coming over here, I think. She doesn't feel judged,' Alexandra agreed.

★ ★ ★

Some hours later, everyone was in the kitchen. Meg, who'd done a pre-dinner drinks party, was sitting with her shoes off, her waitress's outfit askew, drinking a glass of wine that David had given her. She was tired. Lizzie felt glad to be back in London and was darning David's favourite cardigan that the moths had got to, and Alexandra was making a ragu for the spaghetti she planned to serve later. She had declared that living with brilliant cooks meant she didn't get enough practice and she needed some.

David answered the door when Vanessa arrived. She had a bunch of flowers and a bottle of wine. When they had both got down to the kitchen she put the bottle on the table. 'I stole it from Daddy's cellar. I've no idea what it is!'

David had a look at the label and choked. 'I hope he doesn't call the police on you, darling, it's a very good vintage.'

'There were dozens like it, he won't notice,' said Vanessa, pulling up a chair. 'But I've got news!'

Lizzie was arranging the flowers. 'What?'

'It's Hugo and Electra! The engagement's off!'

'Oh my God,' said Alexandra, looking at Lizzie, who put down the freesia she was holding.

'Do you know why?' asked Meg, apparently re-energised by this news. She got up. 'I'll finish those for you, Lizzie. Find yourself a glass of water.'

'Water?' said Vanessa. 'Let's have the wine! If David's right it'll be rather marvellous.'

'Water's good!' said Lizzie, knowing that London tap wasn't famous for its flavour.

'Let's not waste this on Lizzie if she doesn't feel like it,' said David. 'I'll get clean glasses.'

'Are you OK, Lizzie?' asked Vanessa.

She seemed so concerned, Lizzie hurried to reassure her. 'Oh, I'm fine. I just seem to have gone off alcohol a bit since . . . ' She felt silent. Meg and Alexandra were looking at her, their mouths open, willing her to say something neutral. David's lips were pursed in stifled amusement but Vanessa just looked worried.

'Since . . .' There didn't seem to be a single word in the language she could utter.

'You sit down, darling,' said David to her. 'Maybe you've got a touch of flu.'

Lizzie sat and let David fuss round her. But Vanessa was still staring. 'Lizzie,' she said. 'Are you . . . pregnant?'

Lizzie exhaled. 'Yes, I am.' It seemed a relief to say it. She couldn't think of a convincing lie anyway.

'Oh God, Lizzie!' said Vanessa. 'Who — oh my God! It's not Hugo, is it?'

'Yes,' said Lizzie. 'But you're not to tell him. He's not to find out.'

'Is that why the engagement was broken off?' asked Vanessa. 'I mean — I thought it was Electra, but maybe it was Hugo — '

'No,' said Lizzie, firm now. 'It can't have had anything to do with me. Hugo doesn't know and I haven't seen him since your dance.' Although she didn't look at them she was aware of Meg and Alexandra fiddling with things; they of course, had seen him.

'Well, I don't know what to say!' said Vanessa. 'If you were responsible for him calling off his engagement I'll be grateful forever. Electra is such hard work and can be so nasty sometimes — and she's so relentlessly thin! She's always making snarky remarks about me being plump when I'm not.' She paused. 'But why don't you want to tell Hugo? I know he's my brother and everything, but he's a nice man. He'd take care of you.'

'Really, Nessa, I don't want him to know,' said Lizzie quickly while the others drew breath to agree with Vanessa. 'It was terribly unfortunate that I got pregnant, but we don't know each other really. After

255

I nearly drowned and he saved me, we got carried away. We were both so grateful not to be dead, I suppose. I don't want him to ruin his life. He saved mine. It wouldn't be fair to him.'

There was a silence during which no one knew what to say and then Alexandra said, 'OK. Time to put the spaghetti on. Does anyone know how much I should cook?'

24

Lizzie was home early having helped Meg with a tea party. Meg was still at the house, washing up, so Lizzie was alone. She let herself into the kitchen via the area steps, longing to get her shoes off. She wasn't sure if they hurt because her feet were swelling (a symptom of pregnancy, she had discovered) or if her shoes were just too small. She'd bought them in a sale to go with her waitress's uniform.

There was someone sitting at the table and she jumped in shock. It was Hugo.

He got up when she came in. 'I'm so sorry to startle you. Alexandra insisted I stayed to wait for you. She and David have gone to the theatre. I suggested coming back tomorrow but she wouldn't let me.' He smiled. 'She's a very determined woman, isn't she?'

Lizzie's mouth went dry. 'Yes. Yes, she is. Would you like some tea?'

'Yes,' he said. 'But I'm going to make it. Alexandra showed me where everything is and said you've been waitressing with Meg and will want to sit down and take your shoes off.'

Lizzie couldn't help laughing. 'She's not only determined, she's also very frank.'

'That's a good thing. And you'd better take them off immediately.'

Lizzie did as she was told. She felt very torn. She had sworn, and truly believed, she didn't want to see Hugo, but now he was in front of her, making tea, her heart lifted with joy. Even though she was determined that he wouldn't learn her secret. Unless he already knew . . .

'Here we are: tea.' He lifted the teapot and poured. 'Should I have left it to brew a bit longer? Is that too weak for you?'

'It's fresh and I haven't made it or poured it.' She sipped it. 'It's lovely.'

'I should have brought cake,' he said. 'There's a lovely little cake shop on the corner, near where I work.'

'I'm full of cake,' Lizzie admitted, wondering why he was being so nice to her. 'Meg and I shared a bit of Victoria jam sponge that had got squashed. It was filled with cream. Actually I feel a bit sick.' The instant she said the word she wondered if this was some-how revealing. She had to stay calm. If he knew she was pregnant, he would have mentioned it by now. Wouldn't he?

He pulled out the chair next to hers and, when he was seated, he poured his own tea. 'I expect you're wondering why I'm here.'

Lizzie nodded and drank more tea. It was easier than talking.

'I've come to say goodbye.'

Lizzie nearly dropped her cup. 'Goodbye?'

'Well, not for ever. But I'm leaving London. I know Nessa told you that Electra and I are no longer engaged.' He looked at her for confirmation so she nodded. 'I don't know if she also told you that I'm giving up the law. I'm going to become an apprentice to a master cabinet maker. I'm going to learn how to make furniture.'

'Oh,' said Lizzie after a second or two. 'That's why you bought woodworking tools at the market that time.'

He nodded. 'I'm surprised you remember, but yes.'

'And why there were tools in the boathouse?'

'I used to hide up there and make things,' he said. 'My parents wouldn't have tolerated me doing anything like that.' He laughed ruefully. 'In fact, they won't tolerate it now. They're not speaking to me at the moment. Four generations of judges and I'm not following on. As far as they are concerned, it's an utter disaster.'

Lizzie had suffered a lot of family disapproval herself recently and knew how horrible it was. 'Oh, I'm so sorry!'

'It's not your fault. First, I disengaged myself from a woman they thought was the perfect wife for me, and then told them I'm going to throw up a very lucrative, respectable profession to whittle sticks. Hardly what they spent all that money on my education for.'

Lizzie couldn't help laughing. She could just imagine Sir Jasper's horror at the thought of his son doing anything manual. 'My parents aren't speaking to me, either. I've done something far worse, and have been far more disappointing — ' She stopped suddenly, aware of what she'd been about to say.

'What?' His gaze was very intense. 'What have you done, Lizzie?'

She closed her eyes to see if that would strengthen her resolution. 'It's not — ' She stopped again.

He took hold of her hand. 'Lizzie?'

'I'm pregnant,' she whispered.

His hand gripped hers. 'Oh my God. That night?'

She nodded. 'Yes.'

He didn't let go of her hand and she was so grateful

he didn't ask questions. He didn't need her to confirm that the baby was his. 'Well, then we must get married,' he said, instead.

'No! It will ruin your life, Hugo! I didn't want to tell you because I don't want your life to be affected by something that was just — I don't know — an instinctive thing.'

'My life won't be ruined, but unless we get married, your life will be.'

Lizzie swallowed.

'I know a little bit about this because of my legal training and bringing up a baby on your own would be very difficult, even though of course I'd support you as much as I could.' He squeezed the hand he seemed to have forgotten he'd been holding. 'Being married won't be so bad, I promise.'

Lizzie bit her lip but didn't dare speak.

'I've got an afternoon off tomorrow. If you're not doing anything urgent I think we should go and see your parents and tell them we're getting married.'

'Do we have to? They've been so horrible.' At that moment Lizzie was ashamed of her parents and their social-climbing ways although she loved them very much. She was worried they might make Hugo feel more trapped than he must feel already.

'We do have to. I must reassure them that I'm a suitable husband for their only, much-loved daughter. Besides, we have to get their permission to get married. You're under twenty-one.'

'I hadn't thought of that,' Lizzie said. 'What about your parents? Shouldn't we see them, too? Although honestly, I think they'll think you marrying me is so much worse than you giving up the law that if you don't marry me, they'll forgive you for everything.'

'Except that I am going to marry you, whatever they say.'

He said it with such quiet resolution that Lizzie's brief plan of going to Hugo's parents and then declaring that she refused to marry their son melted. It wasn't that she didn't want to marry him, but she wanted his happiness more than she wanted her own. Discovering it was possible to love someone so much was a revelation.

She licked her lips, preparing to say something to indicate that he mustn't marry her just because she was pregnant and he was honourable, but she couldn't think of the words. She was certain that was his only reason but was there anything she could say that would stop him making this sacrifice? If there was, she didn't know what it could be.

They arranged that he would collect her the following afternoon at four o'clock. He apologised for not being able to make it a bit earlier, but he said he had a lot to do. And so it was that the next day, Lizzie was ready. She was dressed in her most respectable clothes, enhanced by a bright yellow jacket from Alexandra that looked lovely with Lizzie's simple summer dress, which was one of the ones her mother had chosen. She was determined to get on the right side of her own parents if she possibly could.

They drove to Lizzie's home town in Hugo's car and arrived at her parents' house just before five. Her mother opened the door.

'Elizabeth! You didn't say you were coming!'

'And who's this?' said her father, emerging from his study with a harrumph.

'Can we come in?' said Lizzie. 'Perhaps we could talk?'

261

'Fine words butter no parsnips, ' said her father enigmatically, but her mother held the door so they could enter.

They were ushered through to the sitting room and Lizzie sat down on the sofa. Her knees were feeling wobbly. She was already convinced that the meeting was not going to go well. But maybe Hugo could rescue it.

'My name is Hugo Lennox-Stanley. And I — '

'You're the man who's besmirched my daughter's good name and made sure this family can never hold its head up again in polite society?' said Lizzie's father.

'I really didn't mean to — ' said Hugo.

'It was your . . . your primitive passion that has ruined — I say *ruined* my daughter's life!' her father went on. 'I know my little girl! I know she wouldn't have dreamt of doing — anything — that would put her in this situation unless she was either forced or seduced! And I don't know which is worse!'

'Daddy! It wasn't like that! Really it wasn't. I told you.'

'Elizabeth, I don't wish to hear from you.'

Lizzie took some calming breaths. Any minute now her father would tell her it was none of her business, although she was the one who was pregnant. He was determined to get out every bit of his anger, disappointment and, possibly, fear and direct it at Hugo. It was easier for him to do this than to acknowledge that his daughter was capable of having passions of her own. Lizzie looked across to her mother and saw that she was crying. She wanted to go over and comfort her but realised she risked being pushed away.

'I'm going to make some tea,' she said to no one in particular and went into the kitchen.

Before she put the kettle on she had a drink of water. She was shaking and felt as if she was suffering from shock. She had once nearly been run over and afterwards she'd felt just as she did now. She had never seen her father so angry. Hugo had come to tell them that he was going to do what they must want — marry her — to save her from the disgrace of becoming an unmarried mother. And her father wouldn't let him speak. She felt perspiration break out along her hairline.

She sat down on a stool, holding her water, trembling and wanting to cry. She was half hoping that her mother would come in and they could hug and weep together and get over it, as they had when she was growing up. But Lizzie had been a biddable daughter and it hadn't often happened, which was probably why she felt so upset now.

Eventually Hugo came in, looking stern. 'I think we should go, Lizzie. Your father is still too angry to listen to what I have to say so we're not achieving anything. I think we probably need to give your parents time to calm down.'

Her parents were in the hall when they came out of the kitchen. Lizzie went to her mother and hugged her. Habit meant her mother's arms went round her daughter but it wasn't a proper hug. Lizzie didn't look at her father. Hugo took her arm and gently led her out of the house.

They drove until they were out of the town and then Hugo found a layby next to some woodland and pulled in. 'That could have gone better,' he said.

Lizzie gave a shuddering sigh. 'I'm so sorry they were so awful to you. I thought they'd be delighted I was going to get married.' She turned to him. 'It

263

was dreadful of my father to accuse you of — those things.'

'He loves his daughter very much and had a lot of pent-up anger to express,' Hugo said. He looked at her for a minute. 'Your hair is beginning to curl.' He moved the little kiss curls that had formed by her ears. '*Curly locks, curly locks, wilt though be mine? Thou shalt not do dishes, nor yet feed kine,*' he quoted softly. 'Except that you will have to do dishes — although I promise you'll be spared the kine.'

She smiled. The shock had faded and she was beginning to feel better about it all. 'I'm used to doing dishes — currently it's a big part of my job. And I could probably feed a cow if I had to, but please don't ask me to milk one.'

Hugo didn't return her smile. 'But seriously, I can offer you very little except my name. Financially, I mean. We're going to be really poor. I have savings and a small income from some money left by an aunt but honestly? I can't keep you in any sort of comfort.'

'So shall we camp on the roadside like gypsies?'

He did laugh now. 'Not quite that bad. I'm going to be renting a little house on the edge of the woods. It belongs to old friends of mine and is quite near the workshop. It's very handy.'

'That sounds lovely! Why are you making such a big thing of it? You're putting a roof over my head.'

'It's not a very grand roof.'

'What? No turrets or castellations? How awful! Tell me what it is like, then.'

'It used to be lived in by the gamekeeper on a big estate that my friends own. It has two bedrooms, a sitting room and a small kitchen that was added later. Oh, and you'll love this — a bathroom.'

'Is it a specially super bathroom?'

'Not at all, quite the opposite, but it's in the house. That is very modern, believe me. The outside privy is still there, but you're not obliged to use it unless you want to.'

'Oh,' said Lizzie, as understanding dawned.

'But I really like it. There's quite a big garden. No lawn, or anything like that, it's just for fruit and vegetables.'

'I'll have to learn how to garden then,' said Lizzie brightly.

'You will. But although we're in the woods the garden is quite a suntrap in the afternoon. The house isn't dark.' He paused. 'But it is very different from where *you've* been brought up.'

'Or where you've been brought up?'

He laughed. 'True, but this is what I want to do and I'm happy to make the sacrifice.' He frowned. 'Perhaps it's unfair of me to ask you to live like that, though. Electra certainly couldn't have. Perhaps I should stay with the law and give up the idea of becoming a cabinet maker.'

Lizzie's hand shot out to touch his sleeve. 'No! You must do what you want with your life! You mustn't give up your dreams for me — I don't care about money. I can cook; I can make my own clothes and clothes for the baby.' She bit her lip. 'Your clothes are probably all such good quality they'll last for generations.'

'You're so right! They will. I have a coat that was my grandfather's. You do make me laugh, Lizzie.'

'And that's a good thing?'

'It absolutely is.' He flashed her a grin. 'Are you up for the second lot of parents?'

'I suppose so. I'm not expecting them — your father

265

anyway — to have had a change of heart though. He's still going to disapprove of me horribly.'

'That's his choice. Now, we must get a move on. I've booked a table at a little restaurant near where my parents live. It's nothing remotely fancy but it's cosy and they're expecting us.'

★ ★ ★

The restaurant was a café during the day, but in the evening served a few early diners. There was a set menu of soup, lamb chops and home-made lemon sponge with ice cream. They ate quickly until Lizzie grew nervous and had to stop.

'Never mind,' Hugo said bracingly on their way back to the car, 'we know it's going to be hell. We'll just tell them we're getting married and get out of there.'

'Are you sure I don't look pregnant?' she asked him as they sat in the car outside the big house. She'd asked Hugo if they could wait a few moments until she felt ready.

'Lizzie, you look lovely! You're wearing the perfect clothes for a girl about to meet her future in-laws.'

'Except they've met me before and they don't like me.'

'It was only my father who took against your short skirt.'

'Are we going to tell them I'm . . .' She paused before saying the word. '. . . pregnant?'

'We'll play it by ear. Now, the sooner we go in the sooner we can get away again afterwards.' He glanced at his watch. 'They eat at eight. Better not to keep my father from his dinner.'

Hugo let them into the house through the side door which was unlocked and led the way to where his parents were sitting. Sir Jasper got up when they entered the room.

Hugo went in first. He kissed his mother and shook hands with his father. 'And here's Lizzie,' said Hugo. 'Who you have met but only briefly.'

Lizzie stepped forward to say hello but although she thought she was speaking no sound emerged. Lady Lennox-Stanley gave her the briefest of smiles. 'Do sit down.'

But Lizzie was too scared to move.

Sir Jasper nodded.

'I'm surprised you've deigned to grace us with your presence,' said Sir Jasper to Hugo. 'You've turned your back on everything we've done for you, after all.'

'Father, I'm following my own course. I'm very grateful for all the advantages you've given me but now I'm using them to do what I've always wanted to do.'

'You seemed perfectly happy with the law until you came across this . . . ' Sir Jasper paused, possibly wondering how he could describe Lizzie in a way that wouldn't be rude but would make his opinion of her plain. '. . . young person.'

'My giving up the law was nothing to do with Lizzie.'

'Drink?' said Sir Jasper abruptly.

'No thank you,' said Hugo. 'We've come to tell you that we're getting married.'

Sir Jasper choked on his whisky. 'Are we to assume that . . . '

'Lizzie,' said Hugo.

'. . . is with child?'

Lizzie sat down suddenly on the chair behind her before she could faint.

Sir Jasper turned his attention to her as she perched on the edge of her seat. 'This is a very unfortunate occurrence. I'm sure there are many other solutions but my son has obviously undertaken to give you his name.'

It took Lizzie a moment or two to grasp that Sir Jasper meant Hugo intended to marry her, which she already knew.

'I am,' said Hugo. 'It is my baby too. Lizzie didn't get pregnant all on her own!'

Both of his parents looked at him in horror. Lizzie didn't know if it was because he'd admitted his part in her pregnancy or had used the word 'pregnant'.

'Have you considered other options?' Lady Lennox-Stanley asked. 'You could release my son from the obligation he obviously feels. We could offer some sort of remuneration for you, if you did this.'

Lizzie longed to say, 'So you'd pay me to have an abortion?' but she couldn't. She couldn't use the word and she didn't dare give them the slightest hint that she was open to offers. She wasn't. 'Hugo and I feel that getting married is the best option for . . . our baby.'

Sir Jasper banged his hand hard on the arm of his chair. 'It isn't a baby yet! And it certainly isn't the best option for my son!'

'I think Hugo can decide what's best for him. He is an adult.' She kept her voice low but clear. She didn't like shouting and didn't want to add to the noise level.

'Hm,' said Sir Jasper. 'Hugo is indeed over twenty-one but are you? Have your parents consented to this marriage?'

'Of course they have!' snapped Lady Lennox-Stanley. 'They'd pounce on a man like Hugo like a tiger on a tethered goat! He's a catch they never could have hoped for. Their daughter, marrying into the upper classes? It'll be their dream come true!'

Lizzie cleared her throat and got to her feet. 'Actually, my parents aren't at all happy about the situation. I do hope they will realise that our marriage is the best thing for everyone — as I hope you will also. However, as you and they seem to be in perfect agreement on the subject, there is no point in staying here a moment longer!' Her anger was seeping past her desire to be completely calm and dignified.

'You sit back down!' roared Sir Jasper.

Hugo was on his feet now. 'Father, I realise that you're unhappy about our marriage — it's not what you expected and it's come as a shock to you. But you must never, ever, speak to Lizzie like that again, or I will genuinely never darken your doors again. Is that what you really want?'

Sir Jasper deflated a little. 'Hugo, you are my son and as such you have duties and responsibilities. I don't want you — either of you — to be trapped in a marriage that is doomed to failure.'

Hugo nodded. 'In which case we'll leave now. Come along, Lizzie.'

He took her arm and swept her out of the drawing room, along the passage to the side door and out of the house.

They walked arm in arm towards the car. Although it had been awful, it wasn't an unexpected reaction. 'Well,' she said. 'I suppose that could have gone worse but I'm not sure how.'

'No,' Hugo agreed. 'I should have made the old

devil apologise to you.'

'No point, it wouldn't have changed anything, even if you had managed to make him do it.'

'You were so impressive, though. I felt so proud of you. Maybe you should take up the law in my place.'

Lizzie giggled. 'No thank you, not if it means I'd have to go through scenes like that every day. I'd rather feed kine, or whatever it was you had in mind for me.'

Hugo stopped. 'My parents really are unspeakable.'

'Don't feel guilty, it's not your fault they're like that. And you can't blame them really. They're bound to connect this decision with you leaving the law and breaking up with Electra, even though I had nothing to do with it.'

'That's not entirely true.'

'What?'

Hugo sighed. 'I suppose we'd better set off for London. I've got an early start in the morning. There are lots of loose ends to clear up.' But he didn't immediately start the car. 'Are you sure you don't mind living in a hovel, Lizzie? That's how Electra would describe it.'

'I think I'm going to love it. It sounds so romantic. I can't wait to see it.'

He looked at her quickly. 'Are you very tired?'

'I will be but at the moment I'm fine.' She was full of nervous energy, fired up by her recent encounter with Sir Jasper. 'Why do you ask?'

'Shall we drive to the cottage? So you can see where we'll live when we're married?'

'I thought you said you had an early start.'

'Yes, but that's tomorrow. If you're game, let's go!'

'I'd absolutely love that,' said Lizzie.

He switched on the engine of the car. 'Try and doze.

270

It's about an hour away.'

Sleep felt very far away, but perfect happiness felt a lot nearer.

25

Lizzie had been feeling extra tired since she'd been pregnant and did actually doze off a bit until Hugo woke her. Being summer, it was still light but there was something magical about being in the country-side as the darkness began to creep in.

'We're nearly there. We're just about to pass where Patsy and Tim live. I was at school with Tim although he was a few years above me and Patsy's parents were friends of my parents so I've known her even longer.' He gestured to a drive which led to a house of a size and type seen for sale in the pages of *Country Life*. It definitely qualified as a stately home.

Lizzie shrank in her seat a little. Were Patsy and Tim (who were probably titled) going to hate her in the same way that Hugo's parents did?

Hugo was unaware of her misgivings as he carried on with his commentary. 'We go through the village, which is very pretty. There's the church, a proper green where they play cricket. I've actually played there myself when Tim needed a batsman.' He slowed down a little as they passed an expanse of grass surrounded by trees boasting a proper pond with ducks.

'You don't have to sell it to me. I can see how lovely it is. The church is wonderful. Look at that beautiful spire!' Lizzie paused. 'I don't suppose we could get married there?' Suddenly she found that she did care about her wedding, a bit, and didn't want to get married in a register office and wear a suit. She wanted a dress and a veil and her friends as bridesmaids.

'I'm not entirely sure of the rules,' said Hugo. 'But Patsy will know. We'll ask her.'

He meant to be reassuring but Lizzie was already a little afraid of Patsy. She would either be like Electra, or be Electra's best friend. Or both.

'How much does Patsy know about — our situation?'

'I did have to tell her everything, but she was very matter-of-fact about it. She even invited you to stay with her and Tim until the wedding. Tim thought it was a huge joke. I don't think he liked Electra much.'

'Right,' said Lizzie, not sure if she liked being a joke.

'I think Tim was just very surprised that I, who he's always teased for being respectable and law-abiding, could make a girl pregnant by mistake and end up having to marry her.'

Lizzie didn't quite know how to answer this.

After a little while Hugo turned off the road and on to a track. 'Now we're getting on to the estate. You can see it's quite wooded but not too densely.'

'You mean it's not spooky?' asked Lizzie, who was wary.

'I don't think so, no. Look how beautiful the trees are! And there's the house.' A few minutes later he pulled the car off the track.

Lizzie stifled a little gasp of delight. It was a dream cottage. It had a pitched roof, a couple of tall chimneys and plenty of windows. There was a garden that was filled with tall flowers she couldn't identify and seemed to include a couple of fruit trees.

Hugo may have misinterpreted the noise Lizzie made. 'I know,' he said apologetically, 'it's not very big and miles from the nearest town. Although it's walking distance to the village.'

Lizzie had a sudden flash of herself walking along the path, through the trees with a pram and a happy baby. 'No! I think it's wonderful! And to be honest, thinking where your parents live, anywhere normal is going to seem tiny to you. Can we go inside?'

'I have got a key so I can get us in, but I'm not sure if the electricity is on. We might have to manage with a torch.'

'Have you got a torch?'

'Of course. In the car. Wait here.'

Soon they'd gone in through the back door and down the passage where several old waterproof coats hung, and into the main room.

With the aid of his torch, Hugo found a couple of oil lamps that he lit and they filled the room with warm light and shadows. 'I promise there is electricity, just not at the moment.'

They were in a good-sized sitting room with a huge fireplace including a bread oven. 'This is quite big!' said Lizzie, surprised.

'Yes, but this would have been the only room,' said Hugo. 'A whole family, with several children, would have done everything in this room, including the cooking. There would have been a range in that fireplace.'

'I almost wish there still was. Think how cosy it would have been! Oh, look, there are a couple of candles on the mantelpiece. Let's light them.'

'There are a couple of bedrooms upstairs,' said Hugo.

'But where are the stairs?' asked Lizzie.

'Behind that cupboard door. Apparently it keeps the draughts down in here, but of course, no heat goes up the stairs unless the door is open.'

She nodded. 'And the kitchen?'

'Now you no longer have to cook on the range there is a lean-to. Through there.' He picked up a lamp and led the way.

The kitchen wasn't very big or very promising, but it was a proper brick extension with plenty of shelves, a large sink with a wooden draining board under the window and a wooden plate rack on the wall next to it. The window looked out over the garden. There was a table with two chairs against the wall and a small separate larder with a zinc mesh-covered window.

'This just needs some jolly curtains and a lick of paint,' said Lizzie.

'I'll talk to my landlady about it,' said Hugo.

'Patsy? No, please don't. I know she's going to blame me for ruining your life like everyone else you know. I would hate to make her hate me before we've even met.'

'She's not going to hate you! Why should she? Everyone except my parents love you! You're very loveable . . .' For a moment it seemed as if he was about to say something else but didn't.

'Where is the bathroom?' Lizzie asked, to fill the sudden silence.

'The bathroom is less inviting than the kitchen. It's through there.'

Lizzie decided it would need more than curtains and a lick of paint to make this little coffin-shaped room cosy but she had hope. Alexandra and David would have ideas about what to do. They could help her make it nice.

'Are you sure you can live here, Lizzie?' Hugo looked around dubiously. 'With a baby? There's no launderette you can go to with the washing. There's probably a dolly tub and a wringer in the shed. Can you imagine washing nappies using those?'

'I love this house!' she said, refusing to think about washing nappies. 'With Patsy's permission, I'll make it into my dream home. Yours too, I hope,' she added quickly.

He laughed. 'If it's your dream home it will definitely be mine too.'

'Let's have a look at the garden,' she said. 'Can we get out through the back door? Oh yes, here's the key.'

A second later she was in the garden, the moon, nearly full, highlighting a rambling rose, a fruit tree of some kind and anonymous shrubs. She could smell honeysuckle but the air was full of other fragrances she couldn't identify. Yet the smell, the moonlight and the falling dew filled her with a strange kind of happiness.

'It's really lovely here,' she said to Hugo a few moments later.

'It is. And the moonlight is so bright. Did you know people used to bleach their clothes in the moonlight?'

'I didn't, no,' said Lizzie. 'Although of course it was terribly kind of Patsy to invite me to stay, I do wish we could stay here now, and just live together and not with Patsy until the wedding.'

He came up and stood behind her so she could feel the warmth of his body against hers. He sighed. 'I know. But we really can't, not in such a small community where we're intending to live. People would be so shocked. No one would talk to you.'

She sighed. 'I know you're right. I just can't wait to call this lovely little house my home.'

While this was true, she was also really impatient for the time they could live together and, if they wanted to, make love among the roses and the honeysuckle in the moonlight. If only it could be now!

★ ★ ★

The drive back to London seemed to go far too quickly. Hugo drove his car swiftly and with certainty and it didn't seem long enough. In the car Lizzie felt she didn't have to face the difficulties being pregnant had produced. She didn't have to think about her parents, his parents, or anything except swooping along, through the night, with Hugo.

'Will they have left the door unlocked for you or do you have a key?' Hugo asked, waking her from her pleasant doze.

'Oh! There's a back-door key hidden in a special place,' she said. 'We all use it.'

'I'm surprised you haven't been burgled!' said Hugo, amused.

'I know! I said that to Alexandra and she reckoned the burglars had been in, had a look around and decided there was nothing worth taking and pushed off again.'

'Well, let's get you inside. You're out very late for a young woman.'

'Who's pregnant,' she added.

'That too.' He put his hand on her arm, concern evident in his expression. 'Lizzie, we're going to have to press on with our plans. There's no time to waste before we get married.'

'I know. And I also know my parents will give permission for us to get married, but all the other things — there's so much.'

'Patsy will help. We must get you down to her as

soon as possible. She'll love having you and a wedding to arrange. She'll steamroller over any difficulties.' He squeezed her arm. 'Trust me. It'll all be fine.' Then he kissed her cheek and opened the back door for her.

26

Two days later everyone was helping Lizzie load her things into Hugo's car. Lizzie was reconciled to going to stay with Patsy and Tim but she was still nervous about meeting them both.

'I wish we could have had a farewell party for you,' said Alexandra.

'No time for that!' said Lizzie. 'There's a wedding to organise!'

Just as Lizzie was about to get in the car, David came out with the sewing machine and found room for it in the boot. 'Alexandra said you must have this. You know you won't be happy without it,' he said. Lizzie tried to remonstrate but was overruled, Alexandra pointing out that she was really the only one of them to use it often.

'Well, if that really is everything,' said Hugo. 'We should go.'

There was another round of hugs, thanks, kisses and promises to visit and then at last Lizzie was in the passenger seat.

'They'll miss you,' said Hugo as he found his way out of London.

'I'll miss them too. They've been like family to me.'

'You still haven't heard from your mother?'

Lizzie shook her head. 'I wrote to her. I told her about the cottage and that we were planning the wedding. I really don't think they'll pretend they don't want us to get married for much longer. They'll have looked you up in Burke's Peerage by now. They'll know who your family is.'

'Just as well Burke's Peerage doesn't rank people by snobbery and bad-temperedness, isn't it?'

'I don't think that would matter to my parents. If you're in there, you're OK by them.' She paused. 'I suppose Patsy and Tim are in there?'

'In Burke's Peerage? I dare say they are, although I haven't looked them up. Why?'

'I'm just a bit — anxious — about meeting them.'

'I promise you, you won't be, the moment you do meet. They are delightful. And so are you!' He looked down at her briefly and smiled, and Lizzie's heart turned over with happiness.

★ ★ ★

Patsy and Tim were on the steps of the big Queen Anne house when Hugo and Lizzie drove up. The front door was open and at least three Labradors were milling about on the grass in front of the drive. With them was a small boy in pyjamas.

Hugo got out and came round to let Lizzie out. Not for the first time, Lizzie was glad of his good manners. They meant he would be by her side when she first met these people who would be so important in their lives.

Tim came over. 'Hugo, old chap.' He clapped him on the arm. 'I have to say, I like this fiancée a lot better than the other one. She's far prettier and probably a lot more fun.' Tim took hold of Lizzie's hand and shook it. Then he kissed her cheek. 'Really lovely to meet you, and I'm so glad you'll be staying with us. It's Lizzie, isn't it?'

Lizzie smiled shyly. Although the welcome couldn't

have been warmer, she was still anxious. She didn't have a lot of experience of hearty, country-based families who tended to have arcane rituals only known to members of the inner circle. And she was not part of the inner circle and possibly never would be.

Patsy joined her husband. 'Hello, Lizzie. I'm Patsy, I've known Hugo and Nessa all my life. And they both speak very highly of you. Say hello to George. George!' Patsy's voice had a carrying quality she probably found very useful. 'Come and meet Lizzie. She's Uncle Hugo's friend. They're going to get married.'

Lizzie couldn't tell how old George was, probably about five. The knees of his pyjamas had grass stains on them and his hair flopped into his eyes. 'Hello.' He looked at his mother. 'Do I call her Lizzie, or Aunt Lizzie?'

'Just Lizzie is fine,' Lizzie said. She took hold of his hand and gave it a shake. 'Hello.'

George nodded shyly and went back to the dogs as soon as he could.

'He's a nice chap on the whole,' said Tim. 'But a bit awkward with the ladies.'

'Timbo, he's only four. What do you expect?' said Patsy. 'Now come along in. Let's get you a drink. I've lit a fire. I know it's summer but for me, a house without a fire is never welcoming. Besides, it's chilly.'

The sitting room was full of tatty sofas and large armchairs. The fire burned in a very beautiful fireplace and there were large family portraits on the walls, but the room was definitely shabby.

'Sit by the fire, Lizzie,' said Tim. 'That chair is quite comfortable. We haven't been in this house long and we're still deciding which furniture to burn and what to keep. That chair is a keeper.'

George and the dogs all flopped on the hearthrug in front of the fire and, suddenly, Lizzie found herself joined in her chair by a small brown dog.

'So sorry, that's Maud,' said Patsy. 'Shove her off if you don't like her. She's quite old and likes to be near the fire but not with the Labs.'

Maud was now sitting on Lizzie's lap. 'I like her. There's a dog in the house in London. Clover. She's always a comfort if you need cheering up. Sits on your lap like a furry hot water bottle.'

Patsy gave Lizzie's shoulder a pat. 'Have a drink. You need something after your journey. What do you fancy? What about a glass of sherry? Always hard to know what's going to taste nice when you're preggers. Timbo?' she called to her husband who was on his way out of the room. 'Don't forget the cheesy biscuits!' She turned back to Lizzie. 'Don't worry, it's all going to be fine.' Lizzie realised that she didn't know if Patsy was saying their pre-dinner drinks would be fine, or if her whole life would be fine. But Lizzie felt reassured on both counts.

Patsy turned her attention to Hugo, who was making himself at home, obviously among old friends. He knew all the dogs by name and George went to him with a train that needed fixing.

Lizzie settled back in her chair, sipping her sherry and eating cheesy biscuits from a bowl that Patsy had put by her side. The others talked easily about events and people she didn't know. But although she felt detached from the scene around her, she didn't feel excluded. It was restful, she decided.

Eventually, Patsy hauled herself out of her chair. 'I suppose we'd better eat something. And Georgie? Time you were in bed.'

George, possibly aware that several people had witnessed him yawning, and therefore wouldn't be convinced by a 'I'm not tired' protest, looked at Hugo. 'Will you read me a bit more of that story, Uncle Hugo?'

'Of course!' said Hugo, getting up. 'I've been dying to find out what Captain Nancy and Peggy did to Captain Flint. Come on. Race you upstairs.'

'Hugo is George's favourite person,' Tim explained. 'I do hope you don't mind. Electra did take exception, rather. She didn't like him paying attention to anyone but her, even when her rival was a small boy.'

'Hugo only brought her here once,' said Patsy. 'Not a success. She didn't quite understand that Timbo had inherited a house and its contents but there was very little money with it, and everything was very dilapidated. She didn't approve of Maud sitting on her lap, either.'

'It's a beautiful house,' said Lizzie, looking around her. 'I can't thank you enough for having me to stay. '

'It's an absolute pleasure! Lovely to have another woman about the place.'

Tim gathered up the dirty glasses on to a tray and took them away, leaving Patsy and Lizzie on their own. 'I know you're in a really difficult situation,' said Patsy. 'But Hugo is a darling man. He will look after you.'

'I know,' said Lizzie. 'He's been so kind already.'

'And we'll get you safely married. Then you can really get to know each other.'

'Do you think we'll be able to get married in the church? It's so pretty.'

Patsy didn't answer immediately. After a moment she said, 'I'm sure we can arrange that. It's unconventional and probably against the rules to marry outside your own parish, but the vicar and his wife are jolly good sorts. This house has always had a strong connection with the church. They have their fête in the garden, the estate has donated a Christmas tree every year and of course the village school is a church school and I'm a governor. I'm sure he'll bend the rules for you and Hugo.'

Her words were reassuring but Lizzie sensed doubt.

Patsy went on. 'Do you have any special skills that might be useful to the church?'

Lizzie nodded. 'I used to help out with the flowers in the church at home. And I can sew. Do you think those things would make me useful?'

'Oh my goodness, they should fall on your neck rejoicing!' said Patsy, happier now. 'Right! Let's see if I've managed to burn the stew. More than likely!'

★ ★ ★

'Do put some butter on your baked potato,' Tim begged her, holding the dish out to her about half an hour later.

'I've got some butter,' said Lizzie.

'Not enough to cover a sixpence!' said Tim. 'Here.' He cut off a lump weighing several ounces and put it on Lizzie's plate. 'I reckon with a baked spud, you need pretty much equal quantities of butter and potato.'

'Only if you're a complete glutton, darling,' said his wife. 'Put the butter back if you don't want it, Lizzie. Tim can be such a pig.'

They were in a dining room that had furniture in better condition. Patsy had put a cast-iron casserole on a trivet in the middle of the table and was doling out stew as if she was serving school dinners. Except,

Lizzie noted, it smelt delicious.

Hugo arrived at the table late. 'So sorry. George and I had to finish the book. It's so good! Have I missed the starter?' he added, looking around at people's stew-filled plates.

'There wasn't one,' said Patsy. 'Although — like Lizzie — I was trained under the terrifying Mme Wilson, I was never good at the fiddly stuff. Now eat up, everyone.'

'I gather Hugo has taken you to see the game-keeper's cottage, Lizzie,' said Tim.

'Yes, but he did it at night, so she wouldn't see how primitive it really is,' said Patsy. 'I can't decide if that's a good thing or just putting off the moment when Lizzie decides she can't live in a hovel.'

Lizzie laughed. 'It's not a hovel and seeing it at night, by lamplight, was very romantic. Seriously,' she added hurriedly, in case her talking about it being romantic would reveal too much about her feelings, 'it's a very nice house, and plenty big enough for two and a baby. Or even two babies,' she added rashly, and then blushed.

'Wait till you see it in daylight,' said Patsy. 'We'll go and have a look tomorrow. See if we can make it habitable.'

'I'd love to make some curtains for it,' said Lizzie. 'I've got a sewing machine with me.'

'Well, I've got an attic full of old curtains. We'll see if there's any you like and could adapt.' She paused. 'I'm afraid there's not much in the kitty for new fabric. We just rely on the shutters but you'll need curtains.'

'I think old fabric would be nicer anyway,' said Lizzie. 'And, if you felt it would be useful, I could adapt some for your windows? Unless you've banished them

285

to the attic because you hated the material, or just hate curtains?'

Patsy threw up her hands in delight. 'I don't hate curtains, it's just the ones here were hanging in ribbons. If you could do anything about them I would be delighted!'

'Anything I can do to help,' said Lizzie.

Patsy beamed with pleasure. 'Darling! I think you're going to make an absolutely terrific wife for Hugo. And don't worry about your parents approving of your marriage. Once they discover he's the most eligible bachelor in London, they'll be chuffed to little mint balls.'

★　★　★

'After breakfast we'll go and see the house. Would you like that, Georgie?' said Patsy, eating well-scraped toast that she had blithely burned. 'I'll give Di a ring first and suggest she meets us there. She's the vicar's wife and if she likes you, I'm sure it will be no problem getting married in the church.'

Patsy fell silent at that point and Lizzie couldn't decide if she had stopped talking because she was worrying about the meeting. Lizzie certainly was herself.

'You're going to be part of the congregation, after all,' went on Patsy, possibly trying to convince herself.

Earlier, Hugo and Tim had gone to look at the cars that Tim had inherited along with the house. Apparently there was a Bentley that Patsy thought would be really useful for the wedding. Patsy, George and Lizzie were dawdling over breakfast.

'We will have to get this wedding going,' said Patsy

rubbing her hands excitedly. 'I do love organising things! It's because I'm so bossy. But we haven't got time on our side.' She paused. 'Does your mother know where you're staying?'

'I wrote to her, giving the address of the cottage, so I expect she thinks I'm there.'

'With Hugo?' Patsy laughed. 'She won't like that. She'll be here as soon as she's worked out how to get here. But don't worry. I'll reassure her.' Patsy sighed. 'Tim and I had a lovely little holiday in a remote cottage in Scotland before we were married. It was delightful. And while that little house is a perfect love nest, you and Hughie can't be there together until you're married. The village wouldn't be able to cope.'

'Hugo explained. I knew it would be like that really, but just for a short time I thought how lovely it would be to just live there while we arranged the wedding.'

Patsy laughed. 'Let's get you married first. And until then, one of you had better live here and the other in the cottage. And I suggest it's Hugo there. It was going to be him on his own before — you know . . . '

'Before he knew I was pregnant?'

'It was a bit of a surprise. A lovely one, obviously.' Patsy sipped her tea, not wanting Lizzie to feel awkward.

'You have been very kind about it.'

Patsy looked Lizzie firmly in the eye. 'I've known Hugo most of my life and he's one of the nicest, kindest, most honourable men I know. I'd do anything for him. And actually' — Patsy seemed pleased — 'now I've met you, I'd do anything for you, too.'

Lizzie looked back at Patsy. This was her opportunity to ask what she had been longing to know: did Hugo love her? He was behaving in a loving way, being so kind, but was that just because he was honourable and she was pregnant? Was he only marrying her because he saw it as his duty?

But she didn't. She returned Patsy's warm smile and said, 'Thank you!'

Patsy brushed off Lizzie's gratitude. 'Nonsense! I think you're going to be such an asset to our little community. It's going to be super having you so near and I know you'll make Hugo very happy.'

'I'll certainly try to,' Lizzie agreed.

Patsy nodded. 'But there's no need to give up everything for him. You won't have time to yourself for years, but it's good to have something that's separate from Hugo, an interest that's all yours.' She gave a smile that suddenly made her beautiful. 'Now, I'll meet you by the front door in twenty minutes?'

27

Patsy, Lizzie and George had pulled up outside the cottage in Patsy's old Volvo estate when a car arrived at speed and screeched to a halt behind where they were parked.

'This is Di Baker, the vicar's wife,' said Patsy quickly, winding down her window as they watched a woman get out of the car.

'Patsy! Hello there!' The woman nodded at Lizzie. 'I'm so sorry but I can't stay,' she said to Patsy, leaning into the car. 'There's been an absolute disaster.'

'Oh, I'm sorry!' said Patsy. 'Anything I can help with?'

Di Baker withdrew from the car window. 'Sweet of you, but no. Two — two! — of my flower guild have come down with a stomach bug. Really, I should issue instructions that they shouldn't eat the same food when we've got a big event coming up in the church.'

Lizzie couldn't tell if she was joking, or really meant it.

'Oh, Di! What event? Don't say I've forgotten something important!' said Patsy, horrified.

Di shook her head. 'Don't worry, Patsy, you haven't. We're having a baptism on Sunday and the bishop's wife is among the guests — the bishop too, for all I know — but it's vital we have good flowers in the church as she was awfully sniffy about our contribution to the cathedral flower festival.

'So, you're short of arrangers?' said Patsy.

'Yes, which is why I'm not asking you to help,' said

Di. 'Flowers are not your forte. No offence.'

'Absolutely none taken,' said Patsy, who seemed excited, 'but before you rush off, let me introduce you to Lizzie — '

'Hello, lovely to meet you but — '

'Lizzie is a flower genius!' said Patsy. 'We were at a very big event a little while ago and the florist cancelled at the last minute — '

'She probably had a stomach bug!'

'— and Lizzie stepped in. Honestly, the flowers were just glorious! She is your woman.'

Lizzie glanced at Patsy. She hadn't known Patsy and Tim had been at the Lennox-Stanleys' ball, but now she thought about it, of course they would have — they were old family friends. Now she looked at Di Baker who was looking back at her, doubt and hope fighting for ascendance.

'Patsy is being very kind,' she said, 'and of course I had masses of lovely flowers then, but I used to help with church flowers a lot when I lived at home.'

'Did you? Have you been sent from heaven?' asked the vicar's wife.

'*God works in mysterious ways, his wonders to perform,*' put in Patsy. 'Lizzie, why don't you go with Di and see what you can do to help? We can look at the house another time.'

'The thing is, we won't have amazing flowers,' said Di, 'we'll only have what people have in their gardens. We don't have a budget to buy flowers.'

'That's what I'm used to,' said Lizzie. 'I'd really love to help if I can.'

'And we haven't cut the flowers yet. We always like to get the flowers done by Friday afternoon, before the church is cleaned on Saturday. We haven't a moment to lose!'

In spite of the need for hurry, the vicar's wife was still dithering so Patsy took control. 'Why don't we start picking in this garden?' she suggested. 'There are some lovely things in there,' she went on, looking at the little front garden, obviously unable to name any of the flowers. 'And more round the back. Probably.'

'That's a good idea,' said Lizzie, getting out of the car. 'Have we got any secateurs?'

'Always,' said the vicar's wife. She went back to her car and found them.

'I really hope she's as good as you say she is,' Lizzie heard Di say as she began cutting anything remotely suitable, greenery or flowers, and putting them into an old bucket she'd found in the hedge. 'I am desperate.'

'Oh, she is,' said Patsy. 'And she's such a sweet girl!'

Lizzie wondered if Di Baker would agree she was a sweet girl once she'd discovered she was getting married because she was pregnant.

★ ★ ★

Lizzie loved doing the flowers. She felt comfortable with the three older women on flower duty and was pleased to be given a large stand to do that would greet the congregation as they entered the church. It was generous, she thought, when no one knew if she had any idea what to do with a block of floral foam and crumpled chicken wire. Luckily the foam had been pre-soaked by Di, who didn't take chances.

When she'd completed her arrangement (declared 'unusual' by her fellow florists), using most of what

291

she'd brought herself, she filled watering cans, swept up and, when asked, went into the churchyard and pulled ivy off a tree for extra foliage.

By the end of it, the church looked stunning, with large displays, and vases of flowers on every window-sill. As it was a special occasion, one of her fellow florists had brought a rich fruit cake, so they could all sustain themselves while drinking tea made with the aid of a gas ring in the vestry.

'You've been an absolute brick,' said Di as they travelled back together. 'God bless Patsy for producing you just at the right moment. Now, would you like to go to Patsy's? Or back to that little house in the woods? It has a Hansel and Gretel feel about it, I think.'

'So do I. And if it's not out of your way, I'd like to go back there. I've only seen it — ' She stopped herself telling Di she'd only seen inside it at night. It sounded too risqué. 'I mean, I'd love to have a good look at it.'

'After what you've done for us today, you can go anywhere you like. It's not just that you work at twice the speed of some of our older guild members but that you cheered them all up, put a bit of heart into them! I can tell you're going to be a real asset to the parish.'

'It is a lovely church. It must be really quite old.'

'Parts of it go back to the thirteenth century, so yes.' Di shot her a glance. 'I gather from Patsy that you want to get married there?'

'I do,' said Lizzie, not daring to look at Di while she said this. 'Although I'm not really a 'spinster of this parish'.'

'Well, I think it's much more important to the

church that you're going to be a 'married woman of this parish'. I'll talk to my husband. I'm sure he can sort something out. Although we must find a date for the wedding. You and your young man will have to go and see my husband as soon as possible. I'll ring Patsy with some times when he's free.' She shot Lizzie a look. 'Don't worry, there are dates available but you'll need to pick one quickly.'

★ ★ ★

It was just as well Lizzie had opted to go to the house and not back to Patsy's, she realised. Because outside the house, looking worried and confused, was her mother. Her car was parked on the lane. Di pulled in behind it.

'Mummy! What are you doing here?' Lizzie called as she was out of the car.

'I got your letter, darling — ' her mother began, but Lizzie did not let her finish. Heaven knew what she was about to let slip.

'Mummy? This is Di Baker — '

'The vicar's wife,' explained Di before Lizzie had a chance to.

'This is my mother, Mrs Spencer.'

'I must congratulate you on your wonderful daughter, Mrs Spencer. She has just saved the day when two of my flower guild ladies fell ill at the same time. She's done a simply splendid job on flowers for the church.'

'Oh well, that's very nice to hear. Elizabeth has always had a gift when it comes to flowers.' Mrs Spencer smiled in a way that meant she didn't know how to go on.

293

'I'm off now,' said Di. 'Lots to do! Probably just as well, the devil makes work for idle hands! Goodbye, my dear,' she said to Lizzie. 'And thank you so much again.'

Di Baker got in the car and drove away before Lizzie had time to wonder what on earth she should do with her mother.

'Do you mind if we go in, darling?' her mother said. 'I'm dying for the bathroom.'

Fortunately the house was unlocked ('Country ways!' commented her mother). The bathroom wasn't exactly luxurious but it was an improvement on Lizzie having to ask her mother to go behind a tree.

Her mother emerged into the kitchen, where Lizzie was waiting for her, drying her hands on her skirt.

'Darling, I had to come. I hated us being at odds with each other!' She held out her arms and Lizzie went into them. They hugged. However, as soon as her mother considered she and her daughter were friends again, she said, 'Is this where you intend to live?'

Lizzie's hackles went up in spite of the hug. 'Yes.'

'Well, I do think Hugo Lennox-Stanley, who comes from a very good family — they go back to the eleventh century, in case you didn't know — might have provided the mother of his child with somewhere a little more up to date. This is not what I expect for my daughter! Although the gentry are often very eccentric.' She gave a little smile. 'To be honest, I didn't expect my daughter to marry the heir to a baronetcy!'

Lizzie tried to keep calm. Personally she preferred not to think of Hugo in this way but her mother was obviously very excited about it. 'The bathroom isn't the best bit of this house. Come and see the rest of it.

The sitting room is charming and quite large.'

'Your father is still sulking,' said Lizzie's mother. 'If you weren't . . . in the family way, he'd be delighted. He refuses to talk about it.' She broke off. 'Elizabeth! This kitchen! It's positively antiquated!'

'The kitchen isn't the best bit either,' said Lizzie, 'although I like it very much. Come into the sitting room.'

They inspected the sitting room together, but that didn't look marvellous either. It was dusty and unloved and although there was room for a gate-legged table and chair as well as the ancient sofa (which was leaking horsehair), her mother didn't seem impressed.

'You'll have to get rid of that open fire. It'll create a terrible amount of dust,' she said. 'You want a nice little electric heater. Clean and easy to use. What's it like upstairs?'

Lizzie hadn't been upstairs so she just opened the door to the staircase and followed her mother up.

'Only two bedrooms? Where will I sleep when I come and stay? And I hope you're not planning to use that bed? It's probably harbouring all sorts of unsavoury things.'

Lizzie looked at the old brass bedstead and thought — with a new mattress and a patchwork quilt, which at that moment she decided to make — it would be perfect. She went over to the window and saw the garden, which looked lovely from here. There was no grass, but flower beds, vegetable beds and fruit trees, with paths in between. There was a fair-sized shed and in front of it a bench. She pictured herself sitting there, shelling peas that she'd grown herself.

'I think this room is lovely, and not a bad size,' Lizzie said, to herself as much to her mother. 'Let's go and look at the other one.'

This was about the same dimensions, but looked out the other way, towards the lane. As she inspected the view, letting her mother huff and puff about making sure she kept the baby in a separate room from the very first day, she saw Patsy's car drive up.

Patsy got out. 'Hello! Are you in?' she called up the stairs. 'Di told me your mother had come, Lizzie, and I wanted to come and invite her to stay.'

Lizzie saw her mother's negative feelings begin to melt as she went down the stairs and was enveloped in Patsy's grand, welcoming aura.

'I'm Patsy Nairn-Williams. I'm a very old friend of Hugo's — known him since we were riding fat little ponies through the woods together as children.' She put out her hand and found Lizzie's mother's, and shook it. 'How do you do? Have you come from miles and miles away?'

'How do you do? I'm Angela Spencer, Elizabeth's mother, but of course you know that, Mrs Nairn-Williams — '

'Do call me Patsy! The other is such a mouthful — I've practically gone to sleep before anyone's got my name out! And I want to take you away from this hovel, which needs so much work doing before it's suitable for our young couple, and take you up to the house. I'm hoping we'll find some lunch.' Patsy took hold of Mrs Spencer's arm and led her out of the house. Lizzie followed.

'Darling?' Patsy turned to Lizzie. 'Why don't you wait here for Hugo? He wants to see the house properly too, and you can explore it together. Now come with me, Mrs Spencer — '

'Angela, please.' 'You must be gasping for a glass of

sherry, if not a perfectly enormous gin and tonic . . . '
Lizzie watched with awe and gratitude as her mother
fell under Patsy's spell. She felt exhausted.

First, she had had to get the vicar's wife on side, and
do quite a lot of flower arranging, and then deal with
her mother, full of criticism and disapproval. While
she longed to see Hugo — so much had happened
since breakfast — she didn't really feel up to going
round the house measuring for curtains or whatever
was deemed necessary.

She went out into the garden and found the bench
she had seen from the upstairs window. She closed
her eyes and turned her face to the sun.

★ ★ ★

'Hello,' said a quiet, deep voice and she opened her
eyes and saw Hugo.

'Hello,' she said back.

'Are you hungry? I've brought a picnic. Patsy
insisted. She felt you needed a break from bossy
women, and she included herself in that.'

'Actually I am hungry. What's the time?'

'Two o'clock. I gather you've had a busy day.'

'I have.' She thought back over what she'd done. 'I
think it will be all right to get married in the church
though. That's one less thing to worry about.'

'That's good. Your mother — who has completely
changed her opinion of me, although I gather your
father still thinks I'm a bounder — and Patsy are
making multiple lists for everything that needs doing.'

'I think Daddy might be a bit overawed by your
background,' said Lizzie, having thought about
this.

'And now he's embarrassed he's been so rude to you.'

'I don't blame him. Anyone would think badly of the man who's carrying off his only daughter.'

He paused. 'Is that bench comfy? Shall we have lunch out here?'

'Yes, let's,' said Lizzie, thinking the bench was quite small and they would be sitting close to each other, which was a nice idea.

'I'll go and get it.'

He came back with two brown paper bags. 'I hope you weren't expecting a Fortnum's hamper sort of picnic. Tim did it while I was talking to your mother.' He paused. 'She has very firm ideas about your wedding, hasn't she?'

Lizzie nodded. 'I'm sure I've told you, but she's known what she wants for me ever since I was tiny. But of course, you mustn't agree to anything you don't like.'

'What about you? Will you agree to things you don't like because your mother wants them?'

'Yes. As long as I'm allowed to make my own wedding dress, I don't really care. Now what's in that paper bag?'

He handed her a bag. 'Two doorstep sandwiches — cheese, I think. An apple and some fruit cake.' He paused. 'And a bottle of wine and a bottle of lemonade, made by our hostess's own fair hands, apparently.' He drew two plastic beakers out of his pockets. 'Wine or lemonade?'

'A bit of wine,' she said. 'Then lemonade.'

A couple of sips of wine felt like enough, she realised. Then she bit into the thick, white sandwich. 'This is delicious,' she said, hoping she didn't sound surprised, although she was.

'Yup. Sometimes when I'm at a point-to-point or something, having a picnic out of the back of someone's car, and they serve crab tart and little vol-au-vents, I long for a proper sandwich. Or 'sangwich' as my father always calls them.'

'They're never going to accept me, are they?' said Lizzie, suddenly less hungry than she had been.

'They will,' said Hugo. 'Give them time. They'll discover what a lovely woman you are and how you'll make me far happier than Electra ever could.'

'Do you really think that?' Then she realised she wasn't sure if she was referring to his parents' feelings about her or his conviction that she would make him happy. She wondered if he knew which question he was answering.

'Absolutely!' he said, sounding surprised that she should be in doubt. 'Good Lord! If it hadn't been almost an arranged marriage, encouraged since we were babies, Electra and I wouldn't have gone further than a few dinner dates. But then it became a habit. Her father's influence could have helped my career, and she was very keen on being married to a barrister.'

'And, of course, she's very beautiful,' said Lizzie, sticking to the subject of Electra, although she knew she should shut up about her.

He nodded. 'Yes, in a racehorse kind of way.'

Still on a path she knew she should steer away from, Lizzie said, 'So if Electra is a racehorse, I must be a sort of pony.' She had in mind a cartoon pony, very round in the middle and hairy. Although she was not yet very round, and her hair was short, she still felt the analogy worked.

'Lizzie!' Hugo was shocked. 'Why on earth would you think that?'

She shrugged. 'I don't know. I suppose it's because things are so odd between us. We hardly know each other but we're getting married. I can't help comparing myself with the woman you'd chosen to marry. After all, if I wasn't pregnant, we'd probably not be still in touch.'

'What makes you say that?'

His expression was concerned and she realised she'd gone down a dangerous path. She couldn't bring herself to say, 'Would you have even asked me out in the normal course of events, if I hadn't been pregnant?' because she didn't want to know the answer, in case it was no. So she tried to pretend she hadn't said anything, shook her head, smiled and shrugged.

He wouldn't let her get away with this. 'Lizzie? What do you mean?'

She desperately wished she'd never started this conversation. And although he'd said she'd make him happier than Electra would, she'd always feel she was second-best. Like the comfortable winter coat you'd get years of use out of instead of the glamorous scarlet one, which would always need dry cleaning but would look fabulous. Nor could she forget his words: *make a girl pregnant by mistake and end up having to marry her.*

She couldn't explain all this. She didn't have the words or the heart for it. 'I don't know! I expect I'm just tired. You should have seen me being helpful down at the church, when I'd done my own stand, filling watering cans, finding extra greenery from the churchyard.'

This seemed to satisfy him.

'Are you too tired to look at the house? I gather

300

from your mother it looks better at night.'

Lizzie laughed. 'I don't think she saw it through the same rose-tinted spectacles that I did. Perhaps another look now, with you, will make me see it more realistically.'

'Oh, I do hope not!' He held out his hand to her. 'Come on. Let's see it at its worst.'

* * *

'Actually,' said Lizzie, a few moments later, 'I still really like it! I know the bathroom is a bit grim and the kitchen isn't exactly modern, but the sitting room is fairly spacious, it doesn't seem damp and the bedrooms are both a good size.'

'Yes,' he agreed. 'Do you remember that flat in Tufnell Park where we first met? Now that really was grim!'

She was surprised he'd remembered that first meeting, but definitely pleased. 'It was horrible! And while this house may not have a proper modern kitchen — my mother's feelings, not mine — it is at least pretty.'

'And I'm sure when you've had a chance to make curtains — I gather from Patsy that that is the plan — and a few other changes as well, it'll be delightfully cosy.'

Lizzie laughed. 'Coming from your background, it's also going to seem small, isn't it?'

'What's more important is that you're happy here.'

'I love it! I even like the brass bedstead, upstairs.'

'We need a new mattress though.'

'Of course.'

'Patsy said we were to make a list of things we need.

301

She has her own list, of course.'

'Of course,' she said again.

'Lizzie, I'm starting my apprenticeship on Monday morning. And on Sunday, I've been told, very firmly, by Patsy and your mother, that we're going to church.'

'Oh good, that means you can see my flower arrangements. And church won't take all day.'

'But Sunday lunch with Patsy and Tim will. They'll insist we're all there for it. Tim cooks the beef — he's very modern; either that or he worries Patsy will overcook it — and Patsy makes wonderful Yorkshire pudding, which goes in a big dish in the middle of the table.' He paused. 'We might have to encourage them to be a bit more formal for your mother's sake.'

'Oh, don't worry — If Patsy does it, it's the done thing, I'm sure!'

He laughed. 'Well, that's good. Now, shall we have a last look round before I take you back? Patsy said you were to have a nap. Apparently they're essential for pregnant women.'

'I hadn't heard that,' said Lizzie. 'But it sounds like an excellent idea.' She hesitated. 'Have we got time for a walk first? I'm just feeling a bit — you know . . .' She couldn't explain herself because she didn't understand her feelings. She should be so happy. She was marrying the man of her dreams, whom she loved so much, and yet instead of feeling ecstatic, she felt a little lost.

'A short one,' said Hugo. 'I don't want to risk the wrath of Patsy.'

'I just want to get my bearings. See what surrounds my future home. I am so looking forward to living here.'

'I'm glad.' He paused, as if he was going to say something else but then didn't.

'Come on!' said Lizzie, partly to cover the awkward silence. 'Let's see if we can find a tree we can climb! I've always loved climbing trees. Strangely, my mother never encouraged it.'

28

Quite soon, however, the lists began to take over Lizzie's life. Her mother, who was still staying, was insistent on them, and Patsy — as they discussed it over the last of the toast and marmalade one breakfast time — agreed that they were important. She and Angela made an unexpectedly good team, which was a relief. No mention was made of Lizzie's father, although Lizzie assumed her mother telephoned him from time to time. Hugo had moved into the cottage so he could leave early without disturbing Patsy and Tim's dogs, and Lizzie felt she hardly ever saw him. Now, Tim was reading the paper, ignoring the women who surrounded him.

'If you don't have a wedding list,' said Patsy, 'your mother is going to be inundated with telephone calls asking what you want as a wedding present. She'll be inundated anyway, but at least she can just tell them to get the list from Peter Jones.'

'And of course,' said her mother, as she seemed to with every second breath, 'time is not on our side. We've only got a month.'

'I know, Mummy,' said Lizzie meekly.

Her mother went on. 'I can help you make the list, darling. You want a nice dinner service — I'll help you find a suitable pattern — and people can just buy parts of it.'

'You'll probably find that someone — possibly related to Hugo — will buy the whole thing,' said Patsy.

'How generous that would be! You'll also need some

good glasses — Waterford for preference . . . '

Lizzie pictured her future kitchen with its stone sink and poor light and thought that possibly something more solid and less precious would be better. Perhaps something bought with Green Shield Stamps. But she knew better than to say this.

'Knives and forks — silver plate will do . . . '

'And don't forget to choose some really good kitchen knives and saucepans,' Patsy broke in. 'I forgot to put them on my list so I'm using the ones that were left in the house. Nightmare! And I'm afraid all the nice glasses we were given got broken in the first year.'

'Oh. Well, I've always brought up Elizabeth to be very careful,' said Lizzie's mother, looking concerned. She was probably picturing Lizzie's kitchen too.

'People can always give me towels if they're stuck,' said Lizzie.

'Very true. We've got towels that Tim had at school,' said Patsy. 'With his Cash's name tape on them.'

'And bedlinen,' Lizzie's mother finished, determined to list everything she had on her mind.

'OK, Mummy, I'll do that,' said Lizzie, wondering if in fact she had to.

'The guest list is my responsibility,' her mother went on. 'But somehow, we must get a list from Hugo's parents.' She paused. 'It's such a shame they're not keen on this marriage.'

'They haven't had a chance to get to know Lizzie — Elizabeth,' said Patsy. 'When they do, they'll love her! How could they not?'

'You're very kind,' said Lizzie.

'I'll have a word with Hugo's mother,' Patsy said. 'After all, she may already have made a list for when he was — ' She stopped, horrified as she realised what she had been going to say.

Lizzie found herself laughing. 'You mean, when they were planning a wedding between him and Electra?'

'I am such an idiot!' said Patsy. 'Why do I never think before I speak?'

'Because you're an idiot,' said her husband fondly, getting up from the table. 'Now I have work to do. And George? If you're quick, I'll come up with you and help you brush your teeth.'

When both Tim and George had left the room, Lizzie's mother said, 'It's wonderful how modern men are so helpful with the children these days. I don't suppose Elizabeth's father ever had anything to do with your teeth, did he, darling?'

'No,' said Lizzie.

'Well,' said Patsy with a firm smile, 'it's probably because George is Tim's child too.'

Lizzie saw her mother send Patsy a quick look and knew she was wondering if in fact Patsy believed in Women's Liberation. It was clearly a worrying thought for her.

'OK, I'll put 'getting an invitation list out of Hugo's mama' on my list,' Patsy said, moving on. 'Lizzie? Have you got the measurements for the curtains for the house? And have you chosen which ones you fancy from the attic?'

'Yes to both,' said Lizzie, noting how her mother hardly winced when Patsy called her 'Lizzie' these days.

'The thing we absolutely need to talk about,' said Lizzie's mother, fixing her daughter with a steely eye, 'is your wedding dress. You really don't have time to make it yourself.'

Lizzie took a calming breath. 'Mummy — '

'I know you want to, and you are quite a good little seamstress, I know that too, but it is far too important a job to be handled by an amateur. Don't you agree with me, Patsy?'

Patsy didn't answer immediately, which was unusual for her. 'Well, the thought of me trying to make my own wedding dress would be so awful, I'd rather get married in my school uniform than attempt it. But sewing is what Lizzie does.' She gave Lizzie a look of sympathy and reached out to pat her hand. 'I do know a good seamstress we could turn to if it got too difficult.'

'I think we need a date that you have to have it done by,' said Lizzie's mother. 'We're only a month away from the wedding. A professional seamstress would need at least a month to do it. If you haven't got it done in two weeks, we'll ask Patsy's person. Is that fair?'

'No! Not really!' said Lizzie. 'You're giving me, an 'amateur', half the time you'd give to a professional. I don't think it's fair.'

'I think what your mother means,' said Patsy, soothing but firm, 'is that if, in a fortnight, you haven't made a good start on the dress — found the right fabric, cut it out, maybe sewn a few seams — then we'll ask my woman so there will be plenty of time for her to do it.'

Lizzie knew her mother hadn't meant that at all, but hoped she would pretend she had.

'Oh God!' said Patsy, leaping up from her seat and looking at the clock on the mantelpiece. 'Is that the time? George is supposed to be playing with a little friend in the village. I mustn't be late — again . . .'

307

She looked at the breakfast dishes.

'We'll clear up, don't worry,' said Lizzie.

'So kind! I know Mrs Wareham will be here in a minute but it's such a big dirty old house she has to look after . . . '

'We perfectly understand,' said Lizzie's mother. 'We'll do it.'

Lizzie's mother spent every second while they were scraping bits of butter off the plates and finding lids for marmalade and jam jars nagging Lizzie about her dress. But Lizzie was not going to give in. She was utterly determined.

★   ★   ★

The little house was Lizzie's sanctuary these days, her mother preferring to make her lists in comfort. Frequently, after Lizzie had arrived, she'd walk along the lane to the red telephone box and ring the London house, talking to whoever answered the telephone. It was quite often David, who showed a lot of interest in her house.

But most of the time, she had her own 'to do' list. This included cutting down several pairs of curtains from Patsy's huge store of worn-out ones, to adapt. She also had a pile of surplices to mend, ones worn by the church choir. She had been given this job — or had she offered? — by Di Baker when they'd been to church that first Sunday. She did wonder if these were a distraction from her hardest, most pressing and worrying task, that of making her wedding dress. She'd been worrying about this even before her mother's ultimatum.

She'd need to go to London for the fabric, she

knew that. She could give Peter Jones her wedding list, having gone round every department picking things in every price range; this was what Patsy said was involved. But John Lewis was better for fabric, although David had been wondering, when she'd last spoken to him on the phone, if there wasn't a supplier for theatrical costumiers she should go to as well. What she really didn't want was her mother coming with her, to help with either of these tasks, but she couldn't think how to stop her.

★ ★ ★

Lizzie was in the garden of the cottage cutting flowers, something she did every time she came, when she heard a car hooting in the lane and then she heard her name being shouted loudly. She looked up to see David's car with Meg and Vanessa hanging out of the windows. Alexandra was driving. She ran to meet them.

The screaming and jumping up and down went on for a little while. So did the questions.

'Alexandra! I can't believe David let you borrow the car to come all this way!' Lizzie said.

'I've passed my driving test. I actually have a proper driving licence. And I'm really good at it.'

Alexandra was obviously very proud. 'David made me drive him right through the centre of London and round Hyde Park Corner the other day and no one hooted!' She stopped. 'He's really sorry he couldn't come, by the way. He's rehearsing for a play.

'I've come to see Hugo,' said Vanessa. 'Is he here? My father is still incandescent with rage! He even made the solicitor check to see if he could break the entail and leave the family estate to someone else. But there's no chance!'

This took the edge off Lizzie's joy at seeing her friends a little. Her own father had not yet come round to the wedding, according to her mother, and she couldn't help being sad about it.

'Patsy knows we're coming,' Vanessa went on. 'She said it was about time you had some people your own age to talk to.'

'I'm afraid Hugo is at work. He leaves the house at about half past seven and doesn't come back until supper. He sleeps here but has all his meals with me and my mother at Patsy's at the moment.'

'Never mind. I'll talk to him about it another time. I'll ask Patsy to ask him to give me a ring,' said Vanessa.

'Actually, I think it's Lizzie he's giving a ring to,' said Meg, and got a push on the arm for her bad joke.

'Oh, you've brought Clover!' said Lizzie delightedly, watching as the dog clambered out of the car, having woken up after sleeping during the journey.

'With us all out all day, we had to,' said Alexandra.

'And we thought she'd like a day in the country,' added Meg.

They all watched as the dog walked along the edge of the lane, sniffing hard, before relieving herself. She didn't seem ecstatic with her change of scene.

'I think she's more at home in Belgravia these days,' said Meg, going to the back of the car and opening the boot. 'We've brought you things from the house. Look!' She was clutching a dressmaker's dummy. 'This should be about your size, Lizzie. And as much fabric as we could fit into an old laundry bag.'

Lizzie hugged her. 'Oh, Meg! I've been wanting fabric scraps so much. I can make a patchwork quilt for my brass bed! When I've made my dress, of course.'

'I'm afraid there's no wedding dress material,' said Meg, who knew that Lizzie was worrying about this.

'Can we go in?' said Vanessa.

'Of course,' said Lizzie, suddenly a bit self-conscious about her future home. 'I don't know what I'm going to feed you on. Or is Patsy doing lunch?'

'No,' said Vanessa. 'She wants you to have time with us today.'

'And don't worry about food,' said Alexandra, 'we've brought food and champagne and Vanessa — very extravagantly — has a special treat.'

'It's a hamper. I'll go and get it,' said Vanessa. 'I thought I ought to make sure the mother of my niece or nephew had plenty to eat. I'm starving!'

'I brought home-made bread,' said Meg. 'A fruit cake, a pork pie, some sausage rolls and some egg sandwiches.'

'That all sounds delicious,' said Lizzie. 'I'm hungry too, now.'

Vanessa came back with a hamper from Fortnum's that was so large she could hardly carry it.

'David sent you cheese and fancy butter,' said Alexandra. 'In case you're short of calcium or something.'

'It was probably a bargain at the market,' said Meg. 'David can't resist a bargain.'

'Let's go in,' said Lizzie, no longer worried, just happy to see her friends.

The hamper was too big to unpack in the kitchen, so they did it on the sitting-room floor, throwing the wood shavings that surrounded each jar, tin or bottle directly into the fireplace.

'A honeycomb!' said Meg. 'Honey on toast is so good. Ooh, tinned ham. And some tongue.'

'And loads of biscuits, of all kinds,' said Lizzie. 'I could now offer George a bit of shortbread if he visits.'

'Is George Tim and Patsy's little boy?' asked Vanessa. 'I've forgotten.

'Yes,' said Lizzie. 'He's sweet.'

'And did you find Patsy scary?' Vanessa went on.

'I certainly did to begin with,' said Lizzie.

To everyone's surprise, Hugo arrived, just when they were having lunch. 'Hello! Patsy told me you were all coming so I've popped back to say hi. I can't stay more than a minute or two.'

'Hughie!' said Vanessa, stepping over the plates of food to get to her brother. She hugged him hard.

Lizzie wished she felt she could show her feelings about him so freely. She smiled shyly at him, delighted he seemed so happy to find his house full of women eating and drinking champagne. Her own father would have been very tight-lipped about it.

'Well, there's loads to eat,' she said. 'What would you like? Some pork pie? A really delicious egg sandwich? You can use my plate. Oh, I'll just give you some nice things,' she finished, hoping she wasn't being unacceptably wifely. After all, they weren't married yet.

'Will you have some champagne?' asked Alexandra. 'There's a drop left in the bottle.

'I'll have the drop,' Hugo said to Alexandra. 'And you just give me what's easy, Lizzie.'

Hugo had to leave very soon but seemed to enjoy his brief picnic. He kissed Vanessa's cheek and Lizzie's, but then he put his hand round her cheek for a moment. 'I'll see you later. I've got a little outing planned.'

Lizzie's heart gave a skip of joy. 'I'd love that!'

'I wouldn't call this kitchen primitive,' said Alexandra, having inspected it. 'It has rustic simplicity.'

She was having a good look at the house while Meg and Vanessa were walking Clover in the woods.

Lizzie laughed at this glamorised description. 'Do tell my mother. She thinks a kitchen without Formica and stainless steel is a kitchen no modern woman could be expected to use.'

'Honestly, by the time you have curtains at the windows and in front of the sink and anywhere else that needs covering, and get some shelves up — is Hugo any good at putting up shelves?'

'He should be,' said Lizzie. 'He's training to be a cabinet maker!'

'Oh well, shelves on every wall, with pretty china, and it'll be completely charming. Now let's look at the bathroom.'

Alexandra agreed this was a bit more of a challenge. 'Honestly? I think this place needs a coat or two of paint, curtains and a good paraffin heater. It's dank even in summer!'

'I know. When I live here, I'll fill that jug that comes with the wash-stand set with flowers.'

'If you're not too busy with the baby . . .'

'Ah yes . . . I'd forgotten about the baby for a minute.'

'But you are excited about it? I mean, now you're getting married and everything, you're pleased?'

'Definitely. I don't often have time to think about the baby but when I do, I'm thrilled really.'

'I think Hugo will make a wonderful father,' said Alexandra. 'He's so caring and he obviously loves you very much.'

'Oh! Do you think so?' Lizzie was as surprised as she was delighted. 'What makes you say that?'

'Just the way he looks at you. It's obvious!'

'He's never said anything,' said Lizzie, wistfully.

'I think perhaps he doesn't like to, in case you don't love him. After all, you're both getting married because you have to. If he says he loves you, and you don't love him back, he's going to feel awful.'

'But I do love him back.'

'Then maybe you should tell him?' Alexandra said this gently, but Lizzie could tell she didn't expect her to take the advice.

'Perhaps,' said Lizzie doubtfully. 'Shall we find the others and go up to the house now? You must meet Patsy. She's wonderful.'

They arrived to find Lizzie's mother talking about bridesmaids' dresses.

'We will need to have dresses made as soon as possible — when Elizabeth has chosen her bridesmaids. Which she needs to do. And don't let Elizabeth say she'll make them. She's insisting on making her wedding dress although the wedding is nearly upon us!'

'Is it?' said George who was playing with his toy cars. 'I thought it wasn't for a month.'

'Oh, hello, Elizabeth, Alexandra,' Mrs Spencer went on. 'We're talking about bridesmaids' dresses. And you're not to say you'll make them, Elizabeth. You won't have time.' Her voice was stern. 'You haven't even made the pattern for your own dress. I do wish you'd let me get a dressmaker organised. We're really very behind on that. We should have a toile.'

Lizzie glanced at her friends, who were looking bemused. 'My mother means a dress made out of muslin or something, to see if it fits, before the dress is made in the expensive fabric.'

'That does sound time-consuming,' said Vanessa. 'If you've got to make your dress twice.'

'I probably won't bother with a toile,' said Lizzie.

'Elizabeth! This is the most important dress you'll ever wear in your life. Think about the photographs!' Then her expression went from horrified to delighted in a blink. 'Oh, Patsy put us in touch with the photographer she used and he can fit us in. He had a cancellation and Patsy kindly put in a good word. You've probably seen his work. He quite often does the portraits of debutantes in *Country Life*.'

'Lovely,' said Vanessa.

'But before that, we must arrange a day to go up to choose your dress material. I have something in mind I think will be very suitable. You want something along the lines of what Princess Grace was married in — you know, with the little stand-up collar. Although of course' — there was disappointment in her voice now — 'you won't be able to have that tight waist band which is so attractive, because of your . . . condition.'

Alexandra sent Lizzie a look of sympathy. 'Gosh, this has been fun,' she said, 'but I'm afraid I think we should go back now. David will worry if we're late. But we'll come again. It's really not that far from London,' she added. 'Now that David lets me borrow the car.'

'You borrow the car from David?' asked Lizzie's mother, very confused. 'I thought he was the butler!'

'He's also the chauffeur,' said Alexandra, not missing a beat. 'He's very possessive about the car.'

It seemed to take ages before Hugo and Lizzie had a moment on their own. Lizzie's mother was full of the visit from the girls, gushing over their loveliness and how surely they would be the perfect bridesmaids if Elizabeth would only hurry up and ask them. But just before dinner, when Tim was bringing her a glass of her favourite sherry, Hugo took Lizzie aside.

'I've arranged to pick you up tomorrow night and take you to meet Harold and see the workshop. I know it doesn't sound terribly exciting but Harold's longing to meet you,' he said.

'I'd love to go! An evening without having to talk too much about the wedding would be perfect.' said Lizzie. 'My mother means well, I know she does, but this wedding — my dress in particular — is making me anxious.'

'Lizzie, just say the word and I'll whisk you off to Gretna Green. The age of consent is only sixteen up there, I think.'

Lizzie laughed. 'I might well take you up on that!'

★ ★ ★

Early evening the following day, she sank into Hugo's car. 'I thought Mummy would go on thinking of things she needed me to think about forever. It was clever of you to say that Harold wanted to meet me. She feels it's very important for a wife to support a husband in his work.'

'That's easy as it's true. I didn't just make it up.'

'I'm so delighted to get away, even for a few hours. It's not that I don't love being with Patsy and Tim, it's the wedding. My mother is doing all the work but if I'm not careful, she'll put me in a wedding dress so I look like Princess Grace of Monaco, and decide what pattern I want on the dinner service. I think I have to

316

do those things myself but I don't want my mother with me at the time. I can't see how to escape!' She laughed, to give the impression she wasn't serious about these doubts.

Although she was.

'Poor you. I'm escaping it all by working.'

'You're enjoying it?'

'I think it was what I should have been doing since before I left school,' he said. 'My parents will take a long time to get used to it, I'm afraid. The generations of lawyers and judges disapproving from beyond the grave.'

'But you have to follow your heart.'

'You do. And I have.'

They travelled in silence for a little bit until Lizzie said, 'I'm really excited now. How long will it take us to get there?' She felt giddy with a sense of freedom, being away from her mother and the endless wedding preparations. Particularly the endless, 'When are you going to London to buy material for your wedding dress?'

'Not very long. The reason we're living here is because it's near to the workshop.'

Lizzie laughed. 'Of course! But it's a shame — I'd like to drive off into the sunset — with you at the wheel, of course.'

He laughed but shot her a thoughtful look.

★ ★ ★

Hugo drove into a lane which led to a pretty double-fronted house. A little way from the house was a barn. He pulled the car up in front of it. 'Harold said he'd meet us here. Ah, here he is.'

Lizzie hadn't formed a clear picture of the man who was imparting his craft to Hugo but had she done so, it would have been an old man with rosy cheeks and a brown overall. She wouldn't quite have added string round his knees but a cloth cap would definitely have featured. She wasn't expecting a man in a very well-made three-piece suit, highly polished shoes and an elegant silk tie. He had a full head of white hair and bright blue eyes. He was smiling.

'Harold,' said Hugo, 'let me introduce you to Lizzie.'

'Lizzie,' he said, taking her hand. 'Now tell me, do your parents insist on your being called Elizabeth?' His voice made it clear he came from the same social stratum as Hugo did.

'They do! How did you guess?' Lizzie felt instantly at home with this man.

He released her hand. 'There's something about you. Now come along in. Let me show you what Hugo and I get up to all day.' Lizzie happily followed him into the barn.

'What can I offer you to drink? Too late for sherry? Too early for whisky? What do you think?'

'Actually, I'd love a cup of tea.' She was aware her mother wouldn't approve of this choice. For her, in polite society, tea was only drunk at breakfast or in the afternoon, even though she quite often had a cup of tea after supper.

'Hugo?' Harold looked at him. 'Would you care to make us some tea? And the biscuits in the tin?'

'The visitor-only biscuits?' said Hugo.

'Of course! We have a visitor; we have an excuse. Come, Lizzie, let me show you what we've been doing.'

The barn was quite full. There was a large table

shaped like a leaf, inlaid with something — Lizzie couldn't tell what — that could have been gold or could have been a pale yellow wood.

'This is waiting to be collected. The owner — we only work to commission — lives abroad and will take it when his house in the South of France is ready for it. This piece' — he took Lizzie to a desk with an open lid and when she looked inside she saw layers of opening boxes within it — 'is what Hugo and I have been working on.'

Lizzie moved across to a table. 'I like this.'

'That's Arts and Crafts in its influence.'

'It's simple, yet beautiful.'

She walked round the workshop which was also a showroom of sorts, looking at each piece with concentration. Harold followed her, supplying bits of information from time to time.

'So, my dear, tell me why you want to marry Hugo? Apart from the fact that you are expecting his child.'

Normally, Lizzie would have been hugely embarrassed to talk about such things with a virtual stranger — a male one at that — but there was something about this kind older man which made embarrassment unnecessary.

'It's quite simple, really. I love him.' She smiled. 'That sounds rather sentimental, I suppose. But it's the truth.'

'And you don't mind him being in a profession — if one can call it, it's more of an art really — that is unlikely to ever make him a rich man?'

'I really don't care about that,' said Lizzie. 'Obviously, I'd prefer it if there was food on the table, but the house we're going to live in has a garden — we can grow vegetables. And I'm good at sewing. People always want sewing done. We'll manage. And I'd rather he was happy than earning a fortune.'

'My dear, do you have any idea of the sort of income you could have expected had Hugo stayed with the law?'

Lizzie shook her head. 'No and I don't need to know. It's not relevant really, is it?'

Harold laughed. 'Well, I'm very pleased he's marrying you. I would never say this in front of him, but he really is very skilled as a cabinet maker and he's only just begun learning. A few more years and he'll know everything I know.'

'Thank you so much for telling me. It makes me feel proud, although his skill is nothing to do with me. But I know it will bring him lots of satisfaction. Ah — here's the tea.'

They drank the tea sitting on stools round an upturned tea chest. 'I'm afraid everything here is for someone else,' said Harold. 'So we have to manage without a proper table.'

'But it does the job,' said Lizzie, putting down her mug and helping herself to a visitor-only biscuit.

When the tea had been drunk, Hugo got up. 'Would you mind very much if I used the telephone, Harold?'

'No, not at all. But come into the house to do it. There's something I want to show Lizzie.'

The house was lovely and was filled with antique furniture. Lizzie would have expected it to have pieces created by its owner. Harold seemed to read her mind. 'Everything I make is for sale. The furniture I inherited does me perfectly well. Now, come and see what's in my linen press.'

Lizzie wasn't expecting to be taken to a cupboard,

but Harold opened the doors on one that sat on a chest of drawers. 'Oh. So this is a linen press?'

'It is,' said Harold. 'Now look.'

The deep shelves were filled with bolts of fabric. Cotton, satin, silk, brocade and lawn. 'Oh my goodness!' said Lizzie. 'Where did all this come from?'

'My mother was a dressmaker and after she died we didn't know what to do with the fabric she left. You would be the perfect person to give it to. Hugo? Come and help me find something suitable to put it all in. Lizzie, you have a look and see if there's anything you don't like. I'll give that to someone whose having a sale of work or some such.'

Lizzie looked through the bolts of silk, satin, fine lawn, poplin. It was all wonderful although there was only a small quantity of many of the fabrics. She was enraptured. Alexandra had given her a bundle of bits and pieces and she had been thrilled with that. This was on another level of loveliness.

Hugo and Harold were gone for a little while but at last reappeared with a large trunk.

'Sorry to be so long,' said Harold. 'We had to empty the trunk first.'

Harold cut through Lizzie's protestations about the trouble she was putting him to and dismissed the generosity of his gift with a wave of his hand.

'Nonsense, child! Call it a wedding present. It may as well clutter up your house instead of mine.'

'But these are really beautiful fabrics.' Lizzie had spotted some oyster-coloured satin in among the prints and stripes which might be just want she wanted for her wedding dress. 'And look at this lace! It's probably really valuable.'

'I hope it's worth a fortune,' said Harold. 'Then

I've given you something worth having. Now, let's see how much we can get into this thing.'

'Will this fit into your car, Hugo?' Lizzie whispered when Harold was out of the way for a moment.

'It should do. I did measure it. Although quite where we'll put it when we've moved into our house is a question for another day.'

'Did you know he was going to give me all this?'

'Not really, but he did grill me about what you liked doing so he knew it was going to the right place.'

'Harold!' said Lizzie quickly as he came back into the room. 'There is so much beautiful material here. I must make you something from it as a thank you.' She wondered if it would be wrong to give Harold an enormous hug.

'Oh well, if you're offering, I do need a new peg bag.'

Lizzie didn't hesitate a second longer. She hugged him. 'A peg bag you shall have. And anything else I think you might like.'

'What a darling girl you have there, Hugo!' said Harold, very pleased with his hug. 'Do look after her!'

'That has always been my intention,' said Hugo.

★ ★ ★

'Well, we don't have to wonder if that visit went well,' said Hugo as they drove away. 'Unlike the other visits we've been on together.'

'What a lovely man!' said Lizzie. 'If only — ' She stopped.

'If only my father was more like Harold?' Hugo suggested.

'Well — I wasn't going to put it quite like that.'

'But I couldn't blame you for thinking it. My father is the product of his upbringing. He's been conditioned to be angry and snobbish all his life. He can't help it.'

'I expect you had a very similar upbringing, Hugo,' said Lizzie. She didn't want to criticise his father more than she could help.

'And I'm not so terrifying?'

Lizzie laughed. 'I did find you a bit terrifying when I first met you.' While she didn't now find him terrifying, she still felt he was a very deep pool she hadn't got near the bottom of yet.

'I can't imagine why. But if it makes you feel better, I found you pretty terrifying, too.'

'What? Me? Why on earth —'

'I'll tell you one day, but now I need to tell you what's happening. I'm taking you to see the girls, in London.'

'What? When did you arrange that? And why didn't you tell me? I haven't got anything with me!'

'I've only just done it. I rang Patsy from Harold's and she's going to tell your mother.' He paused, and Lizzie was silent for a moment, taking it in. She was imagining the scene back at Patsy's house: her mother's outrage, Patsy's matter-of-factness. A sudden rush of happiness made her catch her breath.

'That's wonderful!'

'I thought you needed a little time away from your mother — even just one night.'

'Will you have to drive all the way back here again? So you can go to work in the morning?'

He shook his head. 'I explained the situation to Harold and he's given me the day off. I don't have to be back in the workshop until the day after tomorrow.'

323

'Do the girls know I'm coming?'

'I'm afraid not. I couldn't get through. But I'm sure it will be fine. I'll give you my card that has the number of the London house on it. If you don't want to stay with the girls you can ring me and we'll make another plan. Or drive home.'

Lizzie began to laugh. 'This is so unexpected and lovely!'

'I'm glad you're pleased. I'm going to stay with my mother who's in town with Nessa. We have to try and heal this breach.'

'Do you think you might be able to? I don't think your parents will ever forgive me for not being Electra.'

'They will when they get to know you. We must just make it possible for that to happen.'

'We probably don't have to see them all that often,' said Lizzie, to make herself feel better.

Hugo chuckled. 'Will a day be enough for you in London? To get the fabric for your dress? And do the ghastly wedding list which I should do with you?'

'Absolutely. And don't think about doing the wedding list. It's enough that one of us should suffer! As long as you won't mind what I put on it.'

'I couldn't care less. It's your wedding-dress material that's important.

The trunk full of fabric in the boot came into her mind. 'If there was enough suitable material in what Harold gave me to make a dress, I wouldn't have to go. Think how wonderful that would be.'

'Harold would be thrilled, I know that.'

'In two days I could design my dress and cut it out on the big table in the kitchen at the house. It would be so perfect! And I wouldn't have to waste my time with the girls going shopping. At least, not so much of it.'

'Don't you like shopping?' He seemed surprised. 'I thought all women did.'

'Sometimes, but the thought of looking at wedding-dress material with Mummy or traipsing round Peter Jones picking dinner services and tea sets — ergh! I could probably choose a couple of things but not a whole house's worth of suitable gifts.'

'But if you don't, you risk getting things you don't like.'

'I don't care, do you? I'm sure if people want to give us presents they can think up nice things they want us to have.'

'Towels and toasters?'

'I always say you can't have too many towels and toasters.'

'I've never heard you say that!'

'I promise to say it at least once a day from now on.'

He laughed and squeezed her knee. It made her very happy.

29

Lizzie was relieved to find the door to the basement kitchen in Belgravia was unlocked, which meant someone was in and still up. It was nearly ten and very late for an unexpected visit. She gestured to Hugo who was waiting in the car to check all was well. He nodded and drove off. The trunk full of material was on the pavement.

Lizzie opened the door and saw Alexandra explaining something to Meg, who was stirring a pan on the stove and then took a separate spoon and tasted whatever was inside it. Clover was lying in front of the gas fire, snoring, even though it wasn't lit. A rush of love for her friends and nostalgia for the time she lived there, before her life changed forever, came over her. She felt tears prick her eyelids although really there was nothing that she'd change about her life now — if there hadn't been a wedding to get through.

Then Alexandra spotted her. 'Lizzie! What are you doing here?'

Then her joy changed to concern. 'Everything's all right, isn't it?'

'Oh yes. Hugo brought me, as a surprise. He thought I'd had enough wedding preparation and needed a night off.'

'How lovely! I told you he loved you. Come in.'

'Actually, I've got a trunk full of fabric with me. If you could give me a hand with it?'

Meg rushed over. 'Don't you dare lift it! We'll bring it in a moment.'

326

David came forward calmly. 'You're here — how wonderful. Come in,' he said, echoing Alexandra. 'Don't lurk on the doorstep. How are you? Lovelier than ever! Come and sit down. What can we get you? Are you very tired?' He drew her to the best armchair. Clover promptly jumped on her lap.

'Oh,' said Meg, 'it's lovely to see you! Do you have a case?'

Laughing and discouraging Clover from licking her face, Lizzie said, 'No! I have a trunk full of material but not a toothbrush, nightdress or pair of knickers otherwise.'

'I suppose you were thinking of running up those necessary items, using the fabric?' suggested David.

'I would have struggled with the toothbrush, I have to say. And I couldn't make the other things, either, because my sewing machine is in the country. Although hand-sewing a pair of knickers would be possible. It's so lovely to be back here with you.'

Alexandra came and perched on the arm of the chair. 'You're not implying that 'love in a cottage' isn't all it seemed to be when we visited? You do want to be married to Hugo?'

'Oh yes! 'Be married' is absolutely the thing I want. But apparently that can't happen before you've been through this monstrous ordeal called a wedding.' Just for a moment Lizzie looked stricken, as she remembered both her mother's oppressive lists and her own niggling fear that for Hugo it was a marriage of convenience.

There was a silence.

'Is it really as bad as all that?' said David eventually. 'Have you run away?'

Lizzie looked at her friends. 'No, it's not so bad I

want to run away, it's just my mother is staying.'

'In that tiny — quite small house?' said Alexandra, more accustomed to larger spaces.

'No, she's staying with Patsy, but so am I! Hugo's staying in the cottage and I hardly ever see him, although he comes to Patsy's for meals. My mother is always there too, talking about the wedding. Hugo brought me up here for a little break from it all. My mother thinks I'm buying dress material and choosing a wedding list from Peter Jones.'

'Hugo is going to be a kind and thoughtful husband,' stated David.

'And what are you really going to do while you're with us?' asked Alexandra. 'If you're not doing those things?'

'Well, I did mean to buy fabric for my dress and get it cut out, on the big table . . . '

'Are you not going to have a wedding dress, then?' asked Meg.

'What?' said Lizzie. 'Of course I'm having a wedding dress! I was also hoping you might be bridesmaids. And Vanessa. Although I won't have time to make your dresses.'

'Oh, that's all right,' said Meg. 'We'd have been most disappointed if you hadn't asked us to be bridesmaids. We've been getting so excited about your wedding. I'm really pleased you asked me to make your wedding cake.'

'And I'm going to ice it, apparently,' said David. 'Because of my skill in making putti, cherubs, swags and flowers. I usually make them in plaster of Paris, when I'm restoring mirrors and picture frames, but Alexandra says the skills are probably the same.'

'I love the idea of a cake with putti on it,' said

Lizzie. 'I hadn't really thought much about the cake apart from wanting Meg to make it.' Then she frowned. 'What are putti again?'

David laughed. 'Same as cherubs only without wings. And you don't have to have all those things on your cake.'

'As long as I can make it,' Meg said again. 'I've been researching recipes.'

'And I want to do something useful towards the event,' David said.

'Oh, David!' said Lizzie, getting up and putting her arms round him. 'You're such a prop to us girls! You're like a father only a lot more fun. I don't know how we'd manage without you. You don't need to be useful.'

'She's right,' said Alexandra. 'I couldn't have managed living here on my own, not for more than five minutes.' She joined in the hug.

'Girls!' said David, obviously moved. 'Stop being foolish and put the kettle on.'

When they were all drinking tea, Alexandra said, 'So, if you don't want to spend your time in London buying fabric' — she was obviously still thinking about it — 'what are you going to make your dress from? I do have some parachute silk left over from the war you could have.'

'No need! Hugo took me to see the workshop and the master craftsman, a really sweet man with snow-white hair, gave me all the fabric his mother had. She'd been a dressmaker and he never knew what to do with it.' Lizzie got up. 'I brought it with me.'

'So where is it?' asked Alexandra.

'In the trunk outside the door,' said Lizzie. ' I told you. I'll get it.'

'And I said you mustn't,' said Meg. 'It's likely to be heavy. We'll do it.'

Soon the contents of the trunk were on the big table that was at the opposite end to the kitchen table.

'Right, so what have we got?' asked Lizzie. She picked out the oyster satin she had seen first. 'I wonder if there's enough here to make a dress? It may not be a complete bolt. It could be just a few yards.'

'You wouldn't have to use just that,' said Alexandra, holding up a bolt of satin the colour of a peacock's breast.

'You mean, have a peacock-blue bodice and a different skirt? Hmm, I'm not sure I could have blue but the idea of having different material for the bodice and the skirt is brilliant.'

'There are some lovely fabrics here,' said David. 'How much is in a bolt?'

'I don't know, but the bolts may not be complete,' said Lizzie. 'But look at this lace!'

'Satin skirt, lace bodice and sleeves. Sounds ideal,' said Alexandra. 'What style do you want?'

'Has anyone got a pencil and paper? I'll draw it. I can see it in my head,' said Lizzie.

David produced the drawing things.

Meg put another cup of tea by her side. 'Do try the madeleines. I'm perfecting my recipe.'

'Oh! I think you've done it! That is absolutely delicious.' Lizzie regarded her friend. 'Meg, will you be offended if I tell you my mother has found some caterers? I didn't ask you to do the catering because it's going to be for so many people and I want you to be at the party, propping me up, like you always do.'

'As long as David and I can do the cake, I'd much rather just be a guest — '

'Bridesmaid,' Lizzie corrected. 'I wonder if Hugo will have anyone else from his side of the family to be a bridesmaid, apart from Vanessa?'

'What about me?' asked David.

Lizzie nodded. 'That would be an unusual choice for a bridesmaid, but I don't see — '

'Not as a bridesmaid, you daft ha'p'orth!' said David. 'I meant as a guest. Do you want me to bring a beard?'

Lizzie looked at him, completely at a loss.

Alexandra bust out laughing. 'He means, do you want him to bring a female friend — known as a beard — to make him look straight?'

Lizzie rolled her eyes. 'If you'd feel more comfortable, and she's nice, you'd be very welcome to bring a beard. But otherwise, just come on your own.'

'Is there a limit on the number of guests you can have?' asked Meg.

Lizzie shrugged. 'I don't think so. Apparently my parents have had a separate account with money for my wedding in it. My mother is now happily spending it.'

'I've always been led to believe that little girls spent their whole lives dreaming of their wedding days,' said David. 'I'm a bit shocked to find that in your case, Lizzie, it isn't true.'

Alexandra and Meg looked at him in horror. 'David!' said Alexandra. 'I'm disappointed in you. That would make Lizzie a very boring, superficial person and she certainly isn't!'

'Sorry!' He put up his hands in surrender. 'I'll get my morning suit cleaned by way of apology.'

'I expect you're right, actually,' said Lizzie. 'I mean, my wedding was always going to be my mother's

331

project and not much to do with me. Mostly I'm going along with it and trying to rebel in any way I reasonably can.'

'I don't see you as a rebel, Liz,' said Alexandra.

'To be honest, we none of us saw you as the type to have a shotgun wedding,' said David.

Lizzie giggled. 'If you had an inkling of the preparations that are going on, you'd never call it a shotgun wedding, even if I am pregnant.'

'And you're rebelling against them?' said David. 'You don't think having a homosexual on the guest list is rebelling enough?'

'No,' said Lizzie, 'not half enough. I'm going to make my own dress and I'm even trying to avoid having a wedding list. Now if you'll excuse me, I'm going to draw what I plan to walk down the aisle in. And, David, if my father doesn't come round to the idea of me being pregnant, you can walk me down it!'

★ ★ ★

The moment her pencil hit the paper the dress began to appear. A round neck, not high, just grazing her collar bones, three-quarter-length sleeves, a full-length skirt starting under the bust (which would help with the bump) and a ribbon with a bow with tails down the front (which would also help with the bump).

'OK,' she said, taking her drawing up to the other end of the room where Meg was adding the final touches to a late snack, ostensibly for David, who had a small part in a play and had not been home long, but of course she'd made enough for everyone. 'Have a look. What do we think?'

'Lovely. It's sweet, suitably demure for a wedding

332

dress and extremely pretty,' said David. 'Well done, Lizzie.'

'I love that!' said Meg, having set down a platter of nibbles. 'You could use the lace for the sleeves.'

'Tell you what,' said Alexandra. 'If you manage to get your pattern made and your dress cut out, we'll come with you to Peter Jones to make a wedding list.'

'That would make it more fun, I must say. Apparently if I don't have one people will be forever telephoning my mother asking her what we want as presents. And as my mother is staying with me at Patsy's that could be difficult.' She laughed. 'Imagine my father having to answer the calls! He'd go mad!'

'Maybe your mother would go home? Once the invitations are out and people start wondering what to give you?' suggested Meg. 'It's going to be short notice for people.'

Lizzie sighed. 'I know. The guest list from our side of the family has been ready since I was born, probably, but Hugo's mother isn't so accommodating.'

'So your mother will be staying with you at Patsy's for a bit longer? Is it driving you mad?'

Lizzie shrugged. 'I'm not sure if Mummy could be wrenched from the house. She is enjoying herself too much. It's funny, earlier today I was almost ready to strangle her but now, after a few hours away from it all, I'm happy for her and Patsy to organise my wedding if they want to — not that I have the slightest chance of stopping them. Hugo and I have the rest of our lives to do what we want.'

'So you *will* make a list?' asked Meg. 'For your mother's sake?'

'If I've got time,' Lizzie agreed. 'But making my dress is my priority.'

'Are you going to make a toile?' asked David. 'I could get hold of some muslin or something if you wanted to.'

'I wasn't going to bother — '

'I think you should,' David said firmly. 'I think you shouldn't go back to the country until you've got a toile that fits and your dress cut out.'

'What's a toile?' asked Alexandra. When Lizzie and David had both explained she said, 'Do you have to make it out of muslin? There are a lot of sheets which are now practically transparent they're so old. Could you use them?'

'They sound perfect,' said Lizzie. 'And then I don't have to wait to get muslin. But my sewing machine is in the country.'

'There's another sewing machine in the attic,' said Alexandra. 'One of my nannies used to make my dresses with it. It's probably pretty antique.'

'The other one is pretty antique too. That won't matter at all.'

'There really is a lot to be said for being part of a family who never throws anything away,' said Alexandra.

'They only never throw anything away because they never come here,' said David.

'This is going to be fun!' said Lizzie.

★ ★ ★

Although it was so late, everyone wanted to get involved. David found her enough brown paper to make a pattern for the bodice, and lining paper for the dress, which didn't need such precise fitting. He also found another Anglepoise lamp so she could see

334

better. Alexandra helped with measurements and Meg supplied everyone with snacks. A second dress-maker's dummy was found with a sewing machine — the one the girls had brought with them when they visited Lizzie was still in the country, of course. It was a fairly good match for Lizzie's own figure round the top. As her bump — very small at the moment — would only show underneath the bust line, it didn't need to be accommodated.

Eventually, Meg told her it was time for bed. 'It's half past two in the morning. You've got plenty of time to finish this and if you do it when you're tired you're likely to make a mistake.'

'Oh. Yes, I suppose you're right.' Now she thought about it, Lizzie realised how exhausted she was.

'We should have made you go to bed earlier,' said Alexandra. 'After all, you're sleeping for two now. Isn't that what they say?'

Lizzie laughed. 'My mother says I'm eating for two when she's not telling me not to eat potatoes as I don't want to put on weight and make my bump show. Although I do get tired. But I was so involved in making my dress I didn't notice I was fading a bit.'

'You see!' Alexandra went on. 'Weddings aren't all bad.'

'You're sharing with me again,' said Meg. 'And I've found you a nightie. We'll have to get you a tooth-brush in the morning.'

'I've loved this evening!' said Lizzie, taking the mug of cocoa Meg handed her. 'Being back with you all. I've felt like a girl again, instead of a soon-to-be mar-ried woman. It's not that I'm not looking forward to that, I definitely am. But if I hadn't got pregnant I could have carried on being a girl for a bit longer.'

'You've got another day to be girl!' said Meg.

'And we'll do the wedding list together. It'll be fun,' said Alexandra.

'Only if I've done everything I can to my dress,' said Lizzie firmly. But she was smiling. Life seemed manageable again.

★ ★ ★

Lizzie came downstairs to the basement kitchen in her borrowed nightie and Meg's dressing gown, which she had taken without asking. It was six in the morning but in spite of her late night she was so keen to get going again she'd been wide awake since half past five. When David came in at seven she was wearing the toile, holding it together at the back with one hand.

'Oh, I say!' said David. 'If that's what you look like when you're dressed in old sheets, I can't wait to see you in oyster satin with a lace bodice.'

'You like it? You think it will be OK?'

'More than OK, love. You'll be the most beautiful bride ever.' David cleared his throat. 'Want a bacon butty?'

'Yes, please,' said Lizzie. 'I'm starving!'

Her toile finished and her dress cut out, Lizzie went back to bed until Meg and Alexandra came and told her it was time to get up again.

'Come on! We're off to Peter Jones to make that list. David is going to meet us afterwards and take us out to lunch.' Alexandra looked thoughtful. 'I'll lend you something to wear. That skirt and blouse you came in is too square for the Kings Road.'

★ ★ ★

Lizzie was alone in the house when Hugo came to fetch her that evening. It was six o'clock and Meg and Alexandra both had jobs serving canapés at a cocktail party. David had left for the theatre. Hugo came to the front door, and as she'd been expecting him to come in through the area, she was slightly out of breath when she greeted him.

'Hello,' he said, seeming a bit shy for some reason. 'Are you ready to leave the big city and come back to our little house in the woods?'

'I am, although I have had a lovely time. Come down to the kitchen. There's food. We can have a little snack before we set off. Unless we're in a hurry?'

'No. Our time is our own.'

She led the way, talking over her shoulder. 'I'm looking forward to hearing how you got on with your mother.' She tried to sound casual as if it didn't matter to her one way or another. She failed. Her anxiety about this was evident in her voice.

'Convincing her that the wedding is a good thing?'

'Yes.' Lizzie opened the door to the kitchen and let Hugo walk in first.

Hugo looked at the plates filled with canapés that were laid out on the table. Some of them were a bit battered at the edges but it was still an impressive spread. 'My goodness,' he said. 'It's a feast!'

'It's Meg. You know she works for a catering company? A box of food fell over in the back of the van. She brought home everything that couldn't be given to the paying customers. David provided these lovely olives from somewhere in Soho that imports them direct from Greece. And there's egg mayonnaise. Alexandra is practising mayonnaise. She never got it quite right for Mme Wilson. Meg said it was a life skill and therefore she had to perfect it.'

'There's enough — '

'For an army. I know! I think they're trying to fatten me up. Sorry. We don't have to eat it.'

'No! I'm delighted. I don't think my mother ever tried to fatten anybody up. Rather the reverse. And she eats very little herself so forgets other people need food.'

'Well, do sit down. Shall I make some tea to go with it?'

'Tea and miniature quiches? Sounds perfect.'

'Sorry. Would you like something else?' Lizzie felt wrong-footed. 'I always want tea if I've eaten something cheesy. I'm sure there'll be wine somewhere.'

'Tea would be fine,' he said. 'You're looking well, Lizzie. Have you had a nice time?'

'It's been just fab. I've really enjoyed myself.'

'But not so much that you won't want to go back to the country?'

Lizzie shook her head. 'London is wonderful! I'll always love it, and I'll always cherish memories of when I lived there. But . . . ' She paused, not sure if he was ready to hear how much she loved making a home, for him, and her, and — soon — for their baby. 'Anyway! I've got so much done since I've been here, my mother is going to be delighted. We even made a wedding list at Peter Jones. I'm sorry you didn't get to choose anything but, to be honest, even with Alexandra and Meg it was pretty grim.' She lit the gas under the kettle. 'Apparently we can take back anything we don't like and choose something else.'

'Your mother will be very relieved. I know it was on her mind.'

'My mother isn't one for bottling things up. If she's

338

worried about something she likes the whole world to worry with her.'

Hugo laughed. 'Yes, but she loves you very much and so I forgive her. But actually, talking about your parents, which we sort of were, I went to see your father. We had a man-to-man talk and he's going to escort you down the aisle very proudly. I think you were right: he was embarrassed that he'd overreacted in the beginning, but he's very happy about it all now.'

'Oh, Hugo! That's amazing! I can't thank you enough! I tried to tell myself it didn't matter and that David would do it if necessary but in my heart — ' Suddenly she couldn't speak.

Hugo came to where she was sitting and put an arm round her and hugged her to him for a few seconds. 'There's something else as well.'

'What?'

'He rang your mother and told her he couldn't cope without her any more and she's going home first thing in the morning.'

'That's a miracle,' Lizzie said, awed. 'And she doesn't mind?'

'Obviously I haven't seen her but I suspect she's delighted to be so needed. But you can see her before she goes and tell her about the wedding list and the dress. She'll leave happy as a grig.'

Lizzie laughed at his archaic language but there were tears in her eyes.

'Let's get this tea, shall we?' said Hugo.

A few moments later they both had mugs of tea. Lizzie sat at the table and ate a miniature quiche. Fortified, she said, 'So tell me. How did you get on at your mother's?'

'I wasn't quite sure what to expect. Sometimes

my mother follows my father and does everything he wants without question. Sometimes she rebels.'

'My mother is the same! I think she does what Daddy wants if she doesn't care but if she does care — like wanting to plan my wedding — she goes ahead and does it.' Lizzie hesitated. 'I can't thank you enough for talking to him.'

'It was my duty as your future husband to reassure him about me. And he is very reassured, believe me.'

This made Lizzie smile again. 'So, your mother? Does she think I've ruined your life?' Another sip of hot tea helped keep her chin from wobbling.

'She still hasn't accepted the idea of my giving up the law, but I don't think she still blames you for that. I think she'll eventually see you as her daughter-in-law instead of Electra. Nessa has helped, obviously, going on about how lovely you are. As did I!' he added, answering her unspoken question. 'She will come to the wedding.'

A wedding without the groom's parents, at least one of them, would have been a bit embarrassing. Weddings, she realised, were terribly public. She didn't want hers spoilt by scandal.

'She also sent you this.' Hugo reached into this pocket and drew out a slim leather box. He handed it to Lizzie. 'It's not a present; she's lending it to you.'

Inside was a delicate tiara of pearls and tiny flowers formed out of enamel and diamonds. 'Oh my goodness, it's so pretty!' 'Try it on?'

She took the circlet to the mirror and set it on her head, threading it through her hair so the jewels were partly obscured. 'It's beautiful.'

'I thought it would suit you.' He paused. 'My mother offered to lend you one of several tiaras that are part of the family jewels but most of them are in the bank. I thought this one was the most you. The others are a bit big and old-fashioned. My mother was surprised I chose that for you. She hardly considers it jewellery. It's not nearly valuable enough.'

'It's perfect! It's so kind of your mother.'

'Not all that kind. It's a tradition in my family to lend the bride jewellery for the wedding, particularly headdresses, which they may not have.'

'But it's a good sign, isn't it? She's keeping with tradition and lending me a crown.'

He laughed gently. 'It's hardly a crown but it looks lovely on you.' He hesitated. 'As we're going to get married, I suppose we're engaged?'

She nodded. 'I suppose we are. We seemed to miss out that part, didn't we?' One minute we hardly knew each other and the next we are planning to spend the rest of our lives together, she thought.

'We did and so we missed getting you an engagement ring.' He put his hand in his other pocket and took out a smaller, squarer box. 'I've taken it upon myself to get you one. But, of course, if you don't like it, it can be exchanged.'

Inside the box was an opal ring that flashed blue and green. Round it were diamonds. It was quite large and yet didn't seem heavy.

'It's beautiful!' said Lizzie, a bit overcome.

'Do you like it? It's Edwardian, so made just at the turn of the century, before the First World War. I got David to help me choose it and he thought you'd like having something a bit different from the single stones that most people have.'

'Oh? When were you in touch with David?' Lizzie was a bit surprised. She hadn't pictured Hugo and

David becoming friends.

'I managed to ring him yesterday and today, after he'd taken you girls out for lunch, he took me to a jeweller friend before he had to be at the theatre. He's nice, isn't he? He's so fond of you all.'

'He's lovely. So is this ring.' Lizzie was staring at it.

'Here,' said Hugo. 'If you think you like it, I'll do this.'

For a horrible moment Lizzie thought Hugo was going to go down on one knee. But he didn't. He took the ring out of the box. 'Lizzie, will you do me the extreme honour of becoming my wife? Will you marry me?'

Lizzie gave a little nervous laugh. 'I think, considering all the preparations that have gone on, I'd better say yes!' She held out her hand, waiting for him to slip the ring on to her finger.

'No,' he said. 'That isn't the answer I want. If no one knew anything about us, there had been nothing booked — no church, no venue — no parents involved, if you weren't pregnant, and I asked you, what would your answer be then?'

She looked up into his eyes. 'Same,' she said. 'I'd say yes.'

'In which case, you shall have your ring.' He put it on and it flashed blue and the diamonds sparkled.

'Thank you so much!' she said.

This was the moment when she should follow Alexandra's advice and tell him she loved him. It was also the moment when he should say the same thing. But he didn't.

There was a short silence. Hugo looked a bit awkward, cleared his throat and then said, 'I'm so glad you like it. Now I'm going to take you back to Patsy's.'

30

Lizzie was aware of being excited when, four weeks later, she woke up and realised it was the morning of her wedding. All her family and lots of her friends were going to gather together today to see her marrying Hugo.

Several of them were here already. There were her parents and Gina, who were staying at the hotel. It had been lovely to catch up with Gina the previous day and she knew that she was planning to have dinner with her parents at the hotel after the wedding. Lizzie hoped Mrs Brinklow, her mother's guest of honour, wouldn't join them; Gina would either die of boredom or suppressed laughter.

David was at the hotel too and Lizzie really hoped her parents wouldn't run into him, although he and Gina had met before and got on really well. But her parents would be very confused if they realised Lizzie had invited Alexandra's butler-come-chauffeur to her wedding. Maybe they would think he was there because of Alexandra.

Alexandra and Meg were staying at the house in the woods. They had reluctantly left Clover behind in London with a neighbour. They didn't think she would be a particularly welcome guest at the wedding, or even in the cottage, which had been hastily redecorated and made fit for guests and was therefore rather vulnerable to dog hair and claws. Vanessa, the third of her three bridesmaids, was somewhere here in Patsy's house; and Hugo was with Simon, who was his best man. She wasn't sure where he lived.

When she saw her dress hanging up on the wardrobe door, covered in a cloth, she felt a rush of emotion that was partly nerves and partly pride that she'd managed to make it in time. Next to it was a cloud of white tulle bunched on to combs and sewn on to the tiara that would be her veil. The veil had originally been her grandmother's. Her mother had taken it to someone recommended by a friend and this person had created something which delighted both mother and daughter — not an easy feat.

Having not particularly enjoyed the preparations, now the day was here, Lizzie wanted to get up and get going. She looked at the little travel alarm clock on the bedside table, thoughtfully provided by Patsy. It was six thirty, hours before anyone else would be up. The wedding was at two, and at twelve, Lizzie's mother was coming over to help her get ready. Hours away!

Patsy said that breakfast would be served at nine, but Lizzie needed something to eat now. She had forgotten to take up a snack with her at bedtime and if she didn't eat first thing, she felt sick. She got out of bed and found her dressing gown.

Although it was so early, she wasn't the first one in the kitchen. 'Nessa! Hello! What are you doing up at this time?' Lizzie said, seeing one of her bridesmaids sitting at the kitchen table with her hands round a mug of something

'Oh, hello, Lizzie. I woke up before dawn and couldn't get back to sleep.'

Nessa didn't seem her usual bouncy self, Lizzie thought, allowing for the hour. When they'd first met, on the cookery course, Lizzie had had her down as a haughty deb, scathing of lesser mortals, but she knew her better now. Vanessa was capable of great kindness and Lizzie was now really fond of her. 'Are you OK, Ness?'

Vanessa sighed deeply and stared into her mug. 'I don't know.'

'Why? What's the matter?'

It took Vanessa a long time to stop mumbling and come out with what was worrying her. 'It's the best man.'

'What's wrong with him?' Lizzie was worried too now. Hugo's best man worked in Switzerland, which was why she hadn't met.

Vanessa was quick to reassure her. 'Oh, there's nothing wrong with him! I've just had a crush on him for years.'

Much relieved, Lizzie refilled the kettle and tipped the tea leaves out of the pot into the bucket under the sink. 'I think that's lovely. The best man is always supposed to get off with one of the bridesmaids.'

Vanessa was cast into gloom again. 'But it won't be me, will it? It'll be Alexandra, who's always so elegant and confident.'

Vanessa seemed really distressed and Lizzie didn't feel she could console her on an empty stomach. 'I'm going to make some toast. Would you like some? Patsy said I should just help myself to food when I wanted it. Apparently when she was pregnant she was starving all the time.' She found the loaf and started slicing.

Although she looked rather longingly at the bread, Vanessa shook her head. 'No toast for me, thanks.'

'Nessa, please relax. You look lovely in your bridesmaid's dress. I think the design suits you best of all.' The kettle had boiled and Lizzie warmed the teapot with a swirl of water before spooning in the tea leaves.

'Do you really think so?' said Vanessa.

'I do! As you know, I didn't make them, but I spent a lot of time thinking about what would suit everyone. And what they could wear afterwards.' The brides-maids' dresses were full length and slim-fitting with boat necks. There were bolero jackets to wear over them so they would look decent and wouldn't be cold in church; churches were always cool even in September. The dresses were made out of raw silk and were the same peacock blue that Alexandra had taken a fancy to in the fabrics that Harold had given Lizzie. It was a colour that suited them all but did slightly favour Vanessa.

'I'm worried I look a bit fat in it,' said Vanessa.

'Oh, come on! You won't. You're bound to look thinner than I do — I'm pregnant!' Lizzie added boiling water to the tea leaves, hoping that Vanessa would now stop worrying and eat something.

'It doesn't show that you're pregnant — hardly at all. But something Mummy said last night made me worry.'

'Last night? How did you see your mother last night? Did you drive over? You must have got back here very late.'

Lizzie had been packed off to bed early before her 'Big Day' and when she'd said goodnight, Vanessa said she wasn't going to be long before she went to bed herself. Hugo was just about to leave to go and stay with his best man.

'Oh? I suppose you don't know. Mummy and Daddy are here. They arrived quite late.'

'What? To stay with Patsy and Tim?' Lizzie felt sick in earnest now. She was prepared to see Hugo's parents at the wedding, when she was protected from them by dozens of people, but not when she didn't even have her mother between her and them. Suddenly Lizzie wished that her parents were not in the local hotel; she needed them here. And Hugo was too far away to protect her.

'Why did they come last night? It's not that far from your house. They don't need to be here before the wedding, do they?' Lizzie suddenly panicked in case there was some ritual to be carried out by the groom's parents she had forgotten about.

'They came because Daddy wanted to talk to Hugo, quite urgently. Tim left them to it in the library with a bottle of brandy. It was all a bit last minute.'

Lizzie's head swam and a cold sweat broke out at her hairline. 'Nessa, you wouldn't be a love and make the toast, would you? I suddenly feel as if I might throw up.'

'Oh God, poor you! Yes, of course.'

Lizzie watched her bustle about and began to feel a bit better. 'Sorry to be a nuisance. I was supposed to be looking after you while you were worrying about the best man. Tell me about him.' It would be a distraction and stop her panicking about why Hugo's parents had turned up so suddenly.

'Simon? He and Hugo were at school together and he used to come and stay in the school holidays. As you know, he lives in Switzerland now and I haven't seen him since then.' Vanessa paused. 'What do you want on your toast?'

'Butter and Marmite, please. But go on about Simon.'

'You know Hugo, he's kind, but of course they didn't want me hanging round in the holidays, so I used to spy on them. But one day we all went to the

347

beach for the day. We had an older cousin staying with us and he was in charge. He had a girlfriend.'

'Wasn't the beach quite far away?'

'Quite far, I suppose, but the cousin, Peter, was all for taking us. I think he wanted to impress the girl, who was terribly keen. Our parents were abroad somewhere, having a holiday. Anyway, on the way home, we three kids were in the back of the car. I pretended to fall asleep and accidentally on purpose rested my head on his shoulder.' She sighed. 'I kept it there all the way home. It was so lovely.' She handed Lizzie her toast.

Lizzie took a bite and decided to focus on cheering Vanessa up. Then she'd worry about what on earth Hugo's father wanted to talk to him about that was so urgent that necessitated coming over last night. There was only one reason she could think of.

'It's really sweet that he didn't move,' she said to Vanessa. 'Or put your head somewhere else.'

'It was, wasn't it?'

'And I think he — Simon — will be very impressed with how you've turned out. You must have been quite young when he last saw you.'

'I was thirteen.'

'Not a good age — spots, puppy fat — but now you're grown up and gorgeous! I expect you'll be asking me to rescue you from him later.'

Vanessa laughed. 'Well, I suppose I have improved a bit since those days. I was rather chubby and my hair was terribly greasy.'

'It's luxuriant now! Do you remember when we first met at the cookery school and I helped you in the dressmaking class? I thought then that you had lovely hair.'

'I was very shy and I know it made me seem a bit stuck-up. You girls seemed different from the others there — a group of friends.'

'We'd only just met. And you're part of the group now.'

Vanessa smiled. 'It's lovely! With you I can just be myself, I don't have to compete to be invited to the most parties and balls and all that stuff.'

Lizzie gave her a warm smile back, confident Vanessa was now happy. 'OK, Ness, can you tell me why you think your parents felt obliged to come over last night? So your father could talk to Hugo on the night before his wedding?'

Vanessa picked up a bit of toast. 'Well, I don't suppose it was so Daddy could tell Hugo about the birds and bees. Hugo has obviously got that one sorted out.'

'Yup. I can confirm that to be the case.'

Both girls giggled and then Lizzie asked again, 'So why do you think they came? And what did your father need to say to Hugo that was so urgent?'

Vanessa examined the crumbs on her plate. 'I don't really know my father very well. I've always been a bit frightened of him, to be honest.'

Lizzie nodded. 'I can understand that.'

'But I think the only thing he really cares about is money. He thinks there's nothing he can't have if he can pay for it.'

Lizzie shrugged. 'Poets say money can't buy you love!'

'Daddy would definitely say that actually, it can.'

'I wonder,' said Lizzie slowly, 'if your father thought, if he offered Hugo enough money, he would pull out of the wedding.'

Vanessa gasped.

Lizzie went on. 'Let's not pretend, Nessa. We both know your father is very unhappy about Hugo marrying me. Hugo is his son and heir. He might very well be prepared to do a lot to stop the wedding.'

'Oh God, Lizzie!' Vanessa began, as if wanting to deny what Lizzie had just said. But she stopped, unable to say it wasn't possible. 'But Hugo . . . he'd never do anything like that — I mean take money to pull out of the wedding. He loves you!'

Lizzie took a breath. Did he? He had never *said* so. Caught up in the whirlwind wedding preparations and soothed by Hugo's gentle kindness, she had mostly managed to bury her concern that Hugo was only marrying her because it was the honourable thing to do, but she had never completely forgotten it. Still, she had no doubt that, whatever his motive, he would do the right thing. 'Well, of course I trust him completely, but I have to know what they were talking about. Could you ask him?'

'No. Absolutely not.' Vanessa didn't hesitate.

'Maybe I should ask him — '

'No!' said Vanessa again, with even more certainty. 'He wouldn't tell you.'

'What about your mother? Would she know? And if she did, would she tell me?'

'No. I'm sorry, Lizzie. If you want to find out you're going to have to ask Hugo. Of course, it would be terribly unlucky to see him before the wedding.'

It took Lizzie less than half a second to consider this. 'Not half as unlucky as me turning up at the church and there being no bridegroom there.'

'True,' said Vanessa. 'So what are you going to do?'

Somehow this question made Lizzie feel a bit better, a bit stronger, as if there was a solution. 'We need

350

to see Hugo. He's staying with Simon. Do you know Simon's address?'

'No. But Mummy will know. She'll have it in her address book.'

'She won't have her address book with her, will she?'

Vanessa nodded. 'She never goes anywhere without it! She's got a tiny one that fits in her handbag. It's in case she's travelling and needs a loo. There's always someone she knows within reach.'

'Goodness me! So, all we need now is an excuse to look at her address book.' Lizzie tried to think up reasons why she might need an address, and quite quickly too, but failed.

Vanessa took on the problem more directly. 'I'll go upstairs and steal it from her room.'

'Is that possible? Won't she wake up and ask you what on earth you're doing, rummaging in her handbag?'

Vanessa shook her head. 'No. She takes sleeping pills. A bomb could go off in her room and she wouldn't wake up.'

'What about your father? Would he wake up? That would be scary!'

'They're not in the same room. They never share a room now. Patsy put him in the room Hugo uses when he's here.'

'Great! So, you go and get her address book and hope she's got Simon's current address.'

'But how will we get there? I can't drive. Can you?'

Lizzie said instantly. 'David will help us. He'll drive us wherever we need to go.'

'He's one of the ushers, isn't he?'

'Yes,' said Lizzie. 'And a very good friend. Now go!'

But before Vanessa could escape Patsy came in, wearing a paisley dressing gown and signs of a bad night. 'Morning! I was going to bring you tea in your room, Lizzie.' She pulled out a chair and sat down, her head in her hands. 'Did I see tea? Could one of you be an angel and pour me a cup?'

'Are you OK, Patsy?' said Lizzie, anxious. Patsy was important to how the day went and if she was ill, someone would need to think of a plan B.

'I'm fine. I just didn't sleep all that well — worried about today I suppose, although I know everything is in hand.' Patsy smiled reassuringly. 'Although maybe the brandy last night was a bad idea. Nessa? If you go through to the scullery you'll find a bottle of Alka-Seltzer. Would you be a love . . . ?'

Vanessa fetched the slim glass cylinder and brought Patsy a glass of water. Everyone watched as Patsy slipped three of the huge tablets into the glass which began to fizz loudly.

'I never thought you could take more than two of those,' said Lizzie.

'I never take fewer than three. They cure everything.' Patsy gulped down the contents of the glass and belched discreetly behind her hand. 'Excuse me. Now I can face anything!'

'Did you have a late night?' asked Lizzie, wondering if they could get the information they needed from Patsy, and not have to dash off across the countryside to find Hugo.

'Yes. Hugo stayed talking to his father for hours — '

'Do you know what they talked about?' Lizzie interrupted. She smiled apologetically as Patsy gave her a surprised look.

'I was just wondering', Lizzie went on, trying to

sound casual, 'why the Lennox-Stanleys felt the need to come here last night? The wedding's not until two.' Lizzie was aware she was sounding a bit unhinged and hoped her status as bride would make this acceptable.

'To be completely honest,' said Patsy, 'I'm not sure. Maybe toast will help me think.'

Vanessa took the hint. Once the bread was under the grill and she had found marmalade to add to the butter and Marmite that were already on the kitchen table, she said to Lizzie, 'Can you make the toast? I just want to pop up and see if Mummy's awake.'

Lizzie got up quickly. 'Of course.'

But before Vanessa could get as far as the door, Patsy shook her head. 'No point, Nessa. Annabel said she was going to take a pill and didn't want to be disturbed until midday and then only in an emergency. She's not coming down for breakfast.'

Lizzie and Vanessa exchanged glances. If only Vanessa had given a different excuse to leave the room.

'While we're talking about Nessa's mother,' said Lizzie, 'I would find it easier not to see her parents before the wedding.' She gave one of those smiles which people use as punctuation rather than because they're expressing happiness or a greeting. 'I expect you know we're not on the best of terms. Would it be terribly rude if I went down to the cottage and had breakfast with Alexandra and Meg?'

'Oh, that sounds fun,' said Nessa. 'Can I come too? We could be bridesmaids together.'

Patsy balanced an inordinate amount of marmalade on to a corner of toast. 'Well, I don't mind, and as the bride Lizzie can do what she likes. But wouldn't your esteemed papa think it rather odd if his daughter doesn't make an appearance at breakfast?'

Vanessa shook her head. 'I don't suppose Daddy would notice if I was at the table if I turned up wearing a suit of armour. He certainly wouldn't care if I wasn't there.'

'Oh,' said Patsy. 'In which case, do go. As long as you promise me faithfully you won't be back late. I need you here on the dot of twelve if not a bit before.'

'I'm sure it can't take that long to put on a dress — ' Lizzie began.

'It's not just a dress and it can take ages,' said Patsy. 'Besides, your mother is coming at twelve and we don't want to spoil her day by giving her conniptions, do we?'

Lizzie agreed. 'She's been looking forward to this day since she first knew her baby was a girl. We won't be late back.'

'Then off you go. Give my love to your bridesmaids. They're great girls.' Patsy smiled, possibly glad to have two fewer people to feel responsible for.

'But before we go,' said Lizzie, 'would you mind if I made a phone call? Just local? I just want to telephone David about something.'

'Oh, David? Lovely chap. Please do. Use the office. The local telephone directory is in there.'

Vanessa ran up the stairs to borrow her mother's address book without Patsy noticing while Lizzie made her call. When the hotel receptionist was putting her through to David's room she realised it was still early. The clock on the wall of the office said it was only ten past eight.

David was very good-natured about being woken by a frantic phone call but after he'd heard Lizzie's tale of woe he said, 'Lizzie, I can't do it. I'd love to help you, but the church has had a panic with the

354

flower rota. They didn't have enough people to decorate it for your wedding, so they roped me in.'

'David! How did the church flower people even know you existed?'

'I went over last evening. As an usher I thought I ought to check the venue and it's a lovely church. There was a woman, Diana . . .'

'Diana Baker. She's the vicar's wife.'

'She was there with another woman and they were wringing their hands. I naturally asked them what the problem was. They told me, and I felt I couldn't let you or that beautiful church down. So I told them I was an actor, but when I started out in rep as an ASM, I'd had to create more than one Birnham Wood for the Scottish Play and offered my services. They were delighted.'

'I'm impressed they knew what an ASM was. I'm not sure I did, before I met you.'

'I did have to explain it meant dogsbody and you had to turn your hand to anything. But anyway, I'm committed.'

'That's so kind of you to offer to help. I'm surprised Patsy didn't say anything about there being a problem with decorating the church.'

'Diana was trying to avoid telling her. She said she had enough on.' He paused. 'I could lend you the car. I know you can't drive but Alexandra can. I could drop the car off the moment I've had breakfast.'

'That's so kind, David,' said Lizzie, biting back her request for him to drop the car off before breakfast. 'Thank you so much. And I'll see you later.'

Vanessa joined Lizzie in the office, bearing her mother's little black book. 'Absolutely dead to the world, she was. So, let's see where Simon lives.'

She found the address quite quickly, and they wrote down that and the telephone number. 'We just have to hope he didn't rent out his house when he went away and we find out that he and Hugo are staying somewhere else.'

Lizzie shuddered at the thought.

'This is all a bit crazy. Are you sure you still want to go?' Vanessa was looking a bit worried. 'We could go off on a wild goose chase and not find them when we get there.'

Lizzie bit her lip and thought hard. Was it crazy? She pictured herself at the church, waiting for the music to start and for a man she didn't know running up with a message from Hugo. She closed her eyes and the picture was so vivid, it was almost as if it had actually happened. 'If you're willing to come, I do want to see Hugo. Although if you'd rather not, I could just go with Alexandra. She could talk to Simon for me.'

Vanessa's eyes widened. 'No, that's all right. I'll come. I really like Alexandra but I'm not having her stealing Simon before I've had a chance.'

'Good. And to avoid the wild goose chase, we'll ring Simon first — at least you will — to make sure they're there.'

Vanessa pretended to be someone from the local council although it was only eight thirty in the morning. Having confirmed that Simon was in the house, she rang off.

'You did that so well!' said Lizzie. 'And Simon must have beautiful manners not to shout at you, considering how early it is.'

Vanessa looked at the office clock. 'It is quite early. But I've always liked acting. I wanted to go to drama school but of course Daddy disapproved.'

They shared a moment of regret for the intransigence of Vanessa's father, Lizzie thinking again about how likely it was that he had tried to talk Hugo out of the wedding. She thought about the baby nestling safely under her blouse. She already felt fiercely protective of it. In Sir Jasper's position, with his attitudes and ingrained opinions, Lizzie might have done the same thing. You would do anything you could to stop your child making what you considered to be the biggest mistake of his life.

She cleared her throat and then said, 'Shall we go?'

31

It was lovely seeing Alexandra and Meg, who were sitting at the table under the apple tree having breakfast and for a few minutes Lizzie stopped feeling that the day was going to be a disaster and that her heart was bound to be broken.

After some initial excitement and celebration Lizzie explained her problem. Alexandra and Meg listened in silence. Meg obviously thought she was absolutely mad but Alexandra was more thoughtful.

'Why would Hugo's father do that?' asked Meg. 'He should be delighted. He wouldn't want his son to abandon the mother of his child, surely?'

'You don't know my father,' said Vanessa. 'He's used to getting his own way.'

'But Hugo!' said Meg. 'He loves you!'

Vanessa had said the same thing, but yet again Lizzie was brought up short, wondering what Hugo really felt for her, and if it was strong enough to withstand his father's possible intervention. Yet again she remembered Hugo saying *end up having to marry her*.

She felt sick once more.

'But there's always the thought that he's been forced into this because I'm pregnant. He might not really want to do it.' Lizzie managed to put on a smile and the thought occurred to her that she was probably going to have to do that a lot today. Her mother had the photographer of her dreams. There would be a lot of pictures. If, of course, the wedding happened at all.

'Actually,' said Alexandra, 'although I'd stake my

life on Hugo loving you to bits, Lizzie, I did know a girl who had an au pair. Her big brother, who was quite a lot older, fell in love with the au pair. I remember my friend telling me that her mother spent all night persuading him to call off the wedding. And he did.'

Lizzie broke out in a light sweat and everyone else looked shocked.

'OK,' said Meg. 'It is remotely possible that Hugo's papa will have done that — or tried to do that — but — '

'I don't want to take the risk, Meggie,' said Lizzie quietly.

They'd had more tea and eaten some pastries that Meg had brought with her and Lizzie was starting to worry about time. She'd got up so early, where was the time going? Surely David should be here by now?

Eventually they saw the big car come down the lane and pull up outside the house. Lizzie rushed to meet him.

'Sorry, I'm a bit later than I intended to be. I met your parents at the hotel, Lizzie, and I had a bit of a job convincing them it was entirely appropriate to invite your plumber-cum-family retainer and goodness knows what else to a wedding, even if it wasn't for the family you were retaining, so to speak.'

Alexandra found this hilarious. 'Oh God! Do you remember? Your parents drove you home and you didn't know how to explain David and he turned into the plumber and then a butler.' She looked at Vanessa who was looking confused. 'You had to be there, really.'

David smiled. 'A bit of quick improv and the problem was solved.'

'I said you were the chauffeur at the last encounter,'

said Alexandra.

'I'm a man of many parts! Appropriate for an actor. I emphasised my role as church decorator. Anyway, Lizzie, don't you want to go somewhere?'

'We do, definitely. Are we all coming?' she asked.

'As I'm driving, I'd better come,' said Alexandra.

'I'm coming. It's my brother we're dealing with,' said Vanessa.

'I'll come if you want me,' said Meg. 'Otherwise I'll stay here, wash up, and keep everyone calm in case you're not back by twelve.'

Lizzie's eyes widened with horror at the prospect. 'We definitely want you, Meg, and I have to be back by twelve. My mother would die if I wasn't! Quick, into the car. We must leave immediately.'

'Hang on a giddy minute,' said David. 'Do you know where you're going?'

'We've got the address,' said Vanessa, heading towards the car.

'But do you know what direction you're heading in?' said David. 'Let's have a look at the map. Lexi? Find the AA book and let's make a quick plan.'

Alexandra went to the car and came back with a yellow book that was filled with maps. David quickly looked up the village where Simon lived. 'It's not that near,' he said. 'You won't have time to get lost. Can anyone find me a bit of paper?'

He jotted down a list of places to aim for. 'OK, which of you is the navigator? Who's going to read the map?'

'Not me,' said Vanessa. 'I feel sick if I try to read in cars, even a map.'

'Me too,' said Meg.

'OK,' said Lizzie. 'I'll do it. I usually do, don't I?'

She took the paper. 'David, you do know I love you?'

'Even though you're marrying someone else?' said David, laughing.

'I really hope I am,' she said. 'We just need to make sure of the bridegroom's intentions.'

'If it will make any difference, I think the chances of Hugo standing you up at the altar are nil, but if running all over the country to make sure will make you happy, there's no harm in it. As long as you're not back late.'

Once they were in the car and had set off, Lizzie looked at her piece of paper more carefully. 'There are a lot of places on here. I hope it's not too far away. We need to set off back home again by eleven at the latest.'

'It can't be that far, or Hugo would have found somewhere nearer to stay,' said Alexandra.

'Not necessarily,' said Vanessa. 'He'd want to stay with Simon, his best friend and his best man.'

'And Patsy and Tim's house is out of bounds as it's got me staying in it,' said Lizzie. 'And his parents,' she added gloomily.

'And a good hotel is out of the question?' said Alexandra.

'There's only one remotely near enough and it's probably full,' said Lizzie. 'My parents, David, and Mrs Brinklow, a friend of the family my mother is most desperate to impress, are all staying there. Anyway, we're going where we're going.'

They had to stop in a little market town to use the public conveniences and for Lizzie to wonder if she shouldn't just trust Hugo and ask Alexandra to head for home.

'I don't think it's much further,' said Alexandra,

when Lizzie dithered aloud about the wisdom of this venture. 'I spotted a signpost to the village. We must be nearly there.' Alexandra glanced up at the town-hall clock and then looked at her watch. 'But have a think.'

Lizzie was finding it difficult to get her brain to work. 'The only thing I can think about is how utterly ghastly it would be if Hugo didn't turn up. I think I really need to know that he's going to.'

'Then on we go!' said Alexandra.

★　★　★

'I think it must be that house,' said Lizzie, looking at a small Georgian house behind a hedge. It had taken them longer than they would have liked to find it.

'It's nice, isn't it?' said Vanessa. 'Shall we knock at the door?'

'I'm not going in,' said Lizzie.

Her companions screamed at her so loudly it was surprising people didn't come rushing from their houses to see who was being murdered. 'I can't!' said Lizzie. 'I really need to know, but I can't actually ask him.'

'Is it because it's bad luck to see the groom before you see him in church?' asked Vanessa, who was a little bit more sympathetic than Alexandra was.

'No!' said Lizzie. 'I just — I mean — supposing he says he can't go through with it? I'll die.'

'All right,' said Alexandra. 'We'll go in and ask him. Come on, Ness.'

'Oh, OK. Do I look all right?' Vanessa asked Lizzie.

'Why on earth does that matter?' asked Alexandra. 'I'm going.'

Vanessa, anxious lest Alexandra ensnare the best man before she had a chance to, hastened after her. Meg followed.

Lizzie sat in the car, her thoughts in turmoil. The bride in her thought this was crazy, and she should be at Patsy's house lying down with slices of cucumber on her eyes, filing her nails and pushing down her cuticles with an orange stick, as recommended in all the bridal magazines. The woman in her desperately needed reassurance that she wasn't making a huge mistake. She wanted to marry Hugo, so very much, but she wanted *him* to want to also. She wanted him to be happy. She didn't want to trap him in a marriage that would make him unhappy. Recently she'd been thinking that it wouldn't . . . but she didn't know any more. She'd just come to the conclusion that the combination of being pregnant and the maelstrom of the wedding preparations had made her a little bit crazy, when the driver's side door opened and a man she'd never met leant in.

'There's been a change of plan,' he said. 'I'm Simon, by the way.'

'I think I'm going to be sick,' said Lizzie. She got out of the car and ran behind a hedge. She retched but didn't actually vomit and felt better afterwards. She got back into the car. 'Tell me the worst.'

'There is no worst. I've got a letter from Hugo. I suggest you read it. Then I'm driving you back to Patsy's as I know the way well and will be quicker. We'll go in my car. But read the letter first.'

Lizzie opened it with trembling fingers.

363

My darling Lizzie,

I've been rehearsing these lines in my head for so long now, never quite daring to say them to you in case you look at me, frightened, embarrassed and generally put off the whole idea of marrying me.

I fell in love with you when we met looking at that horrible flat in Tufnell Park. I wasn't a free man and when I met you again, at Nessa's dinner party, I knew that I should have stayed away for ever. That was why you terrified me. I knew my destiny had changed the moment I met you.

As you know by now, my family are very stuffy and buttoned-up, no one ever talks about feelings, but in spite of that, we do feel things. Meeting you jolted me out of the path other people had chosen for me. I decided to give up the law and, fortunately, this was enough to make Electra realise I was not the dream husband she had thought I was.

When you became pregnant and I found out about it I knew I had to marry you, for your sake as much as mine, but I was worried that I'd somehow trapped you into settling down far too young.

I know I should have told you how much I loved you long before this but I found the words so difficult. I tried to show you I loved you, though, and deeds are supposed to be more meaningful than words.

But now I know that you're worried my father may have tried to talk me out of our marriage. He didn't; he wanted to arrange an income for me so we're not quite so poverty-stricken while I do my apprenticeship. But if he had — and he might well have done, he does like his own way — he would never have succeeded. I love you so much, more than I can

364

ever express, and will never stop trying to show you how much that is.

Your ever- (and ever!) loving husband-to-be,
Hugo

Lizzie was sniffing and wiping her nose before she was halfway through it and was crying by the end.

'OK?' said Simon. 'Now we're going to get going because you're the bride and you can't be late. Hugo will go with the girls in the other car. As bridesmaids, they're not so important.' He looked at his watch. 'Eleven fifteen. We're cutting it fine. Hold on to your hat!'

Neither of them spoke for a while. Lizzie needed time to pull herself together. Simon was concentrating on the road.

Eventually Lizzie felt enough in control to take the opportunity to inspect her driver. He was good-looking, tall, with very blue eyes and dark curly hair. She could see what Vanessa saw in him. He seemed nice, too. Kind, certainly. She really hoped he would take a fancy to Vanessa — provided of course that she still fancied him.

'I'm sorry about this,' she said eventually. 'I think all the wedding preparations must have made me a little crazy. Of course I know Hugo wouldn't leave me at the altar.'

'To be fair, I don't blame you for thinking that Hugo's father might have tried to talk him out of it. But even if he had tried, he'd have realised that he'd met his match. Hugo loves you to distraction. He'd never give you up.' Simon drove on for a while. 'Can I tell you what I was worrying about?'

'Of course.'

'I was worried that you might not love him half as much. It worried him, too. He thought you'd been bounced into this wedding and that you might not be happy about it.'

Lizzie sniffed, hoping she wasn't going to cry again; her mother would tell her off if she appeared with red eyes. 'I could have done without the wedding but I do really love Hugo. He said in his letter — he may have told you — that he loved me the first time we met. Well, it was the same for me. I was worried about him being trapped into marrying me, too. Alexandra — you met her briefly — she knew how I felt about him, and she told me I should have told Hugo. But girls don't do that, really. Not unless the other person has said it first. So I didn't.' She sighed. 'I probably should have.'

'It is hard to tell someone your feelings. You two haven't known each other very long, after all.'

'I wish we could have just got married, the two of us, with no fuss.'

'But you couldn't?'

'No. My wedding day has obsessed my mother since I was a little girl. I couldn't deprive her of it.'

'That's kind.'

'I don't know about that.' Eager to change the subject, she said, 'Do you remember Vanessa, Hugo's sister?'

'Nessa?' He spoke enthusiastically, which was a very good sign. 'Of course! I'm looking forward to catching up with her. She's turned out quite lovely, hasn't she?'

'I didn't know her when she was — however old she was when you last saw her.' In fact, Lizzie remembered perfectly well. Vanessa had been thirteen. 'But she's turned out to be a real friend.'

'Yes?'

'Yes. She was so helpful finding out your address from her mother, and of course came with us on our mad adventure.'

Simon didn't speak for a while. 'It wasn't as mad as all that. I mean, Hugo's father is a difficult chap. He wasn't at all happy about his son letting his wife live in 'some damned servant's cottage and being a damned embarrassment to the family'. It offended his pride.'

Lizzie laughed. There was something in the way that Simon spoke that made it seem like a direct quotation; he had Sir Jasper's tone of voice perfectly.

'He's a bully,' Simon went on. 'But Hugo is more than a match for him when he cares about something, or in this case someone. I think Sir Jasper knew that and didn't even try to talk him out of it.'

'I am so relieved. Hugo's father being against the wedding has been a bit of a dark cloud over it. Not that Hugo and I ever talked about it, but I know he felt it. My father wasn't keen at first either, but I knew he'd come round, once he'd got over showing such an eligible man the door!'

Simon smiled. 'I'm so pleased I've had a chance to get to know you a bit. I can see that you're going to make Hugo very happy. And I'm prepared to make sure he does the same for you.'

Lizzie laughed.

'Now, why don't you shut your eyes and try to have a doze?' Simon went on.

'Why?'

'Because I'm going to go faster than you might be comfortable with.'

Lizzie shut her eyes.

Simon parked the car in front of Patsy and Tim's house with a slight skid. It was twelve fifteen. Before Lizzie could even think of getting out of the car, the front door opened and people and dogs streamed out. There was her mother, her hair revealing that her perm hadn't been given long enough to relax and so the curls were too tight, wearing her dressing gown over her wedding outfit. Behind her, carrying a glass of water, was Gina, wearing a very dashing headpiece complete with veil, looking harassed, obviously having had a hard time keeping Mrs Spencer calm. There was Patsy in a smart, close-fitting dress with a matching jacket all covered with an apron, worn with very old driving shoes. Then there was Diane Baker, the vicar's wife. She was dressed for a wedding but was currently missing a hat. She was there to take the bridesmaids to the church; she had a big enough car.

Lizzie's mother didn't know if she should scream at her daughter or just be relieved she'd arrived. Her tone vacillated between outrage and happiness.

'Elizabeth! Darling! Where have you been? Now come upstairs and get dressed this instant!'

Lizzie got out of the car. She felt very calm. She knew it wouldn't take an hour to get ready, let alone the two originally scheduled. All would be well. It was going to be the perfect wedding in the country.

★ ★ ★

At last the time came for people to leave for the church. Lizzie, who had been ready for ages, had vacated the bedroom so her mother could put her hat on in peace, and observed the departures from the doorway of the morning room.

First to go were Hugo's parents. His mother looked tired but extremely elegant in a wonderful hat with a long feather secured by a diamond brooch.

His father looked distinguished in his morning suit, holding his top hat under his arm. He paused on his way out of the house, saw Lizzie and turned back. He looked her over critically. 'Hmm, yes, very simple, very nice, covers your knees.' Then he winked before he led his wife out to the waiting car.

Lizzie nearly fainted with shock.

The vintage Bentley lent by Tim and Patsy was being driven by a local man in a chauffeur's uniform. When it returned from taking Hugo's parents, it was going to take Patsy, Tim and Lizzie's mother. Lizzie was glad that her mother had someone to go with as, having been the centre of the day in her important role as mother of the bride, there was suddenly no role for her now the wedding was about to take place. Lizzie thought she looked lovely in her closely fitting hat covered with flowers with a little veil.

Patsy looked elegant too, now wearing heels and a veil secured by a large bow on her head. Tim, like Sir Jasper, looked timeless in his tailcoat and he took the mother of the bride's arm with great kindness.

At last, everyone else had left so it was just Lizzie and her father, waiting for the car to return.

'It's not too late to change your mind,' said her father gruffly. 'Well, of course it is, but I'm supposed to say that.'

'I don't want to change my mind, but thank you for asking!'

'Ah, the car is here,' said her father, relieved that

there was no longer any danger that feelings might become apparent. Feelings had always been his wife's department.

★ ★ ★

A few minutes later Lizzie glanced up at her father and saw he was trembling. He was more nervous than she was. She gave his arm a reassuring pat; then her bridesmaids assembled behind her and after a certain amount of whispering and 'good luck' messages between them, they were ready. The vicar gave the signal and everyone in the church stood up.

Lizzie looked down the aisle and saw Hugo waiting for her. His arm was half held out to greet her.

Purcell's 'Trumpet Tune' began and Lizzie and her father set off. A moment later, Hugo had hold of her hand. 'I love you,' he said, quite audibly. Lizzie gave a sigh of deep happiness.

All was going to be well.

370

We do hope that you have enjoyed reading this large print book.

Did you know that all of our titles are available for purchase?

We publish a wide range of high quality large print books including:
Romances, Mysteries, Classics General Fiction Non Fiction and Westerns

Special interest titles available in large print are:
The Little Oxford Dictionary Music Book, Song Book Hymn Book, Service Book

Also available from us courtesy of Oxford University Press:
Young Readers' Dictionary (large print edition) Young Readers' Thesaurus (large print edition)

For further information or a free brochure, please contact us at:
Ulverscroft Large Print Books Ltd., The Green, Bradgate Road, Anstey, Leicester, LE7 7FU, England. Tel: (00 44) 0116 236 4325 Fax: (00 44) 0116 234 0205

Other titles published by Ulverscroft:

A SPRINGTIME AFFAIR

Katie Fforde

Gilly runs her own B&B business from her much-loved family home, which she doesn't want to part with — at any price. But that's before she meets handsome estate agent Leo, and soon she begins to wonder whether selling up might not be such a bad idea after all. Meanwhile, Gilly's daughter, Helena, has a budding romance of her own. A talented weaver, she's becoming very close to her new landlord, Jago, who's offered to help her at an upcoming craft fair. It's what friends do, and they are just friends. Aren't they? With spring in full bloom, Helena and Gilly begin to ask themselves the same question: might their new loves lead to happily ever after?

A COUNTRY ESCAPE

Katie Fforde

Fran has always wanted to be a farmer, so how she ended up a chef in London is anyone's guess. However, her childhood dream is about to come true. She has just moved into a beautiful — albeit very run-down — farm in the Cotswolds, currently owned by an elderly relative who has informed her that if she manages to turn the place around in a year, the farm will be hers to inherit. But Fran knows nothing about farming. She might even be afraid of cows. She's going to need a lot of help from her best friend Issi, and also from her wealthy and very eligible neighbour — who might just have his own reasons for being so supportive. Is it the farm he's interested in? Or Fran herself?

A SECRET GARDEN

Katie Fforde

Lorna is a talented gardener and Philly is a plants-woman. Together they work on the grounds of a beautiful manor house in the Cotswolds. They enjoy their jobs and are surrounded by family and friends. But for them both, the door to true love remains resolutely closed. So when Lorna is introduced to Jack at a dinner party, and Lucien catches Philly's eye at the local market, it seems that dreams really can come true and happy endings lie just around the corner. But do they? Troublesome parents, the unexpected arrival of someone from Lorna's past, and the discovery of an old and secret garden mean their lives are about to become a lot more complicated . . .